"The power we call the Magia," said Forgoyle, "is nothing less than the Divine capacity for creation and destruction. As a source of supernatural energy, it is neither good nor evil — until an adept taps that power through his magestone. Why do you suppose the Order has so rigorously insisted the Magia be used only for healing? Because healing is selfless. If the Magia were tapped for selfish ambition, there is no way of predicting what evil might follow."

He gave Caradoc a searching look. "That is also why we open our ranks only to those who can be relied upon to uphold the Order's values — peace, wholeness, sobriety.

"You have it in you to become the greatest mage of your generation. In all the years you have studied with me, I've yet to find the limits to your potential.

"You have the power, Caradoc. But not the discipline.

"And this makes you, potentially, a very dangerous man."

Book One of the THE MAGES OF GARILLON

The Burning Stone

DEBORAH TURNER HARRIS

Futura

An ORBIT Book

Copyright © Deborah Turner Harris 1987

First published in Great Britain in 1988 by
Futura Publications, a Division of
Macdonald & Co (Publishers) Ltd
London & Sydney

*All characters in this publication are fictitious, and
any resemblance to real persons, living or dead, is purely
coincidental.*

ISBN 0 7088 8253 6

Printed in Great Britain by
The Guernsey Press Co. Ltd, Guernsey, Channel Islands.

Futura Publications
A Division of
Macdonald & Co (Publishers) Ltd
Greater London House
Hampstead Road
London NW1 7QX

A BPCC plc Company

DEDICATION

For my husband, Bob, who suffers manfully the trials of being married to a writer.

ACKNOWLEDGMENT

I would like to thank Betty Ballantine for all her help and encouragement, and for her magical ability to make silk purses out of sow's ears.

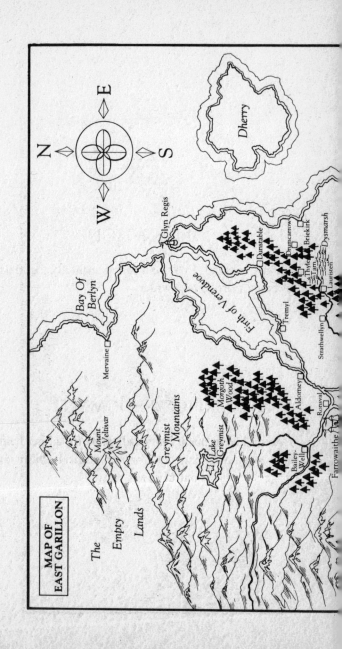

MAP OF
EAST GARILLON

The

Empty

Lands

Greymist Mountains

Mount
Veltivar

Bay Of
Berlyn

Mervaine

Lake
Greymist

Morgoth
Wood

Bailey-
Well

Frith of Veréndue

Aldorney

Romsval

Farrowraithe

Glyn Regis

Dunstable

Tremyl

Strathwellyn

Drumcarrow

Briekirk

Thyle

Tarn

Laursten

Dysmarsh

Dherry

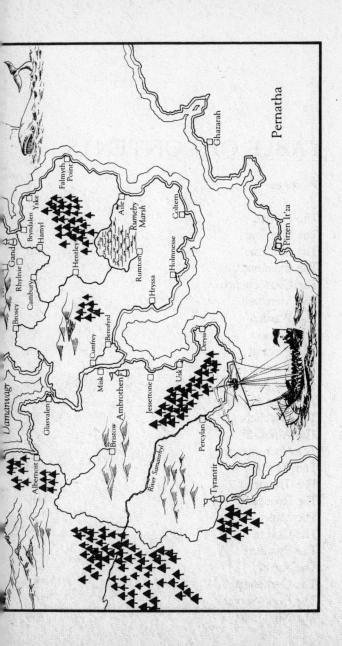

Pernatha

Ghazarah

Pirzen It'za

Falmyth
Point

Bryndalem Yske

Hamyl

Hentley

Alie

Rumeby
Marsh

Coltern

Holmnesse

Rumton

Hryssa

Cambury

Rhylnie

Brosey

Gand

Damavagr

Cumfrey

Beresfyrd

Misk

Glasvalen

Ambrothen

Jessettone

Usk

Deryss

Albernost

Bristow

River Samanrhyl

Percylan

Tyrantir

TABLE OF CONTENTS

CAST OF CHARACTERS

The Nobility

Delsidor Whitfauconer—Lord Warden of East Garillon
and Seneschal of Farrowaithe

Evelake Whitfauconer—Delsidor's elder son and heir
by Delsidor's deceased first wife

Gwynmira Du Bors Whitfauconer—Delsidor's second
wife

Gythe Du Bors Whitfauconer—Gwynmira's son by
Delsidor

Fyanor Du Bors—Gwynmira's brother, the Seneschal
of Ambrothen

Arvech Du Penfallon—Seneschal of Gand

Devon Du Penfallon—Arvech's crippled son

Kherryn Du Penfallon—Devon's sister

Khevyn Ap Khorrasel—Baron of Kirkwell, a friend
of Gwynmira's

The Clergy

Caradoc Penlluathe—a novice of the Order of Mage
Hospitallers of Ambrothen

An'char Maeldrake—Grand Master of the Order of
Mage Hospitallers of Ambrothen

Forgoyle Finlevyn—Magister of the Order of Mage
Hospitallers of Ambrothen, Caradoc's teacher

Ulbrecht Rathmuir—Magister of the Order of Mage
Hospitallers of Ambrothen, a friend of Forgoyle's

Baldwyn Vladhallyn—Arch Mage of East Garillon

The Military

Commander Jorvald Ekhanghar—Marshall of Gand

Commander Galledan—an officer in the Farrowaithe
    Guard
Cergil Ap Cymric—Galledan's young lieutenant
Geston Du Maris—Cergil's fellow cadet
Lord Aldehron Ashfyrd—Marshall of Farrowaithe
Captain Llew Ap Connacht—an officer in the Far-
    rowaithe Guard
Sir Manfred Du Bourne—Llew's superior
Commander Ildevek Winsaddel—Marshall of
    Ambrothen
Captain Vergild Du Coverlay—an officer in the
    Ambrothen Regulars
Captain Tergoth Marhc—Vergild's colleague, assigned
    to prison duty
Rogan and Aelfhere—sentries of Ambrothen Keep

The Commoners

Serdor Sulamith—a friend of Caradoc's
Margoth Penlluathe—Caradoc's sister
Arn Aldarshot—owner of the Beldame Inn
Gudmar Ap Gorvald—a merchant prince
Harlech Hardrada—a seaman and friend of Gudmar's
Vult Hemmling—a farmer from Rhylnie
Rhan Hallender—a bond-servant
Tarlton—an old miner
Tobe Greenham—Gudmar's chief steward

The Rogues

Borthen Berigeld—a brigand-leader
Muirtagh—Borthen's lieutenant
Haskel Tohr—an innkeeper, Rhan's master
Valoran Trace—a fugitive from justice
Perne and Uskan—two of Borthen's henchmen

PROLOGUE

On the twelfth day of February in the year of the Red Boar, 1347, a storm swept westward out of the Straits of Pernatha into the Bay of Ambrothen, punishing the south coast of the Garillan mainland with howling winds and lashing rains.

During the four days it took for the storm to blow itself out, no ship of any description ventured out past the breakwaters of Ambrothen Harbor, and only three vessels succeeded in navigating the dangerous passage through the channel reefs to seek haven within reach of the city's seawalls.

Two of these vessels were fishermen returning home in the teeth of the gale. The third was a galleass of Pernathan design, with the name *Yusufa* picked out in faded script beneath her figurehead.

Masked by tempest-driven racks of mist and rain, her presence went two days undetected both by the city's customs agents and by the watchmen on the walls of Ambrothen Castle. By the time the weather had moderated sufficiently to allow a customs inspector to pay a visit to the *Yusufa*'s hold, there was nothing left on board to give rise to suspicion except perhaps a surprising amount of empty space between the decks.

When questioned about this, the captain of the *Yusufa* explained that they had just come from dropping off a shipment of raw timber at Holmnesse and were looking to take on a fresh cargo of cured hides, raw wool, and salt fish for their return voyage to Pernatha. Since the vessel's papers were all in order and since the customs inspector had his own private reasons for not wanting to spend any more time than he had to aboard, the formalities were speedily concluded, and the customs inspector went back to make a routine report in the *Yusufa*'s favor.

Harlech Hardrada, owner as well as captain of the *Yusufa*, watched his guest's departure with a narrow gleam in his berry-black eyes. His true cargo—a lucrative consignment of illegal Pernathan juju'bi—had been ferried ashore under stormy cover of darkness the previous night and was now safely hidden away under the floor of a supposedly unused warehouse, not far from the waterfront. His commission fulfilled, he had only one remaining appointment to keep before the *Yusufa* and her crew would be free to weigh anchor.

Despite the considerable amount of money he expected to receive for his services, Harlech was not looking forward to the meeting. While his employer was a liberal enough paymaster, it was not comfortable to be long in the same room with him. Harlech, recalling several previous encounters, caught himself gritting his teeth at the memory and cursed himself for a fool. Nevertheless, as the time drew nearer he thought twice, then opened up a bottle of Mervainian pine-mead.

Nightfall came early under the still-lowering sky, and the cold fog rolled in, settling thick as porridge over the murky, white-flecked water. When the mist had become so dense that the lights from shore were no more than pale smears in the darkness, Harlech tossed off the last of the liquor in his glass and sent word to the men on deck to clear away the longboat.

A quarter of an hour later, muffled to the eyes against the damp, Harlech sat stolidly in the bow of the boat and listened to the soft dip and swish of the moving oars as his men steered a wandering course among the dark hulls of the neighboring ships. The quay itself became gradually visible as a line of yellow lights. Cutting along the reinforced embankment, they fishtailed gently into a narrow canal and, eight oarstrokes later, coasted to a halt next to a sloping ramp of broken stones.

The ramp led upward to the rear entrance of a disused boatyard. Leaving his men huddled together under a tarpaulin, Harlech trudged up to the gates and rattled the rusty chain. A dark figure popped into view and thrust a peering face at him through the bars. "Oh, it's you, is it? Come in. 'is Eminence is expecting you."

A key grated corrosively in the lock, and the gate swung creakily inward. Following the sentry, Harlech set off through a graveyard of skeleton keels toward a long two-story building on the far side of the compound. Upon their arrival his companion exchanged words with someone on the other side of a bolted door. A moment later, Harlech stepped inside the temporary headquarters of the League of the Night-Raven, the most notorious band of criminals in all of East Garillon.

From there he was ushered up a flight of stairs and deposited with a word of explanation at the half-opened door of a square, firelit room. The man just inside the threshold, a flat-faced giant with shoulders like a bull's, gave him a long look through colorless eyes, then stood aside to allow him to enter.

The source of the firelight proved to be a portable brazier standing in the middle of the floor. Beyond the red gleam of its glowing embers, the master of the League—the individual quaintly styled as "His Eminence" by his followers—was seated at a table with his back to the wall.

Behind him, magnified by the light, his shadow spread up and outward, brooding over the room like the wings of some nocturnal bird of prey. The flickering firelight gave the image an uncanny suggestion of independent movement. His fascinated gaze drawn momentarily toward the ceiling, Harlech failed to notice that the other man had raised his head until a mocking, inimitable voice said doucely, "You're late, Captain. I was beginning to wonder if you might have undergone a change of heart."

Harlech thought it best to ignore the gibe. Bringing his eyes level with his employer's, he shrugged and said sourly, "We made what speed we could. It's a rare dreichit night out there."

The man known as "His Eminence" bared white teeth in a soulless smile. "Delayed by mere weather? You astonish me. Or was the success of last night's maneuvers due to some genius other than yours?"

Recalling several wet and harrowing hours spent escorting a highly perishable cargo ashore through a maelstrom of rain and high seas, Harlech squared his jaw till his beard bristled. "Och, I'm the spark that dreamed up yon scheme, right enough. And seein' as how we got the goods into the city by the fifteenth, like ye asked, I'm lookin' t' collect the bonus ye promised over and above our usual fee."

"You sound as if you expected me to quibble." The man behind the table seemed genuinely amused. Shifting forward in his chair, he lifted a thick brown envelope from the stack of papers in front of him and tendered it to Harlech. "By all means count it if you wish. But you will find it a waste of your undoubtedly valuable time."

Accepting the packet gingerly from his employer's manicured fingers, Harlech weighed it long enough in his palm to allow pride to overcome suspicion before stowing it away in the breast of his jerkin. "I'll allow goin' back on a bargain isna your style."

"Your trust is heartwarming." A smile, half-mocking, half-malicious, played about the corners of the other man's full red lips. "But as to my good faith, I assure you that it depends entirely upon the nature of the bargain. Speaking of which—you were boarded this afternoon by a customs agent named Gaultry. Did you have any difficulty with him?"

Harlech consulted his memory. "No. Not t' speak of. Mind, I did think for a moment he was goin' t' insist on takin' soundings down in the hold. But then he seemed to think better of it and let be." He paused, then inquired sapiently, "One of your pensioners? Ye must have a mighty interestin' collection of 'em."

"A hobby of mine. Perhaps one day I may even contrive to add a seneschal to their number." His Eminence was gazing pensively at the magnificent green gem that graced the ring on his right hand. "As for Gaultry—he is, regrettably, subject to periodic attacks of conscience. So far he has managed to withstand them, but one of these days I may have to take him personally in hand."

He tilted his wrist, and green fire sprang up from the stone in his ring, his eyes resting still upon the jewel's deep color. "It may interest you to know," said His Eminence dreamily, "that I have a decided gift for . . . persuasion."

CHAPTER 1

The Novice

"Well, no luck today either," announced Caradoc bitterly as he entered the dingy little room. Closing the door behind him with an irritable backward thrust of wide shoulders, he settled his weight against the doorframe and folded his arms. "This makes—what, three weeks now, and still no prospect of work. I hope you have some suggestions to offer. My ingenuity and my patience are just about exhausted. Not to mention my feet."

His companion was sitting tailor-fashion on the floor, with a lute resting across his knees. Made from honey-colored maple-wood, it was a thing of rare beauty, and the elegance of its craftsmanship contrasted oddly with the threadbare state of the room. He paused in the act of fitting a new string to the ivory-inlaid neck, and said, "I'm sorry. Did you try the silversmith—the fellow Arn mentioned?"

"Yes, I tried the silversmith." Abandoning the lintel in favor of a nearby chair, Caradoc seated himself with an audible huff. His long limbs extended in a negligent sprawl, he said to the ceiling, "I also tried the master-clerk at the customshouse in Chantry Street. I also tried the mercer—you know, that friend of Forgoyle's—but he's gone up to Gand to inspect a new consignment of raw wools from Mervaine and won't be back for another three weeks. I also tried a dozen or so equally respectable establishments. With comparable results. I can recite the entire list if you're interested."

"That won't be necessary. I take your point," said his friend dryly. Holding the string in place with thin, practiced fingers, he added, "Cheer up. Something's bound to turn up sooner or later."

"Then it had better be sooner," said Caradoc tartly. "That crimp-faced landlord stopped by earlier this morning, and he made it none-too-delicately clear that we could either pay him the rent we owe him by no later than next Friday or go make up our beds in the street. I'm telling you, Serdor, that's only the beginning. If I don't turn up a source of ready money by the end of the week, I won't answer for the consequences."

He drew a deep breath and let it out again in a wave of disgust. "God, I wish the examinations were tomorrow, instead of a month away. Once I'm formally admitted to the Order, all our troubles will be over—" He bit the last word short.

Serdor, his grey eyes abstracted, adjusted the tuning peg at the head of the lute, strumming the tightening gut with his thumb. Listening as his friend brought the new string unerringly into harmony with the others, Caradoc glanced around and said, "By the way, where's Margoth?"

"Margoth?" Serdor struck a full chord, then muffled it with his palm. "She went out about two hours ago. I don't recall if she said where she was going."

"That sounds like Margoth," said Caradoc. "I hope she has sense enough to hurry up. It'll be dark in another half hour."

He stood up and went to the window. Outside, the red rays of the mid-February sun were radiating upward from beyond the adjacent rooftops. The muted light playing lightly over his face lent flattering emphasis to the handsome bones, the ruddy coloring. Sitting beyond him in the middle of a widening pool of shadow, Serdor was momentarily reduced to an outline of angular shoulders and a bent brown head. Laying aside the lute, he took out a small penknife and a disreputable stub of a writing quill. Softly humming a plaintive air in a minor key, he began to trim the nib.

After a moment or two, Caradoc turned away and crossed

the room to where two stubby yellow candles stood in dull metal holders on either end of the narrow mantel. He lit both of them from a single match. As he snuffed the flame between finger and thumb, the sound of the door opening and closing below them at the level of the street made both men look around.

Quick footsteps tapped up the stairway and came to a halt in the hall outside. A hand tripped the latch and pushed the door inward. Heralded by a draught of chilly air, Caradoc's red-haired sister stepped briskly over the threshold.

Guileless blue eyes scanned the room. "Oh, are you still here, Serdor? I was afraid you might have gotten tired of waiting and gone home," said Margoth. "Hello, Caradoc. Did you have a good day?"

"No," said her brother baldly. "What about you? Where have you been?"

"Didn't Serdor tell you?"

"No," said Caradoc. "He said only that you'd gone out."

Margoth's glance slid past Caradoc and lighted upon the minstrel. "Craven," she said.

Serdor shrugged, his steady gaze unruffled. "I make it a rule never to borrow trouble without asking permission," he said, and flipped the penknife into the air with a quick-wristed juggler's toss.

Margoth caught it neatly. Cradling it in her outstretched palm, she said, "Always the soul of discretion. Very well, I'll break this ground myself."

Her fingers flickered, and the knife disappeared from view. An instant later, it materialized in her opposite hand. "Stop playing around," growled Caradoc. "Margoth, what the devil have you been up to?"

Margoth clapped her hands lightly together, and the knife vanished again. "I've got a surprise for you," she said. "I've got a job."

There was a moment's dead silence.

"Would you mind repeating that?" inquired her brother.

"Certainly," said Margoth cordially, and reproduced the knife from the pocket of her dress. She handed it to Caradoc, then reached up to adjust the rumpled line of his collar. "I have got a job."

Her gaze shifted expectantly from Caradoc to Serdor and back again. When neither of them spoke, her smile curdled to a grimace. "What's the matter?" she demanded tartly. "Do I need to repeat it a third time?"

"No," said Caradoc. "I heard you quite distinctly, thank you."

"Then why are you looking so sour?" asked Margoth with some asperity. "I thought you'd be pleased."

"I hope that's not your idea of a compliment," said Caradoc. "Who 'hired' you?"

"There's no need for you to look so affronted," said Margoth. "Arn did. He wants me to help cut at the Beldame: giving him a hand in the kitchen, making sure the customers have everything they need—"

"In other words," said Caradoc, cutting in, "being a common serving-maid. "

His tone brought a flush to his sister's cheeks. "What if I am?"

"That question is irrelevant," said her brother austerely, "in view of the fact that the whole thing is completely absurd and doesn't bear thinking about."

"Oh, indeed?" There was a veiled flicker of annoyance in Margoth's blue eyes. "Would it be stretching the point to ask why?"

"In the first place, it's not necessary for you to take on employment," said Caradoc. "We can get by without it."

"I'd like to know how," came the curt reply. "And in the second place?"

"In the second place, you have no business in a place like a tavern," said Caradoc. His color had risen.

Taking a closer look at her brother's face—"What are you really objecting to?" asked Margoth, dangerously.

"If you were as worldly-wise as you think you are, you wouldn't have to ask," said Caradoc. "Tavern wenches have a name for being loose, drunken sluts. And men who drink in taverns expect no better of them. Do you think I want to see your reputation put at risk in such a place?''

Margoth shrugged. ''It's preferable to being turned out-of-doors for indigence. And anyway, it's the Beldame we're talking about, not some Mackerel Wharf grog-den. Arn—''

''Can't be everywhere at once. Left on your own, unprotected, you could very easily find yourself the butt of some pretty rude gallantry,'' said Caradoc sharply. ''Maybe you don't have much regard for your reputation, but I, at least, value mine. And I tell you I won't have any sister of mine trailing her skirts around a taproom!'' He ended on a snort.

''Just who do you think you are?'' demanded Margoth indignantly.

''Your elder brother,'' said Caradoc. ''And head of this household. Give it up, Margoth. You're not going to go to work at the Beldame, and that's final—''

''I don't recall asking your permission!'' snapped Margoth. ''I'm your sister, not your chattel. It's not for you to say what I will or will not do!''

Her challenging gaze clashed with Caradoc's, and for a bristling moment neither of them spoke. Then Caradoc gave a long-suffering sigh. ''Look, Margoth, I appreciate your trying to help, but it simply isn't on. Just be patient for a few more days. Once I'm working—''

''Once you're working,'' said Margoth, ''I will be only too happy to stay home and keep house. In the meantime, however, I intend to accept Arn's offer. Unless, of course, you'd rather I took up picking pockets.''

She presented her brother with a small leather pouch.

It was his purse, empty. Caradoc swore, and slapped reflexively at the front of his jerkin where he had last bestowed it.

Behind him, Serdor made a stifled noise in his throat. Turning on the minstrel with a forbidding glare, Caradoc said frostily, ''I fail to see anything funny about this. It's bad enough that you had to go and teach her these gutter-tricks in the first place, without encouraging her to cultivate a criminal proficiency in them.''

''Oh, do take a damper, Caradoc,'' said Margoth in exasperation. "Sleight of hand may not, admittedly, be a terribly respectable accomplishment, but I'm not seriously considering entering into a life of crime. Unless, of course, you refuse to listen to reason."

Caradoc glowered at her. "Don't be ridiculous."

"Then stop being so almighty dogmatic," retorted Margoth. "Arn's a good friend, and the Beldame's an honest, well-run house. Anybody listening to you would think I was planning to go into competition with the Cod Street whores!"

"If you aren't, I suppose it's because you're lacking that particular natural talent," said Caradoc nastily.

Margoth's chin shot up. Meeting her brother's smoldering eyes, she said evenly, "I might be tempted to say the same thing about you, *apprentice*. You certainly didn't display any excess of natural talent last September when you went up before the Magisters to try to prove your worth to the Order."

Caradoc's face suddenly went dangerously pale, but Margoth was for the moment too angry herself to notice. Her blue eyes sparkling, she continued in the same deliberate tone, "All you did display, in fact, was arrogance, and that in copious supply. Well, the Council wasn't impressed, and neither am I. You can strut about playing cock-of-the-walk all you like, but that won't pay the rent, and it certainly won't enhance your chances of passing your examinations *this* time. So take my advice, and try to listen less to your pride. Then maybe—just maybe—you might be able to convince the Council that you should, after all, be admitted to the Hospitallers' Order."

She paused for breath. White about the mouth, Caradoc said, "Bravo. Are you quite through?"

Seeing his expression for the first time, Margoth swallowed and drew herself up. "I've said all I'm going to say."

"It isn't necessary to say more," said Caradoc, turning on his heel and starting for the door. "You have won your point, Margoth. By all means, take the job at the Beldame, or do anything else you please. In the meantime, permit me to relieve you of my incompetent presence."

With this parting shot, he turned and wrenched the door

open with a vengeful twist of a strong wrist. Margoth put out a restraining hand, then let it fall again as the door slammed shut behind him.

His footsteps rang out hollowly in the stairwell as he descended. Then there was silence. After a moment, Serdor recited softly,

"Wythe swerd y-brok and riven scylde,
Sir Bleys waes harried fram the fylde. . . .

"I think you've carried the day.

"Ande hys woundes like rubees ryche and rede . . ."

Margoth didn't turn around. "He didn't mean half of what he said. I wish I hadn't lashed out at him like that."

"Your choice of weapons *was* a bit heavy-handed," agreed Serdor quietly, watching her back.

"He's been so worried about the upcoming trials. . . . I thought if I could take up the burden of supporting us till then, it would make things that much easier," said Margoth. "Except that I lost my temper, and now matters are worse than before."

She turned and gave Serdor a watery smile. "Poor Caradoc. He always seems to have to learn his moral lessons the hard way."

"I suppose it's one of the penalties for his being exceptionally gifted," said Serdor wryly. "Would you like me to go after him?"

"Yes—though I expect he'll be about as approachable as a bear with a sore head." Margoth was looking visibly relieved. She tilted her chin and said, "Don't you ever get tired of playing the peacemaker?"

"Frequently," said Serdor with a grimace. "But I don't suppose that alone will absolve me."

Seeing the contrition deepen in her face, he gave her a whimsical grin. "Don't worry. But give me a few hours. It's going to take time to talk him into anything like a state of resignation. . . ."

CHAPTER 2

The Warning

Margoth's first three weeks at the Beldame proved more difficult than she had foreseen—not because the work was hard or the customers impertinent, but because Caradoc had appointed himself to be her chaperone.

Protective to the point of belligerence, he was all too ready to take offense on her behalf. Unwilling to provoke another painful scene, Margoth endured his unwanted solicitude in silence, but it was becoming apparent that something was going to have to be done to ease the situation.

Solutions didn't come easily. Sitting at her sewing table late one afternoon, Margoth was sourly playing games with a handful of small copper coins to aid her concentration when a knock at the door roused her from her reverie.

It was Serdor, carrying his lute, his face whisked pink by the stiff breeze outside. "Arn's invited me to play at the Beldame tonight," he explained as he stepped across the threshold. He set the lute carefully against the wall and cast a wary eye around the room. "Where's Caradoc?"

"With Forgoyle, at the hospital. He won't be finished until some time after eight o'clock," said Margoth.

"Is he planning to come along to the inn afterwards?" inquired Serdor.

"I don't know what's to stop him," said Margoth acidly. "Unless you can suggest some new strategy we haven't tried yet."

"We've exhausted hints, threats, and cajolery," said Serdor. "I'm afraid the only recourse left to us seems to be physical violence."

"We've had more than enough of that already." Margoth rolled her eyes. "You know, I wouldn't mind if Caradoc would be satisfied just to keep watch over me from a distance. But as it is, he quarrels with just about anyone who has the audacity to make conversation with me."

Serdor grimaced. "He certainly has developed a marked predilection for fisticuffs. Arn's lucky his furniture's still intact."

"Oh, Caradoc is not entirely without discretion," said Margoth, looking down her nose at him. "He always invites his victims to step outside."

Serdor drew a deep breath, held it, and let it out again through his nostrils. "That's too bad. It would solve a lot of problems if Arn would ban him from the premises."

"You know as well as I do that Arn would never do that," said Margoth. "He's always saying how much Caradoc reminds him of our father. It would take more than a few shouting matches to convince Arn that any son of Bran Penlluathe could have his fair share of faults."

Silence fell. After a long moment's reflection, Serdor said thoughtfully, "I'm surprised Forgoyle hasn't had something to say about this."

"With any luck," said Margoth, "he hasn't heard anything about it."

"I wouldn't count on that," said Serdor. "He knows Caradoc far too well not to guess that something must be up. And that may not necessarily be a bad thing: Forgoyle understands Caradoc and is bound to know how to talk to him."

Forgoyle, however, was just as baffled as anyone else by Caradoc's unlooked-for capacity for violence. Tactful at first, he attempted to broach the subject as a hypothetical issue but failed to elicit anything like a satisfactory response. He was still debating the merits of a more direct approach when matters came to a head of their own accord.

The situation erupted on a Sunday afternoon, one week before the scheduled examinations, as they were working together in one of the ateliers in the south wing of the Hospitallers' College. The review session had to do with general pharmacology. Forgoyle was bending down to take an experimental sniff at a beakerful of liniment that Caradoc had just finished preparing when an explosive exclamation from his favorite pupil made him look sharply around.

Caradoc was glaring hot-eyed at the alembic on the counter in front of him. An instant later, before Forgoyle could forestall him, Caradoc snatched it up with a growl and hurled it at point-blank range into the bin at his feet.

There was a splintering crash, and shards of broken glass leaped up like a fountain. Caradoc, fists clenched before him on the countertop, was still glowering at the wall in front of him. His long nose twitching at the rising reek of antiseptics, Forgoyle waited until his protégé's color had returned almost to normal before inquiring mildly, "And what, may I ask, was all that about?"

"Stupidity!" Caradoc spun about on his stool and tossed a hand into the air. "Sheer, bloody stupidity! I added camphor where I should have added tincture of iodine and spoiled the whole bloody lot. . . ." He drew breath and abruptly closed his mouth, his eyes still smoldering.

"Pardon me for saying so," said Forgoyle evenly, "but I fail to see why such a minor mistake should warrant such a major display of temperament."

"I know," said Caradoc savagely. He drew breath again and said in a softer voice, "I'm sorry. I shouldn't have flared up like that. But I can't seem to keep my mind on what I'm doing today. I don't know what the problem is."

"Don't you? I think I could hazard a guess," said Forgoyle a trifle tartly. "It appears to me that you are presently suffering from a marked lack of self-discipline."

Caradoc blinked. Then, dropping his eyes, he said stiffly, "I'm afraid I don't follow you."

"Oh, yes you do," said Forgoyle grimly. "And it's about time you and I had a talk about it."

Caradoc's profile remained obstinately uncommunicative. "About what?"

"Don't be obtuse," snapped Forgoyle. "In the course of the past few weeks you've gained a reputation the commonest tavern bully might boast of. If the fact has escaped your notice, I assure you it has not escaped mine."

There was a moment's appalled silence. Seizing his advantage, Forgoyle continued. "Public use of profane language, disorderly conduct, personal assault—I can only marvel that you haven't yet been summoned to appear before a court of law. It makes me wonder if the ten years we've both invested in your training haven't been a criminal waste of time!"

He glared expectantly at his errant pupil, who by this time was looking decidedly uncomfortable. His cheekbones aflame, Caradoc lowered his chin and muttered defensively, "It wasn't . . . I can explain."

"All right. I'm waiting," said Forgoyle, and folded his arms.

Caradoc knotted his long fingers together. "You know Margoth's job at the Beldame? Well, it isn't working out."

"She seems to think it is."

"Yes, but . . ." Caradoc groped for words, then went on in a rush. "She doesn't really know the half of it. She doesn't hear the lewd comments that go on behind her back. She doesn't see the way some of those men eye her up and down when her head's in a different direction. . . ."

"Doesn't see it?" said Forgoyle, "or simply doesn't heed it?"

"It amounts to the same thing, doesn't it?" said Caradoc. "Look, I know as well as you do that most of the talk and the looks are harmless. But there's always the danger that one day somebody might mean what he says. And I can't seem to get that out of my mind."

"I see your point," said Forgoyle quietly. "But it's one thing to be looking out for your sister. It's another thing entirely to be looking for trouble. Apparently you don't yet know the difference. And that really worries me."

Caradoc gave him a puzzled frown. "Why?"

There was an odd glint in Forgoyle's deep eyes. "Because you're gifted—the most gifted pupil I've ever had. And because you haven't yet grasped the fact that great gifts carry with them a proportionate degree of moral responsibility."

He sighed and sank down on a nearby stool. After studying his hands for a moment, he looked up and said softly, "You don't need me to tell you that the affinity for the Magia varies considerably from one individual to the next. With some, it's a degree of sensory acuity that makes them able diagnosticians. With others, it's a high level of rapport with their patients that gives them the ability to relieve pain and dispel fear. Still others have a strength of will that gives them power over the physical bodies of those around them—power to set right what has gone wrong. It is part of the task of the magister to help his pupils discover their own strengths—and their own limitations."

The glint in his eyes deepened. "With most students, it soon becomes evident that their personal power extends only so far and no more. But you, Caradoc, are different. In all the years we have worked together, I have tested you time and time again, trying to determine your limitations. And to this day, I still don't know the extent of your potential.

"This is what worries me. You have the power, but not the discipline. And this makes you, potentially, a very dangerous man."

His voice hardly stronger than a whisper, Caradoc said, "In what way?"

"In many ways," said Forgoyle. "Broadly speaking, the power we call the Magia is nothing less than the Divine capacity, as yet unrealized in time, for both creation and destruction. Simply as a source of supernatural energy, it is neither good nor evil. Its nature becomes a matter for moral debate only when the adept, tapping its power through the agency of his magestone, seeks to apply that power to accomplishing an end he himself has conceived. If his is a selfless intention, the Magia will sanctify him and his actions. If, however, his intention is self-interested, he will corrupt the Magia, and it will corrupt him.''

There was a gravity in his look that Caradoc had seen before but rarely. ''Why do you suppose the Order has so rigorously insisted, down through its history, that the power of the Magia must be used exclusively for the purpose of healing? It is because it is the one office one human being can perform for another that is essentially selfless.

''And therein lies our safeguard. For if the raw power of the Magia were to be tapped to serve the selfish ambitions of any mere mortal, outside the governance of the Order, there is no way of predicting what evil might follow as a consequence.''

He gave Caradoc a searching look. ''This is likewise why we cannot afford to admit to our ranks anyone who cannot be relied upon to uphold the values espoused by the Order: peace, wholeness, and sobriety. For the Order is, and will remain, only as sound as the individuals who comprise it.

''You have it in you to become the greatest single gift to the Order of your whole generation. We need you—but only if you can demonstrate that your self-control is commensurate with your ability to wield the power of the Magia. *Now* do you understand?''

Caradoc nodded slowly, his face overshadowed in thought. ''I believe I'm beginning to.'' He spread his hands before him, their indwelling strength manifest in the structure of the bones. Staring at them, he said softly, ''You know, when the Council first confirmed that I had the gift, I felt somehow—oh, I don't know—hallowed. As if the ability had been given to me for a special purpose. I never doubted it for a moment— until the examination last fall, when I—I failed.''

When he looked at Forgoyle again, there was pain in his eyes. ''What seemed to come so hard to so many people came so easily to me. I suppose I got overconfident. I don't feel like that now. I've never been so anxious before in my life.''

"And so you're exorcising your own anxiety on Margoth's behalf," said Forgoyle.

Seeing the arrested look on his pupil's face, he gave a wry chuckle and clapped an affectionate hand to Caradoc's bowed shoulder. "Believe me, you have nothing to fear from this examination. Your mistakes are behind you now; stop worrying about them. Just keep calm, and all will be well."

CHAPTER 3

The Beldame

The four days that followed Caradoc's talk with his teacher passed without incident. On the evening of the fifth day, leaving Caradoc to finish his rounds at the hospital under Forgoyle's direction, Serdor and Margoth set out from Candlewick Lane and made their way to the Beldame Inn through the soft apricot glow of a springtime sunset.

Serdor had his lute with him. His first appearance at the inn had been received with enthusiasm, and Arn had promptly issued a standing invitation for him to repeat his performance. It was a happy compromise: lacking the means to buy into the Most Worshipful Company of Ambrothen Musicians, Serdor was barred from engaging in regular work for regular wages, but he was not prohibited from accepting the offices of charity.

Arriving at the Beldame as the light was fading, Serdor and Margoth went in through the back door and discovered Arn Aldarshot, the proprietor, sitting at the kitchen table, staring sadly at a handsome gilt-finished horologe, which normally occupied the mantelpiece in his own small sitting room.

Seeing them, he pointed to the clock. "It's stopped," he announced glumly. "I think it must be broken."

The horologe, brought back to Ambrothen from Pernatha by Arn's maternal uncle, was one of his most prized possessions. Hands on her hips, Margoth subjected the clock to a critical scowl. "Let me take a closer look at it," she said. "Maybe I can find out what's wrong. Have you got a key to the casing?"

"Not anymore," said Arn sourly, and slid down the bench to make room for her.

"Hmmm." Margoth turned the horologe between her hands and bent down to inspect the tiny ornamental keyhole at the base of the back-panel. "Do you mind if I have a go with a hairpin?"

Arn glanced dubiously over at Serdor, who gave him an affirmative nod. "Go ahead, then," said the little innkeeper to Margoth. He winced slightly, and added, "Just don't expect me to watch."

"Don't worry," said Margoth. There was an intent, faraway look in her blue eyes as she gave herself over to her task. Watching her face as she delicately inserted the end of the pin into the miniature lock, Serdor knew she was already reaching beyond the immediate question of the lock toward an intuitive apprehension of the greater problem.

It was Margoth's particular gift: an instinctive understanding of and affinity for material things, especially for mechanical devices. Her skill at sleight of hand was only one aspect of a more complex ability. While he by no means fully grasped the extent of her talent, Serdor suspected that it was closely akin to the mysterious sympathetic powers that promised to make her brother a great healer.

Her guiding fingers light and sure, Margoth gave the pin a calculated half twist. There was a silvery click as the lock yielded, and the back of the horologe swung open, revealing a bewildering array of cogs and gears. Admiring Margoth's dexterity as she probed unerringly through the fragile maze of the clock's moving parts, Serdor wondered if he alone knew enough to appreciate her potential.

Growing up in the back streets of the city, he had learned as a child all the thieves' arts of legerdemain, and practical experience had rendered him an expert in their use before circumstances and the timely intervention of Forgoyle Finlevyn had rescued him from his precarious career. When he had first been introduced to Margoth and her brother, he had amused her by teaching her the tricks that had been his means of livelihood, little dreaming that they would prove the keys to unlock her own inner resources.

A small mutter of satisfaction from Margoth now told him that she had solved the difficulty at hand. There was a synchronized sequence of clicks as she adjusted the set of the clock hands and gently nudged the master-ratchet into motion. Leaning forward, Arn cocked his head to one side and listened. "It's ticking again!" he exclaimed. "What did you do?"

The redheaded girl gave him a twinkling smile. "I removed some fluff from the wheel that advances the hour hand," said Margoth. She closed the back of the horologe and gave her father's old friend a quizzical look. "I'll set it properly the next time St. Welleran's rings out the hour. In the meantime, shall I go open up the common room?"

By seven o'clock, the Beldame's tables and benches were nearly all full. Surveying the scene from the second-floor gallery overlooking the common room, Serdor sipped at the ale in his tankard and waited to see if his services were going to be called for.

The company was by no means exclusively male. Noting the number of bright, quilted skirts among the soberer array of work-smocks and jerkins, Serdor remarked to Margoth, "Caradoc can hardly complain of your being conspicuous tonight."

"Yes. Comforting, isn't it?" said Margoth with a grin. "I hope you've got a few dance-tunes tucked away under your hat. Somebody may well demand a jig or two before the night's out."

The call for musical entertainment was not long in coming. Wryly acknowledging the assortment of friendly gibes, Serdor picked up his instrument and started down the stairs.

Scattered hand-clapping followed him as he made his way across the length of the room and hoisted himself one-handed

onto the end of the bar. Running nimble fingers over the
strings, he cast a searching look around the room, seeking to
catch the prevailing mood of his listeners.

Many of the faces in the crowd were familiar, but there
were some strangers present as well. Almost before he was
aware of it, Serdor's eyes were drawn to the opposite end of
the floor, where a tall figure sat in shadowy isolation at the
table in the corner.

Darkly anonymous in unrelieved black, the figure had,
even at rest, a tigerish poise suggestive of uncommon strength
and agility. Struck by the singular intensity of the impression
he had received, Serdor peered through the smoky air in an
attempt to capture a glimpse of the stranger's face.

His failure to do so left him oddly unsettled. Only the
realization that his audience had gone expectantly quiet kept
him from yielding to the impulse to walk back to where the
stranger was sitting.

A hand touched his arm. "I think you know the song that I
would like to hear," said Margoth softly.

Her smile dispelled the chill of his brief moment of disquiet. Returning smile for smile, he bowed his head over his
lute and played to please her:

> "My love, her eyes are like the sky
> When it is mirrored in the sea.
> My love, her face is like a glass
> That brims with light for none but me. . . ."

There were other songs to follow, some old, some new.
Slender, unspectacular, Serdor managed nevertheless to dom-
inate the room with his command of his music. The thin,
clever fingers, with all their inbred artistry, lent freshness and
poignancy even to the melodies his listeners knew by heart.
Work-hardened hands curled motionless around cup and bottle, the audience gave him their rapt attention, in the form of
laughter or silence, as his inspiration moved them.

Attentive to the shifting currents of interest among his
listeners, Serdor moved on effortlessly from ballad to lyric,

exchanging the plaintive laments of unrequited love for the strong music of the sword, the chase, and the winecup. As the ale flowed more freely, the latent rhythms of the dance flowered spontaneously into action; whooping appreciatively, the livelier members of the company pushed the wooden benches to the walls and formed up for the reel, the round dance, and the galliard.

Serdor by this time had been joined by a fiddler from Cumfrey and an impromptu percussion section armed with an assortment of plate and cutlery. As she threaded her way along the edge of the forming dance-set, Margoth was abruptly relieved of a trayful of empty mugs and swept onto the floor.

Her captor was a gangling, good-natured saddler, who said, "Come on, hen—we're needin' another lassie," and locked his elbow firmly through hers. Catching at a distance the mischievous gleam in Serdor's dancing eyes, Margoth cast one wary glance at the size of her partner's feet, then abandoned herself recklessly to the boisterous patterns of a country jig.

At the end of the set, pink and breathless, she adroitly ducked out of an importunate group of the saddler's rivals and beat a hasty retreat to the bar. Arn was bent double behind the counter, trying to coax a few last drops of brown ale out of the cask into the mug he held under the spout.

"It's no good—I'm going to have to go down to the cellar for another barrel," he said. "That fellow by the door—yes, that's him in the red doublet—wants a brandy, and his three mates want cider. Can you take care of them while I'm gone?"

A unanimous "Heuch!" from the dancers on the floor made the rafters ring.

"Oh, I suspect I'll manage," said Margoth.

"Well enough. I won't be long," said Arn. He craned his neck for another look, and added, "Just make sure they pay on the spot."

He passed her the unfilled glass and disappeared through the door leading back to the kitchen. The music reached a crescendo, then skipped to a timely halt. As the after-echoes settled, a voice said in her ear, "If no one wants that half-pint you've got in your hand, I'll take it."

It was Serdor, flushed with success and exertion. "The fiddler can carry on from here: I've earned my keep for the night," he said, tipping a cupful of coppers into the pouch at his belt. "What would you say to a dance or two when Arn gets back? I promise I won't tread on your toes."

"In that case, I accept," said Margoth. "Where are you off to just now?"

"To put my instrument away," said Serdor. "If Caradoc should happen to come in and mistake me for some presumptuous upstart, I want all the breakables safely out of his reach."

"Don't be unkind," said Margoth reprovingly. "You know Caradoc's been the model of good behavior since Forgoyle took him to task."

"Not entirely without some difficulty—but I suppose that's all the more to his credit," said Serdor. "Never mind. It's only two more days till the examination. After that, we can all breathe easily again."

He gave her a whimsical look and departed. Left on her own, Margoth gave a businesslike tug to her apron strings and plucked three mugs and a brandy-glass off the shelf behind the bar.

Someone had wedged the front door open, admitting a stream of cold March air. Picking her way through an obstacle course of outstretched legs and displaced furniture, Margoth came to a smart halt next to the man in the red doublet and deposited his glass on the table in front of him.

The three men with him leaned forward to rake in their tankards as she set them down one at a time. Her gaze traveling impassively over the stained cuffs and loutish unshaven faces, Margoth drew back a pace, and said briskly, "There you are, masters. That will be half a crown, if you please."

The man in the red doublet sat up and draped a negligent arm over the back of his chair. Favoring her with an insolent stare, he said, "We ain't done yet. Tell the host tō chalk up an account and we'll pay it before we leave."

One of his companions passed a remark behind his hand to the man sitting to the left of him. Both of them sniggered. Grimacing inwardly, Margoth summoned the effort to be pleasant, and said, "I'm sorry, sir. Master Aldarshot doesn't make a habit of extending credit."

"Don't he? That's too bad." The man's slate-colored gaze traced the line of her bodice like a dirty finger. Taking up his glass, he said, "I bet you could talk him into it."

The glass was within easy reach of her hand. Margoth restrained the impulse to cause an accident and smiled through set teeth. "Now why on earth should I want to do that?"

The man shrugged. "I just thought you might do a favor for a friend."

"For a friend," said Margoth shortly, "I might. But you don't qualify even as an acquaintance. And so I'm afraid you're going to have to pay by the round, like everyone else."

One of the other men at the table gave a hoarse bark of derision. "Watch it, Mordi. This filly means business."

At neighboring tables, heads were beginning to turn. Grinning still, Mordi shifted his weight in his seat. "That's all right by me—as long as there's a bit of pleasure to go with it."

His eyes narrowed speculatively. An instant later, he lunged forward.

Margoth leaped aside, but his fingers snagged her left sleeve. Trapped amid the tangle of chairs, she wheeled sharply and whipped her arm out of his grasp, but a second later he caught her 'round the waist and jerked her backward into a stale-smelling bear hug.

Mordi's companions exploded into bellows of ribald laughter. With her captor's alcoholic breath streaming down the back of her neck, Margoth shot a harassed look in the direction of the bar.

Neither Serdor nor Arn was anywhere in sight. Crimson with indignation, Margoth was about to jab a disciplinary elbow into the pit of her assailant's stomach when there was a sudden flurry of shifting furniture and a choked squawk of astonishment from the man who was holding her.

His grip dragged at her shoulders. As she fought for balance a familiar voice, honed to a cutting edge, said, "Let her go, scum. Or you'll be bald before your time."

There was a brief pause, punctuated by an oath from Mordi. He pushed her from him with a snarled epithet and pivoted, fists upraised. "Caradoc, *no!*" cried Margoth, then dived out of the way as her erstwhile assailant sailed backward through the air and landed flat on the floor among the rushes.

Shrieks of alarm broke out on all sides as the bystanders scrambled for safe distance. Eyes smoldering with single-minded ire, Caradoc bore down on his sister's attacker and caught him by the collar.

The table by the door went flying as Mordi's three associates lunged to the rescue. "Look out!" called Margoth sharply, and winced as two of them piled onto Caradoc from behind.

The third man stopped to snatch up a stool. "Oh no you don't!" said Margoth grimly, and took aim with a pewter tankard.

It bounced off her victim's left temple and clattered to the floor. As she reached for another, a long-fingered hand caught her firmly by the wrist. "For God's sake, get back before you get hurt," snapped Serdor, and bounded on past her.

He was purposefully weighing something in his other hand that Margoth recognized as the kitchen pepperbox. Sidestepping the groaning form of the man Margoth had dinted, he stalked over to where the main struggle was still in progress and emptied the contents of the box over all concerned.

Combat came to an immediate and shattering halt. Whooping and sputtering, with red eyes streaming and nasal passages on fire, the four men on the floor abruptly abandoned their differences and subsided into fits of agonized sneezing.

Serdor waited a minute or two until most of the dust had settled, then waded in. Hooking Caradoc under the armpits, he disentangled him from his helpless opponents and dragged him, still detonating, out through the open doorway onto the step.

The novice mage had a cut lip and a blooming black eye. Surveying the damage, Serdor wordlessly handed him a cloth. Dabbing at the blood on his chin, Caradoc gulped air, then said stuffily through his nose, "Is Margoth all right?"

"Yes, I'm all right," said Margoth from behind them. Joining them, she inspected her brother's face. "That's more than we can say for you. I'll get you a piece of raw meat for that eye. That should help until Forgoyle can treat it properly." She added soberly, "Let's hope he's got a recipe for canceling bruises. Somehow, I don't think the Council of Magisters would believe you if you told them you'd walked into a door."

CHAPTER 4

The Examination

Twice a year, once in the autumn and once in the spring, all the members of the Order of Mage Hospitallers of Ambrothen—servitors, ordinaires, preceptors, and magisters— met together in Council to witness the selection of new members for the Order from among the novices trained in the stone-walled courts of St. Welleran's.

Steeped in tradition, in wealth and reverence, the Hospitallers occupied a privileged place in Garillan society, and membership was a coveted honor. Coming from virtually every town and village within the environs of Ambrothen, crowding elbow-to-elbow the long benches in the chapter houses adjoining the cathedral's south transepts, the aspirants were many, the vacancies few.

The utilitarian rigors of early instruction—the reading and writing, the anatomy, pharmacology, and theology—eliminated at the outset the foolish, the frivolous, the easily discouraged. Eliminated also, in later stages of the training, were those who failed to exhibit the depth of memory, the single-mindedness of concentration, the strength of will, and the degree of self-discipline necessary for the effective practice of the art of healing. Those who remained faced their ultimate challenge in the conciliar examinations.

It was Caradoc's second chance.

That he had been given a second chance was a minor

miracle for which Forgoyle Finlevyn was largely responsible. Sitting now in eminent discomfort among his nine fellow magisters on the left side of the chancel, Forgoyle surreptitiously scanned the sea of faces below. Failing to locate Caradoc's among them—the back ranks were clustered among the pillars and beyond the reserve of candlelight from the high altar—he eased his shoulders away from the unaccommodating back of his chair and made an effort to attend to the final phrases of invocation.

A chorus of well-drilled "amens" rumbled through the columns in the wake of the last word. Closing the vellum-bound volume before him, the preceptor allowed his palms to lie reverent on the jeweled covers for an extra instant in honor of the occasion before glancing deferentially sideways in the direction of An'char Maeldrake, Grand Master of Ambrothen.

Smoothly taking his cue, An'char left his seat in a rustle of heavy ceremonial satin and paced solemnly forward, his measured footfalls echoing a little on the marble mosaics as he took his place on the edge of the tongue-shaped dais at the base of the pulpit. From where he sat, Forgoyle could, with difficulty, make out the design under the Master's feet: three six-rayed stars strung along a common axis, enclosed by an eye-shaped frame. Trinity and unity—the emblems of the faith by which the Hospitallers lived their lives.

Unlike the preceptor, An'char bore no book in his hands. What he was about to say had long ago been committed, syllable by syllable, to memory; and custom had served to deepen the groove of the mind until the words flowed freely as water in a well-worn channel.

It was of the Hospitallers' history that he first spoke. Fingers loosely curled in his lap, Forgoyle listened quietly to the quaint, time-worn phrases as, using the language of another time, An'char recalled a Garillon of the past.

"In the ancient days of the kingdom of East Garillon, when Dunsinar was still its name, there lived between the mountains and the sea a race of seers, the Corrianon in the tongue of old, they who by their arts first unlocked the mystery of the smaragdi, the magestones of power, and taught their descendants the use of them for the commonweal of all the land.

"And for many long years there was peace in Dunsinar, and prosperity under the rule of the Corrianon, the seer-kings. But in the end, lore waned in Dunsinar, and after a time, a new race came east from over the mountains. Their chieftains, the Gerys Ap Lliar, made war upon the Corrianon and wrested from them the sovereignty of the land, laying waste to the hallows of the conquered peoples, and forbidding the teaching of the ancient wisdom.

"Thus were the Corrianon driven into hiding, and thus perished much of their learning. But that which was preserved was handed down in secrecy from master to master, till the coming of the Wardens from over the eastern sea, and the renewing of the covenant of the Magia. . . ."

It was a story the youngest novice knew by heart before he had been six months an apprentice of the Order: how the last kings of Vesteroe, the now-legendary Empire of the East, had sent one Evelain Du Morrigan with five great ships to establish a new kingdom in the lands to the west, how Evelain had enlisted the aid of the remnants of the Corrianon, and how together they had succeeded in overthrowing the descendants of the Ap Lliar warlords.

In the early years of his reign as first Warden of East Garillon, so renamed in honor of his king, Evelain had fulfilled the terms of his alliance by marrying a daughter of the Corrianon royal line, taking her name—Whitfauconer—according to the custom of her people. He had then further demonstrated his gratitude by founding the Order of Mage Hospitallers to perpetuate the religion and teachings he had come to revere.

The members of the new Order in time set up their infirmaries, their dormitories, their almshouses, libraries, and schools, carrying their skills and their expanding wealth, spiritual and material, into the sister-cities of East Garillon, so that now all five towns—Farrowaithe, Ambrothen, Tyrantir,

Glyn Regis, and Gand of the Bells—had each her chapter house, her college, and her cathedral.

And her manners. And her morals, the latter governed according to the written canons of the old Masters: temperance and chastity, reverence and self-governance; sobriety, piety, courtesy, compassion—the four seals of wisdom, the four signs of the upright life.

It was not enough that the initiate should be proficient in the mage's healing arts. Consecrated to the right and proper use of extra-personal power, the novice must be prepared to submit himself unconditionally to the dictates of reason and religion as taught by the Order he served.

And because the Order was itself pledged to guarantee the right and proper use of the Magia, the Council of Magisters, of whom Forgoyle was one, were exceedingly careful in making their choices from among the novices under their tutelage.

The anteroom was too warm for comfort. Running a finger around the inner circumference of his tight collar, Caradoc glanced obliquely at the other two young men who shared with him the long padded bench.

They wore, as he did, the green robes of a novice, but neither was well-known to him. It cost him a pang of discomfiture to recall that both were younger than he by more than a year. They sat unmoving, their tensions, if they had any, masked by their silence. Caradoc uncomfortably fingered the fading bruise under his left eye. Forgoyle's ministrations had reduced the swelling and the discoloration, but he knew he still bore the visible shadow of combat.

But he could not afford to worry about that now. Withdrawing his gaze, he set his mind deliberately not to dull its edge by attempting to recall ten years of instruction in the few minutes remaining to him. Lost in the effort, he did not hear his name called until the proctor repeated it, then tapped him peremptorily on the arm. "Caradoc Penlluathe? Hurry up. The magisters are waiting."

Having been in the Examiners' Hall before, he knew what to expect. Familiar, the remembered details leaped to his eyes as he crossed the threshold and heard the double doors fold together at his back: the long, slablike table, its white marble surface tinctured with spilled residues of others' essays in the Hospitallers' art; the tall shelves to his right crowded with bottled herbs, essences, and elixirs; basins, flagons, and cups made from glass, earthenware, wood, and stone.

And directly in front of him, beyond the table, the two shallow steps leading up to the level of the Examiners' Circle—not, in fact, a circle, but a crescent formed of eleven straight-backed wooden seats, arranged so that their occupants would have full view of the rest of the room. And before the central chair, somewhat more ornately carved than the other ten, a short-stemmed lectern upon which rested, open, the Book of Caer Ellyn.

Forgoyle was in his appointed place, two chairs to the right of the Grand Master. Glancing involuntarily in Forgoyle's direction, Caradoc experienced a brief and wholly impersonal instant of eye contact before Forgoyle turned his attention to An'char.

Acutely conscious of the disfiguring marks on his face, Caradoc bowed low as custom demanded. An'char, however, did not allude to them. Forefinger holding its place lightly among the illuminated capitals on the page before him, he fixed upon Caradoc a penetrating pair of discerning black eyes, and said, "Master Penlluathe, good day. If you feel yourself prepared, we shall begin with matters of general knowledge. What, if you please, is the first degree of Orison?"

Caradoc drew a deep breath and recited, "The first degree of Orison is that of Interior Silence. Its purpose is to compose the mind for the task at hand."

"And the second?"

"The Orison of Sensibility, which permits the mage to identify the nature of his patient's complaint."

"And the third?"

"The Orison of Affinity, which allows the mage to establish physical rapport with his patient so that he may effectively enter into the Orison of Healing."

"These four degrees of Orison," continued Caradoc, "comprise the Quadrivium of Bodily Physic. The higher Trivium of Spiritual Revelation is composed of the Orisons of Seeing, or Union, and of Restoration. . . ."

He was soundly grounded in theory. All that books could teach him he had learned as well as any other examined by the Council that day. But his true skill as a healer had yet to be proven, not on the basis of correct answers to hypothetical questions, but on the living bodies of sick men and women.

On the table in front of An'char stood a small silver gong, together with a silver hammer. He lifted the hammer and struck a single bell-like note. In response, a grey-robed serving brother stepped into the room from an alcove to the left of the door. In his hands he bore a length of thick undyed silk.

A second serving brother emerged silently from another alcove to the right of the door, carrying on a silver tray a silver flagon, a tall-stemmed cup of clear crystal, and an orb crowned with the symbol of the Order: a silver star surmounting the intersection of two crossed staves of flowering wood.

The two brothers bypassed Caradoc on his right and on his left, leaving the sacramental objects on the table in front of the Grand Master before retiring. An'char waited until they had left the room before lifting his hands palm-outward to the level of his shoulders, intoning, "The Magia is the breath of God, power supernal, in which is vested life and health. We, His acolytes, do herein dedicate ourselves anew to the husbandry of the power entrusted to our keeping, not for our own enrichment, but for the welfare of all in need of healing, irrespective of degree."

He bowed his head, bringing his palms together before his face. The other members of the Council followed suit. After a meditative silence, An'char prayed, using the traditional words of dedication.

Raising his head, he took the flagon and the cup and poured out a measure of deep-red wine. Then he lifted the cup in his left hand and sketched the Mages' six-pointed star in the air over the brim of it with the three middle fingers of his right hand. "May he who is to receive this cup remain ever true to thy designs. And may thy blessing be ever upon him in his performance of thy will."

Lifting the cup to his lips, the Grand Master took a single sip, then extended the cup to Caradoc. Stepping forward, Caradoc accepted it. Under the grave, watchful faces of the members of the Council, he drained it at a long draught and returned the cup to the table.

An'char next took the orb and spoke the formal words of blessing over it before placing it in Caradoc's outstretched hands. The metal cool against his skin, Caradoc knelt to utter his response. "I, Caradoc Penlluathe, aspirant to the Order of Mage Hospitallers, do here pledge myself ready to submit to such tests as may prove me worthy of acceptance to the brotherhood. To that end, I do hereby swear solemnly before this company that I do undertake this calling most soberly, asking and receiving the sanction and protection of God that I may serve His people in reverence."

He rose and returned the orb to An'char. The Grand Master laid it on the table next to the flagon, then took up the silken blindfold. Caradoc bent his head submissively as the primate of the Order in Ambrothen bound the blindfold securely over his eyes. Then he took seven steps backward to await the onset of the test.

An'char struck a second chiming note off the gong and immediately two of the chapter's brothers ordinary brought in the first patient. There was a rustle of displaced bedding and a soft bump as the attendants set down the bier on the floor. Out of the ensuing silence, An'char's voice spoke sonorously: "Caradoc Penlluathe, you may begin."

The final test. Raising his head, the soft silk heavy against his face, Caradoc twitched back the sleeves of his robe and took his smaragdus between his cupped hands. Flesh-warm to the touch, the magestone pulsed softly against his fingers. Holding himself erect, Caradoc brought his body gradually under the rod of his conscious will.

The autonomic reflexes of his body yielded first to external control. The rapid action of his lungs subsided; the anxious pounding of his heart eased itself into slow, rhythmic beats. As his body acquiesced to the preternatural quiet he asked of it, his senses began to quicken toward superlative acuity. Using the smaragdus as the focus, Caradoc called a nexus of refined impressions into his mind from touch, smell, and hearing.

"Are you ready, Caradoc Penlluathe?" said An'char.

"I am, Your Eminence."

"So be it, then," said An'char. "May the Lord God be your mentor. Where is your patient?"

Caradoc pressed the smaragdus more tightly between his palms. At once, the nerves along his arms and face took on the heightened sensitivity that allowed him to locate by sensation what his eyes could not see: a consciousness of warmth, distinct from the coolness of the floor and the surrounding air. Caradoc said aloud: "He is lying five feet from me, to my left, on a bed raised two feet off the floor."

An'char neither confirmed nor denied Caradoc's announcement. His voice without expression, he said, "What is the patient's ailment?"

Caradoc took two steps forward. The power of the Magia, channeled through the smaragdus, enhanced his nonvisual perceptions until he could hear even the drafts in the room, could smell even the slight pungency left behind on the blindfold by the touch of the brother's hands. Releasing his grasp on the smaragdus, he dropped to one knee beside the man on the bier and laid his fingers lightly on forehead and breast.

At once his ears and fingers relayed a jumble of information—the drum-throb of the heart, the roaring of the blood as it raced in circles through veins and arteries, the reed-whistle of air through the passages of the lungs, the healthy turbulence of the stomach. The man was asleep—the fragrance of poppies identified the narcotic he had been given. And beneath the quiet induced by the drug, the sharp frangibility of damaged nerves.

Directing his voice toward the Grand Master's chair, Caradoc said, "This man has a compound fracture: tibia and fibula of the right leg, with some internal splintering. No other injuries beyond bruises to the right thigh."

There was a pause that might have been approval. "The leg has not yet been set," added Caradoc.

Again the not-quite-neutral pause. "Then it remains for you to set it," said An'char.

It promised to be a demanding task. His brow creased with concentration, Caradoc bent forward. Leaf-light, his fingertips located, one by one, the shards of bone in their matrix of flesh. Fixing the position of each in its relation to the others, he again grasped his magestone in one hand while the other rested on his patient.

The force of the Magia mounted within him in response to his need. Slowly, slowly, but ever more surely, he felt the glowing power infuse his whole being. When the glow reached his fingertips, he began to direct, painstakingly willing the jointure, piece by piece, of splintered bone, repairing torn cells, healing and sealing with the power at his knowledgeable command. Some part of him had entered the body lying before him, his strength flowing from a never-ending source, his own body a paean of joy in the practice of his craft. Suffused with power, he lingered momentarily, rejoicing in the healed flesh under his hand, then gently withdrew, first releasing the magestone, allowing the glow to gradually fade, and finally bringing his hands together, head bowed in peace.

As the smaragdus cooled he rose and turned his head to where he knew An'char would be.

"It is complete," he said, and smiled.

CHAPTER 5

The Consequence

"Come away, my love, for now 'tis May
And roses in their prime.
Come away, my love, for life is short
And swift the pace of time.
And if you come, I'll give to you
A crown of gold to wear,
All twined from the branch of the yellow
   rose,
All on your raven hair.

"And thus sang I to my true love
All in the month of May,
But autumn sorrow rings me now,
For she has gone away.
She has gone, I see, with summer
   time,
With the waning of the year,
And the flowers that I gave to her
Are withered, dry, and sere."

The pure tenor voice that had lifted the melody from the lutestrings gave it back again with consummate grace and then ceased. For one jeweled firelit moment longer, Serdor's long fingers gentled the chords into silence before he relaxed and laid the lute carefully aside.

From her vantage point by the opposite wall, overlooking a dozen dark, featureless heads, Margoth smiled a little tremulously as her blue eyes rested on his planed, half-averted face, with its lightly-hollowed cheeks and expressive mouth.

The applause broke out from every corner of the Beldame's big common room, stirring the smoke-scented air with a strong current of appreciation. She saw Serdor smile somewhat self-consciously before he swung himself off the edge of the table where he had been sitting and made his way past the crowded benches to her side.

He greeted her with a mock groan. "Ale! Water! Anything wet you happen to have handy. What time is it?"

Margoth filled a tankard to the brim and handed it to him. "Almost ten o'clock." Her eyes following his movements as he took the cup and raised it to his lips, she said, "They certainly aren't rushing things, are they? The Council of Magisters, I mean."

Serdor shrugged and upended his tankard, exposing the strong sinews of his throat as he tilted his head to drink. Dropping his elbow after two swallows, he gave her one of his quizzical looks over the tankard's rim. "Did you expect them to be quick about it? Don't forget how important they are. Only little people like you and me have to do things in a hurry."

His tone was cheerful, but Margoth wasn't entirely convinced. Seeing her dubious expression, Serdor said quietly, "There's nothing to be gained by worrying now. Remember Caradoc's talents, and trust him to prove his own worth."

For a moment, Margoth was silent. Then, summoning a determined smile, she nodded. Satisfied, Serdor finished his ale and gave her back the empty cup before delving into the pouch at his belt. "My rent's due tomorrow," he said wryly. "That means I'd better pay my shot while I still can. How much?"

"Nothing at all, you bantling-brained nightingale," said a third voice, from behind him. "Whatever gave you the notion that I expect you to pay for the miserly pint or two you allow yourself in a night?'' inquired Arn.

"I beg your pardon. I was under the impression that it was customary,'' said Serdor, turning around. "Don't tell me I've been in error all these years.''

Arn snorted. "If I'd known you'd be drawing a full house every night of the week, I'd have hired you instead of Margoth. I've sold more ale and wine in the two weeks since you started playing here than I did in two months previous. The least I can do by way of gratitude is furnish sops for your vocal cords.''

"Thank you. In that case, I'll have another,'' said Serdor, and wandered off with a replenished mug in hand to talk with some travelers who had arrived from Farrowaithe the night before. Her eyes following him, Margoth saw him take a seat at their table and embark upon what was evidently an animated conversation.

"I'll say this for our Serdor: He's got talent enough to spare,'' said Arn thoughtfully, wiping his brow on the hem of his apron. "That old lute-maker—what was his name—Holbeyn?—really knew what he was about when he took that lad on as an apprentice. Pity the old man's nephew couldn't see any farther than the end of his own jealous nose when he took over the shop from his uncle. Serdor'd be well on his way to master-journeyman by now.''

"Which is precisely what our young Master Holbeyn *didn't* want to see,'' said Margoth sourly. "Well, at least Serdor's still got his music. That's just as well, since the few odd jobs he manages to pick up these days don't pay enough to keep a rat in cheese-parings.''

"Aye. What fairly puzzles me,'' said Arn, "is why some lord high-muckety-muck hasn't swept him off the street-corner and into the manor house to lead a fat, pampered life as the family songbird.''

"There are all kinds of reasons,'' said Margoth. "For one thing, he has no influential connections. For another, he's not nearly decorative enough.''

"Decorative? Well,'' said Arn fair-mindedly, "I'll admit

he's not your usual butter-faced choirboy. But there's nothing wrong with the lad's looks that a haircut, a new suit of clothes, and a couple of months' extra feeding wouldn't cure. What he needs to do is worm his way into the Swan or the White Pelican. If the fine ladies and gentlemen once got a chance to hear him play, he'd be on his way to a comfortable future."

"Assuming that he got a chance to be heard before they ordered him to be flung out on his ear and thrashed for his insolence," said Margoth tartly.

She glanced at the clock on the mantel. Catching the sudden flicker of anxiety in her eyes, Arn said, "What do you suppose is keeping Caradoc? Shouldn't he have been back here by now, beaming with good news?"

"You'd have thought so," said Margoth, and produced a rather unconvincing smile. "Ceremonial congratulations undoubtedly take time. . . ."

Another hour went by.

The overnight lodgers retired one by one to their rooms, and the regular company evaporated. Left sitting by himself on the bench with a dry tankard and a growing sense of uneasiness, Serdor stood up and walked over to the window, trying not to notice the unconcealed worry in Margoth's blue eyes as she and Arn went from table to table collecting empty plates and cups.

The street outside was too dark to be revealing, and it was not until they heard footsteps on the front steps that they realized that there was anyone coming.

An instant later, the door to the common room flew open, propelled by a grandiloquent flourish of vigorous hands. A tall, broad-shouldered figure stood outlined in the doorway. Light from the fire and the lamps picked out the ruddy sheen of his hair and the almost feverish glitter in his eyes. Margoth gave a muffled exclamation and ran foward as Caradoc swept grandly over the threshold.

"Good evening, my friends," he said, his shadow magnificently magnified on the wall at his back, the proud bones of his face gilded with light. "I suppose you're wondering what's been keeping me."

Serdor watched, speechless, as Caradoc flung back his head, a strange, disturbing smile playing over his curled, splendid mouth. "Allow me to convey the results of today's examinations," he said in a voice razor-edged with ghastly triumph. "The Council of Magisters have determined that despite my undeniable ability, I am too ill-mannered to be admitted to the Order. . . ."

CHAPTER 6

The Merchant

As the river-barge—affectionately, if inaccurately, named *Thistledown*—plied its leisurely way toward Farrowaithe along the upper west bank of Lake Damanvagr, it was the sight of fruit trees in blossom, planted row on row to the water's edge, that signaled the barge crew that they would shortly be within sight of their destination.

Gudmar Ap Gorvald—who owned the barge, and the orchards, and the big country house yet hidden from view—had made the lake voyage from Ambrothen to Farrowaithe many times before. But the peripatetic life of a merchant-adventurer who was also a diplomat had never wearied him of the pleasures of homecoming, and when the barge's master came aft with the news that they would be putting into shore in a few minutes' time, Gudmar laid aside the documents he had been reviewing without so much as a second glance, and went out to watch for his first glimpse of Valden Manor.

Presently his eye caught the red gables, the half-timbered walls, the tall window bays with their mullions catching the sunlight like mirrors. The gardeners, he noticed, had been turning the earth along the paths. As the barge glided to a halt next to the dock, the humid odors of soil and grass were stronger than the scent of lake water.

Tobe Greenham, the manager of the estate, was waiting for them on the landing, perspiring in the warmth of the day.

Vaulting the barge's portside railing with a negligible expenditure of effort, Gudmar clapped two vigorous hands to the smaller man's shoulders and grinned down at him through a thick golden beard. "Hello, Tobe. You're looking well. I take it you got my message?"

The little man nodded. "Aye, Master Gudmar. The day before yesterday. Your rooms are all aired and ready for you. But . . ."

He stopped, his round face puckered in disapproval. "But what?" inquired Gudmar warily.

Tobe's scowl deepened. Looking his employer squarely in the eye, he said, "Do you know a man with only one hand, sir?"

It was Gudmar's turn to frown. "Why do you ask?"

"Because," said Tobe, "there's a one-handed fellow arrived up at the house two hours ago, demanding to see you."

Intrigued in spite of himself, Gudmar thought a moment. "Is he still there?"

"Aye, sir. He refused to leave, even though we told him you weren't expected home before nightfall. Said he had something important to discuss with you that wouldn't wait." Tobe made a sound not unlike a snort. "Shall I have Perry and Wyatt put him out, sir?"

"No," said Gudmar. "If it's who I think it is, one-handed or no, it would cost everyone involved far more trouble than it's worth. No, I'll go and see him. Where is he now?"

"In the Green Room, sir. I didn't know where else to put him. . . ."

"Never mind. It doesn't matter," said Gudmar. "Go tell our nameless friend that I'll be joining him as soon as I've finished here."

When Gudmar arrived, his tenacious guest was standing at the window with his back to the room. Taking in at a glance the undisciplined shock of black curls and the empty left coat sleeve, Gudmar set one broad shoulder comfortably against the right-hand lintel and said cheerfully, "Well, I'll be damned! So it *is* you."

Harlech Hardrada turned at the sound of his voice and

flashed several gold-capped teeth in a broad grin. "Aye, we're all of us entitled t' a pleasant surprise now an' again."

" 'Nasty shock' was the phrase I had in mind," chuckled Gudmar, coming forward to exchange handclasps. He looked his friend up and down and said, "God, it must be two years since I last saw you. How have you been, you tarry old villain?"

"Oh, well enow," said Harlech, and raked a bright eye around the room. "If ye were tae offer me a drink, I might tell ye more."

"This isn't the Red Lion, but I think we could probably find something potable on the premises," said Gudmar. Stepping aside, he gave two tugs at a tasseled bellpull. "What's your fancy? Malmsey? Arrack? Ale? We've a tolerable home brew here. . . ."

Some time later, halfway down a bottle of aqua vitae, Gudmar poured them each another measure, then settled back in his chair. "I'm sorry if my steward wasn't very cooperative. But you might at least have given him your name."

Harlech sucked in a mouthful of liquor and swallowed. "That's where ye're wrong. The fewer people ken I was here, the better."

Arrested with his glass suspended between the table and his mouth, Gudmar gave the other man a long look. "You're not joking. Harlech, are you by chance in some kind of trouble?"

Harlech showed teeth in an expression that bore no resemblance to a grin. "That's puttin' it mildly. And if I cannae take steps tae get me and my lads out of it, we just might all wind up kissin' the hangman's daughter. Or worse."

His brown, hook-nosed face was seamed as a walnut. "Ye ken I'll be for askin' ye a favor? Before I do, ye'd best have the tale from the beginnin'."

He drew breath. "Remember the arrangement we had wi' that spicer-chappie out of Gand? It was sweet: all we had tae do tae earn our pay plus commission was tae make two runs a month into Pirzen It'za an' back as long as the orangeries were in fruit. Nothin' easier—till we ran into a bugger of a gale off Deryss and lost th' whole bloody cargo.''

"And that," said Gudmar, "is where the trouble started."

It wasn't a question. "Aye, ye've said it," agreed Harlech. "Tae get our commission in the first place, we had tae sign articles sayin' we would stand responsible for goods damaged in transit. When we limped into port wi' our hull awash wi' brine-pickled oranges, we discovered we had tae raise a baron's ransom practically overnight or go to gaol. I was actually considerin' sellin' the *Yusufa* when I got a chance at another job. I was that desperate I decided t' take it. But I wish now I'd just sold off an' been done wi' it.'' He paused and glowered into his glass.

"What kind of job was it?" asked Gudmar.

Harlech's black-bearded face lifted. "What d'ye think? Runnin' juju'bi. Into Ambrothen."

There was a moment's silence. "You sap-headed fool," said Gudmar in measured tones. "I don't suppose it occurred to you at the time that you might have come to me."

Harlech grimaced. "Aye, I did think on it. But there was the spicer howlin' for his compensation, an' me not knowin' where ye was t' be found . . . well, I had tae decide in a hurry."

"And made the wrong choice," said Gudmar.

"We were told it would just be a one-off thing," said Harlech defensively. He added bitterly, "That turned out t' be a lie, of course. When we got back wi' our first cargo, we were given a choice: make a second run, or have all our names passed on to the magistrates."

He fell abruptly silent. "How many trips have you made since then?" asked Gudmar.

"Four," said Harlech. "Wi' a fifth comin' up. But I don't want tae make it. An' I'm hopin' ye're just the man t' get me out of it."

Gudmar digested this. "I'm certainly willing to try. But first I'll need some solid information. Who hired you in the first place?"

"A tall, black-heided chiel wi' a tongue like a graver's

burin. He gave his name as Rothben, but that'll no' be right,''
said Harlech. "Ye'd be better inquirin' after him by his title:
his lads refer t' him as 'His Eminence.' ''

This was the title normally reserved for high-ranking members of the Hospitallers' Order. "Why that, I wonder?" said
Gudmar, frowning. "Could it be that this Rothben used to be
in holy orders?"

"That I couldna tell ye. But ye could doubtless find out,"
said Harlech. "For my part, I'm willin' tae give whatever
information I can about where this Rothben might be found—
provided ye can guarantee me an' my lads won't have t'
stand trial for yon smuggling charge."

"I'm scheduled to pay a call on the Lord Warden tomorrow morning," said Gudmar. "If I know him as well as I
think I do, we ought to be able to hit upon a satisfactory
arrangement. Do you want to stay here tonight?"

"Thanks, but I've taken enough risks for one day," said
Harlech. "As soon as we've finished that bottle, I'll be off."

"Whatever you think best. But you'd better let me know
where I can find you again when I need to," said Gudmar.

The twinkle suddenly reappeared in Harlech's black eyes.
"In Ambrothen, of course. At the sign of the Red Lion."

CHAPTER 7

The Warden

The fifth of April dawned brightly. Since he was expected at Farrowaithe Keep shortly after ten o'clock, and since he had an eight-mile ride between him and his destination, Gudmar breakfasted early and set out from home while the moon was still visible in the morning sky.

Well-mounted, he reached the outskirts of the city with plenty of time to spare. Beyond the South Port, the traffic became noticeably thicker, as wagons, handcarts, and live-stock jostled for position between the buildings and the waterways. Keeping a tight rein on his big roan stallion, who showed signs of taking exception to the noise, Gudmar struck out along the east bank of one of the main canals and arrived three bridges and several avenues later on the south bank of Castle Tarn.

Built on the island in the midst of the Tarn, Farrowaithe Keep stood wall-within-wall above the waters, with its pennoned towers reflected on the surface of the lake, as on a mirror. In the early days of its builders, the castle had been accessible only by boat. Now, however, the Tarn was spanned to the south by the seven graceful arches of the Warden's Brig.

Both the Brig and the Keep were patrolled and defended by the Farrowaithe Guard, an elite branch of the city's standing militia whose loyalty was pledged to the person of the

Warden. There was a contingent of the Guard on duty at the mainland end of the Brig and another stationed on the other side below the gatehouse. As Gudmar was a frequent visitor to the Keep, and was known, moreover, as one of the Warden's closest friends, he was escorted with deference past these and two other checkpoints, and in due course reached the donjon itself.

Here, dismounting in the cobbled courtyard in front of the main entrance, he was met by the Warden's personal secretary and conducted inside along a cloisterlike gallery to the door of the Warden's personal solarium. Beyond the threshold the air was moist and fragrant with the scent of growing things. Catching sight of a tall figure in brown on the far side of a small marble fountain, Gudmar said, "Three equerries, two lieutenants, a captain, a groom, and a clerk: unless I'm much mistaken, the number of staff between you and the outside world has multiplied in the three months I've been away. Anyone would think you were trying to discourage visitors."

Delsidor Whitfauconer, Seneschal of Farrowaithe and Lord Warden of East Garillon, turned and smiled, his grey eyes lit by a rare warmth. "A necessary precaution, I'm afraid. Not all visitors are as welcome as you are. Did you have a good trip?"

Which was simply another way of asking for news. Side-stepping a pot of plumelike ferns, Gudmar strode forward to receive the Warden's firm handshake, and said, "That depends entirely on your point of view. As merchants, we fared no worse than usual. As diplomats, we might have done a good deal better."

"I take it His Serenity the Commander of the Faithful of the Princedom of Pernatha was less than enthusiastic about lending us his aid in regulating the cultivation of juju'bi weed within his domains," said Delsidor dryly. "There are seats in the window bay over there. Once we've made ourselves comfortable, you can tell me the whole story."

"There isn't really much to tell—at least as far as the Sultan is concerned," said Gudmar, gently pushing aside a delicate spray of white orchids as they moved toward the window the Warden had indicated. "The morning after we put into port at Ghazara, I presented myself and my credentials at the palace. After a fortnight of kicking my heels on the fringes of the court, I was eventually invited to attend a general audience in the imperial throne room and was permitted to deliver your letter to the Sultan in person."

"Two weeks . . . that confirms one or two of my less-than-charitable suspicions about my esteemed counterpart," said Delsidor. "Did he read the letter in your presence?"

Gudmar shook his head. "He merely examined the seals and announced that affairs between princes were best reviewed in private. He then handed the letter, unread, over to his grand vizier and instructed me to return to the palace the following day to receive 'the pearl' of his 'wisdom.' "

Though he was far from pleased, Delsidor's thin lips quivered slightly at this literal rendering of Pernathan court language. "What was it worth?"

"The pearl of his wisdom? Not a lot," said Gudmar frankly. "The Servant of the Servants of the Prophet appreciates your growing concern over the increasing availability of juju'bi and similar narcotics in the coastal cities of East Garillon. However, while he would gladly render you the assistance you require, as a courtesy from one prince to another, he is in this instance hampered by the fact that there exists no Pernathan law forbidding either the growth or export of the weed in question."

"In other words," said Delsidor grimly, "it isn't only the odd peasant farmer who is getting rich off the juju'bi trade. I was afraid of this. I wonder which of His Serenity's eminent courtiers is involved."

"I couldn't even begin to guess. And even if I could, what good would it do?" Slipping down in his chair, Gudmar planted his bootheels on the windowsill. "No, if you're seriously hoping to put a stop to this smuggling, you're going to have to tackle the problem on our own home ground."

"The thought had occurred to me," said Delsidor with bleak irony. "We—the other seneschals and I—have already discussed what might be done to enhance the general effectiveness of our maritime patrols. But without the cooperation of the Pernathan government, it's not going to be easy."

"Oh, I don't know . . . it might prove less difficult than you think," said Gudmar thoughtfully.

Delsidor gave him a penetrating look. "What have you got in mind?"

"A suggestion," said Gudmar with a wry smile. "I have a friend who is in a position to do us a favor—for the right price."

He proceeded to outline Harlech's proposal. At the end of his recital, as Delsidor sat silent in thought, Gudmar said, "I realize the success of this plan involves what might be considered an undesirable compromise, but as far as I know, this man Harlech represents our only real lead in this whole affair so far. It seems to me that it might be worth thinking about."

"What's there to think about?" said Delsidor. "You may tell your friend he has himself a bargain."

He stood up. "So our elusive master-criminal operates out of Ambrothen? You know, I believe it's time I paid a visit to my brother-in-law."

At the mention of Fyanor Du Bors, Seneschal of Ambrothen, Gudmar quirked an eyebrow. "So you're planning to take part yourself in the investigation? Wouldn't it be simpler to let Fyanor handle it?"

"Simpler perhaps," said Delsidor, "but likely to prove less effective. Fyanor is able enough in his own way, but I have reservations about his good judgment. He's too ambitious to be patient, and that could spoil everything."

"You'd better not let him suspect as much," said Gudmar. "I don't think he would take it as a compliment."

"Don't worry: I am quite accustomed to dealing with tender Du Bors sensibilities," said Delsidor with a grimace. "An overwhelming degree of personal vanity is the family vice."

He flexed his shoulders. "Evelake will look after affairs here in Farrowaithe in my absence. He's old enough now to profit by the experience. And he's earned the chance to show what he's made of."

Delsidor's older son had been from earliest childhood a favorite of Gudmar's. "Is Evelake at home then?" asked Gudmar. "I thought he was still in Gand."

"He is," said Delsidor. "But I'm going to send Galledan to fetch him home. The trip there and back should take no more than a fortnight. By that time, I shall have made all my arrangements."

"What about Gwynmira?"

"She'll be coming with me," said Delsidor. "I have no intention of leaving her here to make mischief while I'm away."

Delsidor's relations with his second wife were known to be strictly formal—a circumstance which sentimental people attributed to a lasting devotion to the memory of her deceased predecessor. More knowledgeable than most, Gudmar said thoughtfully, "That will certainly make things easier for Evelake. But I doubt that she'll approve."

"I'm not asking for her approval—merely for her acquiescence," said Delsidor. "She has lately taken to complaining of boredom. A visit to Ambrothen should at least provide a respite from the tedium of hunting parties. . . ."

CHAPTER 8

The Consort

Compact and powerful, the falcon was visible as a brown and white cruciform against the blue of the springtime sky. Borne on shifting air currents, it swooped and circled, its piercing telescopic gaze raking the distant undergrowth of the vale below.

Gwynmira Whitfauconer, consort of the Lord Warden of East Garillon, reined in her horse on the crest of a low wooded hill and paused to watch the falcon's progress. Her escort, Khevyn Ap Khorrasel, Baron of Kirkwell, came to a halt beside her.

The other members of the hunting party had drawn off to the lower slope of the hill, their velvets showing as patches of rich color among the trees. Withdrawing his attention from the floating mote in the air overhead, Khevyn turned and said pleasantly, "Now, Lady Gwynmira, what was it that you wished to discuss with me?"

His companion adjusted her veil with a gloved hand. "A matter of literary conventions, my lord. Are you fond of fairy tales?"

As an opening gambit, it had a certain piquancy. Intrigued, Khevyn shook his head. "I'm afraid I must plead ignorance, my lady. My acquaintance with such stories is slight."

"Indeed? What a pity," said Gwynmira silkily. "Often they have more art to them than one might suspect."

The peregrine disappeared momentarily behind a feathery screen of pine trees. "I would be honored," said Khevyn, "if you would instruct me."

"Gladly. It is important, first, to bear in mind that fairy tales are often rooted in fact," said Gwynmira. "For instance, see if you can guess something of the origin of this story:

"Once upon a time in a kingdom by the sea there lived a king. This lord married and had a son, but shortly after, his wife sickened and died. Two years later, this lord married again, and in due time his second wife also gave birth to a son.

"As these two boys grew, the younger rapidly outstripped the elder in beauty and accomplishment. It was then that people began to whisper that it was a pity that the inheritance of the kingdom should depend upon the order of birth rather than on the degree of merit each possessed."

"An unfortunate accident of circumstances," agreed Khevyn. "Is there more?"

"There is," said Gwynmira. "After a while, some of the more perceptive nobles of the kingdom, among them the younger boy's uncle, decided that it would be in the best interests of the realm if they could contrive to set aside the old laws of inheritance. Accordingly, they made a pact among themselves, pledging that when the old king died, they would work together to put the abler of his two sons on the throne."

"Interesting," observed Khevyn. "But wouldn't these men be guilty of treason?"

Gwynmira toyed with her riding whip. "If one regards sovereignty as residing in a particular person, yes. But if one regards sovereignty as residing in the government itself, then the answer is no."

"I see you are a philosopher," said Khevyn.

"Hardly. Merely a realist," said Gwynmira composedly. She turned to Khevyn and suddenly smiled brilliantly. "Let me put a question to you, my lord—purely out of academic curiosity. Suppose the younger boy's uncle came to you and

offered you certain . . . concessions . . . in return for your
support. What reply would you give him?''

Khevyn considered the matter unhurriedly. ''That would
depend on the nature of the concessions he offered me.''

''Then let me be more specific,'' said Gwynmira equably.
''Suppose the younger boy's uncle offered you, first of all, a
substantial sum of money with which to hire and equip a
large company of retainers. Suppose he agreed to supply you
with additional funds to aid in maintaining this company in
the advancement of his interests. Suppose, beyond this, that
he guaranteed you a political appointment of importance
upon his attaining his object. And suppose he would be
willing to grant you certain mercantile revenues as a token of
his gratitude once he became solidly established. Supposing
that all these were the inducements offered, what would your
answer be?''

Her magnificent eyes challenged him. ''In view of this
lord's evident generosity,'' said Khevyn, ''I should be either
a churl or a fool to decline. However, having agreed to lend
him my support, I would make my unstinting cooperation
contingent upon his faithful observance of the terms of the
contract.''

''It would hardly be wise to do otherwise,'' said Gwynmira
serenely. ''But in this case, you may rest assured that the
nobleman in question will honor his bargains to the letter.''

After that, it was merely a matter of arranging the particulars.

If the Warden's consort found reason to be satisfied with
the fruits of her morning's work, she found cause for alarm
when, upon returning to Farrowaithe Castle, she received
word that her husband wished to see her without delay,
concerning a matter of importance.

The phrasing of the summons was sufficiently curt to be
disquieting. Face-to-face with her own peerless reflection in a
large silver dressing mirror, she spent the time it took for her
maid to comb out her black-amber hair wondering if there
was any conceivable way some hint of her brother's dangerous aspirations might have come to her husband's attention.
When, at the end of a quarter of an hour's internal debate,

she was no nearer to finding an answer to the question, she laid aside her riding habit for more conventional attire and marched out to confront the father of her son in a spirit of veiled defiance.

Half-prepared to expect the worst, she was considerably relieved upon entering his sitting room to discover nothing more sinister in his manner than a slightly heightened degree of aloofness. Relief gave way to waspish irritation, however, when she learned what was about to be expected of her.

"I anticipate leaving for Ambrothen no later than the twenty-second of April," said Delsidor with cool civility. "If you will be so good as to furnish me with an account of your personal requirements, I shall see to it that everything will be provided for your comfort on the road." His tone was maddeningly final.

"And what if I do not choose to go?" inquired Gwynmira sharply.

He merely lifted an eyebrow. "In case you haven't noticed, I am offering you an opportunity to amuse yourself. If there is some particular reason—other than the desire to annoy me—why you would prefer to remain in Farrowaithe at the moment, say so. But don't waste time engaging in melodramatic utterances."

To force the issue any further was to risk arousing unwelcome speculation. Curbing her rising temper with an effort, Gwynmira said, "What about Gythe?"

He looked surprised. "What about him?"

"Will he be coming with us?"

"No," said Delsidor. "Why should he?"

"To learn." Gwynmira showed small, even teeth. "To acquire valuable experience. Evelake is not the only member of the family likely to profit from traveling abroad."

"What makes you so certain that Gythe has nothing to gain by remaining at home?" said Delsidor. He added calmly, "If you ask me, it wouldn't do him any harm to be deprived of your society for a while."

Gwynmira caught her breath, then glared at him. "Just what do you mean by that?"

"There is really no need to look so affronted," said Delsidor.
"I merely point out that Gythe is rapidly approaching the age
when he needs to start establishing his own independence."

"Indeed." Gwynmira gave a trill of brittle laughter. "I
suppose that is why—in your infinite wisdom—you propose
to make him answerable to his brother while we are away."

Delsidor's deep eyes held a glint of repressed fire. "So
that's what galls you? You know, you haven't done your son
any favors by encouraging him to contemplate his own eminence. Sooner or later, he is going to have to accept the fact
that he is not, as you have led him to believe, master of all he
surveys. And now seems as good a time as any to introduce
him to the idea. . . ."

That proved to be the last word on the subject. Her anger
smoldering on the edge of incandescence, Gwynmira returned to her own chambers and spent the next three hours
pacing the floor of her bedroom in hot-eyed resentment.

Then she sat down and began a letter to her brother,
Fyanor Du Bors.

CHAPTER 9

The Brigand

Early in the evening on the ninth day of April, a man wearing the look of a traveler sauntered down a malodorous back street in the waterfront district of Ambrothen and stopped in at a tavern known locally as the Daisy.

Dimly lit and reeking of rancid fat, the common room of the Daisy had little to recommend it. Nothing daunted, the traveler made his way to the knife-scarred bar and apparently ordered a drink compounded of several unusual ingredients.

The shock-headed proprietor shifted a pendulous paunch and wandered off muttering. A few minutes later he returned with a brimming tankard. The traveler accepted it, and a small scrap of paper changed hands under the base of the glass. After paying, the traveler left the drink untasted on the bar and headed for the door.

His next stop was an apothecary's shop wedged between two larger buildings at the end of a rubbish-strewn cul-de-sac. From there he moved on to a dingy hostel lurking among the warehouses above the wharfs. There he received his final set of instructions and set out to keep his projected rendezvous.

His destination proved to be a dark, three-story house not far from the city's principal abattoir. Ushered inside, he was subjected to a systematic body-search and taken upstairs. Here— stripped of hat, cloak, gloves, belt, and weapons—he was ushered into the presence of the man referred to by his confederates as "His Eminence."

After the preliminaries had been disposed of, Borthen Berigeld, a study in sumptuous black from his gleaming hair to his polished boots, leveled a penetrating gaze upon his visitor and said placidly, "You wish to engage my services? Very well. Behold me open to instruction. What is it that you require me to do?"

The visitor, who had been left only slightly ruffled by the cruder aspects of his reception, answered readily. "Undertake a political murder."

Borthen's full red lips collected themselves in derisive admiration. "Interesting, if not highly original. The prospective victim?"

The other man's pale eyes were steady. "Evelake Whitfauconer of Farrowaithe."

If Borthen was startled, or even surprised, there was nothing in his manner to indicate as much. "A rather ambitious undertaking. To what do I owe the honor?"

"Your reputation," replied his visitor, folding his arms.

Feral black eyes veiled themselves as their owner toyed with the emerald on his right hand. "Good lord, is that the only reason?"

"Do you need another?" countered his guest.

"No," said Borthen. "Why do you want me to murder the Lord Warden's son?"

The visitor lifted his chin. "My personal motives can hardly affect either your decision or your performance."

"Forgive my vulgar curiosity," said Borthen. "Let us henceforth be impersonal. So?"

"I was about to ask," said his visitor, "if you have the necessary resources to guarantee success. Should you accept my offer."

"I have the resources," said Borthen, and the insolent, black gaze hardened. "Have you sufficient means to pay me the exorbitant price I would demand in exchange for my expertise?"

"Name the amount," said the visitor promptly.

Borthen did so. When the other man neither winced nor offered to haggle, he added, "This is, of course, only if I succeed in carrying out my part of the bargain. In the unlikely event of failure, you would be under no obligation to pay me anything."

The visitor inclined his head. "I can hardly find fault with that arrangement."

"I didn't expect you would. I shall require a good deal of information of the most practical kind," said Borthen, his manner marginally more decisive. "The young gentleman in question is presently in Gand, is he not?"

"Not for long," said his guest. "I have it on unimpeachable authority that Evelake will be leaving Gand within a fortnight's time, en route to Farrowaithe by the Old High Road. He will be traveling under escort, of course, but I don't suppose you would find that an insurmountable obstacle."

Winged black brows turned sardonic. "If I may be permitted a certain amount of professional pride," said Borthen, "the matter hardly seems a worthy challenge. Why not simply hire a pack of ruffians and do the job yourself?"

"I require strict anonymity," said his visitor, "and I want the job done properly."

Borthen did not pursue the matter. "Your grievance against the Lord Warden must be of considerable magnitude."

His visitor shrugged. "It suffices."

"I will take your word for it," said Borthen. "There will be a considerable hue and cry. We shall have guardsmen and spies nosing every square inch of sod between Mervaine and the Bay of Esk. Nothing like it for exercising one's surplus energies. Your proposal has a certain appeal, if only for training purposes."

His visitor tilted his head. "May I take that to mean you are accepting my proposition."

"You may take it," said Borthen, "that I will discuss the matter with my colleagues."

He rose from his chair and moved toward the door. Hand resting lightly on the lintel—"Kindly remain here until I return," said the leader of the League of the Night-Raven.

"Should you feel lonely in my absence, you will find two of my men outside in the hall."

In the passageway Borthen was joined by a massive individual with grizzled, tightly-curling hair and bare arms knotty with muscle. "Ah, Muirtagh," said Borthen. "How is Gaultry, the customs clerk?"

Borthen's second-in-command curled a disparaging lip. "He sang like a bird when we put him to the question. You were right: he'd lost his nerve and squealed to his superiors. And they went squealing to the seneschal's justiciar."

"Whose province it is to pursue and chastise the ungodly— namely us." Borthen was looking thoughtful. "So firsthand information about our operations has filtered through to the higher authorities. I wonder . . . have you seen our friend in the green baize cloak?"

"The fellow who wanted to arrange a meeting? Not yet," said Muirtagh dourly.

"He has just made me a very tempting offer," said Borthen, with the tenderest hint of a smile. "So tempting that it savors of red herring. He's obviously only an errand boy. I believe I should like to know the person he's working for."

Muirtagh, who had some knowledge of Borthen's resources, accepted this declaration with a growl of assent. Hooking large thumbs in his broad leather belt, he asked, "What about this Gaultry?"

"I leave that matter to your discretion," said Borthen, and the smile broadened unpleasantly. "I'll join you when I've finished here."

Muirtagh, after a glance at the other man's face, grunted and beckoned to the two men standing guard outside the room where Borthen's visitor was waiting. At his signal they left their post and followed him down the stairs.

Alone in the corridor, Borthen turned to face the door and raised his right hand palm-outward so that the ring on his finger drew the torchlight. For the space of several minutes he stood unmoving, his concentrated gaze fixed on the green stone in front of him. Then, drawing breath as if to re-collect himself, he opened the door and stepped across the threshold.

His visitor had seated himself in one of the chairs. As Borthen entered he rose smoothly to his feet and raised his eyebrows inquiringly. "The matter is settled. The boy," said Borthen, "is no longer a matter for your concern."

He extended his right hand. After a marginal hesitation, his visitor stepped forward and took it. His eyes went blank.

First emotions.

Then images.

Then, as Borthen probed more deeply, a scene unfolded:

. . . A spacious study paneled with windows. Behind a marquetry-wood writing table, a slender man in a crimson doublet whose lean, clever face is framed between cropped black curls and a trimly-pointed beard. The Seneschal of Ambrothen, Fyanor Du Bors.

"My sister," says the seneschal, "writes with considerable urgency. Are you familiar with the substance of her letters?"

His sister's envoy nods. "The Lady Gwynmira honors me with her confidence. As a postscript to her missive, I am instructed to add the following message: 'The season of waiting is past, and the harvest is upon us. In the ripeness of the time, let us not hesitate to reap what we have sown.' "

Fyanor smiles. " 'Lest unthrift despoil us of our hopes, and negligence dispossess us of our portion.' I shall not presume to argue with the wisdom of Caer Ellyn. Concerning her stepson, my sister shall be apprised of my decision to act. . . ."

. . . Releasing his visitor's hand, Borthen wished the now alert man a sardonic farewell and allowed him to take his leave. Coming into the room a few minutes later—"Well?" said Muirtagh.

Borthen laughed out loud. "We are about to become the spearhead in a political conspiracy. Our real employer is none other than the Seneschal of Ambrothen himself!"

CHAPTER 10

The Bargain

"By the power vested in this tribunal, you, Caradoc Penlluathe, have been tried and found wanting," the Grand Master had said. "In view of the evidence presented, it is the considered opinion of this Council that you are unfit to assume a place among the ranking members of the Order. . . ." His tone would have struck sparks from steel.

Not even the raucous din of a murky dockside tavern could drown out the words that beat over and over in Caradoc's mind as he sat hunched over a table in one dark corner, staring bleakly into the most recent of uncounted cups of bad wine.

He had spent the past many days—how many, he had no idea—drinking in the back rooms of this and other anonymous dens like it, in a futile attempt to deaden the savagery of his bitterness over the decision of the Council against him. Despite his grim efforts, he could not get drunk. And he was still no nearer to coming to terms with the Council's verdict than he had been on the night he had come away from the examination, bearing the triumphant proof of his healing talent like a gift to the altar, only to have the offering dashed from his hands.

Forgoyle, not troubling to hide his personal dismay, had pleaded that his pupil should not be formally dismissed until the matter had been reviewed by Baldwyn Vladhallyn, Arch

Mage of East Garillon. An'char Maeldrake, grudgingly, had agreed, and they were now awaiting the arrival of an archiepiscopal legate from Farrowaithe. But Caradoc cherished no illusions concerning the outcome of his appeal.

His fury was all the harder to bear for being laced with grief—grief that the gifts which would have made him a great healer should go to waste because those sitting in judgment upon him could not themselves abide a normal human reaction. I gave you ten years of my life, he thought bitterly. And you expect me now meekly to accept that it was all for nothing!

He looked down the long ruin of the years ahead, and his tired anger curdled to despair, to a desperate yearning that left him choked, eyes blurring. He fought for control. Oblivious to the smoke, smells, and noise around him, he drew out his magestone and gazed at it. For a decade, since the early days of his novitiate, he had carried it about his person, and it was now as much a part of him as his hands or his eyes. Through its agency, he had been permitted to taste, even to wield, a power kings might envy, and to contemplate the prospect of giving it up, now, was itself a special agony.

"That's an interesting bauble," remarked a light voice at his elbow. "Did you come by it honestly?"

There was something faintly chilling in the quality of the voice—the remotest suggestion of dissonance, like chimes played out of tune and heard over great distance. The hairs at the nape of his neck prickling for no apparent reason, Caradoc raised his head.

The individual looking down at him projected an impression of height, of expensive, somber clothing, of cold unimpassioned eyes. In no mood to discuss his affairs with anybody, let alone officious strangers, Caradoc defiantly swallowed the last grainy mouthful of wine in his glass and growled, "Have you got some honest reason for asking?"

The newcomer swung one flawlessly booted leg over the bench and sank uninvited into the empty space across from him. "I have a reason, yes. I may be in a position to help you."

It didn't sound like altruism. His jaw hardening, Caradoc demanded belligerently, "What makes you think I need help?"

The other man smiled, not warmly. "Some people would say that the fact you're drinking the house wine speaks for itself. But let's be realistic: a failed Hospitaller can't have many options left open to him."

Coming from a total stranger, this deliberate piece of brutality was as damaging as it was unexpected. Unable to keep from flinching, Caradoc controlled the impulse to lash out with both fists, and said, "I would be interested to know how you came by your information."

"I'm sure you would," agreed his tormentor. "But there are limits to my generosity. What are you going to do, now that your future with the Order is nonexistent? Or haven't you been able yet to summon the fortitude to consider the problem?"

This time the taunt brought Caradoc to his feet. His eyes glinting a dangerous emerald, he said, "If my fortitude is to be the topic of conversation, perhaps you'd like a demonstration," and struck out at the other man's face.

Just short of contact, his wrist was caught and pinned in a lightning grasp so painful that for an instant it took his breath away. Before his fury could reassert itself, the other man's voice, glacial with scorn, said in his ear. "Don't be any greater a fool than you can help. Haven't I said I may be in a position to do you service? Then stop behaving like an oversized juvenile before other people begin to take notice."

The grip on his forearm burned like a bracelet of hot iron. Forced against his will to yield, Caradoc stopped resisting. "That's more like it," said his assailant cordially, and released his wrist. "Now sit down and listen to me."

As Caradoc settled sullenly back in his seat, the man leaned forward and clasped black-gloved hands before him, his voice dropping to an undertone. "While I do not belong to the Hospitallers' Order, I am not entirely a stranger to its internal affairs. If rumor is to be believed, you are a young man of exceptional talents. One wonders what prompted the Council to dismiss someone of such promise."

Caradoc's handsome mouth twisted. "I have bad manners."

"Demonstrably." The other man was unruffled. "Even so, I gather you see yourself as the victim of injustice."

The fire in Caradoc's green eyes had died back to a sullen smolder. "Let's just say I would have appreciated being given the benefit of the doubt. But it's all over and done with now."

"Is it?" There was a gleam in the stranger's dark pupils. "You still have your magestone, don't you?"

Caradoc hunched a petulant shoulder. "Not for long. It's only a matter of time before I'll be forced to give it up."

"Not necessarily," said his companion softly. "There is an alternative."

It suddenly dawned on Caradoc what the other man was suggesting. He straightened his spine with a snap, his eyebrows contracted in protest. "What are you saying? That I should defy the Order and retain possession of the stone?"

"Why not? Don't you want to?"

"Of course I want to! But that's . . ." Caradoc's voice trailed off. Taking a deep breath, he said, "I can't go against the Rule of the Order like that. The Council would see me stricken down like—"

"Only if they caught you." The stranger's smile was provocative. "Once beyond their reach, you would be your own master."

"You make it sound so easy," said Caradoc derisively.

"It could be far less difficult than you imagine," said the man in black. "As you will discover if you leave it to me to make the arrangements."

There was a long pause. The blood high in his cheeks, Caradoc asked flatly, "What exactly is it that you're offering me?"

"Freedom," said the stranger, his smile deepening. "Freedom, and the chance to make the most of your gifts, unhampered by the restrictions of the Order."

A long silence followed.

"An attractive prospect," said Caradoc. "What's in it for you?"

The man in black threw back his head and laughed. "You learn quickly. Very well: I am about to embark on a business venture, the success of which is contingent upon my securing the services of a mage. For my part, I am prepared to provide horses, protection, and money—money enough to buy independence. Are you interested?"

Again there was a silence.

But the decision had really been made already, somewhere in the depths of outraged shock and savage anger, in the endless days and nights of sodden, bleak despair, so alien to his nature. Suddenly it was an enormous relief to act rather than try not to think.

"Tell me," said Caradoc grimly, "what exactly do you have in mind?"

"With pleasure," said the man in black. "But first let me introduce myself. My name is Borthen Berigeld."

CHAPTER 11

The Fugitive

The door-latch stuck, as it always did on wet mornings. Fingers scrabbling over cold metal, Margoth steadied her hand for the additional second it took to shift it, then swept out onto the step.

A thick dawn-fog lay white about the shops, chilling the April morning, cushioning dark squares of window glass with cottony damp. Drawing her cloak against the penetrating air, Margoth shot one worried glance backward at the house she was leaving, then stepped down into the street.

It was difficult to keep to a walk. Blinking through mist-beaded lashes, she paused only twice, once to readjust her cloak, and once when a soot-colored cat shot hissing out of the gutter and into her path. And because the streets were empty at this hour, she arrived at Madrigal Court minutes faster than usual.

Jammed with high, timbered shop-fronts, the Court was hardly wider than an overgrown alley. Scuffing impetuously through the litter strewing the cobbles, Margoth marched past several instrument-maker's studios and turned abruptly into a constricted gap between two tall houses.

Several paces farther along, the gap widened out into a small, weedy courtyard formed by the back walls of the four surrounding buildings. The western wall was broken by the presence of a narrow, crookedly-hung door at the bottom of three muddy steps. Descending the steps, Margoth balled one hand into a fist and rapped resoundingly on the central panel.

There was no immediate response. Tapping one foot in her impatience, Margoth drew a quick exasperated breath and knocked again. This time a muffled voice from inside called out an unintelligible syllable of acknowledgment. A moment or two later, the door opened with a petulant squawk of badly-oiled hinges.

There was a pause. "Margoth?" said Serdor's voice dubiously from beyond the threshold.

He was standing barefoot on the wooden floor, naked except for a cloak which he was holding draped around his waist with one hand. His bare ribs and arms were stippled with gooseflesh, and one glance at his eyes told her that she had wakened him out of a sound sleep. "Yes, it's me," said Margoth. "Let me in. I've got to talk to you."

"Yes. Of course. Excuse the early morning stupidity. What time is it?" asked Serdor, stepping aside.

"What difference does that make?" Moving past him on her way to the center of the room, Margoth turned, her palms pressed together, and spoke to his back. "Serdor, Caradoc's gone."

Serdor froze in the act of closing the door and looked around. "Gone? You mean he didn't come home last night?"

"No, he didn't," said Margoth flatly, meeting the minstrel's sharpening gaze. "At least, not long enough to do more than slide this under the crack of the door."

The message had been hastily scrawled on a torn sheet of foolscap. Her hands unsteady, she dragged it out of the inner pocket of her cloak and proffered it for his inspection. He took it, but did not immediately look at it. Instead, he clasped her chilled wrist in his light fingers and steered her toward the nearest chair before drawing up a stool for himself.

He seated himself without ceremony, despite his awkward attire, and unfolded the letter she had given him. Watching his lowered face intently, Margoth saw a puzzled crease appear between his eyebrows as he studied the writing before him. He was evidently reading it twice over, for it was a long moment before he looked up again.

"Well, what do you make of it now that you've seen it?" she asked.

"Not a great deal," said Serdor frankly. "Caradoc seems to have outdone himself in the interests of brevity this time."

"Yes, hasn't he?" said Margoth acrimoniously. Twitching the paper out of the minstrel's hand, she flicked selected phrases with a distracted forefinger. " 'I've succeeded in finding employment . . . should be gone only a matter of a fortnight or so . . . don't worry . . .' God! Not a word about *who* hired him, or why, let alone where he's gone, and he says 'don't worry'!"

The sudden stinging sensation along her lower lids warned her that she was closer to tears than she cared to admit. Swallowing, she said grimly, "What Forgoyle is going to say about this when he finds out, I shudder to think. . . ."

Forgoyle Finlevyn was in the hospital refectory eating his noonday meal when a solemn-faced servitor approached him with the message that he was wanted immediately by the Grand Master.

Since the legate from Farrowaithe had arrived the previous evening and had had time enough in which to consider the problem of Caradoc Penlluathe's dismissal, Forgoyle thought he could guess the reason behind the summons. Prey to instant misgivings, he pushed aside his half-empty plate and followed the servitor out of the dining room and along an adjoining corridor which brought them to the door of An'char Maeldrake's quarters.

The Grand Master, he discovered, was alone. "Come in quickly and close the door," snapped An'char, dismissing the servitor with a curt flick of the hand. "You and I have got some serious talking to do."

His heartbeat accelerating, Forgoyle did as he was told and moved toward the center of the room. "What about? What's happened?" he asked. Then, seeing the iron expression on

the older man's face, he added with fatalistic bluntness, "Is
it about Caradoc?"

"I'm glad to see this won't catch you entirely unpre-
pared," said An'char acidly. "Yes, it's about Caradoc. Your
protégé appears to have cast all moral responsibility to the
four winds and has fled the city."

Feeling suddenly weak at the knees, Forgoyle clamped
both hands firmly to the high back of the nearest chair. "I
can't believe it," he said flatly. "There must be some
mistake. . . ."

"There is no mistake," said An'char testily. "The Grand
Prior of Maeldune gave me his verdict shortly after eleven
o'clock this morning, confirming the decision that Caradoc
should be cast out of the Order. When we sent two preceptors
to fetch him from the dwelling he shares with his sister, they
returned with the report that he went out yesterday evening
and never came back. A note he passed to his sister suggests
that he left Ambrothen sometime during the night."

"That's unthinkable!" protested Forgoyle. "His sister—"

"Knows no more of his whereabouts than we do," said
An'char. "The preceptors verified as much when they questioned her. Nor did Caradoc confide, as far as we can tell, in
any of his acquaintances. Clearly he intended to disappear as
quickly and as quietly as possible. Which makes it all the
more imperative that we find him—and speedily—before he
has the chance to make mischief."

For a long moment Forgoyle was silent, his dark eyes
deeply troubled. "I hold you ultimately responsible for this
gross breach of faith," continued An'char sternly. "Had my
better judgment prevailed, this wayward young man would
have been deprived of his magestone on the very day that his
membership was suspended. But you gave us your repeated
assurances concerning his integrity, and because your fellow
magisters respect you, they allowed themselves to be persuaded. If we now have a renegade on our hands, it is
because you valued your own judgment too highly to reckon
realistically with the flaws in your pupil's character."

Have I really been as blind as that? wondered Forgoyle. A

pulse throbbing dully in his temples, he said aloud, "If you tell me Caradoc has fled the city prompted by a sense of wounded pride, I will accept your word for it. But that he has gone intending to exorcise his mortification through acts of criminal violence I will not believe."

"Believe what you like," said An'char shortly. "But I am assigning you to go after him and bring him back to Ambrothen. Your long association with him will give you a stronger tie to the penumbra of his magestone. We do trust you to perform your duty."

Forgoyle let this pass. "Is he to be tried according to the laws of the Order?" he asked quietly.

An'char looked suddenly weary. "No, my friend," he said. "If Caradoc surrenders without violence and gives up his magestone of his own free will, the Order will take no further action against him."

It was an astonishing concession, perhaps compounded in part by the Council's respect for Forgoyle, but which also recognized the formidable talent of the pupil and the dire consequences that might result if the smaragdus were not returned. Carrot and stick, thought Forgoyle, and, prepared to breathe more easily, said, "I understand. When do I leave?"

"As soon as possible—before his penumbra has a chance to fade away," said An'char. "Say, in one hour's time."

He subjected Forgoyle to critical inspection. "The strain of maintaining to the Orison of Seeing for long periods of time will be considerable. You will require the assistance of at least one other magister, apart from the three preceptors I intend to send with you. Have you any suggestions?"

"Yes," said Forgoyle, and pulled his shoulders straight. "If he gives his consent, I should like Ulbrecht Rathmuir to accompany me."

Caradoc Penlluathe, as far as anyone could determine, had last been seen at the Daisy, a tavern of questionable repute located in the heart of one of the rougher areas of Ambrothen. Something more than an hour later, riding knee to knee with Ulbrecht along a narrow, evil-smelling thoroughfare, Forgoyle cast a worried glance at the buildings around them, and said, "Thank you for agreeing to come along. It's a singularly thankless task, playing the bloodhound."

"Especially when your personal feelings are divided against one another. Still, I can understand An'char's sense of mission," said Ulbrecht with a grimace. "Remember, he was with the Order in Farrowaithe when one of their novices used the Magia to blind a fellow student, then fled, taking his magestone with him."

"Of course. You're right, I had forgotten." Struck by the thought, Forgoyle frowned. "God, that must be fifteen years ago! There was quite a hue and cry—" He broke off abruptly.

"That's understating the case," said Ulbrecht. "The search party finally cornered their runaway in a ruined broch somewhere up in the far north. He refused to give himself up, and when they tried to take him by force, he unleashed a storm of power that leveled the broch and left three of his pursuers for dead. The destruction was so complete, they couldn't even find his body afterwards."

His gaze connected with Foygoyle's. "Can you honestly blame An'char for seeing Caradoc's flight as a prelude to a similar incident? Why else do you suppose he's declared himself ready to waive the Order's right to prosecute in the event that Caradoc yields himself up without a fight? He knows how dangerous this mission might prove, and he's hoping to give us every chance to succeed without anyone's coming to harm."

"That's assuming we can find him in the first place," said Forgoyle. "We'd better quicken our pace."

By day the Daisy proved to be a ramshackle two-story tavern, one street removed from a sprawling tangle of warehouses. Uncomfortably aware that not all the attention they were attracting was merely curious, Forgoyle was relieved to discover that there was a stableyard of sorts at the back of the building, accessible by means of a garbage-strewn lane.

Leaving the other three members of the party to keep a watchful eye on the horses, he and Ulbrecht returned to the front of the tavern and tried the door. "Locked," said Ulbrecht with sour resignation. He removed a riding glove and rapped sharply on the paneling.

For a long moment there was no response. Then a shutter banged open overhead and a surly voice called down, "Be off! We ain't open for business till sundown."

Forgoyle looked up. A heavy, blue-jowled face glowered back at him over a window box of dead geraniums. "Indeed? I'm afraid we're going to have to ask you to make an exception," said Forgoyle.

The owner of the Daisy produced a gap-toothed sneer. "And just who d'you think you are?"

"We're from the Order of Mage Hospitallers of Ambrothen," snapped Ulbrecht, with a glance at Forgoyle. "You have exactly one minute in which to open this door before I declare this establishment under quarantine as a pesthouse and order your doors to remain locked for a month!"

There was a fulminating pause, then the head disappeared abruptly from view. Thirty heartbeats later, they caught the sound of stumping footsteps and a muttering voice. A key rattled angrily in the lock and the door opened with a groan. "Come in then," growled their host, shuffling aside with ill grace to allow them to enter. "What d'you want?"

"Information," said Ulbrecht unceremoniously. "Last night a tall man with red hair came in for a few drinks. He thinks he left something behind. Do you remember where he was sitting?" Ulbrecht held up a gold piece.

The owner of the Daisy wiped his nose on his sleeve. "If he left anything, it won't be there now. But please yourself—he was sittin' in my back room there, in the right-hand corner."

"Thank you. That's all we require of you for the moment," said Ulbrecht, and dropped the gold piece into the other man's soiled palm. "You may leave us. We'll call you when we're ready to leave."

Alone in the shabby room where Caradoc had spent several hours the night before, he and Forgoyle exchanged glances. "I'll take the first turn," said Forgoyle.

"All right," said Ulbrecht. "I'll watch at the door to make sure there aren't any interruptions."

Standing over the corner table, Forgoyle sighed and drew out his magestone. Gazing down at it as it lay warmly glimmering in his two hands, he wondered if he himself would have had the courage to part with it, had that act of renunciation been required of him. Grateful that he had never been confronted with so painful a dilemma, he closed his eyes and willed himself to enter into communion with the Magia according to the Orison of Seeing.

First, the clarity of audible sounds: the buzzing of a fly three rooms away . . . the whisper of water in a drainpipe somewhere underground. Then, once sound was laid to rest in interior silence, vision became unencumbered.

. . . As he opened his eyes again, a shimmering brightness took shape in the space between the table and the wall. As he continued to gaze upon it, its outline became steadily more human, hanging like a bright shadow in the air . . .

The penumbra. The nimbus of power that descended upon the novice at the moment when he first took his magestone in his hand and called upon the Magia.

As a man standing in the light of the sun casts his shadow upon the ground, so the mage living on the threshold of power projected his penumbra upon the fabric of time and space, a token of his passing presence visible to those gifted with the skill to See, until, with the passage of time, the residual image dissipated like smoke upon the wind.

Like footprints in soft sand, the penumbra—while it lasted—could be followed to its source. But its duration was unpredictable and the energy required to hold it in view for long was considerable. Because Caradoc would know this as well as they, the chase was bound to prove grueling.

Ulbrecht calculated that their quarry had had at least twelve hours' head start, and probably more, which meant that timing would be critical. Resigning himself to the idea of spending at least half the night in the saddle, he allowed his gaze to come to rest on Forgoyle's rapt profile.

In the same instant, Forgoyle stiffened suddenly and shuddered, the air hissing sharply past his teeth on his indrawn breath. Instantly alert, Ulbrecht leaped to his side.

The deflected focus of the other man's eyes told him that the Orison was yet unbroken. Laying his hands lightly over Forgoyle's, he waited until he felt the tingle of power through his fingers, then framed his unspoken question: "What is it? What has so disturbed you?"

Then, as Forgoyle wordlessly opened his mind to him, he saw it for himself.

Caradoc's penumbra, silvery as moonlight. And superimposed over it, another, glowing red, like coals in the night . . .

CHAPTER 12

The Heir Apparent

"Parry! . . . Fall back! . . . Beat! . . . Lunge! Better, but keep your blade up. Let it trail like that in battle," said Jorvald Ekhanghar sourly, "and I promise you, you won't repeat the mistake. Now try it again."

Conscious of seven other pairs of eyes at his back watching and analyzing his every move, Evelake Whitfauconer shook aside his sweat-soaked hair and took a firmer grip on the hilt of his drill-rapier while he tried to remember a host of admonitions from previous lessons ("point level with your opponent's eyes" . . . "weight on the balls of your feet" . . . "wrist *under* the hilt" . . .).

The Marshall of Gand backed away and resumed his threatening stance at the opposite end of the fencing strip. Evelake dropped his blade briefly to ease his aching forearm, then snapped it up again into guard position, waiting for Jorvald to give the word to begin.

The fencing drill recommenced with a thin chink of blade on steel-light blade. From his vantage point on the sunlit terrace overlooking the green and the drill yard, another boy watched with dark, thoughtful eyes as the figures on the strip danced forward and back, engaging, disengaging, engaging again to the accompaniment of barked instructions from the master-at arms.

Once, as Evelake twisted sharply to avoid a well-aimed

stop-thrust, the watcher gave a small jerk and caught his lower lip between his teeth. Evelake leaped clear, and the boy on the terrace abruptly subsided and continued to watch, hands folded in his lap above the twisted ruin of his crippled right leg.

The flashing dialogue of motion, with its tense clatter of point, blade, and handguard, absorbed all other sounds. It was not until a long shadow sprang up on the ground in front of him that Devon Du Penfallon realized he was no longer alone.

It was his father. "There is no need to disturb yourself," said the Seneschal of Gand as Devon made a clumsy attempt to rise. "I was told I would find Evelake out here."

Before Devon could respond, a collective whoop from the fencing strip drew their eyes downward. Evelake, locked blade-to-blade with his teacher, dropped neatly to one knee and twisted his weapon free of the bind. An instant later he was on his feet again, springing forward into a well-balanced lunge.

The two fencers parted, testing the ground as nerve and sinew collected themselves in the short breathing space. Following Evelake's movements with an experienced eye, Arvech Du Penfallon found himself admiring the natural quickness, the ingrained dexterity.

Not that Evelake would ever match his father's muscular height: in the company of his peers he looked slight and undergrown for the fifteen years of his age. Still, he was no weakling: he had speed and agility, and there was promise of strength to come in the well-set shoulders and supple limbs.

Arvech withdrew his gaze from the scene below and transferred it almost against his will to the boy who sat so quietly beside him on the cushioned bench, the sunlight revealing with painful clarity the pallor of his face, the frailty of an invalid's frame.

And Devon, who had been forced all his life to sustain comparisons, read in his father's eyes, cloudy beneath the obligatory solicitude, the repressed avoidance, the dislike imperfectly concealed by self-conscious decency.

Devon was only too well aware of his father's resentment that some malignant turn of circumstances had left his son helpless with a condition that not even the most skilled Hospitaller could cure. The knowledge made it no easier for Devon to bear his own bitter frustration that he could never share in those commonplace activities that were so thoughtlessly easy to the sons of other men.

The dark, inescapable moil of emotions was as familiar as the recurrent ache in his crippled leg. Resisting it with all the resolution of sixteen years' enforced discipline, Devon clasped his thin hands a little more tightly and waited in silence.

His father, after a brief instant of eye contact, looked away again, as he always did. "What did you want with Evelake, sir?" asked Devon.

Arvech had returned to watching the fencing. "Commander Galledan has just arrived from Farrowaithe," he said, without looking around. "He brought letters from the Lord Warden, apprising me of the fact that he wishes Evelake to return home. As soon as is conveniently possible."

Two days later, alone with Evelake in the tower room that had been assigned to him since his coming to Gand Castle, Devon said, "So, you're taking horse first thing in the morning." He idly fingered the gemmed hilt of the ceremonial sword Evelake had left lying in the window seat.

"As soon as it's light." Frowning, Evelake paused briefly in the act of stuffing a rather disreputable brown doublet into the open mouth of the pack lying at the end of his bed. "Breakfast in the saddle, and off to Farrowaithe."

"You don't sound too daunted by the prospect," said Devon. He rocked back in his chair and clasped his sound knee between his hands. "Still, it's a pity you're not going to be here for the Midsummer Festival this year. Jorvald still hasn't figured out who it was who set the rockets off the roof of the East Tower last year."

Evelake's expression was owlish. "I hope for my sake he never finds out," he said feelingly.

Devon laughed, but the laughter didn't reach his eyes. "I

wonder why your father's summoning you home six months ahead of schedule."

Evelake scooped up three books from the window ledge and stowed them on top of the doublet. "I don't know. I asked Galledan, but he seemed to feel that the question was badly timed and wouldn't tell me anything. I suppose I'll find out soon enough."

Whistling tunelessly, he took a last look in the wardrobe, then closed the door. "By the way, I have a gift for Kherryn—if you think she'll accept it."

"I'm sure she'll be delighted," said Devon. "What is it?"

Evelake took something small off the top of the dresser and held out his open hand. "This," he said.

Cupped in his palm was a small box, carved from clear rock-quartz in a delicate design. Hair-thin, the etcher's traceries swirled in ice-crystal patterns over five of the six surfaces. The lid itself was surmounted by a lozenge-shaped panel upon which, perfectly drawn in low relief, was the image of a striking hawk, the emblem of the Whitfauconers.

The workmanship of the thing was exquisite. Devon looked up from the box. "It's beautiful," he said. "I can't think of anything she would like more."

Evelake smiled. "I'm glad you approve."

He put the box gently back in its place, then returned to the bed. He closed up his pack and straightened up, arms akimbo. "There. That's everything, I think. No, wait a minute."

He picked up the ornamented rapier by the hilt and scowled at it. "Now what am I going to do with this?"

"Aren't you going to wear it?" asked Devon.

Evelake shook his head. "Too fancy. I'll be carrying the one Father sent me, on the road."

He lowered the blade, and his gaze met Devon's. For a moment neither of them spoke. Then—"I wonder," said Evelake. "Would you keep it for me?"

A bright flicker of something like eagerness sprang into Devon's dark eyes. His fingers curling almost fearfully about the hilt Evelake held out to him—"Yes," he said. "I'll take good care of it."

CHAPTER 13

The Watchers

The sun's heat was a steady hammer beating down on the baked, white stones of the jagged valley below. Even several hundred feet above the valley floor, in the shelter offered by the caves that honeycombed these arid hills, it was hot and airless as a forge, though it was scarcely mid-April.

Caradoc plucked his sodden jerkin away from his chest and leaned forward, blinking around him in the glaring daylight at the campsite they were shortly to abandon. Three days ago, arriving just before sunset, he had been too sick of the heat, the riding, and his own conscience to appreciate fully the strategic advantages of the spot Borthen had chosen as their base of operations. Now, however, relatively more rested, he was in a more perceptive frame of mind.

Only a high spine of ground separated them from the road that drove a dusty serpentine westward over the trailing hemlines of the hills. Turning his head, Caradoc could see above him the tarry outlines of the desiccated evergreens that crowned the ridge, scrabbling for root-space among the boulders. As he looked he caught a flicker of camouflaged movement between a rock and a tree-trunk: one of the lookouts Borthen had posted several hours ago.

Borthen was evidently expecting action after three days of waiting. At dawn they had all packed and saddled the horses now tethered in the shelter of a narrow ravine a hundred yards down the slope from the camp. From this, Caradoc gathered uncomfortably that the culmination of Borthen's expedition was only hours—perhaps mere minutes—away. By the terms of his agreement with Borthen, he was not to take any direct role in the fighting. But there were other ways of striking a blow than with a broadsword.

He didn't know the name of the man they were out to capture. He gathered from the speculative hints and rumors dropped about the cookfires that Borthen's quarry was a person of considerable importance, but the rest of the company seemed as ignorant as he was himself. Muirtagh, Borthen's massive lieutenant, had been more than usually taciturn on the subject, and even Caradoc knew better than to question Borthen.

In any case, the time for demanding information had been that last night in Ambrothen. He had not done so. Instead, he had made a thief's bargain, and he was now bound to keep it, little though he might relish the thought; Borthen was unlikely to release him, and his own manhood rebelled at the notion of flight.

Not far away lay six readied crossbows, each bolthead a spiked crown of bristling metal. In the course of his healer's apprenticeship, he had witnessed the havoc such a barb could wreak among ligature, nerve, and muscle. He knew, perhaps better than any other man among them, where a shot could cripple, or kill. . . .

Someone was sharpening a blade. Caradoc became abruptly aware of the fretful whine of a grindstone above the distillated silence of the noonday sun. Irritably brushing away a fly, Caradoc jerked himself to his feet and strolled out into the open, taking the weight of the sun on his dampened shoulders. Setting one foot on a convenient rock, he studied the brown silhouettes—dun, sorrel, chestnut—of the horses moving sluggishly among the scrub below. . . .

"Admiring the view?"

The ponderous, basso profundo irony was Muirtagh's. Discarding a rude rejoinder, Caradoc half turned as Borthen's leviathan lieutenant moved into his shadow. "Borthen's just come down from the ridge," said Muirtagh dourly. "You'd better come inside to hear what he's got to say. If you've finished what you're doing."

It was pointless to take offense. Shrugging, Caradoc removed his foot from the rock and trudged back across the dusty yards to the mouth of the cave.

Inside, sitting and standing, ringed round about with torch-light and stacked weapons, were thirteen of the fifteen hire-lings that made up Borthen's attack force. At the center of the group, cool and unruffled, his sumptuous black clothes hardly creased with the hard usage they must have endured, stood Borthen himself.

He raised an eyebrow as Caradoc entered, then proceeded smoothly to business, his habitual air of languor for once in abeyance. "Gentlemen, the party from Gand is on its way. They should reach the vale within the hour. . . ."

He gave them, then, individual instructions to supplement the overall plan of attack they had all been obliged to memorize. Moving from point to lucid point, he might have been issuing stage directions to a group of playactors. His matter-of-fact tone—far from being reassuring—served only to emphasize the cold-bloodedness of the venture they were here to carry out. Catching Caradoc's sidelong glance, the man sitting next to him grinned unpleasantly and thumbed the edge of his bared poniard. Disgusted, Caradoc stiffened and looked away. Then he remembered that he was now to be numbered among these reprobates.

He was not given time to pursue the reflection. "You men have your instructions. In the absence of any questions, I shall assume that you understand them. That goes," said Borthen, "for you as well."

Caradoc, rousing himself from his reverie, realized that the remark was directed at him. Meeting Borthen's heavy-lidded gaze, he said, "As long as you recall the fact that I will serve your purposes only so far as I may without inflicting any injury."

"Your restraint is duly noted," said Borthen dryly. "Far be it from me to place uncalled-for strain upon your moral conscience."

CHAPTER 14

The Ambush

It was blisteringly hot. Evelake shifted uncomfortably in the saddle, acutely conscious of the way his breeches clung sweat-soaked to his legs wherever they touched leather. He ran his tongue over dry lips and glanced sideways at Commander Galledan riding stiff-shouldered beside him. Ahead of them the air was rippling with the heat that bounced off the bare, boulder-strewn hills.

It was their fourth day on the road since leaving Gand. Hampered by baggage wagons, their progress had been slow, the accommodations variable. The inn where they had spent the night had been indifferently appointed and the clientele mixed, but it was not the memory of an ill-cooked meal and a hard mattress that was occupying Evelake's attention at the moment.

They all wore light cloaks over their chain mail to keep off the sun. Lifting a hand from his reins, Evelake fingered the clasp at his throat, tracing by touch the design of gold interlacing in whorls about an oval bubble of crystal. Inside the crystal was an interwoven knot of what looked like dark silk. The sheen of it was the sheen of a girl's long hair.

The hair belonged to Devon's sister, Kherryn; the brooch was a parting gift to her brother's best friend. Evelake's brown eyes were thoughtful as he rode on in silence through the noonday sun.

Stark as the bleached bones of giants, the hills rose steadily up on either hand, cutting off, both north and south, the mild airs of spring. The road began to wind as the gaps between the hills began to draw together. At the end of another hour's riding, the party came to a point where the road made a humpbacked hop and plunged sharply downward for fifty yards into a narrow, steep-sided valley.

"Here's where we stop a moment," said Galledan. Drawing rein economically with one hand, he signaled to the men behind to halt.

Squeaking leather and germinating dust, the rest of the company checked their mounts to a standstill while their commander studied the terrain in front of them. Piebald with hot shadows, the gorge wound an erratic course between two running bluffs. In the still air the silence was unbroken.

"What's the matter?" asked Evelake.

Without taking his eyes from the road, Galledan smiled tautly. "The habit of suspicion—I don't like the look of this. If I wanted to waylay somebody, I could hardly pick a likelier spot. Cergil!"

"Sir?" A young officer kneed his horse forward from the back ranks.

"Take Wyn with you and ride on ahead," said Galledan. "Take as much time as you need to give this valley a good looking-over. We're in no particular hurry."

"Yessir. What exactly are we to look for?"

"If I knew that, I wouldn't need to send out scouts," said Galledan sharply. "This isn't your first foray—*you* decide what needs investigating. Go as far as that spur of rock you can see from here. Yes, that's it. Beyond that, the land opens up, so we shouldn't have any trouble."

Evelake watched silently as Cergil and Wyn wheeled their horses and started down into the vale at a trot. The dust of their passing hung in a thin sheen of white behind them until their moving forms were lost in a drifting cloud. The rest of the company unlaced their helmets and dismounted to drink a few spare swallows of water. The murmur of subdued voices sounded like the hum of bees in the unnatural heat.

High up on the ridge, crouched like armed boulders among

the dwarfed pines, men shifted their weapons with expectant stealth. The sun hung white-hot over the western gap of the valley. In the shimmering calm, Muirtagh made a sudden movement. "Here they come. There's their dust rising."

The men about him reached for their bows. Muirtagh nocked an arrow, waiting loose-handed for the riders to draw near enough to afford him an accurate shot. The sound of hoofbeats filtered up to them from below. The two men closest to the edge of the bluff raised their bows, hands poised flexibly on the bowstrings.

"Not now," hissed a voice behind them, drawing their eyes backward. "Must I teach you your business?" demanded Borthen. The words were a plaintive whisper, but his eyes were menacing. "There are only two riders down there, as we can all see. That means that the rest of the party is hanging back to allow these two to reconnoiter. I need not point out to you that if they fail to return in the same condition in which they left, we are not going to get a second chance. Kindly curb your eager impulses."

The speech lost none of its sting from being delivered in an undertone. "You heard him," growled Muirtagh. "Lay your weapons by until you hear me tell you otherwise. I'll personally flay anyone who makes a move before then."

There was a shame-faced ripple of motion as they obeyed. The two scouts passed directly beneath them, supple-handed and easy in the saddle. The helmeted heads turned from side to side, watchful and intent.

They were about to move on past when the foremost rider suddenly checked his horse with a quick twist of the wrist. The still air suspended the sound of his voice as he turned to mutter something to his companion sidling up from behind. For a long moment the two huddled together as if in consultation. Then, leaving his companion to continue on alone, the first wheeled his mount around and kneed it toward the southern slope.

Loose gravel slewed away from beneath the animal's hooves as it struggled up the first stage of the steep incline. Motionless among the pine-shadows, Borthen's men waited in tight-lipped silence. Feeling Borthen's gaze upon him like the mark of a firebrand, Caradoc took a deep breath and took his magestone in his hands . . .

. . . thoughts are like leaves whirling in a column of wind. Lay the wind to rest and the thoughts will settle to the earth and be still . . .

. . . and in interior stillness, you shall hear what is sealed from the ear and discern what is veiled from the eye . . .

. . . The rider was still ten yards distant when Caradoc rose to his feet and stepped into the gap left between two ragged pines. Startled by his sudden appearance, the horse came to a stiff-legged halt. Its rider, scowling, laid a hand to the hilt of his sword. "Halt! Who are you?"

To Caradoc, on the threshold of the Orison of Affinity, the spoken words boomed like an avalanche. He sensed the force of the other man's suspicion like a gust of hot wind. "A traveler," he said gently, and stepped forward so that the rider could see that he was unarmed.

The rider stiffened but made no move to spur his horse aside as Caradoc left the shadow of the pines and began to walk toward him. Forestalling a half-fledged resolution, Caradoc said, "There's no need to draw your sword. I can do you no harm."

He halted at the rider's saddlebow and held out his hand. For a moment the rider sat mesmerized as if torn between two conflicting desires. Then, as their fingers met, his eyes went wide and blank as Caradoc's voice, soothing as the sound of falling rain, laid his fears to rest . . .

. . . here is nothing save the raven in the rock . . .

The return of the scouting party was heralded by telltale plumes of rising dust. Evelake's horse raised its head and whickered softly. Evelake gave an admonitory twitch to the reins, then glanced around as Galledan started forward. Seeing no reason why he shouldn't follow, Evelake allowed his gelding to have its head, closing in behind Galledan's mount.

"Well?" inquired the commander as Cergil and Wyn drew up in the road in front of him.

Cergil shrugged. "We didn't see anything, sir."

Galledan gave him a sharp look. "You're not satisfied?"

"No—I mean, yes." Cergil hesitated, then scowled. "I thought I saw someone moving up on the ridge to the left, but when I rode up to take a look, I didn't find anything. It must have been a trick of the light."

Galledan lowered his chin. After a moment's consideration, he said slowly, "All right. We'll go ahead. Give the men the order to remount. But tell them to keep plenty of daylight between them until we reach the other side of this vale."

They rode forward in double file. His skin prickling under his damp clothing, Evelake glanced behind him. The men toward the rear of the company had drawn scarves up over the lower halves of their faces to filter out the dust cast up by the horsemen in front.

They rode well-spaced, as ordered. Loose stones skipped and slithered away from under steel-shod hooves. Wyn was riding at his side. Hearing him loosen his sword in its sheath, Evelake laid his free hand on the hilt of his own rapier. It came to him in that instant that he had never drawn it at genuine need.

The bluff rose steeply on their left. Another fold of land jutted up in an uncompromising incline on their right. The light seethed on chalk-white stone. Evelake eyed the southern ridge, studying the dark line of the evergreens that ran in clumps among the rocks.

A flurry of wings off to his left startled him. He glanced around as a small flock of black birds broke from cover, spiraling up out of the trees with harsh cries.

He opened his mouth to speak to Galledan, but before he could utter a sound, a dull *thunk!* beside him made him look left in time to see Wyn tumble sideways out of the saddle, a black-feathered arrow quivering in the flesh at the base of his throat.

For a split second, Evelake stared in mesmerized horror at the man choking out his life on the ground. Then suddenly the air was alive with whistling shafts.

All around him men screamed and fell, clawing at the black-winged barbs. A hard hand struck him a heavy blow between the shoulder blades. "Get back to the wagon!" ordered Galledan's voice in his ear.

Half-dazed by the suddenness of the onslaught, Evelake moved to obey. The commander spun his horse around and charged back down the line, marshaling the men who were still unharmed.

A second volley of arrows followed the first, interspersed with crossbow bolts. Three horses crashed to the ground in a tumult of squeals and thin, splintering legs, but most of the men had now dismounted and were using their animals as shields. Evelake, in a lightning tally, counted twelve still on their feet. Bending low over the saddle, he spurred toward the nearest baggage-cart.

An arrow struck the ground in front of him and skidded out of sight. A second one took the gelding squarely in the chest. The horse gave a wet, breathless sob and plunged forward, blood gushing over its knees. Evelake kicked his feet free of the stirrups and leaped clear as the grey somersaulted into the dust, hooves flaying the air.

He landed hard on his back a few yards away. The fall almost winded him, but he managed to get to his knees, gulping painfully for air as he scrambled for shelter among the boulders at the side of the road.

From where he knelt, he could make out Galledan shouting orders from the protection of the first wagon, his gaze roving frantically over the confused jumble of horses and corpses. Looking, Evelake realized, for him.

He called out, waving a signaling arm, then shrank back as a spent arrow grazed his cheek. The commander's gaze focused and, dropping low, he began to work his way back in Evelake's direction, using rocks and fallen horses for cover.

Someone, raw-throated, gave a warning shout of alarm. Wheeling, the beleaguered remnants of the escort party saw the trees on the south crest burst apart to emit a racing gaggle of armed men.

There was no time to weigh numerical advantages. Evelake picked himself up and flung himself and his dust-dimmed blade into the forming melee.

Striking and parrying, as he had been taught, he bore his way through the ringing confusion, seeking wildly for Galledan. Then he saw him, locked in a vicious blade-to-blade contest with the black-clad leader of the attackers.

Balanced breathlessly between running steps, Evelake gave a startled exclamation as a sudden lancet of hot pain scored his right shoulder from behind.

He whipped around, blade raised in defense, and found himself confronting a short, powerfully-built figure garishly dressed in blood-splashed blue and yellow. Sallow teeth showed themselves in a broad leer as the man jabbed at him a second time with the point of a heavy curved saber.

It was a brigand's weapon, not a gentleman's, never intended for the deadly courtesies of the fencer's art. Countering a solid thrust with a hit off the handguard of his own light rapier, Evelake was forced to leap back, wrist badly jarred by the impact.

His adversary took a slapping step forward, lashing his blade sideways so that the half-turned edge cut the air from under the boy's left arm. The rising dust caught grittily between his teeth, Evelake chased the stroke with a quick beat of his rapier, hoping to drive the saber far enough out of alignment to win himself time to lunge, but his opponent, instead of resisting the deflected momentum of his weapon, allowed it to carry him into a spin.

Coming smoothly around full circle, he landed heavily in Evelake's path again, blade aimed not high, as Evelake had been taught, but low, presenting a threat to the legs. For a split instant they faced each other across six feet of trampled ground before the man gave a hoarse whoop and sprang forward, the saber sweeping viciously for the boy's left thigh.

To a man lightly armed, there was only one countermove. His right hand meeting his left on the hilt of his rapier,

Evelake slashed upward, using the combined strength of both forearms to crack the force of the blow. And because it could only partially succeed, dropped under the stroke to the ground.

Twisting, he struck clumsily at the gaudy exposed side, and in spite of the awkward angle, he made contact.

The brigand shuddered as the sword slid greasily through fat and muscle. Two bloodshot eyes stared at Evelake in ghastly incredulity before the man pitched forward, flattening the boy beneath the weight of his body as he fell. Impaled, he writhed once in a paroxysm of anguish and then went limp.

Gagging at the smell of spilt blood, Evelake managed to thrust the heavy body aside. Dragging himself free, he sat gazing numbly at the inert, reeking shape beside him and the foreign stains on his own clothes. It was the first man he had ever touched in genuine combat, and the wound had been mortal.

A sudden nausea swept over him, but he mastered it long enough to wrench his drenched steel free of the corpse. He discovered that the blade had been snapped six inches from the point.

Clutching the hilted fragment in his hand, he rose shakily to his feet. The dust in the air was now so thick that he could hardly see what was happening around him. Metal still skidded, shrieking, over metal to the accompaniment of grunts and cries. Somewhere nearby, a voice was moaning in pain.

"Milord Evelake?"

He turned sharply at the sound of his own name. Outlined in the eddying dust stood a tall, slender figure dressed entirely in black, watching him composedly through a pair of hooded black eyes. In a sick instant of recognition, Evelake identified him as Galledan's adversary.

He had little time to digest the grim implications of this. The brigand-leader advanced, slowly, but with every appearance of assurance. Heartsick, but resolute, Evelake stood his ground, his broken sword wavering between himself and this new threat.

He knew from the outset that his chances were almost

nonexistent. Breast to breast they struggled for a brief moment before the brigand made a swift chopping motion with the edge of his free hand. The paralyzing blow caught the boy's sword arm between the elbow and the wrist.

Evelake cried out as his broken blade went spinning among the rocks. The next instant, he found himself pinned with heartrending ease by a pair of sinewy hands employing a grip that even Jorvald hadn't known. His wrists suspended agonizing from behind, he aimed a kick backward at the man's ankle and heard the hiss of an intaken breath as his foot struck home.

The pinioning grip promptly shifted, and a hard set of knuckles smashed with brutal precision into the wound in his arm. Evelake made a strangled sound through his teeth and sagged toward the ground, his vision going cloudy. While he was still fighting to keep from fainting, his captor efficiently lashed his arms behind him.

The same rough, efficient hands hauled him upright. "May I suggest that you come along quietly?" murmured a suave voice in his ear, punctuating the remark with a knee jerk from behind.

Imprisoned, sick with pain, he was hustled rudely back up the southern embankment. "If you struggle, you will only prolong the carnage down there, and I assure you," continued the same malicious voice, "that your associates are getting the worst of it— Ahh!"

The voice broke involuntarily as Evelake succeeded in smashing the heel of one boot into his captor's instep.

There was a perilous pause.

"Not wise, sweeting," said the voice grittily.

A leg shot out in a scything motion too swift for the eye to follow. His feet cut violently from under him, Evelake landed abrasively on the ground. He caught a brief glimpse of a tight-furled fist driving straight for his face before the world splintered into blackness, and he remembered nothing more.

CHAPTER 15

The Necromancer

The nature of the tool is known by the purpose which it serves.

Oblivious to the broken-backed landscape passing around him, Caradoc rode through the glare and grit of the late afternoon like a man stricken blind.

All around him the survivors of the foray laughed and cursed and coined lewd epitaphs for their fallen adversaries as their horses jostled one another along a disjointed succession of trails that wound like vipers northward toward the dark and distant outline of forested foothills. His ears ringing with their rough-tongued gibes, Caradoc left his horse to choose its own path, his mind clogged with sickening images of blood and death:

A chestnut gelding trying to run on a shattered foreleg . . .

A man looking on aghast as blood fountained in heart-stopping bursts from a gaping wound in his thigh . . .

Another staring vacantly up at the sky, a crossbow quarrel protruding from his ruptured chest . . .

In his own recklessness, Caradoc had not foreseen such carnage. Nor the bitter anguish of guilty inaction as, trained to read and to respond to human suffering, he had been constrained to stand helplessly by while men died who otherwise might have lived.

Six hours earlier, prompted by an uneasy sense of his own

dereliction, he had told Borthen, "I will serve your purposes only so far as I may without inflicting any injury"—little dreaming that he had already yielded up his honor.

And thus the decision of the Council of Ambrothen had, after all, been vindicated.

It was not an easy truth to accept. Pressing on grim-faced through the anonymous dusk, Caradoc fought to an exhausted standstill the stubborn desire to deny it. And once the painful concession had finally been made, he discovered, to his wondering surprise, a new sense of resolution.

A mistake cannot be recalled. But it need not be repeated.

The moon was rising when Muirtagh, riding at the head of their ragged column, signaled a halt. Dismounting with the rest, Caradoc peered over the heads of the men in front of him and caught sight of a square, dark tunnel-mouth cut into the moon-whitened rock of a low cliff.

It proved to be the entrance to an abandoned mine. Leading his horse under the arch of the entryway, Caradoc flexed his aching legs and threw a searching glance around him.

Cathedral-like in the light of newly-kindled torches, the roof soared away into the upper darkness. The cavern itself was more than eighty yards across, a huge orb of empty space propped up by stalagmites. On the far side of the great chamber, the torches picked out the black maws of two adjoining passageways leading farther into the womb of the hill.

They set up camp quickly, some bedding down the exhausted horses in the southwest corner of the cavern, others fetching bracken to feed the cookfire someone had kindled in a hollow in the center of the floor. Left to himself just inside the entryway, Caradoc looked for Muirtagh and realized that Borthen's second-in-command must have stepped back outside. The thought was not particularly reassuring.

No one had seen either Borthen or the prisoner since the battle, but Caradoc was certain they couldn't be far behind. Contemplating his next meeting with the brigand-leader, he experienced a pang of foreboding. All the way from Ambrothen, he had been able to assuage his uneasiness with the thought that once the foray was over, he would be his own man. In the cold light of his new perspicuity, however, he was forced to admit that his association with Borthen might be far from over.

In his uneasiness, he yielded to the urge not to stray too far away from the opening. He was in the act of setting out his bedroll in a shallow alcove ten yards to the right of the mouth of the entryway when a sharp scuffle of movement and a muffled exclamation from the passage made him look up in time to catch sight of an unnaturally bulky human form blocking the opening: Muirtagh ducking head and shoulders as he passed under the rude arch.

And behind him, upper arm bruisingly viced between the big man's clamped fingers, a slight figure, motley in the soiled rags of what had once been a fine suit of clothes.

Fed by fresh air currents, the flaring torchlight showed up the gentility of buckskin breeches and cambric shirt, blood streaked liberally along one sleeve. Catching a brief glimpse of the prisoner's face, Caradoc went rigid, a sudden cold sweat of enlightenment prickling the warm skin between his shoulder blades.

Borthen's captive was only a boy.

He was allowed scant time in which to ponder his discovery. Following hard upon his prisoner's heels, Borthen himself stepped briskly through the gap and stopped, dark eyes flicking from face to inquiring face as his men turned to look at him.

"Perne. Uskan. You may leave your blankets where they are for the moment. I require your services. Yes," said Borthen, glimmering gaze devolving, "and also, I think, yours."

Caught in the intransigent malice of Borthen's smile, Caradoc in that instant did not trust himself to speak. Schooling his face, he straightened up and waited, hoping that the brigand-leader would not read his eyes too closely. "For someone who has just executed a masterstroke against conventional authority, you don't look particularly pleased," said Borthen.

"Never mind. I have another, possibly more instructive, diversion for you."

Remembering the scout on the hillside, Caradoc said tonelessly, "What do you want me to do this time?"

"Nothing," said Borthen genially, "except watch. . . ."

At his gesture, Muirtagh and the others began to move off, taking the prisoner with them. With an ironic flourish of one hand, Borthen invited Caradoc to follow them. "Keep Muirtagh amused in my absence. I shall join you shortly."

Threading a wandering course through the disorganized flotsam on the floor of the cavern, Muirtagh led the party into the right-hand passageway. Shunted along, reeling with exhaustion, the prisoner was clearly drawing near the end of his strength, but he retained spirit enough to balk at the mouth of the tunnel, flinging his slight weight backward against the thrust of Muirtagh's arm.

Muirtagh's answer was a swift kick, shrewdly administered from behind. Jolted into forward motion again, the boy stumbled and almost fell. Catching a fleeting glimpse of his white face from behind Muirtagh's slablike shoulder, Caradoc locked his teeth against the hotly-worded protest that rose to his lips, and strode grimly on.

The passage they entered was narrow, and the breadth of Muirtagh's shoulders seemed to fill it from side to side. Coming immediately behind him, Caradoc could no longer see the prisoner, but the continuous rasp of boot-leather on stone, the leaping of the shadows that followed their torches, and the sound of the boy's ragged breathing told him as much, or more, than he cared to know.

The tunnel took them fifty yards deeper into the heartrock of the mine, then cut obliquely to the left, running on for an indeterminate distance into oppressive darkness. Twenty yards farther along the left-tending off-branch, there gaped another opening in the left-hand wall.

It proved to be an entrance to a chamber of sorts, roughly rectangular, its walls displaying the scars left by picks and mattocks. Pausing on the threshold, Muirtagh launched the boy through the opening with force enough to send him sprawling.

The impact jolted a wordless exclamation from the prisoner's broken lips. As Borthen's lieutenant stepped back from the opening, Caradoc snapped, "Damn you, that was completely unnecessary!" and made a push for the threshold.

An arm like a small tree-trunk barred his way. "And just where d'you think you're going?" demanded Borthen's second-in-command.

"Where does it look like I'm going?" Meeting Muirtagh's colorless eyes with a blistering glare, Caradoc was too angry to be circumspect. "If that boy in there is worth as much as you all seem to think he is, you'd better stop playing cat and mouse with him and let me see to his injuries. I'll need to free his hands, for a start."

For a long moment, Muirtagh merely stared at him. Bracing himself for a potentially disastrous tussle, Caradoc was surprised when the bigger man dropped his arm and shrugged, his broad face inscrutable. "Have it your way, leech-boy. Just be thankful His Eminence has a use for you."

Nodding to the two other men present, he stepped back from the doorway, leaving Caradoc free to pass. Shaky with unspent adrenaline, Caradoc shook off an instant's relief and entered the improvised prison-cell.

The prisoner was huddled in the far corner of the room, his head bowed over his upraised knees. At the sound of Caradoc's approaching footsteps, however, he stiffened and looked up, his brown eyes hostile.

He did not flinch as Caradoc knelt down beside him, but beneath the dirt and the bruises, his face held a shrinking expectancy. After a glance over his shoulder, Caradoc said reassuringly, "Don't worry. I'm not going to hurt you. Hold out your hands."

He reached for the knife at his belt. The prisoner drew a sharp breath and held it. Reading the mistrust in his attitude, Caradoc halted, knife lying flat in his palm. "Hold out your hands," he said again. "Please."

The brown eyes studied him searchingly for a moment. Then the boy relaxed and extended his bound arms.

Caradoc inserted the knife-point between the ropes and gave an upward jerk to the blade. Freed, the boy's swollen hands dropped apart, wrists livid with rope burns.

He made a determined effort to flex his fingers. Surveying the visible battery of cuts and bruises, Caradoc said gently, "I'm sorry you've been so roughly handled."

The boy's response was a cold glare. "Unlikely as it may sound," continued Caradoc, "I have some skill as a healer. I can treat your injuries. If you'll let me."

This time the brown gaze flashed at him. "If you show me," said Borthen's prisoner icily, "any reason why I should trust you."

"Fair enough," said Caradoc. "Perhaps this will satisfy you."

He plucked open the collar of his shirt and light winked through his fingers as he gathered his mage's pendant into his hand. Bending forward, he offered it for inspection.

The boy stared at the green stone. "A smaragdus," he said softly. "Very well. I believe you."

"Good," said Caradoc. "May I examine your shoulder?"

The boy hesitated a heartbeat longer, then nodded. But as Caradoc reached out to draw aside the tatters of his right sleeve, the boy said abruptly, "If you're a mage, what are you doing here?"

Caradoc paused. Unable to keep the bitterness out of his voice, he said curtly, "It's a long story."

The boy considered this. Watching as Caradoc laid bare the wound in his upper arm, he said, "Then perhaps you can at least tell me what your leader intends to do with me."

"I don't know," said Caradoc. "It might help if you'd tell me your name."

"Anything to oblige," said a mellifluous voice at Caradoc's back. "His name is Evelake."

The boy started involuntarily, his face draining of color as he stared past Caradoc's bent shoulder. Caradoc, who had no need to look, snapped in a profane breath between his teeth and pivoted slowly on his haunches.

Borthen lounged in the entryway, one black-damasked shoulder propped negligently against the right-hand support of the opening. Smiling unpleasantly, he said, "More to the point, Evelake Bran-Gelleryn Whitfauconer. Of Farrowaithe."

CHAPTER 16

The Victim

Whitfauconer? His mind cracking like a pennant in the wind, Caradoc laid hold of the significance of the name. My God, he thought. The Warden's son . . .

"Precisely," said Borthen affably, as if he had spoken. "Never let it be said that we do things by halves. Who, may I ask, gave you orders to unbind him?"

Before Caradoc could think of a rejoinder, Evelake said, "Whatever your plans may be, I have no intention of cooperating." Despite his appearance, he retained an unlooked-for dignity.

"No?" said Borthen. "Then perhaps it's just as well that your cooperation won't be necessary."

"What are you planning to do to him?" demanded Caradoc.

Borthen lifted an eyebrow. "Nothing terribly painful. The Whitfauconer heir is merely going to assume a new identity."

"Just like that," growled Caradoc. His mouth dry as a desert gully, he added, "Has it occurred to you that he might not play along with it?"

Borthen's smile was untroubled. "He won't have any choice. When I've finished with him, he will retain no recollection of who he really is."

Unhurriedly he raised his right hand, turning the ring on his thumb so that the stone, a vitreous dark green, was uppermost. For a moment he gazed upon it fondly, his full lips sustaining their malicious uplift. In the same moment, with a shock that surpassed anything else he had experienced that day, Caradoc suddenly realized what it meant . . .

Incredulity jarred him into protest. "You're no mage!"

"That," said Borthen, "depends entirely on the exclusive nature of your definition." He lifted his chin, amusement glinting deep in his heavy-lidded eyes. "Surely you ought to have noted by now that an affinity for the Magia is not necessarily confined to those in holy orders."

But training in the use of the smaragdus had to begin somewhere. Again it was as though Caradoc had spoken. "Every institution has its renegades," Borthen said smoothly, watching Caradoc's face. "A fact which should come as no surprise to you."

It registered as a direct hit. With a sinking feeling in the pit of his stomach, Caradoc found his tongue. "If you are yourself capable of drawing upon the Magia, what was the point of engaging me as your accomplice?"

Borthen's expression was genial. "An appreciation for my own genius. Your talents and your circumstances marked you out as a likely apprentice. You could learn a great deal from me."

"Maybe," said Caradoc, his jaw hardening. "But I'm not at all sure I can afford the price."

"Oh, come now," said Borthen reprovingly. "After your princely performance earlier this afternoon, there can't be that much left of your sacred principles."

Which explained only too clearly why he had been directed to use his mage's skills to put the scout off the scent. Aloud Caradoc said, "I gather I passed the test."

"You did indeed," agreed Borthen, "which is why I've invited you here to witness a demonstration."

He turned his head, his gaze coming to rest thoughtfully on the white, defiant face of the boy, Evelake. "Paramnesia," he said gently. "Have you ever come across the term before?"

The question was directed to the prisoner, but it was Caradoc who answered, his voice flattened to a monotone. "It means 'false memory.' "

"Exactly." Borthen seemed pleased. "Most people are subject to it insofar as we all tend, mentally, to reshape the character of past events to suit the way we wish to interpret our own actions. Under the proper circumstances, it is possible to expand the mind's capability to delude itself to the point where it will accept any amount of false information and adopt it as truth."

He smiled down at the boy in the corner. "First, however, true memory must be extinguished. As you, Caradoc, are about to observe."

He took three unhurried steps in the direction of his prisoner. Kneeling defensively in the brigand-leader's shadow, Evelake flattened himself to the wall, but Borthen made no immediate attempt to lay hold of him.

Instead, he stood at ease, his head slightly bent, his shoulders relaxed as if he were pondering some matter of small importance. But Caradoc, recalling his own training, recognized in the brigand's attitude of contemplation the prelude to something sinister.

Silence reimposed itself upon the room. The silence deepened until small sounds—the brush of leather on cloth, the furtive crackle of the orange torchfire—attained preternatural distinction. Frozen in horrified fascination, Caradoc could only watch when Borthen moved at last, stretching out his hand before the boy's upturned face.

The stone in the brigand's ring flashed with a sudden viridian intensity. For a suspended instant it hovered like a sullen star in the still air of the room. Borthen extended his arm full-length and lowered his hand, palm pressing deliberately downward as if to lay itself on the prisoner's forehead.

Brown eyes uplifted in mesmerized revulsion, Evelake shrank from contact until the last moment, dropping lower and lower until his shoulders met the floor. An instant before Borthen actually touched him, he made an abortive effort to strike the brigand's arm away. In the same instant, Borthen's free hand intercepted the blow with a sinuous snatch that pinned the boy's chafed wrist grindingly against the wall.

Evelake gasped and struggled, his face drawn with loathing. With a delicacy that contradicted the hard left-handed wristlock, Borthen touched the fingertips of his right hand caressingly to the boy's temples.

The touch was palpably light, but Evelake started as if he had been stung, his lower body leaving the floor in a convulsive leap. Maintaining contact, Borthen dropped to one knee beside him as the boy writhed again, his back and chest arching upward at an acute, unnatural angle.

Aghast, Caradoc clapped a hand to his own magestone, gripping it till his knuckles showed bleached as picked bone. Hardly aware of what he was doing, he drew breath and held it as the power from the stone coursed along his fingers, sweeping his senses toward a perilous clarity of perception.

The air in the room was alive with spitting crackles of energy. Caught on the periphery of the duel between two wills—Evelake's and Borthen's—Caradoc went rigid as their opposing voices shrieked at him from the threshold of Union . . .

. . . Taste with me the sweetness of dominion . . .

. . . Help! . . .

. . . Share with me the moment of surrender . . .

. . . *Help me!* . . .

Powerless for an instant to direct the responses of his own mind and body, Caradoc shuddered under the assault of two conflicting sensations—a white-hot agony, and a seductive sense of omnipotence. Poised on a knife-edge between the one and the other, he fought his own paralysis for the freedom of choice as the pressure mounted from either side toward a crisis.

Disadvantaged from the outset, it was Evelake who first showed signs of yielding under Borthen's sustained and formidable attack. As the balance of power shifted, Caradoc seized his chance to enter the field.

Not to second Borthen, but to oppose him.

At once the spirit world leaped at him with terrible clarity. Where Borthen's face had been, there was a twisted mask of living darkness. As Caradoc stared, horror-stricken, out of the fathomless eye sockets shot twin arcs of searing flame that fastened themselves like vampires to his face and neck.

Momentarily blinded, he reeled away, clawing at the fiery network of teeth and talons that was threatening to rend away his throat. With the blood bubbling into his mouth, he knotted his fingers among the coils of flame and ripped them away, but the smoke of his own charred flesh doubled back on him, clogging his windpipe with its stench.

Beating the air, he choked and spat, and in that instant caught a fleeting glimpse of his leering adversary as Borthen raised a hand in a gesture of command.

Clutching his magestone, Caradoc felt it cleave to his palm like a live coal. Fed by the surrounding blaze, it seared its way to the bone. Unable to bear the agony, he hurled it from him.

Arching through the incandescent air, it struck the wall beyond. There was a booming rumble, and rock exploded in all directions. A flying shard struck Caradoc hard on the temple, and the light in his eyes went dead.

CHAPTER 17

The Traitor

The hour was late. Fyanor Du Bors of Ambrothen, having repaired to his library, was anticipating company and bore the waiting period with an impatience that he did not trouble to hide now that he was alone.

The windows on the east side of the room were open. Outside, a thunderous wet wind was blowing off the sea in the wake of a late spring storm. Lightning flickered red on the horizon, branching in patterns like ignited kelp among the turreted clouds. Within, the room contained a salty stickiness of the wind that left a lusterless glaze on wood and glass. Everything smelled strongly like the inside of a seashell.

Fyanor, a glass of wine at his elbow and a book lying open in his lap, was paying no attention to either one. After a while, he roused himself with an irritable shake of his shoulders and left his seat, crossing over to the window to study the ominous sky.

As he did so, there was a soft knock at the door. Pausing in midstep, Fyanor gave a muttered exclamation and turned around. Capturing his glass on his way back through the center of the room, he said, "Come in," and waited.

The door swung inward. Outside, a figure swathed in a hood and cloak stood in somber relief against the lighted hallway. "It's high time you put in an appearance," said

Fyanor shortly, coming forward. "What kept you? Did you run into any difficulty?"

The figure on the doorstep did not immediately reply. Stepping over the threshold, he closed the door gently behind him and set his back against it. Placing one slippered foot on the brocaded saddle of a nearby stool, Fyanor balanced one elbow on his raised knee and said with an edge on his tongue, "Your report, please. Was your mission successful?"

The figure by the door lifted a pair of finely gloved hands and deftly folded back the concealing hood. "Eminently," said his visitor, stepping forward into the light.

The appalled silence lasted only a second. Too far from the bellpull and unwilling for the moment to shout, Fyanor remained where he was and slashed out in a voice like a scalpel, "Who the devil are you?"

His visitor smiled—not pleasantly. "Shall we say, an employee of yours?"

"Oh, really? That's very interesting," snapped Fyanor, "because I don't know you."

"Oh, yes, you do—if not on an intimate basis. I," said his visitor, "am Borthen Berigeld. We are by way of being partners. Don't tell me you've forgotten our business arrangements already?"

"What arrangements?" Pale above the embroidery of his collar, Fyanor was glaring in imperious indignation.

"Come now—it hasn't been much more than a matter of weeks," said his visitor reprovingly. "I'm sure if you consult your memory, you will recall the trifling matter of your inconvenient nephew."

There was a knife-edged letter-opener lying unnoticed on the table not far from his hand. Flinging his glass at the interloper, Fyanor made a sudden dive for it and experienced the humiliation of being rudely intercepted by a trained arm and shoulder.

Borthen did not retain any hold on him, but the letter-opener went flying out of reach with a calculated flick of a supple wrist.

Massaging his forearm, Fyanor uttered a word that was

supposedly current only in dockside conversation. Mastering himself with an effort, he said grindingly, "All right, fellow. What do you want here?"

Borthen selected a chair and sat down with a gracile lack of ceremony. "Money, of course."

"Oh?" Fyanor was beginning to recover some degree of composure. "Would it be impertinent to ask what for?"

"For my services," said Borthen, settling his shoulders against the back of his chair. "At any rate, I made a bargain with a man named Aedron on the assumption that he was acting as your agent."

"Then you are laboring under a misapprehension. If you made any agreement with such a person," said Fyanor, "that has nothing to do with me."

"Well, that certainly simplifies things," said Borthen, with evident satisfaction. "Since Aedron—regrettably—is no longer in any condition to fulfill his part of our contract, then I shall assume that my obligations to him are at an end. And that leaves me free to make a new agreement with you."

"Aren't you taking rather a lot for granted?" inquired Fyanor brittlely.

"Not at all," said Borthen. His smile broadened. "You see, I have Evelake. Alive."

There was a pause.

"That's very interesting," said Fyanor evenly. "One wonders, however, why you are coming to me instead of going at once to Delsidor, the boy's father."

"I have always prided myself on my business acumen," said Borthen. "I rather imagine that you would pay more—in the long run—to keep the boy permanently out of sight than his father would pay to get him back. Particularly in view of the fact that you stand to lose a great deal more than money if it should be brought to the Lord Warden's attention that you were the one who hatched this plot in the first place."

Fyanor sneered. "It would be very difficult for you to prove that."

"It would be easier than you might think," said Borthen. "Aedron was obliging enough to leave behind him a signed testimony, implicating you to a rather alarming degree. He has himself suffered an unfortunate accident. But I'm certain a magister-inquisitor could get to the truth easily enough.''

Anger flared in the seneschal's fine eyes. ''Not even Delsidor would dare order me to submit to such an examination.''

''Should the issue be raised,'' said Borthen blandly, ''anything less than a voluntary offer to undergo questioning would generate serious suspicion. You would fare better if the matter were never mentioned.''

He flicked an imperceptible mote of dust from the sleeve of his doublet. ''The boy is as good as dead. And will remain so, as long as you continue to meet my requests. In return, you will have what you want: an unobstructed highway to power.''

The seneschal's gaze was dangerous. ''I want to see him.''

Borthen raised an eyebrow. ''Take my word for it: we have him.''

There was another grating pause. ''How much?'' demanded Fyanor between clenched teeth.

''Far less than it would cost you to finance an army, which is the only other way you could ever hope to accomplish your designs. I have no desire,'' said Borthen, ''to drive you to rebellion by wholly unbridled extortion.''

And he proceeded to name his price.

CHAPTER 18

The Renegade

The afternoon sun was kind to the shabby furnishings of the two small rooms that Serdor called home, lending an illusion of polish to the bare floorboards and lying only lightly on the threadbare upholstery of the dilapidated armchair Serdor had rescued from the rubbish-heap a few months before. It did little, however, to dispel the cloud of anxiety overshadowing its two occupants.

Margoth, settled in the armchair, was single-mindedly sewing a patch over the elbow of Serdor's one spare shirt. Serdor himself was sitting a few feet away at a scarred wooden table, idly sketching in the margins of a musical score-sheet he was working on. A breath of air from the open window ruffling the page under his hand made him abruptly aware of his lack of progress. Giving himself a slight shake, he straightened his shoulders and turned his head so that his eyes came to rest on Margoth's downcast profile.

Absorbed in her task, she did not immediately look up. In an effort to cast off his gloom, he allowed himself the pleasure of watching her.

The sunlight, spilling honey-gold around her, kindled the latent rutile fire in her hair. The rich sheen of it framed the left side of her face, and within its loose silken shadow, her cheek and throat took on the warm hue of tinted ivory.

The severe purity of her brow was mitigated by the

unconscious tenderness of her mouth. Studying her, Serdor experienced a familiar pang. Quiet where they lay, his fingers tingled with a sudden longing to touch her bright hair, to prove its fine-spun texture.

She was close enough that he could have done so, had he yielded to the impulse. But the inescapable poverty of their surroundings—the cracked walls, the lopsided chair in which she was sitting, the coarseness of the shirt she held in her lap—restrained his hand. Margoth of the cinnabar hair deserved a richer courtship than his.

Yet his longing for her, once awakened, could not easily be silenced. And there was only one vehicle worthy to express it. Moving quietly, he rose from his seat and reached for his lute.

As his shadow passed by her she lifted her head and, seeing the instrument in his hands, smiled up at him. "I thought I might as well play as sit and brood," he said. "You don't mind?"

Still smiling, she shook her head and returned to her work. Trusting in her preoccupation, he went back to his seat and ran his fingers thoughtfully over the strings. Then sang, to ease his heart's desire:

> "Forget me not, though I be long
> A pilgrim in a distant land,
> Though heart must hunger long for heart,
> And hand be sundered long from hand.
> Though song be stilled and mirth be mute,
> I pray your grace, for I shall be
> True as a hermit's holy vow,
> The mirror of all constancy.
>> I loved you long before this hour,
>> And though these weary days shall try
>>   my love,
>> Yet it shall neither faint, nor fade, nor fail,
>> Nor die.

Forget me not. Though lips be mute,
Yet see the promise in my eyes
Worth more than any spoken pledge
Or vows delivered up with sighs.
Transplendent as the summer skies
With stars unnumbered, silver-lit,
My love shines waverless, a flame
That burns and has no end to it.
    I loved you long before this hour,
    And though these weary days shall try my love,
    Yet it shall neither faint, nor fade, nor fail,
    Nor die. . . .

" 'Where there is water, look for sweet vervaine,' wrote the
poet Isembard, 'And where there is music, look for heartease.'
. . ." Acquiescent to the promptings of his fancy, Serdor
played on through the lengthening shadows, his supple hands
plucking inventions like garlands from the well-tuned strings
of the lute he had made himself.

It wasn't until Margoth stirred in her seat and sighed that
he realized so much time had gone by. As he broke off in the
middle of a chord, Margoth said, "I'm sorry to interrupt you,
but if I'm going to get to the Beldame on time, I'd better be
on my way."

The light in the room had mellowed from gold to orange.
"You should have called me to order sooner. I had no
idea it was so late," said Serdor. He set the lute carefully
aside and stood up. "I'll walk you as far as Candlewick
Street."

"What, not all the way to the front door?" inquired Margoth,
affronted. Then, seeing his nonplussed expression, relented
with a small gurgle of laughter. "No, I haven't forgotten.
Though I'm sure when Forgoyle arranged for you to run tame
in the lay section of the Hospitallers' library, he had no
notion what he was letting the curators in for."

Still grinning, she reached for her shawl. "What's it to be
tonight? History, literature, or languages?"

"Languages. One never knows," said Serdor with dignity,

"when a working knowledge of Pernathe may come in handy."

The sky overhead was banded with rose-colored clouds, and the breeze from off the bay was fresh. "Tell Arn, if he asks, that I'll be along in a few hours' time," said Serdor as they parted company at Candlewick Cross.

It was half an hour's walk from the neighborhood of the Beldame to the front gates of St. Welleran's, the combined priory, cathedral, and hospital of the Order of Mage Hospitallers of Ambrothen. In the massed shadow of its stone walls, Serdor paused and drew out a piece of parchment, rather dog-eared from much wear. Signed by both Forgoyle and the Grand Master of Ambrothen, and sealed with the triple star, it was a writ authorizing him to make use of the cathedral library within the limits prescribed by the Rule of the Order. He presented the writ to the servitor on duty at the gatehouse, and was given permission to enter.

In the early days of St. Welleran's, all the books and manuscripts belonging to the Ambrothen branch of the Order had been housed in the western end of the Hospitallers' living quarters. Over the years, however, the number of holdings maintained by the Order had grown steadily larger until it had finally become necessary to find more space to accommodate them. Accordingly, a new building had been erected on the level plot of ground adjoining the hospital and adjacent to the herb gardens. The books had all been moved, and the old library had been converted into quarters for the Grand Master.

The new library was accessible by a gravel path that ran past the guesthouse and then turned right, running the length of the dormitory, through the garden. The garden itself was enclosed by a protective hedge, broken at opposite ends by wooden gates set into tall arbors. Entering through the west gate, Serdor closed it behind him, then paused as his quick ears picked up the sound of footsteps coming toward him down one of the sidepaths from the direction of the main building.

The footsteps were moving quickly, striking down hard on the gravel. Frowning slightly, Serdor lifted his hand from the gate-latch and stepped out of the arbor.

The dark-robed figure on the path to his left came to an abrupt halt. "Who the devil are you?" snapped a deep voice testily.

The voice was familiar. "Forgoyle!" exclaimed Serdor. Re-collecting himself, he lowered his voice. "It's me . . ."

"Serdor? Good God," said Forgoyle, peering forward to get a better look at his face. "What are you doing here?"

"I was just on my way to the library," said Serdor. His frown returning, he added, "I didn't realize you were back in Ambrothen. When did you arrive?"

"About two hours ago," said Forgoyle. "Since which time I've been in conference with the Grand Master."

He sounded weary and on edge. "I see," said Serdor. He hesitated. "Is Caradoc . . ."

"No. We never caught up with him," said Forgoyle shortly. He ran a hand over the back of his neck, then returned his gaze to the minstrel's expectant face. "Look, this is hardly the place to discuss it. Come back with me to my house, and I'll give you the story. . . ."

Forgoyle's house in Maulden Court had been a bequest from a childless uncle. Although, like the other unmarried members of the Order, he had been allotted quarters at St. Welleran's, it was at the Maulden house that he kept his personal library, and it was there that he spent much of his time when he wasn't on duty either in the hospital or in the lecture-room.

The house was shrouded in darkness. Pausing in the hall-way to kindle a lamp, Forgoyle led the way into his study and closed the door behind them. Motioning the minstrel to one of two armchairs, he sank heavily into the other one.

His face in the lamplight was seamed with fatigue. "It was my original intention to summon you and Margoth together," he said, "but I'm glad now to have the chance to talk with you first, alone."

Serdor sat down, but his back remained straight. His grey eyes unwavering, he said, "So, the news is bad. You may as well let me know the worst from the outset."

"The worst?" Forgoyle gave a mirthless laugh. "You

don't know what you're asking. For starters, there's the fact that the Lord Warden's elder son was abducted twelve days ago on the road from Gand to Cheswythe.''

Sharpened by shadows, the minstrel's thin face went momentarily blank. After a careful pause, Serdor said, ''That's going to come as a shock to a good many people. Privileged information?''

Forgoyle nodded. ''Until tomorrow, when the seneschal's heralds break the news to the general public.''

''I see,'' said Serdor. ''Would it be out of place to ask how you come to know about it before anyone else?''

''No. Seeing as how you've already guessed,'' said Forgoyle. He drew breath. ''It was in following Caradoc's trail that Ulbrecht and I stumbled upon the remains of Evelake Whitfauconer's escort.''

''And the evidence suggests that Caradoc was somehow involved,'' finished Serdor. He was looking rather white.

''I wish I could deny it,'' said Forgoyle.

Extending an arm, he lifted a roll of parchment from the desk and opened it on his knee so that Serdor could see it was a map. ''The signs we were following led us across the Laranrhyl and on into the Grey Hill country. Eventually, we wound up here.''

He pointed to a spot on the map where the mapmaker had recorded the presence of a deep, narrow valley. ''That's where the ambush took place.''

Serdor wordlessly held out his hand. Passing him the map, Forgoyle said, ''Seventeen dead out of thirty, including the commander. Everything the young lieutenant was able to tell me seemed to indicate that the brigands had had help from someone possessing a high level of mage-craft. I would have pressed on that very night, but something happened. . . .''

''And what,'' inquired Serdor, ''was that?''

Forgoyle's jaw hardened. ''This won't be easy for you to hear.''

''At this point,'' said Serdor grimly, ''it hardly makes any difference.''

Forgoyle nodded. "If any of this is going to make sense, I'd better explain a few things: Whenever a mage calls upon the Magia to perform a task, his act generates certain . . . resonances. The Magia serves as a conductor for these resonances—rather in the same way that water conducts sound. Under these conditions, it is possible for one mage in a State of Orison to make contact with another. Provided that both parties are willing, and that the distance separating them is not too great.

"Generally speaking, the closer one mage is to the other, the easier it is for them to achieve mutual awareness. And the more coherent the degree of communication. But in some cases, when one or both of the mages are exceptionally gifted, physical distances become negligible."

He stopped for a breath, then went on. "That night I succeeded in making contact with Caradoc. Not long enough for any specific communication to take place. But long enough to know that he was under attack and in deadly danger."

His fingers came together and locked. "I've never experienced anything like it. The pain was agonizing—as if he'd been swept into a firestorm. I caught a brief impression of a room. Or rather, a cave. And then there was an explosion—" He broke off with a shudder.

His face a study in stark black and white, Serdor asked softly, "Are you telling me that Caradoc is dead?"

Forgoyle forced his fingers apart. Staring at them, he said, "I don't know. Whether the fire was real, or some kind of a projection, I can't say. But the backlash of that explosion was enough to knock me senseless. When I recovered, I tried repeatedly to reestablish contact, but it was so much wasted effort."

He looked at Serdor. "I'm not going to enjoy breaking this to Margoth."

The minstrel's grey eyes were bleak. "Then don't. Leave it to me."

Something in the way he said it caught Forgoyle's ear. He said, "You won't be doing her any kindness by not telling her the whole truth."

"Until we know for certain what's happened to Caradoc, what we've got," said Serdor, "is a half-truth. And a half-truth is just about all it would take to make Margoth do something foolish—like setting out on her own to see if she can learn the whole truth for herself."

His gaze met Forgoyle's. "If you don't think she's capable of doing just that, you don't know her as I do."

Forgoyle digested this. "What are you going to tell her then?"

Serdor grimaced. "Only that you lost the trail in the midst of the hill country. That much we're sure of. The rest can wait."

He stared at the floor for a moment, then said thoughtfully, "Now that they've heard your story, what action does the Council intend to take?"

"The Council here in Ambrothen has been relieved of that particular responsibility," said Forgoyle. "The question of whether or not to pursue the investigation further rests now with the Arch-Diocese of Farrowaithe. I myself am forbidden to take any further part in the affair."

Some time later, Arn Aldarshot was in the kitchen of the Beldame Inn forking potatoes into a large pot of bubbling stew, when a voice hailed him by name from the back door.

It was Serdor, one boot on the doorsill. He had his lute with him, wrapped in the folds of his old cloak. "Come in," called Arn, wiping his hands on his apron. Then, as the minstrel stepped across the threshold, Arn got a better look at his face. "What's the matter?" he inquired sharply.

"Nothing," said Serdor. He set his instrument down on the nearest bench. "Arn, I have a favor to ask of you. Will you let me borrow Briona?"

Briona was Arn's own saddle horse, a sturdy bay mare with a silken mouth and a sensible expression. "I haven't got much money," continued Serdor, "but my lute should be worth something—at least enough to pay for her hire. Will you trust me with her?"

Arn was eyeing him with gravest disapprobation. "I most

certainly will not! At least, not until you give me something like a decent explanation for what this is all about."

"Spoken like a man of sense!" declared a female voice from the doorway. "What's going on?" demanded Margoth, leveling a penetrating look at Serdor. "Why this sudden impulse to take to the high road?" She added suspiciously, *"You* haven't taken up with some mysterious stranger, have you?"

"No," said Serdor. He moved the lute aside and sat down, his sharp chin raised so that he continued to meet her gaze. "Forgoyle's back. I've just come from talking with him. Caradoc's not with them. They lost his trail somewhere up north in the hills between Tavenern and Cheswythe and had to turn back."

Margoth was looking paler than she had a moment before. "Is that all?"

Serdor shook his head. "There's more, but I promised Forgoyle we'd keep it to ourselves until the news is officially released. There's been a rather spectacular political abduction—the son of the Lord Warden himself. Forgoyle thinks that Caradoc was somehow mixed up in it."

"Caradoc! But that's nonsense!" exclaimed Margoth. "He would never—" She stopped, her blue eyes wide and dark.

"I gather that the evidence is somewhat unconventional," said Serdor. "But in any case, Caradoc's defection is no longer the private concern of the Order. From what Forgoyle told me, it seems that the plot to kidnap the boy may well have originated here in Ambrothen. Lord Delsidor himself will be arriving shortly to direct the investigations."

He paused a moment, then said, "The Warden has already stated that any and all accomplices in the raid will be sentenced to a traitor's death."

An image of hanging, drawing, and quartering leapt irresistibly into Margoth's mind. Her gorge rising— "But Caradoc, whatever he may have done, is still a member of the Order," she choked. "Surely that means he would have to be tried in a court of canon law."

"That all depends," said Serdor, "on who finds him first." Assuming he can be found at all. . . .

He crossed one booted leg over the other, his face somber. "With the Warden's men leading the field, the Order has called in their hounds. If Caradoc is apprehended by agents of the crown, Forgoyle is fairly certain that Arch Mage Baldwyn won't interfere on his behalf."

He studied both their silent faces. "I realize it's probably going to prove a bootless errand, but I want to see if I can locate Caradoc myself."

"It seems to me," said Arn, "that a snowball in a soup-kettle would stand a better chance than you would. And even if you succeeded, what good would it do?"

"If I could persuade him to yield himself up voluntarily," said Serdor, "it just might save his life. Especially if Caradoc could furnish information leading to the recovery of the missing boy."

Margoth said nothing. Rising, Serdor moved to her side and laid his hands on her shoulders. "I won't ask you to put your trust in me," he said softly. "The chances of my failing are too great. But we have nothing to lose by my trying."

She nodded and pressed her forehead to his shoulder. Looking past her bright head to Arn, Serdor raised an eyebrow.

"You can have Briona, with my blessings," said Arn. "And don't worry about the lute; it'll be right here waiting for you when you get back."

CHAPTER 19

The Miner

It was approaching evening when a lone traveler on a bay mare rode into the village of Thurby and asked the first person he met for directions to the nearest inn.

Since there was only one hostel in Thurby, his informant called his attention to the sign of the Black Hawk at the far end of the high street. The traveler, who had a civil tongue despite his threadbare appearance, thanked his guide and rode on.

Strangers were normally rare in Thurby, which was well out of the way of the main road. In the days of its founding, it had been prosperous, thriving off the brisk trade generated by the ore mines in the Grey Hills to the north. But it was many years since the ore veins had run dry, and Thurby had dwindled to a sleepy hamlet of shepherds and small farm-steaders. In recent times, few wayfarers had any reason to come there anymore.

Until nearly a month ago, when the son and heir of the Lord Warden of East Garillon had disappeared.

First it had been a party of mages traveling north on a mysterious errand of their own. Then, after the news of the boy's abduction, there had been soldiers in burnished helmets and bright surcoats. And after the soldiers, other men, less openly, whose keen interest in local occurrences marked them for what they were: agents of the Warden.

The one-handed man standing in the middle of the dusty street watched the stranger's receding form with thoughtful eyes until it disappeared from view around the corner into the innyard. Then, not hurrying, he followed after.

Of the six guestchambers on the upper floor of the Black Hawk Inn, two were already occupied and another was reserved for a third guest who was not due to arrive until some time the following day. Mindful of the limited extent of his resources, Serdor inquired about the price of lodgings and took the cheapest accommodation available.

The room, which was hardly more than a closet, had only a single window, overlooking the stableyard, but Serdor was not disposed to be overly critical. Grimy and saddlesore, he considered the advantages of retiring early, but a hot bath and the meal that followed it took the edge off his fatigue, and he decided instead to pay a visit to the common room downstairs.

It was busier downstairs than Serdor had expected to find it: the Black Hawk was evidently a gathering place for a number of local inhabitants. His entrance drew one or two curious glances, but most of the Black Hawk's customers seemed to take little interest in him. He ordered a pint of ale from the innkeeper's wife and looked about for a place to sit down.

The three tables near the windows were largely full. His gaze bypassing the circle of stools and benches drawn up around the hearth on the south side of the room, Serdor caught a glimpse of another table tucked away in the opposite corner, between the edge of the fireplace and the end of the bar.

The man who was sitting there alone might have been, at first glance, either a shepherd or a farmer. Well past middle age, he was short and broad, with sun-seamed eyes and a thinning thatch of white hair. Like most of the other men present, he was dressed in homespun and leather. But, the big hands encircling the base of his mug were not those of a farmer, but those of a builder or a stonemason.

Intrigued, Serdor noted the telltale scars on the gnarled fingers and broad thumbs. Before it occurred to him to look away again, the other man gave him a wry grin and beckoned him over.

Serdor accepted his invitation to sit down. "You'll drink alone in this place if you've not got the smell of the cow byre about you," remarked his new companion with a disparaging glance at the heavy-booted men grouped about the fireplace. "Whatever else you may be, lad, you're no more a ploughman than I am, so we might as well get acquainted. Where are you from?"

Serdor sipped his ale. It wasn't up to the Beldame's standards. "My last stop was Brosey."

"That doesn't quite hit the nail on the head," said the old man. "But you've every right to be cautious if that's the way it is with you."

The shrewd twinkle in his blue eyes made Serdor smile in spite of himself. "It isn't really worth the trouble," he said. "Let me revise that: I'm from Ambrothen."

The twinkle brightened. "That's better," said his new acquaintance equably. "I'm from up around Merrow myself."

"You're fairly far afield, too," said Serdor.

"And not for pleasure either—more's the pity," said his companion with a rueful grimace. "I'm a miner and metal-lurgist, and there's a man I know from Farrowaithe who's paying me to do some exploring for him in these parts."

He settled himself more comfortably in his chair. "What d'you know about the hill country up north of here, lad?"

Serdor shrugged. "Not a lot. Beyond the fact that the iron ore they used to bring out of the mines was reputedly of very high quality. The armorers of Ghazara, I understand, had a decided preference for it, as long as they could get it. But that was a long time ago—before the mines closed."

"Not bad—for someone who's never handled a miner's pick," said his acquaintance with a nod. "D'you know why the mines closed?"

"I always assumed," said Serdor, "that it was because the ore ran out."

The old man grinned. "I thought so, too. But the fellow I'm working for thinks differently. So here I am to prove one of us wrong."

It was Serdor's turn to grin. "You must know your business better than most."

"I know the country," said his companion. "Thirty years ago—when I wasn't much older than you—I used to work these mines. And I know most of 'em like they were kin to me."

"Do you?" said Serdor, his expression suddenly very thoughtful. "Then maybe you can help me."

The old man's blue eyes were sharp as a fox's. "That depends on what you want."

"Nothing that will interfere with your work," said Serdor. He hesitated, then went on. "I'm looking for a friend of mine. He went missing nearly a month ago, somewhere between here and Tremyl. I'm trying to find out what might have happened to him. I'm afraid he might have tried to take a shortcut through the hills and got lost."

"A month ago . . . That would have been about the same time as the Lord Warden's son was kidnapped." The old man whistled softly through his teeth. "Your friend picked a bad time to go traveling north. If he ventured off the road, getting lost might well have been the least of his worries." He cocked his head. "Did you report your friend's disappearance to the authorities?"

"Oh, they know about it," said Serdor a shade grimly. He swallowed the last mouthful of ale in his mug and set it down. "I don't pretend to be well-equipped for this venture," he said, "but if my friend did run afoul of brigands, it seems to me that an old mine shaft could be a good place to start looking for clues. If I supply the paper, would you be willing to draw me a map?"

"I'll do my best," said his new acquaintance. "But first we'd both better have another pint. . . ."

Three-quarters of an hour later, the two of them sat contemplating the chart the old miner had sketched. "You know, I ran into one of the patrols about four days ago," he said. "I could have told them a thing or two if they'd wanted to hear it. Like where to pick up some of the old mining trails. And where to find water. As it was, they didn't want to spend the time, so I decided to save my breath."

He lifted his eyes from the paper. "Do you carry anything like a weapon, lad?"

Serdor's eyebrows went up. "Just a dagger," he said. "And this."

It was an old-fashioned sling. "I haven't used one of those since I was a boy," said the old man, fingering it thoughtfully as it lay on the table between them. "Are you any good with it?"

"When I was younger," said Serdor dryly, "I could put a stone through a window as well as the next one."

The old miner didn't laugh. "I used to use a sling to kill rabbits for the pot. But it's not much good against a man-sized target."

"Perhaps not," said Serdor. "But I don't intend to do any fighting. If I can help it."

By then the common room was emptying out. "Well, you've plainly had enough advice from me for one night," said the old miner, pushing back his chair. "I hope you find your friend. *And* manage to stay out of trouble yourself. Good night."

"Good night," said Serdor. "And thank you."

He watched in silence as the old man headed unhurriedly for the door. Then he got to his feet and stretched.

The innkeeper was bustling about collecting empty tankards. "I'd like to go out and check on my horse," said Serdor. "Will that interfere with your routine?"

The innkeeper looked at him quizzically. "Lord bless you sir, not a bit. It'll be another quarter of an hour before we're finished here. Go out through the kitchen. I'll tell my wife not to lock the back door until you come back."

Guided by the light showing through the cracks in the stable door, Serdor crossed the yard and spent a few minutes conferring with the groom who slept under the same roof. By the time he was ready to return to his room, the only lights showing from the main building were two dim lanterns hanging on either side of the scullery door. Blinking to allow his eyes to adjust to the darkness, Serdor closed the barn door and turned around. As he did so, he caught a flickering glimpse of something moving along the inn's steep rooftop.

Instantly alert, he halted and waited, his body tensing. A few heartbeats later, his straining ears picked up the stealthy scrape and rustle of boot-leather on tiles. A head and shoulders appeared briefly in inky silhouette against the stars. Then the man on the roof began to lower himself down from the eaves.

There was a ledge of sorts running along the back of the inn, where the old stonework of the original house gave way to the newer plaster of the second-floor addition. The mysterious intruder scrabbled his way to the ledge and stopped. Then he began to inch toward the nearest window to his right.

Serdor's teeth came together with a click. It was the window of the room assigned to him.

The figure was visible only as motion in the shadows. Standing feet apart in the middle of the innyard, Serdor stooped for a stone. Then he reached for his sling.

Alerted by the sudden whine of moving air, the figure at the window shrank and froze, but Serdor had already marked its position. The stone left the sling with a hiss and hurtled toward its target.

There was a dull *thud!* and a squawk from the shade under the roof. Grinning mirthlessly, Serdor let fly again.

There was another yowl and some fluent cursing. The black shape of the intruder teetered for a precarious instant on the ledge, then abruptly lost its grip.

There was a haycart parked directly under the window. The intruder landed in the midst of it with a crash and an explosion of hayseeds. Sweeping his dagger from its sheath, Serdor made a purposeful run for it.

In the dark, he stumbled and fell. By then the noise had summoned the groom. Ignoring the other man's demands for information, Serdor shook off the hands that were helping him up and plunged on.

But by the time he got to the haycart, there was no sign of his target anywhere to be found.

CHAPTER 20

The Cavern

The sixteenth of June dawned sultry, with heavy slate-colored clouds hanging low over the sandy ridges of the Grey Hill country. Riding along the ghost of an old mining track at the snail's pace Briona had chosen for herself, Serdor licked the salt from his lips and scanned the terrain before him, doggedly trying to ignore the fact that his clothes were already soaked through with sweat.

Sticky as warm porridge, the air was very still, and the hills themselves seemed interminable. A quarter of a mile in front of him lay the mouth of a switchback canyon tending north and east in a dry series of zigzags. It was the first of three landmarks that—if he could find them—would eventually lead him to the threshold of yet another mine.

He had visited five mines since leaving Thurby many days before, exploring by the light of makeshift brushwood torches to conserve the dwindling supply of oil he had brought with him to fuel his small woodman's lantern. It had been a laborious and time-consuming task, not enhanced by the very real and ever-present danger of losing his way among the networks of intersecting tunnels. And so far, all his efforts had proven singularly unrewarding.

Had it not been for the incident at the Black Hawk, he might have been tempted, after the first week, to give up the search as a waste of time. But the knowledge that he possessed nothing worth stealing had prompted him to dismiss out of hand the possibility that the intruder had been nothing more than a common thief. And the alternative suggestion—that someone had been interested enough in his movements to risk breaking into his room—indicated that there might yet be something to gain by persevering.

And so he had been careful, not traveling by night, camping under cover whenever possible, keeping watch for any signs that might show that he was being followed. So far he had neither seen nor heard anything to arouse his suspicions. But the memory of the shadow on the roof kept him vigilant.

The sky stayed heavy and overcast. Shortly after midday, Serdor came upon the second landmark, a shallow stream only a few yards wide. A narrow ribbon of ferns and green mosses marked the way to its source: a rocky crevasse twenty feet up on the left-hand side of the canyon. Serdor dismounted and gave Briona her head.

She waded in eagerly and dropped her nose. Listening to her thirsty slurping, Serdor stripped off his shirt and bathed his face and chest. Leaving her to crop hungrily at the lush grass by the waterside, he went upstream to drink his fill and replenish his water bottles before preparing to move on again.

A mile beyond the streambed, the canyon gave way to a bowl-shaped valley. After checking his map, Serdor turned to the left, following the western wall of the bowl. After another furlong, he came upon an eroded marking-stone set at the mouth of a narrow defile.

By then there was thunder in the air. Glancing around at the sky, Serdor sighted to the north a ripple of pale sheet lightning. Watermarks about the mouth of the ravine suggested that the valley might well become a flood-lake during a heavy rainfall. Keeping a wary eye on the clouds, Serdor urged Briona up the ravine toward the rising ground beyond.

The upper end of the gorge was a good thirty feet higher than its base. Guiding Briona through a patch of fallen boulders, Serdor emerged onto a flat saddle of hard rock between two sloping banks. Faint, but unmistakable, the trail picked up again, heading north.

Briona, scenting lightning, snorted and tossed her head uneasily. Hands ready on the reins, Serdor looked around for some possible place of refuge. There was a gap in the rocks to the west, a long stone's throw away. Kneeing the mare to a quicker pace, he made his way toward it.

The gap proved to be a natural archway leading into a pocket-sized amphitheater. On the south side of the enclosure, the stone had fallen away to leave a moon-shaped cave of sorts, sloping fifteen feet back toward the parent-rock of the projecting hill. Above the mouth of the cave, horizontal layers of stone formed a natural overhang.

Breathing a sigh of relief, Serdor swung out of the saddle and led Briona across the convex floor of the amphitheater. Outside the shelter offered by the surrounding rocks, he could hear the wind rising. Ducking under the overhang, he turned and looked back.

A brilliant flash of lightning, bursting off the table-rock beyond the north rim of the enclosure, illuminated the landscape in all directions. Directly above the sheltering roof of the amphitheater, a low white cliff flared into sudden prominence. His hand on Briona's nose, Serdor caught his lower lip between his teeth. It was the third landmark he was seeking. And there was a rectangular opening cut into the rock at the cliff's base.

It was only a short climb, but it was a steep one, likely to prove treacherous when wet. Stripping the saddle from Briona's steaming back in a few quick, practiced moves, Serdor gave the matter sixty second's intense consideration. Then he bent down and unhooked his lantern and a length of rope from his saddlebow.

Leaving Briona at the back of the cave with her reins looped securely around a boulder the weight of a man, he raced to the opposite side of the amphitheater and looked up, marking possible handholds and footholds. Then, cat-light, his strong musician's fingers finding sure purchase among the fissures in the rock, he vaulted four feet to the first outcropping and rapidly began to climb.

The wind struck him broadside as he reached the top.

Clutching rope and lantern, he picked himself up and made a dash for the mouth of the mine. He gained the shelter of the entryway as the first heavy raindrops began to splatter like overripe berries on the ground.

Within seconds all that could be seen of the outside world was a solid curtain of pelting rain that turned the dusty soil overlaying the rocks into a thick, grey paste. Retreating several feet back from the arch of the entrance, Serdor hunkered down and struck a light.

He was standing at one end of a great natural cavern, whose dimensions extended beyond the reach of his small lamp. Keeping close to the right-hand wall, Serdor began to work his way widdershins around the cavern's perimeter.

Stalagmites sprang into sudden solidarity at the touch of the light. He continued for a few dozen steps, then stopped short as his lamp showed up a blackened depression on the floor twenty feet away.

A fire-pit.

His breathing quickening, Serdor walked over to it. The ashes were relatively recent. Stirring the dead embers with the toe of his boot, he unearthed bits of recognizable rubbish: a half-burned boot-sole, a bent fork, the neck of a bottle that might have held wine.

The floor beyond was similarly littered. Some time in the not-so-distant past, the cavern had sheltered a large number of men.

A sudden, eldritch scuffling from the shadows sent Serdor groping reflexively for his dagger. Swinging the lamp aloft, he caught a glimpse of a pair of malevolent red eyes above a sharp-toothed snout before the creature vanished into a small gap at the foot of the nearest pillar. Exhaling in mingled relief and disgust, he left the fire-pit and continued on his round.

Eighty paces farther along the right-hand wall, he met with a tunnel. Another sweeping pass of the lantern illuminated a low-ceilinged stretch of corridor beyond. He hesitated a moment under the archway and listened, but heard nothing. That in itself was not particularly reassuring: a sense of brooding menace emanated from the dark beyond the reach of the light.

Light-footed, his eyes intent in his sunburned face, Serdor advanced slowly, halting every few steps. Fifty paces farther, he came to a point where the corridor took a sharp turn to the left. Gulping, he came to a full stop as his nostrils picked up the sudden reek of corruption.

The old stink of death.

It delayed him the few seconds it took to override his instinct to retreat. Peering ahead, he could dimly discern an opening ten yards farther along the left-hand wall. Taking a fresh grip on his resolution, he went on to investigate further.

As he stepped into the opening, the stench struck him with a virulence as physical as a blow. The light of the lantern exploded in the confined space beyond, and in that illuminating flash, he recoiled, lips drawn back over his teeth in a half snarl of horror and disgust.

Sprawled within a few feet of the entrance lay the body of a man. Or rather, what was left of it. Among the foul rags of clothing that still remained, the bones lay raw and dismantled on the stones. In the brightness of the light, Serdor could see the marks of small scavenger teeth.

For a moment he remained where he was, choking back a spasm of nausea. Then, ruthlessly mastering himself, he set out to do what necessity demanded.

The body was not Caradoc's.

The skeletal remains obviously belonged to a man far shorter. Limp with an almost overwhelming sense of relief, Serdor rose shakily to his feet again.

As he did so, he caught sight of something glimmering on the floor a foot or two beyond one outflung arm of the dead man.

It was a gold chain, curiously wrought in a series of interlocking mullets. The design was characteristic of the chains worn by the members of the Hospitallers' Order, but now the metal was blackened, as if by fire, and the chain itself had been broken.

The last time Serdor had seen this particular chain, it had been hanging about Caradoc's neck. But the magestone pendant that had gone with it was missing. Scowling, he knelt down and reached out to take it. Then he caught sight of the dead hand outstretched inches from where the chain lay, and received his second unpleasant shock of the day.

The dead man's hand was missing all four fingers past the first knuckle. The deficiency was neither the result of amputation nor of natural defect. The stumps of bone that remained had been burned black.

Using the point of his dagger, Serdor raked the necklace away from the maimed hand of the corpse. His own fingers shrinking a little, he drew a breath and picked it up swiftly.

It felt oddly warm to the touch. He thrust it hurriedly away into the pouch at his belt and stood up.

He was about to withdraw from the chamber when his keen ears picked up the noise of a disturbance from the direction of the main cavern.

Movement. And voices.

Magnified to a reverberating echo by the bare rock of the mine shaft, the voices were confused and incoherent. And coming closer. Serdor snatched up the lantern and blew out the flame.

Inky darkness sprang up in a dense, enveloping shroud. Placing his feet carefully, he stepped to the left and came into contact with the wall. Using the wall as a guide, he inched toward the opening and listened.

Whoever they were, they had not yet reached the mouth of the tunnel. Slipping around the entryway so that he was facing the curving interface of the passage, Serdor moved foot over foot to the right, palms flat against cold stone, counting silently as he went. . . .

One . . . two . . . three . . .

Nine . . . ten . . . eleven . . . twelve . . .

His right hand shot abruptly into empty air. Recovering his balance with a start, he pulled himself back from the opening and investigated by touch.

His outstretched fingers, brushing wood, told him he had come to a doorway rather than an intersecting tunnel. Praying that the floor beyond was solid, he stepped across the threshold mere seconds before a bobbing brightness and the firm slap of boot-soles on stone heralded the arrival of the newcomers.

The floor under Serdor's feet was mercifully intact. Drawing noiselessly away from the light in the corridor, he stationed himself two feet to the right of the door and pricked up his ears, his thin body tense as a bowstring.

The newcomers were making no special attempt to be secretive. "Whew! First the rain and now this!" remarked the first voice in patent disgust. "Either I've got a polecat up my nose, or there's somethin' dead in here."

"Right the second time," said his companion. "See for yourself."

There was a pause.

"Bloody hell!" said the first voice, impressed. "Well, that's one that didna die o' natural causes. What d'ye suppose nippit the nether ends off his fingers?"

"I haven't the faintest idea," said the second voice with grim simplicity. "But one thing's certain: we've come to the right place—thanks to old Tarlton's memory."

"Aye. It's a muckle great shame he didna ha' sense enough tae keep it in the family," said the first voice sourly.

"That he didn't is hardly his fault. For all he knows, my interest in these old mines is purely commercial," said the second voice. "Still, I wouldn't worry too much about that youngster from Ambrothen. If Tarlton took enough of a liking to him to do him a favor, the lad's probably harmless."

"Harmless!" The first voice pronounced with emphasis an extremely pungent epithet. "Ye wouldna be so free wi' the term if it had been *you* up yon roof, wi' the stones flyin' around ye like crows to the corncrib."

"It couldn't have been as bad as that—he only winged you twice," said the second voice with a touch of malice. "Don't worry. If our paths ever cross in the future, I won't let him do you any mischief. . . ."

Brangling intermittently, the two men made a thorough survey of the room. "See yon stains on the wall there—that's dried blood, or I've never seen it before," said the first voice, this time without any trace of macabre levity.

"And some strands of rope-fiber. They were holding a prisoner in here, all right," said the second voice grittingly. "Well, they didn't kill him, so they must want him for something. It appears that the underworld rumors concerning His Eminence spoke true. Let's see if we can find anything else."

They finished with the death-room and returned to the passageway. "My guess is they did no more than spend the night here," said the second voice. "I rather suspect they didn't go much beyond this point, but we'd better take a look just to satisfy ourselves."

Light danced over the walls of the tunnel. "There's another room," said the first voice. "Show a light and let's see what's in there."

Serdor locked his jaw. Shoulders pressed hard against stone, his flat middle sinking toward his spine, he jammed himself flat to the wall. A strong hand thrust a lantern between the doorposts. He held his breath.

"Empty as a beggar's purse," said the first voice. "Let's keep going."

The lantern was withdrawn. The footsteps carried on down the passageway.

To light his own lamp was to court instant discovery. To attempt to leave the room without a lamp to guide him was to court disaster. Serdor remained where he was, listening to the sound of the intruders' voices receding deeper into the mine.

It was some time before he heard them coming back again. "Clean as a whistle. There doesna seem t' be much point in staying on here," said the first voice as they passed the doorway to Serdor's hiding place. "It looks as if from here we'll just have tae do things the hard way. . . ."

They drew away. Serdor counted to thirty, slowly, then slipped out into the hallway. The intruders' light was a pale shimmer beyond the bend in the passage. Taking care not to let his own lantern knock against the wall, he started after them.

When they came to the main cavern they did not, as he had done, cling to the other edge. Instead, they made directly for the light that marked the opening. Serdor watched them leave from the safety of the tunnel's mouth. Then, trusting to luck, followed in their footsteps.

By the time he reached the outer archway, he saw that the rain had stopped. The two intruders were nowhere to be seen. But the wet earth about the mouth of the mine was pocked with footprints.

The footprints, clearer than any beacon, led away down the path to the left. Grinning mirthlessly, Serdor made his way quickly back to where he had left Briona.

From their conversation, it was clear that the newcomers knew far more about Caradoc's mysterious associates than he did.

And it was just barely possible that they might, eventually, lead him to Caradoc.

All he had to do was follow their trail.

And, at least for the moment, nothing could be easier.

CHAPTER 21

The Prisoners

It was late afternoon and the rays of the descending sun fell full upon the western wall of the stone circle of Thyle Tarn. Like an alchemist's tincture, it drew the fire out of the heart of the dark rock in tiny flecks so that the steep natural bastions glittered with motes like a powdering of jewels.

Fortuitously far-removed from the nearest settlement, Thyle Tarn was a geological curiosity, its great stone ramparts forming a roughly circular curtain wall, broken only by a single narrow gap in the south face. Inside, short-turfed as a castle courtyard, lay a wide open area with a deep spring-fed pool at its center.

Its foundation rising out of dense woodland, the tarn offered great natural potential as a fortress. That no one had ever bothered to fortify it as such was due to the fact that there was nothing for miles in any direction worth defending.

Nothing except the continuing privacy of the eighteen men who had taken up residence within the security of its beetling walls.

The gap in the circle was overshadowed by a spurlike outcropping of stone. The two figures standing sentry-duty on top of the Horn Rock enjoyed a wide view of the surrounding terrain.

Below and behind them, within the compass of the walls, lay a scattering of low stone buildings crudely roofed with thatch. Beyond the northern and western perimeter of the tarn, the land dipped into a broad hollow, then rose again in a series of densely-wooded ridges. To the south, the direction the sentries were facing, the ground lay open for several furlongs before giving way to more trees and thick undergrowth.

The sun was resting level with the treetops when a flicker of motion among the hazel-brakes to the south attracted the attention of Perne Latham. He gave his counterpart a jog in the shoulder and pointed. "Look there: can you make out what that is?"

His companion shaded his eyes with his hands. "I don't see anything. No, wait a minute—it's a party of horsemen."

Perne scowled and craned his neck sideways. "How many of 'em are there?"

His companion squinted. "I count four."

"Four? That's all right. It'll be the hunting party," said Perne, satisfied. "I hope they brought down a deer. I'm so bloody sick of salt pork, the very thought of it makes my gorge rise."

His companion was still peering out across the open ground to the south. "Don't get your hopes up . . . hell and damnation!"

"What is it?" demanded Perne sharply.

"It ain't four riders," said his companion. "It's five."

Perne swore floridly and looked for himself. Close-packed as a blackberry, there were indeed five riders converging on the entrance to Thyle Tarn.

"I'll call Rogan," said his companion tightly, and started to move away.

"No, don't," said Perne, his brow clearing. "That's the Big 'Un himself down there."

The massive deputy of the Master of Thyle Tarn was not to be mistaken for anyone else. "Then who's the fifth man?" asked Perne's counterpart. "You don't suppose it's His Eminence himself."

Perne sniggered nastily. "If it is, I know one fine young gentleman won't be so well-suited."

His companion spat. "Redheaded bastard. If it'd been up to me, he'd have been dead meat by now."

Perne peered over the edge of the Horn Rock. "Looks like his day of reckoning's been postponed. That's not His Eminence, it's another prisoner."

The fifth man was riding empty-handed, his reins in someone else's grip. From his vantage point, Perne could see that the newcomer was tall and strongly made. Above and below the muffling folds of a blindfold, thick hair showed golden, like the tawny pelt of a lion.

The party passed through Thyle Gap at an easy unstressed canter. "Where d'you suppose they picked him up?" remarked Perne's companion dubiously.

"That matters less than who he is," growled Perne. "Come on. Let's go hear what he's got to say for himself."

The two men moved to the Horn Ladder and started down. By the time they reached the foot of the steep rock-stair, the horses were being led away. Muirtagh, at the prisoner's back, cut through the knot at the base of his skull so that the blindfold fell away. Blinking, the blond man shook himself like a large, gold-furred dog and bestowed, somewhat unexpectedly, a broad smile on his growing audience.

Unabashed by stares and anonymous personal remarks, the newcomer pivoted slowly, studying his new surroundings. "What a bonnie hideaway you've got here," he announced admiringly as he returned to his original position. "It's a rare marvel some Lord somebody or other hasn't laid claim to it and turned it into a castle. Ten men in here could just about hold off five hundred . . ."

"Nobody knows about it," said Muirtagh repressively, "and we'd like to keep it that way."

"I suppose it wouldn't be worth the trouble, though," continued the prisoner, pursuing his point. "There's not much of interest out here. No roads, no trade, no towns, no inns . . ."

"No reason, in fact, for anyone to come this way. Why did you?" inquired Muirtagh.

"Maybe he's a hermit," suggested a rude voice unwisely, and subsided, quelled by Muirtagh's silent snarl.

The golden-haired man preserved a smile shading into rue as he stood at ease, his broad shoulders relaxed. "Hardly a hermit. If I were, I wouldn't have gotten into this fix in the first place. . . ."

"What fix?" said Muirtagh, arms folded like stacked codfish over the muscular mat of his chest.

The prisoner grimaced. "You would have to ask. Back where I come from I had the singular misfortune to damage a lady's husband. Rather badly, I'm afraid. . . ."

The rest of the sentence was drowned out in an outburst of catcalls and sniggers. The bluff voice of the newcomer emerged from the tail end of the derision, saying cheerfully, ". . . was purely unintentional. I really was very sorry about it. But how the devil could I possibly have guessed," demanded the captive of his increasingly appreciative audience, "that the wretched little snirp had a skull like an eggshell?"

Muirtagh was not charmed. "Where did all this take place?"

The prisoner looked slightly pained. "If you must know, Strathwellyn. But I'd be pleased if you wouldn't mention it again—"

"You were forced to leave home. Were you followed?" Passionless as an oyster, Muirtagh ignored any and all side issues.

The newcomer dismissed guardsmen, sheriffs, knights of the shire, and their like with a good-humored chuckle. "Don't worry. I left 'em behind three days ago. A bit of pepper and the dogs fair sneezed the scent of me out of their noses once and for all."

He grinned disarmingly. "To tell you the truth, I'd as lief stay here as anywhere—till the local interest dies down."

"Oh, you won't be leaving for quite a while," said Muirtagh. "There's room for you in the guardhouse. You'll stay there till we've had time to check your story."

The prisoner was marched away under guard to one of the grey stone bothies on the western side of the compound and hustled without ceremony into the front room where two more men were sullenly playing cards at a crooked table. The larger of the pair, eyeing the prisoner with sour dislike, fumbled under his jacket and produced a rusty key. Taking his cards with him, he shuffled over to the wooden door in the opposite wall and fitted the key into the lock.

The lock yielded reluctantly with a tooth-setting squawk, and the prisoner's captors propelled him inside. He had just enough time to register the fact that the room was already occupied before one of his attendants, to save trouble, clipped him on the back of the head with a fist-sized block of wood.

When he came to his senses, he was wearing a set of wrist-manacles. The manacles were attached by a three-foot length of chain to a rusty bolt driven into the wall. Focusing his eyes with some difficulty, he eventually realized that there was a second length of chain strung out to the left of the bolt. The chain led to another set of manacled hands.

"Nothing very subtle about our friends' methods," said a voice with weary acidity. "Especially since they have every reason to distrust strangers. Have you got a name?"

Despite an aching head, Thyle Tarn's latest arrival felt a surge of curiosity. He propped his chin on his forearm to broaden his angle of vision and encountered a hollow pair of green eyes. "The name's Valoran Trace," he said thickly.

"Welcome to purgatory," said his fellow prisoner with bitter cordiality. "Are you anybody important? Or did you simply have the ill fortune to cross paths with the lord of the manor?"

Valoran fingered the nape of his neck and winced. "I wouldn't raise even a potboy's ransom, if that's what you mean. Is that big fellow with the flat face the 'lord of the manor'?"

"Oh no," said his fellow prisoner. "Muirtagh is merely an attendant demon. His Eminence, the Black Prince, is himself away from home—for which we can both be truly thankful."

The tone of his voice robbed the metaphor completely of humor. Valoran sat up carefully and took a better look at his cell-mate.

The other man was young—certainly no more than twenty-five years of age—but his face behind the silken floss of a dark red beard showed an unnatural sharpness of bone. Below the haggard, undershadowed eyes, his sunken cheeks were slick with sweat. Abruptly aware of a new source of discomfort, Valoran realized that the air in the room was stiflingly warm.

It took him ten seconds longer to figure out why: even though it was still daylight beyond their narrow window-slit, there was an oil lamp burning at full intensity, standing on the floor a few feet out of reach.

"We practice an enforced brand of asceticism here," said his new acquaintance with the same merciless irony. "His Eminence, you will discover, has his own way of encouraging fasting and vigils."

Fasting . . . lack of food. And vigils . . . lack of sleep. Recognizing in his companion's ravaged appearance the visible signs of privation and sleeplessness, Valoran said, "If you're hoarding the secret of the Philosopher's Stone, I'd advise you to strike a bargain."

The other man showed his teeth. "If I were hoarding anything, he'd have had it out of me by now. With or without my consent. I hope for your sake you have nothing to hide."

The man calling himself Valoran shrugged, but his golden eyes were wary. He said, "I was not aware that brigand-leaders were gifted with omniscience."

"Normally they aren't," said his companion shortly. "But Borthen Berigeld—to give him his right name—is a renegade mage. And his affinity for the Power is—believe me—formidable."

It was a startling revelation. "How do you know?" asked Valoran.

"How does one wolf smell out another?" said his companion. "I am myself a mage. But, demonstrably, one of lesser proficiency."

A renegade mage . . . "Who the devil are these men?" demanded Valoran.

"Haven't you guessed by now? They're the ones," said his companion, "who kidnapped the Lord Warden's son."

There was a long moment of dead silence, broken only by the hiss of the flames in the lantern. "God almighty!" said Valoran. Then added a less pious expression. "Is the boy actually being held here?"

His companion shook his head. "No. That much I'm sure of. According to the snippets of gossip I'm occasionally privileged to overhear, Borthen spirited the boy away to a place known only to himself. I gather no one in the outside world is any wiser than I am."

"No," said Valoran.

"That's hardly surprising," said his informant. "Evelake Whitfauconer has been rendered unable to identify himself."

A hard glint showed in Valoran's golden eyes. "How is that?"

"How else, but by means of mage-craft," said his companion. "The mechanics of the actual process, I'm afraid, are beyond me."

Valoran digested this. "Where do you fit in?"

The other man's handsome mouth curled in savage self-derision. "I was—if you can believe it—hired by Borthen. I suppose he was looking for a likely apprentice. Anyway, I was in some trouble with the Order at the time: it seemed likely that I might be dismissed, and I was desperate and foolish enough to accept the offer he made me. He didn't tell me very much, of course, but what he did tell me I didn't bother to examine too closely until it was too late. By then the ambush was over, thirty men were dead, and I was partially responsible for Borthen's success."

"If that's so," said Valoran, "why are you chained up in here instead of running free with your share of the spoils?"

The red-haired young man grinned mirthlessly. "I discovered my moral conscience still had some life in it. When Borthen set to work on the boy, I tried to intervene—"

He closed his teeth abruptly, his gaunt face haunted by the memory. When he spoke again a moment later, his voice was grey. "Somehow they got my magestone away from me. For all I know, Borthen may have destroyed it—or at least its capacity to conduct the Magia. In any case, I no longer have it. And I have been assured that when Borthen comes back, he intends to make of me his creature.''

It was all beginning to make sense: the heat, the glaring light, deprivation of food and sleep—all calculated to break down an individual's innate resistance. ''I'm apparently scheduled for the same treatment,'' said Valoran. He added thoughtfully, ''I wonder how much time we've got.''

''I couldn't say. But if you're no more than you claim to be,'' said his companion, ''you'll probably be spared the fate that seems to be in store for me.''

Valoran's face was grimly sardonic. ''I wouldn't count on that. And I'd certainly prefer not to put it to the test.'' He stirred restlessly like a large hound in a small kennel. ''I didn't catch your name, lad. If we're going to put our heads together to some good purpose, we might as well not stand on ceremony.''

His companion blinked at him wearily, then extended one grimy hand. ''I'm Caradoc,'' he said. ''Caradoc Penlluathe, of Ambrothen.''

CHAPTER 22

The Agent

The day following Valoran's arrival was heavy and humid, and that night, shortly after sunset, the rain came on in a cloudburst. Breaking like a black wave over Thyle Tarn, the storm drowned the cookfires and drove men indoors to make what they could of a half-cooked meal, while outside the lightning flickered and flashed in a white-hot display of raw power.

There was wind enough even to freshen the stale air of the cell Caradoc was sharing with the newcomer from Strathwellyn. Funneling through the narrow window in whistling gusts, it rocked the lantern and sent the flame spitting. There was a pool of rainwater forming on the hard-packed floor below the window-ledge. It served only to remind Caradoc that it had been weeks since he had last bathed.

Beside him, within a few feet of the spreading puddle, his fellow prisoner was sitting with closed eyes. Since their guards were under orders to rouse them at regular one-hour intervals all through the night, Caradoc first assumed that Valoran was merely resting while he could. Then he saw that the other man's lips were moving. Far from being asleep, Valoran was counting to himself.

A loud crackle of thunder overhead made Caradoc flinch. As its echoes died away, Valoran suddenly opened his eyes and grinned wolfishly.

As Caradoc watched in silent bemusement, Valoran rocked forward onto his knees and unstrapped the worn leather belt from about his waist. Catching up the drab, base metal buckle in one hand, he thumbed one dented corner. To Caradoc's surprise, the face of the buckle sprang away from the back, disclosing a small compartment inside.

Seemingly oblivious to Caradoc's astonishment, Valoran plucked out a tiny metal phial and a little packet of carefully folded paper, held together with a length of what looked suspiciously like quick match. Without turning his head, Valoran said, "I don't know about you, but I don't much fancy waiting about to have my brain picked."

Caradoc stared hard at Valoran's averted profile. "You have some rather unusual equipment for a simple fugitive," he said.

Valoran was thoughtfully studying the ringbolt above his head that was holding their chains to the wall. Without speaking, he reached out and fingered the surrounding masonry.

Small crumbs of loose mortar sifted toward the floor. "At the next crack of thunder," said Valoran, "I want you to start counting out loud."

"All right," said Caradoc. "What are you going to do?"

"You'll see in a minute," said Valoran. He edged closer to the wall and wedged the packet between the base of the bolt and its matrix. "Pour me half a cup of water and hold it ready till I call for it," he added over his shoulder.

Caradoc did as he was told. Returning his attention to the packet, Valoran inspected the dangling six inches of match-cord, then with great care took the cap off the phial.

The air was promptly suffused with a strong reek of mingled sulphur and niter. "What is that?" asked Caradoc.

Valoran smiled thinly. "The Pernathan alchemists call it 'dung of the fire-djinn.' In the presence of water, it—"

The end of his sentence was lost as another roll of thunder burst overhead. "Start counting," said Valoran.

As Caradoc told out the seconds out loud, he dipped the end of the match-cord in the noisome dark substance contained in the phial, then took the cup out of Caradoc's hand.

144

The count became a chant—"One hundred and seventeen
. . . one hundred and eighteen . . . one hundred and nine-
teen . . ."

The end of the quick match disappeared into the cup.
There was a hiss and a flare of sudden light as the cord came
into contact with the water.

Sparks shot up the match toward the packet. "Look away,"
hissed Valoran, "before—"

His words were swallowed up in a deafening crash of
thunder. In the same instant, the packet detonated with a loud
bang of its own.

A small cloud of gritty dust spewed outward in a puff of
noxious smoke. Fanning away the fumes with one hand,
Valoran inspected the base of the bolt. Peering over his
shoulder, Caradoc muttered, "That was close. Do you suppose they heard that?"

"If they had, they'd have been in here by now," said
Valoran. "Look here."

Caradoc bent closer. New stone showed visibly paler where
the explosion had chewed away a quarter of an inch of dirt
and mortar. "That's going to be difficult to explain," said
Caradoc. "Those guards aren't blind."

"No," agreed Valoran. "But they are careless."

Sitting down flat on the floor, facing the opposite wall, he
shifted himself eight inches to the right and leaned back so
that his head was almost touching the ring. His shadow
formed a corona of darkness on the stones behind him,
masking the scar left by the miniature blast. "It wouldn't
escape the notice of a trained officer of the peace," said
Valoran with a wry face, "but it would surprise me very
much if our present gaolers bother to look that closely."

He picked up his belt again. "I've started a promising
crack, but it's going to take work to widen it enough for our
purposes. We've still got half an hour before the guards put
in their scheduled appearance. Let's see how much damage I
can do in that time."

Valoran's prediction concerning the guards proved well-
founded. Working in turns, he and Caradoc spent the rest of

the night chipping away at the weak spot in the wall, using Valoran's buckle as a chisel. By dawn Caradoc's fingertips were rubbed raw, and the crevice around the stake in the wall was half an inch deeper.

Shortly after sunrise, their gaolers brought in their one meal for the day. Staring down into the bowl of porridge and pork fat in front of him, Valoran exclaimed in triumph, "The very thing!"

Mixed with loose grit, it made an admirable substitute for the mortar they had succeeded in removing. After packing out the hole they had made, they took what rest they could and waited for nightfall.

At dusk they started in again. The time passed slowly, measured out between half-hour work-shifts and rest periods timed to coincide with the hourly intrusions from the guards. They kept their work camouflaged with applications of their improvised paste, but Caradoc was by no means convinced that they could go another day without being discovered.

A short time after midnight, he was startled out of an uneasy doze by a muttered exclamation from Valoran. "What is it?" he whispered huskily. "What's wrong?"

Valoran did not reply. He had the ring entrapped between two sinewy hands and was working it up and down, the tendons bulging between wrist and elbow. Beneath the hard knot of his fingers came a muffled grinding as the stake that held the ring in place began to move counterclockwise.

Caradoc held his breath. Teeth exposed in a grimace of concentration, Valoran increased his leverage. . . .

There was a gritty sound, like two millstones meeting, and loose mortar began to flake away like breadcrumbs. Bearing down from the shoulder, Valoran gave a sudden wrench. The ring jerked like a dog at its tether and slid painfully out of the wall, trailing a ten-inch spike behind it.

Valoran caught it as it dropped, and lifted his head. His face in the lamplight was glazed with perspiration, but his golden eyes held a leonine glint of determination.

Before they had time to savor their success, there was a

thud and a clank from the other side of the door. God in heaven! thought Caradoc with a wild surge of alarm. They're early!

He leaped to his feet, gripping a length of loose chain between his shackled hands. Valoran, matching his movements, caught him by the shoulder and gestured vehemently toward the door.

The key turned stiffly in the lock. Flinging themselves against the wall to the left of the doorframe, they waited for it to open.

The guard had just enough time to register the fact that the prisoners were not in their proper place before a doubled bight of rusty chain smacked him squarely in the mouth. Fountaining blood, he went down like a felled ox. Dragging Caradoc after him, Valoran leaped over the body in his path and charged into the next room.

The second guard started up from the table and fumbled for the knife at his belt. The blade hung itself up in the sheath and with a snarl, its owner kicked a stool into the path of his oncoming attackers, then made for the door to the yard outside.

The stool caught Valoran across the shins. Diving past him as he fought to keep his balance, Caradoc launched himself recklessly into a flying tackle and flung both arms around his victim's chest.

Pinned, the guard spat and cursed. Unable to break free with a forward lunge, he threw his weight sideways and jabbed a punch over his left shoulder. It connected and his assailant let go with one hand. Before the guard could press his advantage, his opponent caught the flesh between his lip and his nose and gave it a vicious twist.

The pain was instantly paralyzing. As the guard sagged toward the floor, his red-haired assailant said through clenched teeth, "One squeak out of you and I'll tear your lip off. You've got the key to these gyves? Then hand them over to my friend here. . . ."

"Slowly," said a second voice grimly, "or it'll take a whole family of master-upholsterers to put your face back on."

Once in possession of the key, Valoran speedily disposed of his shackles, then set to work on Caradoc's. Caradoc's face had gone a sickly white. "I'll take over now," said Valoran, methodically locking their captive's hands behind him with one set of cast-off manacles. "You sit back and catch your breath while I see what I can get out of this misbegotten mawworm."

Nodding numbly, Caradoc took a step backward and let the wall take a share of his weight. As he waited for the tingling sensation of faintness to subside, Valoran stole a glance out the window. "All clear—for the moment," he said. "Keep watch for me. This shouldn't take long."

He dropped to the floor and set a knee in their prisoner's back. Wrestling the other man's dagger free from its casing, he inserted the point into his captive's ear. "Now," he said thinly. "You are going to tell me where they are keeping Evelake Whitfauconer."

The guard, mouthing, made an effort to pull away, then jerked as the knife's edge nicked his earhole. "That was just a warning," said Valoran, his voice like steel. "I haven't got all night."

The guard, white-eyed, spat out an epithet, then flinched. "I dunno!" he said thickly.

"All right," said Valoran. "Who does?"

"Nobody! None of us . . . ow! You bloody bastard!"

"The next time I'll finish what I've just started," said Valoran. "Who knows where the boy is?"

The guard was panting wildly. "Nobody but His Eminence! I swear it!"

"Now that," said Valoran, "is unfortunate for you."

He struck out with his free hand. The guard's head snapped sharply sideways. There was a crack like breaking bone, and he went limp.

"Is he dead?" asked Caradoc.

"Regrettably not," said Valoran, with a grimace of distaste. "Are you all right now?"

"Yes," said Caradoc. He added, "But I don't know how fast I could run. Or how far."

"Then we'll just have to create a diversion," said Valoran.

Using his boot, he rolled the unconscious guard toward the door, then turned back to Caradoc. "You know the layout of this place? Good. When I give the word, step outside and make for the gap, keeping as close to the west wall as you can. I'll catch up with you as soon as I've finished here."

Normally Caradoc would have protested, but the brief tussle with the guard had taught him, mortifyingly, the extent of his own weakness. He nodded and took a step toward the threshold. "Wait! Take this before you go," said Valoran, and handed him the guard's dagger. "Now!"

Caradoc slipped out into the darkness. Left alone, Valoran stripped the second guard of his poniard and deposited him next to the first. Then he went back to the room that had served as their prison-cell.

The lantern was still burning brightly. His eyes hard as citrines, Valoran picked it up by the handgrip and tested its weight. Then he swung it around him in a whistling arc and sent it hurtling toward the roof.

The casing shattered on impact. There was an angry puff and a sizzling flare of hot oil igniting. Diving back out of the way of a searing shower of broken glass and burning rush-straw, Valoran waited just long enough to make sure the thatch had caught fire before making his exit.

He overtook Caradoc fifty feet from the hovel. "Easy! It's me!" he hissed as the young mage instinctively wheeled, knife upraised to strike. "Just keep moving and don't look back—"

"Hold it right there! Who the hell are you?" demanded a suspicious voice out of the darkness to their left.

Light from an unshuttered lantern licked toward them across the grass. "Tugge Hensley, of course. Who the hell did you think it was?" countered Valoran, without stopping.

"Tugge—who? . . ." The voice trailed off in indignant bafflement, then skirled, "Hey! Wait a minute!"

Catching Caradoc hard by the arm, Valoran broke into a run.

They gained another fifty feet before the howls from behind them began to take effect. There was a rattle of opening doors and shutters. Lights jumped from wide-flung windows as men demanded to know what was going on.

The owner of the first voice was still shouting. "Somebody's got past the sentries! Where's Muirtagh? Somebody go get Muirtagh!"

There was a deep-throated boom and a backlash of hot air. The west wall of the tarn went suddenly crimson as a column of flame shot upward from the thatched roof of the prison-building.

Stumbling along beside Valoran, Caradoc tripped and measured his length on the ground. Valoran manhandled him to his knees and half dragged him ten yards farther, into the shadow of a large fallen boulder.

Fire was leaping in sheets from the roof of the burning cottage, its hungry roar mounting above the hubbub of disorganized shouts and conflicting orders. As Caradoc and Valoran huddled back in the darkness, running footsteps pounded toward them from the direction of the gap.

Firelight glanced redly off drawn weapons as two men flashed past. "That's our cue," breathed Valoran. "Come on!"

The tingling sensation was back in Caradoc's hands and feet, and his lungs burned as if he had inhaled fire. Clutching at Valoran's sleeves, he hung on grimly to consciousness, making each stride an act of will.

The gap opened up before them, lit from above. Valoran hustled Caradoc past the flanking lintel-rock, then skidded to a dead halt.

There were two men waiting for them at the opposite end of the gap.

Swords glinted bare in the watch lights. Valoran swore under his breath and let go of Caradoc's arm.

The men began to advance, blades flicking like adders' tongues. Keeping a close eye on them, Valoran sidled warily to the left, passing his dagger back and forth from hand to hand. Caradoc did not move. Blindly gripping the hilt of his own weapon with numbed fingers, he waited for the shock of cold steel.

Something cracked hard off the rock face to the right and bounced to the ground. Startled, the nearest sentry jerked his head up. An instant later, he dropped his sword with a strangled cry and fell forward, a poniard imbedded to the hilt in his back.

Valoran roared and charged. As the remaining sentry whirled, snapping, to meet him, he dived to the ground and rolled under the sentry's stabbing blade. Sparks leaped up as the sword-point nicked stone. Valoran got fingers like a vise around the other man's sword-wrist and slashed his dagger through the vein at the base of the hand.

The sentry howled and dropped his sword, blood spurting in gouts from the wound. Valoran hurled him aside. As the sentry scurried for the inner edge of the gap, a small dark figure detached itself from the shadows outside and ran forward.

His throat constricted, Caradoc croaked a warning cry. Valoran spun around, then gave, incongruously, a raucous whoop of welcome.

"Why did ye no' burn the place to the ground while ye were about it?" inquired the newcomer with no particular admiration. "Man, did yer ma never tell ye it was bad luck t' leave a job half-done?"

"In this case," said Valoran tartly, "it would have been worse than unlucky to hang about."

He eyed the fallen guard. "I'm glad to see you haven't lost your touch."

"Practice," said his companion with a grin. Then he noticed Caradoc for the first time. "God, there's another one. Want me tae finish him off?"

"No," said Valoran, hauling him back by the arm. "This one's a friend. I'll introduce you once we're well away from here."

There were two horses tethered among the trees on the edge of the wood. As Valoran's short associate neatly flipped the reins loose with one hand, Caradoc said to Valoran,

"This was all part of a prearranged plan. You're both agents for the Lord Warden. Aren't you?"

The blond man chuckled. "At least your brush with this Borthen hasn't addled your wits. My friend here is Harlech Hardrada—you'll have to ride double with him. My real name is Gudmar . . ."

CHAPTER 23

The Lieutenant

On the twenty-seventh day of June, Lord Aldehron Ashfyrd, Marshall of Farrowaithe, received a message by special courier from an accredited agent for the Lord Warden.

Dated a week earlier, the note was brief, but the matter of it was stirring enough to cause the marshall to mutter under his breath and give the contents a second reading:

Commander:

Information has reached me concerning the existence of a brigand stronghold three days' journey north from the village of Lauristen, on the edge of the Dysmarsh. Since I suspect its present occupants were involved in the abduction of Evelake Whitfauconer, I intend to make my way there with all dispatch, passing myself off as a fugitive from justice.

A contact of mine will be on hand to relay messages. If you do not hear from me again within a week of receiving this first communication, it will be likely that I have met with some mischance. Should you decide to send in a contingent of the Farrowaithe Guard, my contact will make himself known to them and will render them whatever assistance he may. . . .

The letter was signed, "Gudmar Ap Gorvald."

Aldehron Ashfyrd, who knew Gudmar well, had, never-theless, his own opinions concerning how affairs of this kind should be handled. After disgesting the information contained in the latter paragraphs of the letter, he consulted the admirably detailed map on the wall of his study. Then he summoned his secretary and set about drafting the orders that would dispatch fifty Farrowaithe Guards, under the command of an experienced adjutant, to Lauristen the following day.

Nine days later, a few hours before dusk, the main body of Aldehron's task force, under the direction of Sir Manfred Du Bourne, reached the wooded outskirts of Lauristen. Sir Man-fred, possessing a sound grasp of protocol, left the billeting arrangements to his second-in-command and rode off in search of the local sheriff in order to render an edited account for their presence in the area.

Sometime later, as night was falling, Lieutenant Geston Du Maris caught up with the rest of the party.

He had been put in charge of the supply wagons, an unfortunate turn of events for which he strongly suspected his immediate superior was responsible. Laboring under a growing sense of ill-usage, he had been forced to witness a whole series of minor mishaps, culminating in a broken wheel and a colicked carthorse. By the time he at last rode ridge-backed into camp, trailing three red-faced and sullen wagoners behind him, he was in no mood to be trifled with.

Ruthlessly bestowing upon a hapless subordinate the task of seeing to the unloading, Geston heaved himself out of the saddle and surveyed his surroundings with a jaundiced eye. "Looking for anyone in particular?" inquired a voice from behind him.

The voice belonged to Cergil Ap Cymric, his fellow cadet. "Yes. A certain Captain Llew Ap Connacht. And when I find him," growled Geston, "we'll see if looks can kill."

Cergil stepped around in front of him and looked him up and down. "Don't waste your energy," he said. "You and I still have one last chore to do."

Geston groaned. "Oh, God, not another one! What is it this time?"

Cergil grinned. "Don't despair until you've heard me out. Sir Manfred's requisitioned three barrels of ale from the Blue Heron Inn in the village. You and I are supposed to go fetch them."

Geston brightened visibly. "It can't be more than a quarter of a mile from here. D'you suppose we'd have time for a quiet pint or two on our own before we had to start back?"

"That," said Cergil, "depends entirely on how quickly we can get one of the wagons brought 'round."

Twelve minutes later they were on their way. Hanging onto the wagon seat with one hand as Cergil guided the two heavy dray horses down the wooded embankment into the road, Geston waited until the going smoothed out before resuming conversation.

"You know, I don't pretend to understand why we're stopping over here in Lauristen when we know for a fact that the raiders we're after are practically on our doorstep," he said. "You had more reason than any of us to volunteer for this mission. How do you account for the delay?"

Cergil had been one of the two scouts sent forward on the day of Evelake Whitfauconer's ambush. That he had survived the battle with only minor injuries was due entirely to the skill of the armorer who had fashioned the helmet he was wearing when a half-spent crossbow bolt had struck him senseless. At Geston's question, his face lost its humor. "I don't know," he said. "I only hope I get the chance to redeem myself when the time comes."

He turned his attention to the road ahead. "Redeem yourself for what?" asked Geston curiously. "The magister-inquisitor was able to prove that your perceptions at the time had been distorted by the renegade Hospitaller they themselves were looking for. There was never any question of negligence on your part."

"No," agreed Cergil grimly. "And that's precisely why I'd dearly love to get first crack at the bastard."

Geston gave up trying to follow his friend's line of

reasoning. "That might not be easy," he said. "You don't have any clear recollection of what he looks like."

"If ever we meet again," said Cergil with perfect conviction, "that won't make any difference."

Two floors high, and broad across the front, the Blue Heron Inn stood at the intersection of the three roads that made up the street-plan of the village. Leaving Geston to apprise the innkeeper of their arrival, Cergil climbed down from the wagon and led the horses around the east side of the building into the half-enclosed innyard at the back.

The back door was open. Scuffing his boots on the mat, Cergil walked through to the kitchen and found Geston conferring with the owner of the Heron. "Hullo—the kegs are still down in the cellar," said Geston as Cergil entered.

"I've set them aside for you. I hope you don't mind bringing them up yourselves, young sirs," said the proprietor apologetically. "It's been busy tonight—the lad and I haven't had a moment to spare away from the common room since we opened our doors."

"That's all right," said Geston resignedly. "Just point us to the stairway and we'll do the rest."

The cellar, they discovered, was to be reached by means of a trapdoor. They had to move the kitchen table aside before the innkeeper could open it. The barrels were heavy. By the time they had climbed the steps down and up for the third and final time, they were both perspiring.

"I can't think why you didn't bring along a few stalwart privates," said Geston plaintively, tipping his end of the last keg into the back of the wagon.

"Economy," said Cergil, dusting his hands. "It's bad enough having to buy drinks for you."

"Oh, are you paying?" said Geston. "Then what are we waiting for?"

The door leading out of the kitchen opened onto an L-shaped passageway. A staircase at the end of the right-hand branch gave access to the upper floor. Eight feet ahead of them, the hallway ended at a half-drawn curtain. Listening to the general buzz of talk, Cergil said, "This way to the common room. Follow me."

Geston didn't have to be told twice. His mind dwelling pleasurably on the prospect of cold ale, he was caught wholly off-guard a second later when Cergil stopped dead at the doorway and rapped out an oath in an icy hiss of pure venom. Geston had barely enough presence of mind to leap back as his companion flattened himself to the wall behind the curtain and stayed there, his face set like a mask.

Geston instinctively dropped his voice to a whisper. "What the devil's the matter with you?"

Cergil had murder in his eyes. "The renegade mage—" he muttered hoarsely. "The one I encountered on the West Road. He's out there. I've just seen him."

Geston stared at him. "You can't be serious."

"I've never been more serious in my life!" said Cergil fiercely. Seeing his friend's expression, he gripped Geston by the arm. "It's got nothing to do with physical appearances. I just looked at him, and somehow I *knew*. I can't explain it. But I know I'm right."

For three heartbeats longer they faced each other in silence. "I must be crazy," muttered Geston. "All right. Point him out to me."

Cergil released the air in his lungs. "The table in the far left-hand corner—the man sitting with his back to the wall. See him?"

"The tall fellow with the red hair? Of course I see him. Goddammit," said Geston in exasperation. "Why couldn't you have picked on someone half that size?"

He took a second look. "If that blond-bearded hulk sitting across from him is a friend of his, I suggest we send for reinforcements. . . ."

"The Lord Warden and his wife are in Ambrothen at the moment. That's where Harlech and I will be heading from here," said Gudmar Ap Gorvald. "I urge you to accompany us—for your own protection."

Caradoc was gazing down into his wine as though it were

wormwood. "Protection? That's a quaint synonym for 'incarceration.' "

"I'm not talking in euphemisms," said Gudmar patiently. "If you were to present evidence against Borthen—voluntarily—before the Lord Chief Justice of Ambrothen, you would be granted immunity from prosecution under the laws related to 'evidence in support of the peace.' "

"My cooperation might satisfy a court of civil law," said Caradoc. "Do you honestly believe that the Order will be so readily appeased?"

Gudmar opened his mouth, thought a moment, then closed it again. "You see the problem, don't you?" said Caradoc with a bleak smile. "The Order has a sacred trust to protect. If the vows they impose on their members are to continue to have any binding force, violators like me have got to be punished."

His eyes were bitter. "They wouldn't be able to kill me, of course: that would go against their moral directives. But then, they wouldn't have to. . . ."

"Don't let your own guilty conscience delude you," said Gudmar. "I've met several mages from Ambrothen, among them a man by the name of Ulbrecht Rathmuir. I think you underestimate the number of friends you still have within the Order."

He leaned forward onto his elbows. "I also think you may be underestimating Borthen's interest in you. The fact that he didn't kill you when he had the chance suggests that he wants you for some reason. If that's so, he may well take steps to hunt you down."

Caradoc laughed, a shade wildly. "Perhaps it would be best if I simply hanged myself."

"Or do the sensible thing," said Gudmar. "Come back with us to Ambrothen."

Caradoc turned his glass between his hands. His gaunt face was showing the strain. "I can't," he said wearily after a moment, "I can't seem to make up my mind."

Something akin to compassion showed behind Gudmar's golden eyes. "Sleep on it, then," he said quietly. "Things may seem clearer in the morning. Harlech and I will share the night watch between us—'' He broke off, frowning.

"Speaking of Harlech," said Caradoc, "where is he?"

"I don't know," said Gudmar, his gaze narrowing. "He only stepped outside for a brief look around." He pushed his chair back from the table and stood up. "I'm going out to look for him," he said.

Behind him, the common room door flew open and slammed against the inside wall. As Gudmar wheeled, a short wiry figure in a dark cloak tumbled across the threshold and clattered to the floor inside.

It was Harlech, his face pinched white, his one hand pressed hard against a growing red stain at the base of his neck. Gudmar's voice boomed across the shocked outcry of alarm from other parts of the room, "Quick! Get that door closed! And draw the bolts!"

Harlech was making a struggling effort to regain his feet, deaf for the moment to any and all demands. Gudmar and Caradoc shouldered their way to his side and plucked him upright.

The little man was panting heavily, but his eyes were hard and bright. "Thought I'd check the back trail a wee bit," he gasped. "Yon oversized lump of bull-beef ye call Muirtagh's a lot cannier than we bargained on. The bastard's out there now, wi' at least half a score o' cronies, and if they didna mean business, paint my neb blue and call me a Mayfair loon—"

There was an explosive crash and a tinkling shower of breaking glass as a building-brick sailed through the right-hand window. Wincing as the brick itself thudded to the floor three feet away from him, Gudmar called, "Everybody get back! There'll be more where that came from."

His voice carried the ring of authority, and men began to scatter hastily toward the larger pieces of furniture in the room. "Wait a minute! What the hell's going on?" bawled a loud voice from behind the bar, and broke off with a howl as another brick bounced off the wall overhead.

Upstairs a woman was screaming shrilly. Harlech was weaving where he stood, the blood seeping down his chest.

"Take Harlech with you and make a run for the kitchen," said Gudmar to Caradoc. "If you can leave by the back door, do it. I'll follow when and if I can."

The door behind them leaped in its frame at a heavy blow from outside. There was a loud report, like a firedog going off, and the topmost hinge burst apart. Through the widening gap they could all see a seething mat of bodies.

Gudmar snatched his dagger from its sheath and lunged for the doorway. Throwing the weight of his shoulder bruisingly against the door, he jabbed his blade through the crack and heard an angry yelp as the point pricked flesh. "*Will* you go on!" he shouted over his shoulder to Caradoc. "There's nothing you can do here!"

Harlech's face had gone the color of pale clay. Torn between conflicting impulses, Caradoc lingered a heartbeat longer, then tipped the wounded man over his shoulder and made a dash for the curtained hallway.

Hooking the curtain out of the way, he plunged down the short, dimly-lit passage. As he emerged into the main corridor, two dark figures stepped out of the shadows into his path.

Hampered as he was, he couldn't move fast enough to evade them. A mailed fist, driven with malice, smashed into his face just below his left cheekbone and sent him crashing sideways to the floor.

Harlech's unconscious body rolled away from him like a sack of potatoes. "You whoreson!" said a withering voice from somewhere overhead.

A hand gripped Caradoc's hair and began to slam his head rhythmically against the wall while the owner of the hand chanted vengefully, "This is for Wyn. And for Corin. And for Commander Galledan. And for Evelake Whifauconer . . ."

The content of Cergil's message to his superior got unaccountably garbled in transmission. Captain Llew Ap Connacht, for whom it was intended, had the innkeeper's son repeat it three times, and eventually concluded that his subordinates were in trouble.

After that, he wasted no more time. Calling a score of his men to horse, he mounted his rawboned sorrel and led the way at a gallop down the road toward the Blue Heron Inn.

They arrived to find the Heron's front windows smashed in and a full-dress brawl in progress inside. Dismounting smartly on cue among the press of hysterical spectators in the street, twenty Farrowaithe Guards rushed the building on foot and within seconds had the inn completely surrounded.

Inside, trapped in the corridor between the kitchen and the common room, with a frightened covey of farmers and tradesmen cowering on the floor at their backs, Cergil and Geston were doing all they could to hold off their attackers.

But they were outnumbered and losing ground. Bleeding from a cut over his left eye, Geston hit back at a broken-nosed thug who was trying to put a knife between his ribs.

The man fell, and someone else stepped in to take his place. His horrified gaze traveling upward, Geston found himself staring into the flat, thick-nosed face of the biggest man he had ever seen in his life.

The giant was armed with a heavy mace. Abruptly casting all hope to the winds, Geston lunged. His bladepoint grated against plate-mail. An instant later the mace crashed down, shattering his sword and his arm with it.

The shock of the impact toppled him to his knees. Paralyzed with pain, he braced himself to have his skull split.

Someone caught him by the shoulders and snatched him back as the air whistled past his nose. There was a sudden lull in the noise, then an outburst of dismay from among the ranks of their attackers. "Praise God!" whooped the voice of his unknown rescuer in his ear. "Your friends have finally arrived!"

They did not, for all their efforts, succeed in capturing the gigantic leader. Sir Manfred, when he got there, received the news with resignation, and said, "He can't have gone far. Divide up the men into groups of five and see if they can pick up his trail."

Then he sent for the man who had identified himself as Gudmar Ap Gorvald.

Alone in the room, the two men eyed each other appraisingly. "Your arrival was timely—I didn't expect to see the Guard here so soon," said Gudmar with a wry twist of a smile. "The Marshall of Farrowaithe seems to have anticipated trouble."

Sir Manfred inclined his head. "Your message to the Marshall was handed on to me. I am relieved to see that you stand in no further need of our services." He paused, then said, "What about the Warden's son?"

Gudmar grimaced. "We're little the wiser, I'm afraid. I'll have to wait until I get to Ambrothen to see what His Grace has to make of it."

He squared his shoulders. "Your men took ten prisoners?"

"Minus your one-handed friend, yes," said Sir Manfred. "Someone nearly succeeded in cutting his throat, but the local mage-servitor says he'll be all right."

"Good," said Gudmar. "What about the boy with the red hair?"

"We've got him separated from the others. Two of them tried to throttle him," said the commander.

"There's a reason for that," said Gudmar. "He helped me escape from Thyle Tarn. And he's prepared to cooperate with us."

Sir Manfred lifted an eyebrow. "That should certainly stand in his favor when he comes to trial. But I'm afraid I can't release him on parole. Cergil Ap Cymric has identified him positively as the man he encountered on his scouting mission."

"I see," said Gudmar tonelessly. He paused, then added, "He is still suffering from his treatment at Thyle Tarn. He should be given medical attention."

"That has already been taken care of," said Sir Manfred dryly, "as he also took quite a hammering tonight. He'll be allowed time to recover. But as soon as he's fit enough to travel, he'll be transferred to Ambrothen under guard. My lieutenant has volunteered to be his personal escort. . . ."

CHAPTER 24

The Bond-Servant

The two mysterious strangers left the mine and headed north along what remained of an old mining road. Riding after them at a discreet distance, Serdor caught his first clear glimpse of them shortly before sunset of the same day, when they stopped to water their horses at a rock-spring in the lowlands.

The bigger man's leonine coloring was as noteworthy as his shorter companion's empty coat-cuff. Recalling with sudden vividness an encounter with a one-handed man in the High Street of Thurby, Serdor thought he could guess the identity of the faceless intruder who had attempted to break into his room at the inn.

City-bred, he had no illusions about his ability as a tracker, but if his two quarries were aware that they were being followed, they gave no sign of it during the course of a five-day journey northward as far as Strathwellyn. From Strathwellyn, they struck out north by northeast toward the vast tract of bog and quagmire known as the Dysmarsh. It was there, beyond the village of Lauristen, that they abruptly gave him the slip.

After several profitless forays into the treacherous border-lands of the marsh, Serdor was forced, eventually, to admit defeat. The ease with which his erstwhile quarries succeeded in eluding him confirmed a rueful suspicion that they might have done so days earlier, had they chosen. Unwilling to risk venturing out across the Dysmarsh on his own, he had only two courses of action left open to him: to follow the edge of the marsh in the forlorn hope of recovering the trail, or, to turn around and start for home. With nothing to lose, he decided on the former.

It proved, unfortunately, only so much wasted effort. By the time Serdor reached the village of Drumcarrow, it was only too clear that he had ridden well out of his way to no good purpose. He spent the better part of the next night wrestling with the cold logic of failure. The next morning he turned Briona's head around and started out on the first leg of his journey home.

Ten days later, the mare went lame.

She had thrown a shoe and picked up a stone-bruise. Lowering her right forehoof to the ground, Serdor sighed and wondered how long it would take him to reach the next village on foot.

The distance proved to be a matter of nearly eight miles. It was well after dark by the time Serdor tramped, weary and disheveled, into the yard of the first hostel he came to on the Aldenfyrd Road.

Seeing no groom in attendance, he tethered the mare to the hitching post under the swinging, ill-painted sign and mounted the steps to the door. Two men pushed past him as he stepped across the threshold, glaring at him with beefy insolence. Serdor ignored them and went on in.

The common room was half-full. Peering through an acrid haze of hanging smoke, Serdor looked about for the proprietor. Seeing no likely candidate, he shrugged and walked over to the nearest table.

"Excuse me," he said to the back of a grizzled head. "Is the innkeeper anywhere about?"

The man half turned on the bench, fixing him with a jaundiced eye. "Who? Haskel. Naw, he ain't here. Leastways, *I* ain't seen him. Was ye wantin' him?"

Serdor suppressed a sarcastic rejoinder. "I'd like to bespeak lodgings for the night."

His informant took ale at a gulp and belched noisily. "I s'pose ye could talk to the boy. Not that he'll be much good . . ."

Never one to pursue a lost cause beyond reason, Serdor turned his back on the unfinished sentence and steered a course for the door at the opposite end of the room. While he was still several yards away, the door inched open as a dingy figure burdened with a heavy tray edged his way through.

Adroitly eluding table-edges and outstretched legs, the figure brushed past him with a muttered word of excuse. Looking after him, Serdor received a composite impression of youth and neglect. Concluding that this must be "the boy," he watched as the shabby youth discharged his duties, and set himself to waylay him on the return trip.

Moving with a kind of dogged haste, the boy tried to slip past him a second time. Serdor made a short spring and got his hand on one thin shoulder. "Wait a minute," he said pleasantly. "I want accommodations for the night, for myself and my horse. Can you handle it, or will I have to wait until your master gets back?"

Seen at close hand, the boy proved to be a grimy, underfed urchin in clothes at least a size too large for him. Arrested in flight, he drew breath, swallowed, and said, "I beg your pardon, sir. The proprietor is presently occupied in the kitchen. If you'll permit me, though, I'll tell him you are here, and he will be with you directly."

Prepared for countrified vowels and a surly delivery, Serdor was surprised both by the voice and the manner of speaking. Before he could garner any further impressions, however, the boy bowed slightly, with an angular parody of grace, and vanished again into the dimness.

Serdor's room proved to be cleaner than he would have expected, judging by the standards downstairs. The following morning he took his time over breakfast, then donned his boots and made a pilgrimage across the yard to the barn.

The groom was nowhere in sight. Since this seemed to be the usual state of affairs around the Manticore, Serdor went on inside and located Briona in a square stall at the far end of the barn.

Her leg was still swollen, and she laid back her ears in displeasure as he handled her fetlock. Judging by what he saw, Serdor calculated that it would be at least three days before she could be ridden again.

As he lowered her hoof to the floor, the back door of the barn burst open, spilling sunlight onto the hay. Startled, Serdor straightened up as a figure flashed past the stall on a pair of flying feet and came to a halt in the shadow of the hayloft.

It was the serving-boy Serdor had seen the night before. Standing with his back to the minstrel, the boy was trembling, the breath coming hard and short between his clenched teeth. Serdor could not see his face, but something in the lad's nerve-wracked stance triggered a flicker of comprehension. Moving softly away from Briona, Serdor stepped out of the stall.

"Hullo," he said quietly. "Is anything wrong?"

The boy gasped and spun around. His face was very pale, his brown eyes belligerent. "Can I be of any help?" asked Serdor.

"No," said the boy gruffly. He dragged a hand across his forehead and added defiantly, "I'm all right."

His color was beginning to come back, though he still held himself stiffly. Setting one foot on a nearby bale of hay, Serdor gave the boy a quizzical look and said, "Pardon me. I didn't mean to startle you. Much less violate your privacy."

The other looked away. "You've as much right to be here as I," he muttered in the same husky voice, but his tone had lost something of its hostility.

"I was looking after my horse when I heard you come in," said Serdor. "Do you happen to know if there's a competent farrier anywhere around here?"

This earned him a penetrating glare. "You don't have to feel obliged to make conversation with me."

"I know," said Serdor calmly. "But I learned a long time

ago that the best way to take your mind off a thrashing is to turn your attention to something else.''

The brown eyes widened. After a brief moment, the boy bit his lip. ''I-I'm sorry. I didn't mean to be rude.''

''Under the circumstances, I think we can safely forget about it,'' said Serdor. ''What's your name?''

''Rhan, sir.''

''We can also dispense with the title,'' said Serdor. ''If I'm going to address you on familiar terms, you may as well do the same for me. . . .''

Serdor saw more of Rhan in the course of the next two days. Enough for him to discover, without asking, that the boy was lonely, unhappy, and in trouble.

For someone in Rhan's position, that was not unusual: indentured servants were seldom given preferential treatment. What was unusual was Rhan himself. Neither his speech, nor his manners, nor the extent of his education seemed in keeping with his station.

The anomaly was partially explained later. When he brought Serdor's evening meal up to his room on the second night after his arrival at the Manticore, Rhan was clearly hoping for an excuse to linger. Prompted almost as much by curiosity as by commiseration, Serdor waited while the boy set out bread, plates, and cutlery, then said thoughtfully, ''I have an inherent dislike of eating alone. Do you think Haskel would miss you if you were to join me?''

The quick flicker in the boy's brown eyes was one of surprise and gratitude. ''Not for a while, anyway,'' said Rhan and sat down gingerly in the opposite chair.

Desultory at first, the conversation became gradually more personal as Rhan relaxed his guard. At length, casually buttering a slice of bread, Serdor remarked, ''I couldn't help but notice your accent. You're not from around here, are you?''

Rhan shook his head. ''No. I'm from Khariswyth—near Farrowaithe.''

That came as something of a surprise. ''You're a long way from home,'' said Serdor. He leaned over to cut himself another slice of cheese. "What about your family? What does your father do?"

The sudden silence told him that he had, unintentionally, touched a sensitive nerve. Rhan gently laid down his knife. "My father," he said, "was a landowner. And a gentleman."

The emphasis on the preterite spoke volumes, but after a single glance at the expression on the boy's face, Serdor refrained from comment. A moment later, Rhan gave him a crooked smile. "My older brother is a gamester—not a very successful one, I'm afraid." He picked up his knife again and began to trace circles on the tabletop. "Within two years of my father's death, the property had to be sold to settle my brother's debts. And when there wasn't anything else to sell . . ."

The wry twitch of his lips only partially concealed the pain of remembrance, but his voice when he spoke was quite steady. "One of Erich's creditors was a magistrate. Erich handed me over to him in return for a remittance. Lord Rothben made out the writ of indenture—all properly signed and sealed. And—here I am."

The stark little narrative had the aching ring of truth. His indignation on the upsurge, Serdor said, "Surely you don't mean to tell me that none of the rest of your family made any effort to stop him."

Rhan's rawboned shoulders rose and fell in a weary shrug. "There wasn't any other family. Erich and I are the last of the line, and no one else was inclined at the time to pay much heed to my objections. When I learned I was to be sent to Haskel, I didn't want to go. But Lord Rothben—persuaded me."

He fell silent. Remembering the ugly little scene in the barn, Serdor let the silence lie for a moment. With Caradoc's problems—and Margoth's—weighing heavily on his mind, he had no business involving himself in a situation that had nothing to do with him. On the other hand . . .

He said aloud, "It sounds to me as if you could do with some assistance. Since you haven't got any relatives to call on, perhaps a friend might do."

The knife struck the table with a muted clatter. Making no effort to retrieve it, Rhan said on an odd, breathless note, "If this is a game, please don't carry it any further."

"It's no game. It's an honest offer," said Serdor. "Provided that you don't mind waiting until I've settled a few affairs of my own first."

Rhan drew a deep breath. "I don't mind." His brown eyes were bright as stars.

The sudden blaze of hope and excitement made Serdor uneasy. "I ought to warn you that I know next to nothing about the law in a case like this," he said. "I also ought to warn you that it may be weeks—maybe even months—before I'll be free to get back to you. Can you trust me so far?"

"Yes," said Rhan. "After all, I have nothing to lose—"

He broke off abruptly at the sound of his own name echoing angrily down the outside corridor. The light in his eyes went out like a snuffed flame. "That's Haskel calling," he said, shoving back his chair. "I'd better go."

"I'm going into the village first thing in the morning, and as soon as I've finished with the blacksmith, I'll be off on the road south," said Serdor. "If we don't get another chance to talk before I go, remember you have my promise."

CHAPTER 25

The Nightmare

The darkness was impenetrable, cold as a crypt in winter. Staring blindly into the thick black air, he could feel the deathlike cold seeping into his bones like slow poison.

His naked body was laid out on a slab of hard stone. His fingers, traveling outward from his flanks, located a wall a few inches to either side of him. He felt upward along the walls and found that the slab on which he was lying had been roofed over.

This discovery sent a surge of pure fright coursing through his supine frame. His breathing ragged in the darkness, he frantically explored the dimensions of his prison-house, only to find that there was no sign of any chink or break in the surrounding walls.

There was no way out.

He had been walled up, still living, inside a tomb.

Panic swept over him. He flung himself howling at the roof of his sarcophagus, attacking stone with bare fists and fingernails. . . .

His clawing hands burst through a fabric of shadows. Rocketing upright, Rhan came to a shuddering halt as his outflung palms struck wood at arm's length. His heart thudding hard against his laboring ribs, he blinked his eyes and looked around him.

It was no longer dark. Moonlight pouring in through the

narrow barred window above his head showed him that he was not, after all, in a tomb, but in the scullery of the Manticore Inn.

It was not the first time he had been visited with this particular nightmare. Badly shaken, he lay back, trying to collect his waking thoughts.

As he did so, he became suddenly aware of the muted rattle of cart wheels coming up the lane toward the inn. Plodding hooves turned the corner into the alley leading from the road to the Manticore's stableyard. A moment later the wheels creaked to a halt just outside the scullery's narrow window.

Low voices exchanged mutters, and shadows bobbed across the scullery's flagged floor. There was a rasping sound and some controlled bumping. Rhan quietly drew himself up and stole a glance out the window.

There was a covered wagon drawn up in the middle of the yard. The door to the stable was open, and light shone dimly across the threshold. As Rhan watched, two men in dark clothes came out of the barn and went to the back of the wagon. Together they bent over the cart's tail and emerged with a packing case cradled between them.

They carried the crate into the barn. Several minutes later, they returned empty-handed for another. Absorbed in following their movements, Rhan was unaware that there was anyone else abroad in the stableyard until a low voice quite close to him said in a sniggering whisper, "Looks like a prime haul this time. What the sheriff of Rhylnie wouldn't give to know what's lying underneath the floor of my corncrib!"

The whisper was Haskel's. Tensing, Rhan shrank back from the window. A second voice, deeper and throatier than Haskel's, growled, "Just you see to it that the deliveries get made on time. If even one of 'em's late, you'll answer for it."

Rhan could not place the second voice, but there was something frighteningly familiar in its roughness. Hugging himself against a sudden chill, he pressed closer to the wall. The whisper that was Haskel's said, "The lads from the village know their business. And there won't be any trouble from the toll-keepers this time."

There was a rumble from his companion. "There'd better not be. You were supposed to have paid them off."

"And so I did!" Haskel's voice rose defensively, then dropped again. "Look, last month's mix-up wasn't my fault. I did everything I was supposed to do to make sure the dealers in Cheswythe got their consignments. It's just that with the Warden's men cracking down, it's not so easy as it used to be. . . ."

"Nobody's interested in your puking excuses," said the second voice shortly. "I've already had a bellyful of 'em from our friend over in Darkyng. Once we've finished here, we're going off to have a chat with him."

There was a pause. "What about the boy?" asked Haskel.

"Keep your eyes on him. We'll be back to pick him up around noon."

"What are you going to do with him?"

"What makes you think that's any business of yours?" The second voice was not remotely amused. "Orders are he comes with us. That's all you need to know."

The voices moved on, out of earshot. Bony fingers knotted together, Rhan was left to contemplate the stark fact that his circumstances were about to be drastically altered.

Serdor, at all costs, had to be told about it. He leaped to his feet and strode over to the door that joined the scullery to the kitchen.

The handle shifted in his nervous grip, but the door remained closed. He tried it again. Then shut his eyes against the grim realization that the door was bolted from the other side.

Someone, apparently taking no chances, had locked him in.

Haskel's nocturnal visitors departed as unobtrusively as they had come. Rhan spent the ensuing hour turning the scullery upside down. Dawn found him little better off.

His findings were meager. Apart from an assortment of

buckets, washtubs, and broken scraps of furniture, the room contained only a large raised sink with a wooden spigot and a disused coal-brazier that had once served for heating wash-water.

A flat strip of copper-binding off one of the washtubs offered some small promise when he discovered it was thin enough to pass through the crack between the door and its frame. He was still pondering whether or not it would be possible to use it as a lever to shift the bolt from his side of the door when a clumping of heavy footsteps down the steps leading into the kitchen signaled Haskel's arrival.

It was by then broad daylight. Acutely aware that time was running short, Rhan waited until the noises from the kitchen subsided, then set to work with his improvised jack.

Meeting resistance, the soft copper began to give way. Carefully working it up and down in a series of small jerks, Rhan caught his lip between his teeth as the metal buckled between his fingers. He pulled it out, straightened it, and tried again. This time, the metal strip broke in two.

Staring at the shard in his hand, Rhan felt his heart sink. It was only too clear that any attempt to leave the room by way of the door was doomed to end in failure. He was still trying to think of an alternative when the sound of running water underfoot attracted his attention.

The Manticore's water supply came from a large cistern on the roof. The water was funneled down to the kitchen and the scullery along pipes set into the walls, and the runoff was channeled out of the building through a drainage gutter built under the scullery floor. . . .

A drainage gutter . . .

His thin body tensing like a runner's, Rhan turned away from the door and darted over to the sink.

Lying flat on the floor, he examined its underside. There was a plughole in the bottom of the sink. And directly below the plughole, a metal grid set into the floor.

Two feet wide and eighteen inches deep, the drain-canal was lined with slimed stones. It looked to be a tight fit for a human body, but not impossible. Trembling in mingled apprehension and elation, Rhan scrambled to his feet and went to fetch a broken length of mop-handle.

The grid came up with surprising ease. Setting it aside, Rhan stared down into the opening. Two feet below the mouth of the drain, the channel branched off at a horizontal angle. There was water trickling sluggishly along the bottom of it from the direction of the kitchen.

The stench of rotting algae filtered up from below. Taking a deep breath, Rhan wriggled under the sink and swung his legs into the shaft.

With cold water seeping through his clothes, he lowered himself with difficulty into a sitting position, his legs stretched out straight ahead of him. Inching his way along on his haunches, he dropped down until he was lying flat on his back, arms over his head.

Reaching up, he drew the grid cover back over the hole. Then he lay back, staring up at the small square of light, his heart knocking against his ribs.

Except for the presence of that light, he might almost have been reliving his nightmare. The recollection of it made him stiffen in sudden dread of being enclosed in the dark.

The damp air seemed suddenly too thick to breathe. His chest heaving, he closed his eyes, feeling the heavy throb of fear behind his lids.

It was a full minute before he could bring himself to move. Gulping, he at last got his breathing under control long enough to calm the heavy beating of his heart. "It's all right . . . it can't be far," he told himself sternly, and deliberately called to mind the alternative.

The reminder was enough to unlock his frozen muscles. Pushing himself away from the wall with his hands, he began to wriggle on his back along the watercourse.

The light receded until it was visible only as a pale blur against the darkness. By no means sure how long his nerve would hold out, Rhan gritted his teeth against the lurking thought of getting stuck and made the best speed he could.

After running level for thirty feet, the tunnel took a downward turn.

Here the stench of rotting weed was stronger. His stomach lurching queasily at the fetid odor of decay, he wormed his way down the slope.

The angle became steeper. Beneath him, the rocks were treacherously slick. His clothes tugged at his body, and he realized, suddenly, that he was sliding involuntarily down a channel that had become a chute.

Scrabbling for handgrips, he found none. The sudden loss of purchase brought his heart to his mouth. Thrashing, he tried and failed to brace himself against the walls. Helplessly gathering momentum, he slithered another few yards, then abruptly tumbled into empty space.

The drop was only a shallow one, but he landed badly, bruising hip and shoulder as he hit. Ice-cold water sloshed up around him. Choking and sputtering, he struggled frantically to right himself, and rammed a knee, hard, into a jutting ledge of stone.

It was the mouth of another tunnel.

Touch told him it was even narrower than the first, but he had passed the point of panic. Driven on by a dogged fatalism, he dropped down on his hands and knees and pushed his way into the opening.

His shoulders scraping the wall on either side, he made a mole's progress. Worming his way on his belly, he dragged himself along by inches, praying that his straining fingers would not meet up with a dead end.

The passage took a turn to the right. Writhing, he got his upper body past the corner, then exhaled on a sob of pure relief.

Twenty feet ahead of him, blinding to the eyes, was another square of light.

The conduit brought him out onto the bank of a small pond. Elbowing his way past the opening, he collapsed on wet sand, trembling with cold and reaction.

He did not allow himself to linger long. Pulling himself up

a moment later, he looked back and saw above the trees the gabled roof of the Manticore Inn.

Already time was against him. Scrambling to his feet, he struck off through the woods in the direction of the road to Rhylnie.

The road Serdor would be traveling.

CHAPTER 26

The Runestaff

The scullery door was bolted and its one narrow window was barred. Comfortably assured that his serving-boy was securely contained within its four walls, Haskel Tohr gave the matter no further thought until it occurred to him, halfway through the morning, that he hadn't heard so much as a squeak out of the brat since dawn.

With a large consignment of the drug juju'bi due to be shipped out that night, Haskel had enough to occupy his mind without worrying overmuch about the welfare of one whey-faced adolescent. A healthy respect for his employer, however, warned him that it wouldn't hurt to look in on the boy.

The brat knew too much for anyone's good about the smuggling operations that went on beneath the Manticore's roof—a fact which explained why Haskel's employer wanted him out of the way. Grinning nastily, Haskel reflected that should his scullion meet with an unpleasant fate, he for one would shed no tears.

These uncharitable sentiments were magnified a thousand-fold a few minutes later when he opened the door to the scullery and discovered, to his thunderstruck astonishment, that the boy was gone.

Incredible as it seemed, it was true. Standing in the center of the room, Haskel stared at the window, its bars intact, and swore. He turned around in a complete circle and swore again, more violently. Then his restraint broke and he turned his baffled fury on the room. Buckets and brushes went flying in all directions. Clamping onto the sink with powerful, hamlike fists, Haskel rocked it loose from the wall and sent it crashing over onto its side. Water spewed from the broken pipe from the roof and ran gurgling into the exposed drain.

The drain.

Haskel's small eyes noticed for the first time the mophandle lying next to the grid. The grid itself was lying not quite even with the floor.

There was no way of telling how long the boy had been gone. And no time to cast about in the woods to pick up his trail.

Fortunately, however, there was an easier way.

Leaving the scullery in shambles, Haskel went straight to his own room. There he fumbled under his bed and drew out a narrow box some twelve inches long, made of polished black jade. Stuffing the box into his shirtfront, he then went to the open window and bellowed for the Manticore's groom.

Ute Baynes was a simpleminded individual, but he knew from the tone of the bellow that something had gone seriously wrong. He saddled Haskel's black gelding as quickly as he could. By the time he brought the horse around to the front of the inn, Haskel had his boots on and his whip in his hand.

It was less than two hours till noon. Laying the quirt to the gelding's rump, Haskel cantered down the hill to the edge of the pond in the woods below the inn.

A quick inspection of the ground around the mouth of the drainage conduit confirmed his suspicions. Mounting up again, he took the black box out of his shirt and thumbed open the lid.

Inside, pillowed on black silk, lay a thin, tapering rod of translucent green stone. It was plain and smooth, except for a curious glyph traced in silver an inch from the tip. Haskel stared at it for a moment, then lifted it out of its cradle.

At the moment the rod left the box, it seemed to lose what slight weight it had. Floating upward, seemingly of its own accord, it hung lightly suspended from the innkeeper's thick fingers. His expression half-fearful, half-fascinated, Haskel said aloud, "Seek!"

From its passive floating position, the rod gave a sudden twitch to the left. Then the tip wavered, steadied, pointing toward the far side of the pond where the trees grew down to the water's edge.

The pointer guided him straight through the heart of the wood. Noting freshly broken twigs among the bracken, Haskel goaded his horse to a quicker pace. In his hand the green rod swung back and forth like a compass needle. A mile from the Manticore, it pointed him out of the woods to the edge of the road.

The boy had bypassed the village. Following the road south in answer to the fluctuations of the rod in his hand, Haskel decided that his quarry must be making for Rhylnie.

The reason seemed clear enough: if the boy succeeded in winning through to tell his story to the sheriff there, Haskel and his associates would be in serious trouble. His face black with anger, Haskel pressed on again with grim determination.

The slope was crowned with trees. His chest heaving raggedly, Rhan stumbled upward through a stand of long grass and came to a swaying halt at the crest of the hill where the shadows were thickest.

His throat felt raw and his eyes stung with the sweat that clung to his lashes. Blinking to clear his vision, he caught hold of a hanging branch for support and looked around him.

Beneath him the road made a wide loop, stretching south-west in a semicircle of gravel and cart-ruts. Looking north, he could dimly make out the line of trees that marked the southern boundary of the Hahrfyrd vale. Nearly three hours had passed since he had fled the Manticore Inn in hopes of intercepting the minstrel from Ambrothen. Though he had kept the road constantly in sight, he had yet to see any sign of the man he was seeking.

The aching cincture of pain about his laboring ribs warned
him that he was rapidly approaching the limit of his endur-
ance. Nevertheless, he dared not pause for rest. He ran a dry
tongue over cracked lips, steeling himself to make the de-
scent to the roadside. As he did so, his ears suddenly caught
the sound of hoofbeats coming toward him around the bend
from which he had come.

The breath jamming in his throat, he flung himself down
behind a shallow windbreak formed by a fallen tree. As he
peered out from the shelter of its leaves, a horse came into
view.

Not a bay horse, but a black gelding.

With its rider sitting heavy in the saddle.

Haskel!

To move was to risk being seen. His knuckles pressed hard
against his mouth, Rhan burrowed farther down into the long
grass and prayed that the innkeeper would pass him by.

Sharply reined, the gelding slid to a halt at the foot of the
hill. Looping the reins about the saddletree, Haskel vaulted
heavily out of the stirrups. From his vantage point, Rhan
could see the rage in Haskel's face as he started up the slope.

He moved as if he knew exactly where he was going. He
can't have seen me! Rhan thought wildly. It's just not
possible. . . .

Then his eyes picked out something else: a rod of green
stone that seemed to float of its own accord between Haskel's
stout fingers.

The tip of the rod was trained on his hiding place.

The mechanics of it defied comprehension, but the purpose
of the rod was clear enough. With no hope now of remaining
hidden, Rhan sprang to his feet and bolted.

He ran blindly, like a hunted animal, tearing through
thickets and underbrush with reckless abandon. Behind him,
heavy boots pounded out a pursuing tattoo.

The bracken did not yield readily. Flinging himself through
a stabbing tangle of thornbushes, Rhan stumbled to the edge
of a shallow gully. Hands snatched at the air behind him.

Panting raggedly, he dropped to his haunches and slid to the bottom, bloodying his palms and tearing his clothes.

The opposite side was overgrown with bushes. Scrambling, Rhan gained the top and plunged through the matted shrubbery.

An instant later, the ground gave way beneath him with a wrench that threw him facedown into a hollow in the grass at the edge of a small clearing.

Pain sliced like a scalpel through the tendons in his right foot. Gasping he tried to pull himself upright, but his injured ankle refused weight.

A black dizziness almost like fainting swept over him. An instant later a hand fastened itself with damaging strength to his shoulder.

"You're a clever little weasel," said Haskel's voice vengefully in his ear. "Too bloody clever for your own good. . . ."

The stench of sweat and the heat of the innkeeper's sour breath were stomach-churning. Sick with exhaustion and despair, Rhan flung aside his last vestige of self-preservation and sank his teeth hard into his tormentor's meaty wrist.

Beyond the environs of the village of Hahrfyrd, the sunny air was charged with the scent of the wood. Riding south toward the town of Rhylnie along the tree-bordered road, Serdor threw back his hood and let the light play warmly on his upraised face.

Ahead of him the road curved to the left, swinging southeast in a long arc. Serdor gave Briona her head and she broke into an easy canter.

As they rounded the bend, the sight of something on the right made Serdor draw back on the reins. Shading his eyes with his hand, he peered ahead.

There was a heavy-boned black gelding grazing by the side of the road. As they approached, the gelding turned its head and nickered.

His eyes narrowing, Serdor took a second look. The last time he had seen that horse was in the stable at the Manticore Inn.

He dismounted to investigate. The soft ground of the right-hand embankment was trampled and bruised in a path-wide swathe leading up toward the top of the hill. Serdor rubbed thoughtfully at the bridge of his nose, then started up the slope in the same direction.

The signs of rough passage led him to the crest of the hill. Serdor was at the point of continuing down the other side when the silence of the wood beyond was shattered suddenly by a shrill cry.

The cry carried a piercing note approaching agony. His flesh chilling on his bones, Serdor clapped a hand to the sling at his belt and broke into a run.

The voice cried out twice more before he reached the foot of the hill. Redoubling his pace, he plunged through the underbrush and emerged at the edge of a shallow fold in the ground.

He stopped briefly to get his bearings. In the same instant, the air crackled with the sound of a blow.

On the far side of the gully, someone was moaning in pain. His eyes like steel, Serdor set out toward the source of the voice.

Light-boned and quick-footed, he gained the top of the opposite bank with a minimum of disturbance. Traveling another twenty yards on his hands and knees, he raised his head cautiously above a thick screen of ground-foliage.

A clearing opened up ten feet ahead of him. The open space beyond was dominated by a grizzled head and a broad back patchy with sweat. The figure flung back a knotted hand and heaved forward from the shoulder, striking with a heavy riding whip at something on the ground that whimpered in protest.

Teeth coming together with a click, Serdor stood up and fitted a stone to his sling. As the figure reared back to strike again, he took aim and let fly.

The slingstone bounced with a crack off Haskel Tohr's right ear. Howling in pain and astonishment, the proprietor of the Manticore Inn dropped the whip and spun around, clutching the right side of his head.

At the sight of the minstrel, his eyes narrowed to slits. Heavy fists clenching, he lowered his head and charged.

Serdor was no fighter in the conventional sense, but he had grown up in the back streets of Ambrothen, where survival was largely predicated on his ability to hold his own, by fair means or foul, against long odds. As Haskel lunged, Serdor dived under a punch intended to fracture his jawbone and came up with a heel-shaped rock in his hand.

Thick-necked as a bull, the innkeeper skidded to a halt and wheeled, his furled knuckles windmilling. Momentarily cornered with his back to a tree, Serdor took a blow in the side that nearly cracked his ribs.

The force of it carried him, gasping, to the ground. As Haskel bent over him, he smacked the other man smartly on the nose.

Roaring, the innkeeper lurched backward, sniveling blood. Rolling out of the way of a hobnailed kick, Serdor caught his adversary's foot above the ankle and jerked with all his might.

Haskel went down on his back. Frothing obscenities, he heaved himself up off his haunches, arms outflung to engulf his slight opponent in a murderous embrace. He got a grip on the minstrel's shoulder and dug his fingers into the thin flesh under the collarbone.

The grip was paralyzing. Writhing, Serdor tumbled backward. A set of knuckles broke open the skin over his left cheekbone as he toppled. A heavy body straddled his chest and hands grappled for his throat.

Wheezing, Serdor fought for breath, arms flailing out at his sides. As Haskel, grinning, bore down on him, he caught up a handful of dirt and slung it into the other man's face.

The innkeeper yelped and reeled back, clawing at his eyes. Levering himself from the shoulders, Serdor locked wrists and jabbed the man under the chin with the point of his left elbow.

There was a grating snap as of breaking teeth. Haskel exclaimed thickly and rocked back. Serdor hit him again and this time the man slumped over.

Breathing hard, Serdor pulled away from his unconscious adversary. Hand pressed to his battered ribs, he heaved himself onto his knees and looked around. A few yards away, a tumbled form lay facedown in the grass, arms and legs helplessly spread-eagled in the abandonment of unconsciousness.

It was the boy, Rhan. His muscles tightening, Serdor dragged himself across the intervening ground and knelt at his side.

Rhan's face in profile carried an ugly spreading bruise under his left eye. Below the unkempt tangles of fair hair, his clothes were in shambles. Grim-faced, Serdor took one of Rhan's icy hands in his own, groping for a pulse.

To his relief, a faint but steady beat throbbed beneath his fingers. In the same heartbeat, Rhan moaned and stirred.

As Serdor bent over him, the shadowed lids flickered, then snapped wide. Half-drugged with pain, the boy's brown eyes wandered blankly upward, then sharpened as they reached the minstrel's attentive face. Rhan's brow wrinkled uncertainly. "Serdor?" he said on a note of painful inquiry.

Sick at the visible proof of Haskel's brutality, Serdor nodded his head. "Yes," he said quietly. "Yes, it's me."

An expression of incredulous relief transfigured Rhan's haggard face. "Thank God," he whispered, then gave a single breathless sob. "My back . . . ."

His voice cracked on the second syllable. "I know," said Serdor soothingly. His grey eyes were fierce with rare, barely governable fury. Dragging his gaze away from Haskel's heaped bulk, he smoothed Rhan's disordered hair with gentle fingers. "Lie still. Don't try to move yet."

Instead of obeying him, the boy clutched at his sleeve. "The wand," said Rhan distinctly. "You've got to get the wand."

His dilated eyes held a feverish sparkle. Chafing Rhan's gripping hand, Serdor said, "What wand?"

Rhan shivered. Swallowing hard, he said huskily, with a noticeable expenditure of effort, "A green rod . . . made of some sort of stone, I think. Haskel used it to trace me. . . ."

Despite pain and shock, he sounded lucid and in earnest. Puzzled, but unwilling to place any further strain on the boy's shattered nerves, Serdor nodded. "All right. I'll see if I can find it."

Disengaging Rhan's cramped fingers, he rocked back on his haunches and stood up. Conscious of the boy's anxious following gaze, he recrossed the clearing to the place where the innkeeper had fallen and examined the surrounding turf.

There was no sign of any such artifact as the rod Rhan had described. Curbing anger and revulsion, Serdor hunkered down beside Haskel and dragged him over onto his back.

The innkeeper's jacket was open. Staring down at Haskel's barrel chest and sagging belly, Serdor saw, thrust through the width of his broad leather belt, a thin wand of pale, translucent green.

His fingertips shrinking slightly, he took it gingerly by its thicker end and slowly drew it free. Turning it over in his hands, he saw that it was marked with a symbol formed from three interlocking runes.

The device was unfamiliar. Frowning, Serdor studied it for a moment longer, then tucked it away in the breast of his jerkin.

When he rejoined Rhan, the boy gave him a fearful questioning look. "I found it," he said. "Haskel had it in his belt but I've taken it."

Rhan drew a shuddering breath and closed his eyes. Shrugging off his cloak, Serdor laid it lightly over him. "I'm going to fetch my horse," he said. "By the time Haskel recovers his wits, you and I will be well away from here."

CHAPTER 27

The Farmer

It was close to twilight when Vult Hemmling climbed the low hill that led up from the back pasture to the herb garden behind his stout, half-timbered house.

He removed his boots at the back door before going in. Passing from the scullery into the kitchen, he was greeted by the sight of well-scrubbed flagstones and the savory sage-and-onion scent of cooking.

The hearth was swept clean, the crockery all in order on the shelves. A quaintly spelled note from his married daughter, left under a vase of marigolds on the kitchen table, informed him that she had finished cleaning the house and would be back in a week or two to see how he was getting on with it. She suggested, for a start, that he keep the new pup *out*side.

Vult chuckled and walked over to sniff experimentally at the bubbling contents of the iron pot hung over the fire. As he straightened his back, a sudden outburst of canine alarm from the yard out front made his eyebrows pull together over his well-defined nose.

Vult had been a soldier long before he had become a farmer, and a series of recent incidents in the villages surrounding Rhylnie had sharpened the suspicions of everyone in his neighborhood. He was just debating whether or not to fetch his sword from upstairs when a voice from the front of the house gave a muffled "Halloa!"

The voice sounded weary and not a little apprehensive. Pausing to light a lantern, Vult stepped out the back door and started around the side of the house. It was almost completely dark beyond the ring of yellow light cast down by the lantern, and he nearly tripped over the hindquarters of the young dog, crouched bristling over the pup tumbling excitedly about his feet. Beyond, his two older dogs were ranged on either side of the solitary horseman who had reined in his mount by the front gate.

The puppy started, growled, and scuttled out of the way as Vult brushed past. Hackling, the other dogs began to bark again. The horse sidled uneasily, ears laid back, forefeet churning the dust from the ground as the rider applied disciplinary pressure to the rein. Vult called the dogs to heel, then strode forward to take stock of the intruder.

Or rather, intruders. Vult corrected himself. There were two riders astride the one horse.

He cleared his throat and said crisply, "Good evening, friends. What might you be wanting here?"

His tone was deliberately brusque. The foremost rider straightened up in the saddle. "Lodging for the night," said a voice from the darkness. "If you're willing to grant it."

Vult pursed his lips and eyed the faceless forms on the horse with some disfavor. "What makes you think I might be?" he inquired. "If it's an inn you're looking for, I don't mind telling you you've come to the wrong place. This is not a hostelry."

"I know," said the voice apologetically. "Normally I'd respect your privacy. But—forgive me—my friend and I are in urgent need of shelter. Could you . . . do you think you might be able to help us?"

"Maybe. If things were different," said Vult, planting his feet with an uncompromising air. "As it is, you'd do much better to ride on. Rhylnie's only three miles farther down the road. There's an inn on the edge of town—the Griffin. You'll doubtless find it suitable for your needs."

There was a pause. "Three miles . . ." said the voice. "If you please, sir, I'm afraid that won't do. My companion is sick, and I doubt he can ride on even one mile farther. You don't have to take us into your house," continued the voice, anxiety showing naked through the courtesy. "Couldn't you at least allow us to occupy your barn until morning?"

The tone was frankly appealing, but Vult was in no hurry to commit himself. "If I'm to do you any favors, I'll have to know a good bit more about you," he said. "We're not so fond of strangers in these parts—not without good reason. Suppose you tell me who you are and what business you have around here."

"My name, for what it's worth, is Serdor Sulamith," said the rider readily enough. "I'm a musician and instrument-maker on my way to Ambrothen—" The voice broke off abruptly, interrupted by a low moan from his companion, hitherto silent.

There was no counterfeiting the pain-laden quality of the second voice. Vult marched forward, lifting the lantern so that its light spilled upward into the face of the foremost rider.

Blinking, the man calling himself Serdor threw up a hand before his face. His companion, muffled in the folds of a threadbare cloak, slumped loosely against him, face half-hidden by the hood.

Frowning, Vult closed the remaining space between them and slid a hand under the second rider's sharp chin. He lifted it gently and the hood fell back.

The second rider was a mere boy. He was also unquestionably ill: the fine skin under the farmer's fingers was burning with fever.

"I can see I'd best not send you on after all—though I've no doubt it's what I ought to do," said Vult. "But mind, I'll want a detailed account of yourselves and your doings once we get the lad taken care of."

"My thanks." As Serdor eased Rhan down, he added, 'Watch his back."

The boy hung limp in the farmer's arms as Vult carried

him indoors. Laying him belly-down on the bench before the kitchen fire, Vult drew off the enveloping cloak, exposing the ruined shirt beneath.

He whistled softly through his teeth, then turned as the boy's companion stepped across the threshold. "Here's a nasty piece of work," Vult said grimly. "We'll have to give him a bath before we can do anything else. You get the rest of his clothes off while I see about heating up the water. . . ."

Clean, their patient showed the full extent of his injuries. Gazing down at him, Serdor said, "Can you do anything for him?"

"I've a bit of salve on hand that ought to draw some of the fire out of those weals. And enough old linen for bandages," said Vult. "He'll need nursing, of course. We can call a mage out from the chapter house in the town, if you think it might help."

Serdor thought a moment. "No," he said heavily. "Let's see how he fares without one first."

Vult digested this. After a pause, he said, "You haven't yet told me his name."

"His name's Rhan Hallender," said Serdor, and stopped.

"What did he do to earn himself such a beating?" asked Vult.

Grey eyes met blue. "He's an indentured servant," said Serdor baldly, "who tried to run away from his master."

The farmer's expression gave nothing away. "Who is his master?"

"The owner of an inn called the Manticore, over toward Hahrfyrd," said Serdor. "A man by the name of Haskel Tohr."

This time he got a reaction. "Haskel Tohr?" said Vult slowly. "Now that puts a new complexion on things."

"You sound as if you've heard of him."

"Heard of him?" Vult snorted. "By all accounts, there's not a bigger scoundrel for miles in any direction. If our sheriff was worth his salt, the rogue would have been gaoled long ago. Your young friend has my sympathies: it's all to his credit that he gave the blackguard the slip."

"Does that mean that you won't turn him over to the magistrate?" asked Serdor.

"If I know Burliss, all he'd do is send the lad back," said Vult sourly. "No, we'll just keep our mouths shut around here. You're welcome to stay on till the boy's well enough to travel. Then I suggest you make your way back to Ambrothen as fast as you can. . . ."

CHAPTER 28

The Trap

The tunnel was bindingly narrow. Lying prone with head to one side, he crawled forward on his belly, the muscles of his neck and back rigid with strain in the confined space of the passage.

Behind him lay fathoms and years of shadow. Before him, the darkness pressed down as if it had physical weight, clogging his nostrils, riding crushingly on his back. Yet he struggled on, knowing that if he once surrendered, he would be devoured by the dark. His fear intensified with every foot he gained. He was on the edge of blind panic when the passage took a turn, and he saw a jagged window into light. Dim though it was, it seemed blazingly bright to his long-sightless eyes. Heedless as a moth before a candle, he thrashed his way toward it, dragged himself through the gap, and collapsed. For a long moment he lay where he had fallen, limbs outflung in an ecstasy of space. Then he looked around him. He was in a room. It had a door.

His heart beating, he rose and walked stiffly over to examine it. His fingers trembling, he took hold of the latch and pulled it open.

Darkness swirled up into his face like a gale of witch's smoke. Arms outflung before him in an instinctive gesture of warding, he stumbled back. Whipping in black streamers about the door, the shadows shot toward the roof and roiled back upon themselves. As he cowered against the far wall, they began to coalesce. Filling the doorway, the churning dark took on the form of a looming manshape. Two eyeslits burned their way through the featureless black of the face and bent the balefire of their gaze upon him.

Paralyzed, he could not flee. Cowled in its own blackness, the figure stretched out clawed hands to seize him. . . .

His scream splintered the darkness. Buffeted by its echoes, he tried to tear himself away from the restraining grip that held him.

"Easy, lad. I'm not going to hurt you," said a deep voice from somewhere above him. The voice had a friendly resonance that was somehow comforting. He stopped struggling and opened his eyes.

The face floating over him was sun-seamed and weathered. Above the jutting nose, two grave blue eyes returned his regard with something like a twinkle in their depths. Seeing his expression, the stranger grinned. "You don't know me, lad, if that's what's troubling you. My name's Vult. Vult Hemmling."

Shaking off the lingering shadows of his dream, Rhan produced a wan smile. "W-where?—" he asked, and broke off, surprised at the weakness of his own voice.

"My house," said Vult cheerfully.

Rhan looked around him. He was lying, deeply pillowed, in a feather bed. Near at hand were blue bed-curtains and a large wooden chest. Above the chest, a bright window stood open, its mullioned glass sparkling in the sun. "You weren't in any fit state to remember it," continued Vult, "but this is where your friend Serdor brought you the night before last."

Two days ago! Rhan swallowed. "Where is Serdor now?" he asked, too preoccupied for the moment to notice that his vocal cords were beginning to function normally.

"Asleep in the next room. I sent him away to get some rest, but he'll be back when he wakes up. Don't look so nattered," said Vult, the twinkle deepening. "Did you think maybe he'd just dropped you on my doorstep and ridden off on his way?"

I wouldn't blame him if he had, thought Rhan. Recalling his conversation with Serdor their last night at the Manticore— "It may be weeks—even months—before I'll be free to get back to you," the minstrel had said. But he had forced himself between Serdor and those prior obligations obliquely hinted-at.

He owed the minstrel his freedom. The least he could do in return would be to relieve Serdor of all further responsibility.

He was still trying to put his feelings into words several hours later when there was a tap at the door and a brown head appeared around the doorframe. "Good afternoon," said Serdor, and stepped into the room. Crossing over to the bedside, he added, "I'm sorry I wasn't here earlier, when you woke up. How do you feel?"

"Very well," said Rhan. Fumbling from beneath the bed-clothes, he reached out and took the hand Serdor held out to him, trying to summon a fitting eloquence.

He longed to do it gracefully, without faltering under the embarrassing surge of emotion that was threatening to bring on an unmanly show of tears, but all his rehearsed phrases deserted him. Fighting his maddening weakness, he avoided the minstrel's eyes for a moment, and so missed seeing the sudden gleam of understanding there.

"Thanks are necessary only between strangers and business associates," said Serdor gently. "Between friends they are superfluous. Or am I wrong in assuming that you and I are friends?"

The next few days passed without incident, but he and Vult, by tacit agreement, rarely left the boy alone. Awake and talking, he seemed in good spirits. His sleep, however, was haunted by inner demons. Often he actually cried without waking. More often, his own screams released him from the torment.

Late in the afternoon on the fifth day after their arrival, Serdor sat in a chair by Rhan's bedside, simultaneously keeping an eye on his patient and trying inexpertly to repair a rip in his one spare shirt.

Rhan had not shifted his position since falling asleep an

hour before, yet his immobility suggested not relaxation, but rather a state of nervous tension. Glancing aside from time to time at Rhan's still face, Serdor couldn't help noticing the signs of strain.

He was laying the last stitch when a sudden movement from the boy in the bed startled him into pricking his thumb. As he dropped what he was doing, Rhan began to breathe in short, constricted gasps.

His hands were crooked into claws. He muttered something, then flinched as from a blow. Serdor bent over him and laid a light hand on his forehead.

Instead of quieting to the minstrel's touch, Rhan gave a choked cry and wrenched himself away with a violence that sent him crashing into the adjacent wall. His back took the brunt of the impact. Dropping forward onto his chest, he gave a sharp murmur of pain.

"It's all right. It's only me," said Serdor. He made no attempt to touch the boy again.

Rhan's brown eyes, focusing, lost their wildness. "Serdor!" he exclaimed shakily. "For a moment I thought—"

He stopped and shivered. "Thought what?" inquired Serdor steadily.

"Nothing. I—it was just a dream," said Rhan evasively.

"About Haskel?"

"No." Rhan shook his head. "It's one I've had before."

Avoiding the minstrel's gaze, he went on in a low voice. "I'm lying on the floor with my hands bound. In front of me stands a figure hooded and cloaked in black. On its shoulder perches a great black bird, like a raven. At a sign from its master, the bird flies at me, tearing at my face. . . ."

He shuddered and clutched convulsively at the hand Serdor held out to him. When, after several minutes, the boy's fingers finally relaxed, Serdor drew a long breath. "Do you have this dream often?"

Rhan lifted a haggard face and nodded wearily. "You'd think I'd get used to it, but I don't. And it's not the only one—"

He broke off without elaborating, and Serdor refrained

from pressing him. Surveying the boy critically, he said in deliberately prosaic tones, "Never mind. You look as if you'd be the better for some food. Vult's off tending his cows, but if you'll give me a few minutes, I'll see what I can find in the kitchen."

Ten minutes later, mounting the stairs with a laden tray, Serdor paused briefly to recover a sliding fork before reentering the room.

The first thing he saw was Rhan's bed, empty. Rhan himself was on the other side of the room, flattened against the wall next to the window.

"What are you doing up? I thought Vult told you—" began Serdor austerely, then abruptly swallowed the end of his sentence as Rhan showed his teeth and gestured vehemently for silence.

Serdor plumped down the tray on top of the dresser and crossed the floor in four quick strides. Stepping past Rhan, he peered out through the curtains.

Cantering up the winding track that led to the farmhouse from the main road were four horsemen. His eyes narrowing, Serdor examined each of them in turn as they drew nearer. Three of them were unknown to him, but the fourth, mounted conspicuously on a big black gelding, was the proprietor of the Manticore Inn.

CHAPTER 29

The Farmer's Courage

In spite of himself, Serdor stiffened. "It is Haskel, isn't it?" breathed Rhan at his elbow. "I thought so."

He drew a deep breath as if to steady himself. "What are we going to do?"

Serdor did not take his eyes from the window. "I'm not sure. I wonder . . ."

His voice trailed off on a note of speculation. Schooling his face and hands, Rhan restrained an impulse to pluck at the minstrel's sleeve. A moment later, Serdor picked up the thread of his own thoughts. "They can't possibly know we're here—Vult's the only one who knows that. I think this may just be an arrow shot in the dark."

His mouth pinched down at the corners, he took another look. "If I'm right, all we have to do is stay quiet and out of sight until they've satisfied themselves that there's nothing here to find."

"If I were any place but here, I'd wish them luck." Rhan shivered slightly. "What about Briona?"

Serdor went rigid. "Oh, bloody hell," he said flatly. "She's in the barn."

For an appalled instant neither of them spoke. Taking his lower lip between his teeth, Rhan turned abruptly and made for the door.

"Where are you going?" asked Serdor in a sharp undertone.

"To Vult's bedroom. He told me he keeps a sword under his bed." Rhan's voice, also strategically lowered, was suddenly no longer that of a frightened fifteen-year-old. "I thought you might feel better, armed with something more than a slingshot. Will you let me have your dagger?"

"Good God," said Serdor, but after a glance at the boy's face, he unsheathed the blade and wordlessly handed it over.

The riders rounded the last bend in the road and fell into single file as they passed down the path bounded by the hedge. A moment later a frenzied chorus of yelps broke out from behind the house.

"Here you are. It's a pity Vult saw fit to tie up Bayard and the others," whispered Rhan, reappearing with Vult's heavy, old-fashioned rapier under his arm. He propped the weapon against the wall, then closed the door and braced it with a chair before rejoining Serdor at the window.

The riders checked briefly at the sound of a large dog's snarling, but when the source of the menace failed to materialize, they rode forward again and drew rein just under the window.

The foremost rider, a veritable mountain of a man, dismounted and scanned the ground around him before allowing his gaze to wander upward. As he did so Serdor received an indelible impression of a broad, flat-featured face, inscrutable above a barrel-chested body, before the man stepped onto the porch and out of his line of vision.

"Have you ever seen that fellow before?" he whispered to Rhan. Rhan frowned, then shook his head.

In the same moment, the silence was splintered as the sound of heavy knocking broke out below.

Beside him, Rhan flinched at the sound, then smiled crookedly over at Serdor as the minstrel reached out and gripped his shoulder. After a brief pause, the knocking resumed with increased vehemence.

After a moment the big man emerged again into the sunlight and addressed his companions. The sound of their voices reached the ears of their unseen observers with near perfect clarity through the open window.

"Well, your farmer's not here. Where's he likely to be?"

Haskel's voice, when he spoke, sounded gravelly and querulous after the other man's sonorous bass. "Out in the fields, most likely, but we'd better wait around for him here. His holdings are wide enough we could waste hours looking for him."

"You'd better be right about that," said the big man ominously. "Meanwhile, we'll see what we can find for ourselves. Perne, you and Uskan go check around the back. Let me know if you see anything I ought to know about. We'll wait here."

The other two men swung out of their saddles and vanished around the corner of the house. "This is the fifth place we've visited today," growled the big man as he watched them go. "If we don't have some luck pretty soon, we're going to have to go back and report. That won't be any too healthy for you when His Eminence finds out how you've botched this whole thing."

Even at a distance of several yards, Haskel's sudden glistening pallor was visible. "I thought it'd be easy enough to find the brat. He was in no state to go far. . . ."

"He had help. You said so yourself," said the big man uncompromisingly. "If it turns out that they've managed to get clean away, you'll wish you'd called me sooner. Or not at all."

Haskel's attempt to remonstrate was interrupted by the return of one of the other men. "Nothing much back there, Muirtagh, but the back door to the house is unlocked. D'you want Perne and me to go on in?"

Muirtagh considered this. "Why not? We can always offer our apologies later."

"That's torn it," muttered Serdor, backing away from the window. "You get back behind the door. I'll hold them as long as I can—don't argue with me, just do as I say."

He stood scowling at the door for an instant, then removed the chair.

"Why did you do that?" hissed Rhan, wide-eyed.

"It wouldn't stop them for more than a minute," said

Serdor, opening the door a few inches. "This way I may be able to put one of them completely out of commission before they realize there's anyone in here—"

He broke off abruptly as another familiar voice broke through the waiting silence. "Good afternoon," said Vult with peppery politeness. "What can I do for you gentlemen today?"

Exhaling audibly, Serdor left the sword where it lay and returned to his post by the window. Vult was standing just beyond the shadow of the house, his grizzled hair feathered by the light breeze. His eyes were on Muirtagh as he spoke. His left hand kept a restraining grip on Bayard's collar.

Haskel regarded the big, rough-coated dog with undisguised apprehension, but the man called Muirtagh seemed unimpressed. "Are you the owner of this place?" he asked truculently.

"I am that," agreed Vult without moving. "And I'd take it very favorably if you'd call your two friends away from my back step, if you please. I don't believe I know what you're after, but whatever it is, I'll guarantee you won't find it there."

Muirtagh didn't bother to apologize. "Perne!" he called. "Uskan! You can come back now." Returning his hard gaze to the farmer's face, he said, "We're looking for a man and a boy. Have you seen any strangers around here in the last few days?"

"I might have," said Vult. "What d'you want with them?"

"The boy's a runaway servant and the man with him's a thief," said Muirtagh. "If you have any information about them, we'll make it worth your while."

"Will you now?" said Vult cryptically. "Let me think a minute. . . ."

"They'd have been riding double. On a bay mare," said Haskel, with a glance at Muirtagh. "The boy's about fifteen years old—brown eyes, fair hair. The man's young, too, Thin, not very tall. Wearing clothes that would disgrace a beggar."

Vult hesitated. "My memory has a tendency to play tricks on me. . . ."

"Perhaps this will help it along," said Muirtagh contemptuously, and tossed a small bag into the dust between them.

Vult picked it up and weighed it in his hand, after a cautionary glance at its contents. "Now that you mention it, I did see a pair of vagabonds skulking around here. That would have been three—no, four days ago. They came up to me as I was mending the gate down the lane there. They didn't stay long, though. I saw at a glance they weren't respectable folk and sent 'em on their way."

"D'you know where they went?"

"I've a notion—though I can't vouch for it. I told 'em they could find cheap lodgings in Valdenbrook, but whether or not that's where they finally ended up, I couldn't say."

Haskel leaned forward. "What more do you want. Valdenbrook's a good ten miles west of here. We'd better hurry, if we want to—"

"Not so fast," said Muirtagh. "You there—we'd still like to take a look around your property."

The statement implied nothing in the way of free choice. Vult shrugged. "Suit yourself. You won't find anything, but if you've got that much time to waste, that's fine with me."

"Start with the barn," said Muirtagh to his two companions, ignoring Haskel's muttered protest. "One of you go in. The other one can wait outside to make sure nobody sneaks past. I'll check out the house myself."

"Begging your pardon, but that's where I draw the line," said Vult. "You've been mighty high-handed, whoever you are, but don't think that entitles you to do just as you please, without so much as a by-your-leave. I've yet to see any legal proof of your authority, and I'm not sure I like either your looks or your manners. Poke around all you like outside, but I'll be damned if I'm going to let you into my house without better cause than I've had so far."

Muirtagh drew himself up. "If I had any doubts about you, this would certainly make me suspicious."

"Well, *you* make me suspicious," said Vult obstinately.

"I gave you what you came for, and I see no reason to give you any more." He eyed the bigger man coldly. "You're welcome to try force, if you think it will work, but big as you are, you'd have a hard time dealing with Bayard here, if I was to let him go. And there's another like him on guard."

Faced with a definite and fairly formidable obstacle, Muirtagh did not immediately react. A moment later, Perne and Uskan reappeared, the former shaking his head.

"Nothing in there, Muirtagh. Nobody in hiding, and no sign of a bay mare. Just a blue roan hack and two plough horses."

"What did I tell you?" demanded Vult. "You've already lost almost half an hour which you might have put to better use, if you'd just taken my word for it. If you want to spend the rest of the afternoon stumping around my fields, go ahead, but I warn you, I'll have you up before the court if you damage any of my crops."

Muirtagh plainly was still not satisfied, but his three companions took a different view of the situation. "Let's go," said the shorter of the two followers.

Muirtagh was staring hard at Vult. "First I'd like to know what's inside the house that you're so anxious to keep hidden."

"We've already been through that, but if you want to hear it again, I'll be happy to—"

"Hold it. There's a couple of men coming up the road," said one of Muirtagh's henchmen.

Stepping around Muirtagh's horse, Vult peered down the lane, shading his eyes with the flat of his hand. "That'll be Joc Vogel and his son," he said. "They're neighbors of mine—coming to take a look at one of my bulls."

Muirtagh favored him with a colorless glare. "All right," he said, after a pause. "We'll ride on over to Valdenbrook and take a look around. But don't be surprised if we come back."

He returned to his horse and remounted. Leading the way through the gate at a canter, he passed into the lane, sweeping past Joc and his son in a flurry of dust.

"Who was yon?" Joc asked of Vult as soon as he reached the front yard. "Man, ye look like ye'd seen a ghost."

Vult wiped a perspiring face with the back of his hand and released Bayard. "It's been a busy day," he said. "I don't mind telling you, you couldn't have come at a better time. Let's go on down to the back pasture and I'll tell you about it."

What Joc got was a carefully edited version of what had transpired. The real account of what had happened, Vult withheld from discussion until he was alone with Serdor.

"That was certainly touch and go," he said, shaking his head. "If Joc hadn't shown up when he did, the fat might well have hit the fire."

"We were lucky," agreed Serdor. "But there's one thing I don't understand."

"What's that?"

"Why didn't they find Briona when they searched the barn?"

"That shouldn't be too hard to figure out," said Vult. "They didn't find her because she wasn't there."

Seeing Serdor's expression, he chuckled and relented. "I thought she was looking a bit restless this morning, so I turned her out in the east field at the back of the hill, to stretch her legs. I'm mighty glad now that I did."

"So am I," said Serdor fervently. "But that settles things: Rhan and I had better be on our way no later than the day after tomorrow. . . ."

CHAPTER 30

The Homecoming

"If you're going to be coming back with me to Ambrothen," Serdor had said, "you'd better know what you're letting yourself in for. . . ."

Riding double behind the minstrel, Rhan peered over his friend's shoulder toward the distant shimmer of city spires, wondering what they would find waiting for them when they arrived.

They had been a fortnight on the road since leaving Vult's house at Rhylnie, traveling south and west from Bredlemead on the Laranrhyl to Cumfrey on the Daman. At Cumfrey they had taken a ferry across the river to Misk. Since leaving Misk, Serdor had become steadily less communicative.

Reviewing all Serdor had told him concerning the mage Caradoc Penlluathe, Rhan thought he could understand the reason for his friend's abstraction. And so he held his tongue as they pressed on due south, with the Daman Estuary glittering off to their left among the trees. It was not until they were within half a mile of the city walls that he at last ventured to speak.

The rooftops of Ambrothen were lost from view briefly as the road ran down into a hollow between two shallow hills. As Serdor guided Briona up the other side, Rhan asked, "What sort of person is Margoth?"

Serdor did not turn around. "Don't worry: she won't hold it against us that I found you and not Caradoc."

The irony had an introspective cutting edge. Apparently that isn't stopping you from holding it against yourself, thought Rhan. Aloud he said, "That you weren't able to trace him wasn't due to any lack of trying on your part."

"Perhaps not," said Serdor noncommittally. He was silent for a moment, then recited, " 'Let the giver be requited according to his gift . . .' Perhaps I haven't mentioned that I owe Caradoc my life?"

"No," said Rhan, then decided to risk a rebuff. "How did that happen?"

Instead of answering, the minstrel abruptly straightened up in the saddle. Reining in at the crest of the hill, he leaned forward in the stirrups, shading his eyes with the blade of his hand as he looked toward the city across a quarter mile of open ground.

"What is it?" demanded Rhan, craning his neck. Then he saw what had compelled Serdor's attention.

The air above the West Port was busy with winged black shapes, diving back and forth in short flurried flights across the High Gate. "Ravens!" said Serdor, scowling deeply. "I wonder what's drawing them on."

Before they had ridden another furlong, they had the answer: the crennelated ramparts flanking the High Gate were gruesomely decorated with several heads.

There were five on either hand, mutilated beyond all recognition by the birds that clustered pecking and cawing around the still-raw domes of exposed bone. Green-faced, Rhan swallowed hard and averted his eyes. Pressing close to Serdor's shoulder as they joined the line of wagons and foot-travelers drawn up before the gate itself, he murmured shakily, "Who do you suppose they were?"

A ruddy middle-aged tinker in front of them overheard him and turned his head. "Traitors, lad—traitors and murderers. Put there as a warning to others o' their kind."

"I thought that sort of thing was no longer common practice," said Serdor. He himself was looking rather white about the mouth.

The tinker shrugged. " 'Twas done by order of the Warden himself. Seems they were amongst them as made off with his son. . . ."

The line moved forward. "My God," said Rhan flatly. "You don't think . . . ?"

"I don't know," said Serdor darkly. "We'll find out soon enough."

He nudged Briona into motion again. As they passed under the shadow of the gatehouse roof, a clipped voice said sharply, "Stop right there, my good fellow. I'd like a word or two with you."

The hard ring of suspicion was unmistakable. As Serdor drew rein, a lantern-jawed captain in the livery of the Ambrothen Regulars stepped out of the guard tower to the left of the gate. Looking down into a pair of chilly blue eyes above a thin blade of a nose, Rhan experienced a sudden qualm of uneasiness.

Briona laid back her ears and backstepped as the guardsman took hold of her bridle. Laying a quieting hand on her neck, Serdor said, "As you please, Captain. We're in no particular hurry."

He sounded completely at ease. "Whether you are or not is of no consequence," snapped the captain. He beckoned and a harried-looking scribe scurried forward. "First of all, I'll have your name and occupation."

Serdor's expression in profile was slightly pained. "The name is Serdor Sulamith—with one *l*. I'm a musician by trade."

The scribe noted it down. "And the boy?" continued the captain with a hard-eyed glare at Rhan.

"My brother," said Serdor. He tilted his chin slightly and inquired, "Is there something amiss, Captain?"

"Don't speak unless you're spoken to. Are you a resident of this city?"

"Yes."

"Your direction?"

"The sign of the Broken Fiddle, Madrigal Court."

"Where's your Writ of Egress, then?"

"My what?"

"Your travel permit: a paper signed and sealed by the constabulary recording the date of your departure and your anticipated date of return. Obviously," said the captain, "you haven't got one."

"No," agreed Serdor. There was a veiled flicker of annoyance deep in his grey eyes. "When I left the city three months ago, it was generally accepted that any honest man was free to come and go as he pleased."

"Ah—that would be before His Lordship the Seneschal issued the decree," said the scribe, glancing nervously up from his ledger. "You see, sir, when all the evidence seemed to indicate that the conspiracy to abduct Lord Evelake Whitfauconer originated here in Ambrothen—"

"Hold your tongue," said the captain cuttingly. To Serdor he said, "We're going to want proof that you are who you claim to be. Is there anyone in the city who would be prepared to vouch for you?"

His tone implied a strong degree of doubt. Serdor said evenly, "I believe Magister Forgoyle Finlevyn of the Hospitallers' Order would be quite prepared to furnish whatever testimony you might require."

"Indeed? Well, that's easily enough verified," said the captain. "Get down off your horse, you two. You'll be detained at the guardhouse until such time as the Magister Forgoyle can be summoned to attend to you."

They had no recourse but to obey. Seating himself next to Serdor on a wooden bench facing the door, Rhan waited until their escort had withdrawn to the doorstep, then hissed, "What are we going to do?"

Serdor grimaced. "We wait until Forgoyle gets here. And trust him not to give the game away."

Then, seeing the expression of naked anxiety on Rhan's pale face, he forced a smile. "Don't worry: Forgoyle's no fool. If anyone can extricate us from this predicament, he's the one to do it."

Rhan dropped his eyes. Staring at his tightly-clenched fingers, he said through his teeth, "I won't be sent back to Haskel. I *won't!*"

There was a hint of mounting desperation in his voice. "Whatever is at the back of all this official rigmarole," said Serdor, "you can be sure it has nothing remotely to do with catching runaway bond-servants. Just relax, and stop looking as if you have something to hide. . . ."

The waiting period lasted nearly two hours. After listening for a seemingly interminable length of time to the droning conversation passing back and forth between the two Regulars outside the door, Serdor at last caught the sound of a familiar voice above the general noise of the traffic passing through the gate.

He unbowed his spine with a jerk. A moment later, a head appeared around the doorframe. "All right, the pair of you," growled the captain. "You've got visitors waiting to see you."

Visitors?

His eyelids narrowing, Serdor risked a brief glance back at Rhan. Hoping the boy's composure would withstand the test, he drew a short breath and rose to his feet.

As he stepped across the threshold into the sunlight, there was a flurry of long skirts and a pair of warm arms flung themselves firmly around his neck. Her cheek pressed against his—"Serdor! Thank God you're home safely!" said Margoth with breathless sincerity.

Her body yielded pliantly to his hungering embrace. For the space of a heartbeat, he held her close, drinking in her nearness. Then, looking over her bright head toward the captain of the Ambrothen Regulars, he said, "I beg your pardon. Family reunions are always so embarrassingly emotional." He gave her arm a warning squeeze.

That, and the slight stress he laid to the word *family* alerted her. Her wits sharpening, Margoth raised her eyes to his and, after the briefest instant of contact, allowed her gaze to travel past his shoulder to where a thin brown-eyed boy stood braced in the doorway.

The boy gave her a strained grin. "Hello, Margoth," he said. "Aren't you glad to see me, as well?"

Serdor's lips brushed her temple beneath the shadow of her hair. Devoutly hoping she had heard him correctly, Margoth laughed and held out her hand to the scrawny adolescent on the porch. "Of course, I'm glad to see you, brat. But your brother would never have forgiven me if I'd greeted you first."

The boy took her hand. His fingers were like ice. "I was expecting Forgoyle," said Serdor. "Isn't he here?"

"Certainly I'm here. How else do you suppose Margoth learned you were back?" said a deep voice from behind them.

Margoth turned and summoned a dazzling smile. "Oh, there you are, Forgoyle. Be a lamb and tell Captain Du Coverlay here that you've known Serdor and his brother since they were infants. Then maybe he'll let us take them home. . . ."

Forgoyle rose to the occasion with consummate aplomb. While the magister was still expounding for the edification of the captain and his men, Serdor edged closer to Margoth and put his mouth to her ear. "I'm sorry about the subterfuge," he whispered. Then added baldly, "I wasn't able to find Caradoc."

Catching a sidelong glance from one of the privates, Margoth smiled roguishly and fluttered her lashes. In a tone wholly at variance with her expression, she said, "That's hardly your fault—considering that he returned to Ambrothen ten days ago." Seeing the nonplussed look on his face, she added, "I hope you don't feel cheated."

"Cheated? Oh, God, no." Aware of an odd glint in her eyes, he said carefully, "Then he's safe and well?"

"Oh, he's well enough," said Margoth grimly. "But hardly safe: he's locked up in the dungeon of Ambrothen Keep."

From the High Gate, they repaired to the Beldame Inn. Tying on her apron with the tight-lipped air of one determined to keep busy at all costs, Margoth went off to attend to her duties in the kitchen, leaving Forgoyle to acquaint Serdor and Rhan with the details of the story.

"Carodoc was taken prisoner, along with ten other men, in a raid carried out by a group of Farrowaithe Guards. The ten have already been tried and sentenced," said Forgoyle. "Caradoc's case comes up before the Lord Chief Justice the day after tomorrow."

"The Lord Chief Justice?" said Serdor. "But doesn't Caradoc come under the jurisdiction of the Order?"

"The Arch Mage," said Forgoyle, "has decided to waive the Order's right to prosecute in this instance. If Caradoc is found guilty under secular law, he'll share the same fate as the other brigands. The Lord Warden is not a forgiving man."

Remembering the row of rotting heads on the walls above the High Gate, Serdor shuddered inwardly. "Have you spoken with Caradoc yourself?"

"No," said Forgoyle bleakly. "An'char Maeldrake examined him, along with the others. But his findings concerning Caradoc will not be aired until the trial."

"I see," said Serdor. Fidgeting with the glass in front of him, he added, "How much chance do you think Caradoc has of surviving the outcome?"

Forgoyle's lined face had the greyness of age about it. "We can only hope. One of the Warden's friends—a man by the name of Gudmar Ap Gorvald—has spoken up in Caradoc's favor. But the Warden himself has been implacable. I can't begin to predict what will happen."

"Do you think I might be of any help?" asked Serdor.

"Not at this stage of the affair," said Forgoyle wearily. "The witnesses have all been named and the procedure has been set. No one who hasn't already been summoned will be allowed to attend."

Serdor's long-fingered hands abruptly stopped moving. "Does that ban apply to Margoth as well?"

"Yes," said Forgoyle. "And before you voice any opinions, let me say that I think it's probably just as well. There's nothing she could do that would influence the outcome of the trial, and her presence in the courtroom would only aggravate the climate of tension that is bound to prevail."

He pushed back his chair and stood up. "I'm sorry to have to leave you, but I have myself been cited as a material witness to this case, and I need time to prepare my testimony. It's doubtful that I will see you again until after the trial, but rest assured that I will do everything I can. You're staying with Margoth?"

"For the moment, yes," said Serdor. "Arn offered to let Rhan and me have a room here, but I don't think she should be left alone just now."

Forgoyle grimaced. "I was hoping to hear you say that."

"It's as much for my benefit as hers," said Serdor wryly. "Here. I'll see you to the door."

Rhan, with commendable tact, did not offer to accompany them. Once outside in the corridor, Serdor said softly, "I know this probably isn't the best time to bring up new business, but there's something I want to ask you about—and not while Rhan's listening."

"Indeed?" Forgoyle's black brows went up. "What is it then?"

Beckoning, Serdor led the way to the far end of the hall where the light was stronger. He fumbled in the breast of his shirt and drew out something long and thin, wrapped in several thicknesses of cloth. "This," he said, and handed it over to Forgoyle. "Have you ever seen anything like it before?"

The magister took it gingerly and unwrapped the bindings. The unraveling revealed a thin rod of pale green stone, not unlike polished jade. Staring at it and the symbols engraved on its surface, Forgoyle frowned. "Not that I can recall. Where did you get it?"

"You've heard Rhan's account of himself. His master had it in his keeping," said Serdor. "Rhan claims that Haskel used it to track him down when he ran away. Could such a thing be possible?"

Forgoyle peered at the rod more closely. "I certainly wouldn't deny it out of hand."

"It had a strange feel to it when I first picked it up,"
continued Serdor. "Almost as if it were alive."

"I'm getting no impressions whatsoever from it at the
moment," said Forgoyle.

Something in his tone caught Serdor's ear. "Isn't that in
itself unusual?"

"Very," said Forgoyle shortly, and began to replace the
wrappings. "Look—you may have stumbled across something rather dangerous here, but just what it is will have to
wait until after the trial. . . ."

CHAPTER 31

The Sentence

Forty hours later, Caradoc Penlluathe was arraigned before the Lord Chief Justice of Ambrothen on charges of conspiracy and high treason.

The trial was convened in the privacy of an upper room in Ambrothen Keep. The attendance was limited to the officers of the court, three representatives of the Order, and a selection of witnesses, along with the Lord Warden and his wife, and the Seneschal of Ambrothen. Apart from these, no one else was present.

Denied admittance, Margoth and Serdor spent the next two days haunting the outer courtyard beyond the castle walls, waiting for news. On the third day, the court passed its verdict, and Caradoc was sentenced to be hanged, drawn, and quartered.

The sentence was to be carried out in four days' time. Hollow-eyed with watching and waiting, Margoth buried her face in Serdor's shoulder and wept herself into a state of nervous exhaustion.

When she asked for leave to pay her brother a last farewell visit, her request was denied. The news was brought to her by a big man with a golden beard who gave his name as Gudmar Ap Gorvald. Sitting opposite her in one of the two shabby chairs in her front room, her visitor said, his golden eyes compassionate, "I deeply regret the decision of the

court. If there is anything you require, I hope you will not
hesitate to call upon me.''

And then, out of deference to her pallor and her silence, he
took his leave.

Gudmar did not think it necessary to mention that it had
been Delsidor Whitfauconer himself who had rejected the
recommendations for clemency put forth by both the Grand
Master of Ambrothen and by the fellow members of his
Council. Why the Lord Warden had proved so inflexible in
view of the evidence was a question to which Gudmar could
supply no satisfactory answer. He thought about it all the
way back to the Keep and decided to tax Delsidor for an
explanation. Perhaps the over-burdened Warden would listen
more readily to a friend.

The Lord Warden had lost flesh and patience in the long
weeks since they had first learned the news of his son's
disappearance. Aware that he was treading on thin ice, Gudmar
said, ''Ten beheadings a fortnight ago, and the skulls exposed for the ravens. You've made your point. What else do
you hope to gain by condemning Caradoc Penlluathe to the
same fate?''

Delsidor's haggard eyes were inscrutable. ''Bargaining
power,'' he said simply, and then refused to say anything
more.

Forgoyle Finlevyn was more disturbed by the fact that
Caradoc had been refused all rights to visitation. ''The decision was the Lord Warden's,'' said An'char with a grimace.
''I don't pretend to understand it. Unless it's to guard against
the possibility that one of his friends might slip him the
means to an easier death than the one marked out for
him. . . .''

Caradoc's other friends, however, had very different ideas.
They were considering very seriously the problem of getting
him out of the Keep alive.

They spent the better part of what remained of the day
discussing ways and means. Using Margoth's front room as
an improvised council chamber, they devised and discarded
half a dozen plans and argued urgently over the relative

merits of several more. Serdor, of the three of them, spent more time thinking than talking, though he listened a great deal: carefully to Margoth's ruthlessly practical suggestions; tolerantly to Rhan's more flamboyant proposals.

Shortly after midnight, Serdor overruled all protests and packed Rhan firmly off to bed. Left alone, he and Margoth squandered another two hours in fruitless debate. The minstrel was at the point of suggesting that they postpone any further discussion until daybreak when a fresh idea presented itself to mind with sudden and forceful clarity.

He sat up with a start. "What is it?" asked Margoth. She took a closer look at his face and said, "So—you think you've finally got it."

Serdor's grey eyes had caught fire. "It's the best notion I've had all evening," he said. "Let's see if you agree with me."

Margoth gave him her undivided attention as he sketched his proposal in stark outlines. She waited until he had finished, then said softly, "This is all very well, but don't you think you're taking too much on yourself?"

"By going it alone?" He shook his head. "No. One of the virtues of this plan is that no one else need be directly involved."

"On the contrary, that's its main weakness," said Margoth. "If no one else is involved, you have no one to fall back on if something goes wrong."

"If something goes wrong," said Serdor, "I don't want anyone else around to share the penalties."

"If the danger is as great as that," said Margoth, "then you'd better abandon the whole venture." She added on a rising note, "Do you think I want to lose you as well as Caradoc?"

"No," said Serdor quietly. "But how well would you think of me if I did nothing and Caradoc died in agony on the gallows?"

Margoth opened her mouth, then closed it again. After a moment, her blue eyes troubled, she said, "If you're going to put it like that, I can't argue with you. But I'm still opposed to your going by yourself.''

"Who could I possibly ask to accompany me on a mission like this?'' demanded Serdor.

"Me," said Margoth simply. "And you wouldn't have to ask."

Serdor stared at her. "You're not serious."

"I'm deadly serious," said Margoth. "Caradoc may be your friend, but he's *my* brother. Surely that entitles me to some say in this whole affair."

"It's out of the question," said Serdor flatly. "Your presence would double the risks—"

"Or double your chances of success. I've got skills," said Margoth, "that would make me a valuable asset."

"But not an indispensable one," said Serdor. "It may be ten years since I last made my living by those techniques you're referring to, but I assure you I haven't lost my touch."

"Oh, you're good, all right," said Margoth grimly. "But I'm better."

Her gaze challenged him. "Can you deny it?"

"No!" said Serdor with suppressed violence. "But . . ." He struggled for words.

"Listen to me," said Margoth. "You and Caradoc and I—we've been sharing our fortunes, good or ill, ever since we were children. My life is bound up with yours. Don't leave me behind—please."

She laid an imploring hand on his arm. He flinched slightly at her touch and turned to meet her eyes.

For a long moment neither of them spoke. Then he reached up and sheathed her fingers with his own.

Margoth drew a wavering breath. "Thanks," she said softly, and added, "I won't fail you."

His hand tightened where it rested. "I'm glad that's settled," said a voice behind them with prosaic satisfaction. "All you need now," continued Rhan matter-of-factly, "is someone to act as lookout. Namely, me."

He was standing in the doorway, one shoulder resting against the lintel, an old blanket thrown sketchily around him. "You're supposed to be asleep," said Serdor ominously.

"Yes. Well, I woke up," said Rhan. He glanced inquiringly from Serdor to Margoth and back again. "When do we make our move? Tomorrow?"

"Oh, God." Serdor cast a jaundiced look at the ceiling. Returning his gaze to the boy hovering in the doorway, he said shortly, "*You* won't be making any move at all. You're not coming."

"Not coming . . ." Rhan's brown eyes registered hurt and surprise. "Why not? You're taking Margoth, aren't you?"

"Yes. But that's different," said Serdor. "Margoth and I have a commitment to keep."

Rhan planted his feet more firmly. "I have commitments, too."

"Don't be silly. You've never even met Caradoc—"

"My commitment," said Rhan, "is not to Caradoc, but to you." He paused, then quoted softly, " 'Or am I wrong in assuming that you and I are friends?' "

Serdor recognized the words as his own. His jaw tightened. "You are not wrong," he said. "But this is still none of your affair."

"It is if I make it mine. You were under no obligation to help me obtain my freedom," said Rhan, "but you did it anyway."

He stood away from the threshold, his expression doggedly determined. "I owe you a debt of honor—whether you choose to accept it or not. Please let me come with you."

"No!" Serdor sprang to his feet, his eyes hot and dark as smoke. "Damn it, Rhan, will you kindly make an effort to be reasonable?"

Such undisguised anger was something Rhan had never heard before from Serdor. The harsh tone recalled a host of unpleasant memories, but he held his ground. "It's not a question of being reasonable," he said.

There was pain in his voice. Serdor drew an unsteady breath, his face suddenly revealed in its weariness. "Oh, God, Rhan. I'm sorry. I didn't mean it to sound like that."

He crossed the room and placed his hands lightly on the boy's angular shoulders. Lifting his gaze to meet Serdor's,

Rhan said, "I may not be much of a hero. But you can count at least on my loyalty."

Serdor gave him a crooked half smile. "I'm not questioning your courage. But I didn't spirit you away from Haskel's clutches merely to embroil you in the more dangerous aspects of my personal life. You've already paid a sufficiently heavy price for your liberty. I intend to see that you keep it—even if that means saying *no* when you want me to say *yes*."

It was his last word on the subject. But Margoth, catching a fugitive glint of recalcitrance in Rhan's brown eyes, had the uneasy feeling that the issue was still far from being settled.

CHAPTER 32

The Confrontation

It did not prove easy for Forgoyle Finlevyn to accept the knowledge that the impetuous red-haired boy he had tutored into manhood was destined to end his life, not as a venerated scion of the Order, as he himself once fondly had hoped, but as a convicted traitor howling out his final hours in blood and blind agony under the knives of his appointed executioners.

By his own admission, Caradoc had betrayed his calling and played a hireling's role in the abduction of Evelake Whitfauconer. But the wealth of mitigating circumstances—not the least the fact that he had risked his own life in an attempt to undo the harm he had helped to bring about—rendered his case too complex for simple justice. Forgoyle could not dispute Caradoc's guilt. But his heart cried out against the exacting rectitude that had dispensed judgment without mercy.

For a time, the dark burden of his own personal grief outweighed all other considerations. But as his training reasserted itself in bitter resignation, he recalled that Caradoc's testimony had pointed beyond political conspiracy and brigandage to the more sinister fact of necromancy.

Necromancy.

The theurgy of forbidden power.

Rooted in the atavistic rituals of a darker age, the antithesis of all the Order stood for: its anathema and its shadow.

In laying down the precepts governing the use of the Magia, the Order had done all it could to outlaw the practice of the Black Arts. But that the Hospitallers had failed to eliminate the evil completely was a fact of their long history, destined—judging by the evidence—to be repeated.

It was an issue that transcended the personal aberrations of a single individual. Having sat through the High Court proceedings, Forgoyle was grimly aware that Caradoc's trial represented only the beginning.

The Council of Ambrothen had already been apprised of the impending arrival of a special envoy from the Arch Mage of East Garillon, in the person of the Grand Prior of Kirkwell. Second in authority only to Baldwyn himself, the Grand Prior was as renowned for the breadth of his scholarship as for the depth of his skill as a mage.

The archiepiscopal missive specified that the special legate would be assisting in all subsequent investigations related to the practice of necromancy in Ambrothen and its environs. Forgoyle doubted very much that it would end there. It was too much to hope that the disease had not broken out in places farther afield.

That uneasy thought was paramount in his mind when he returned home at the end of the day following the court's pronouncement of justice. It was still with him when he entered his library and discovered a cloth-wrapped bundle lying amid the books and papers on the desk.

Puzzled, he did not immediately recognize it. Then he recalled the rod Serdor had given him.

Conscious of having been remiss, he removed the wrappings and examined it again. Exposed to the light in the room, the rod had a curiously greasy sheen, like the mucous trail of a slug. He turned it over so that the symbols were uppermost. Then, after tracing them over several times with a forefinger, he scowled and laid the rod aside.

The runes were unlike anything he could recall ever having seen before. He spent the ensuing three hours ruffling through the holdings of his personal library but found no pertinent clues to their significance.

The following morning, after conducting his rounds at the hospital, he took the problem to the cathedral library. Several more hours of sifting through treatises on the subject of historical hieromancy proved equally unproductive. It was getting on toward evening when he at last came across an ancient grimoire, bound up in black velvet, tucked away into an obscure corner of one of the side-rooms.

Dust filtered up into his face as he removed it from the shelf. After a glance at its flyleaf, he carried it over to the curator's desk. Oblivious to the curator's curious look, he signed his name to the book-registry and departed without comment, taking the volume with him.

Once at home, he repaired to his library. Setting the book down on the desktop, he sat down and began to leaf through its crackling pages.

The book was an encyclopedia of arcane signs, drawn up at Kirkwell three centuries earlier by the Ninth Synod of Magisters. The compilation had followed a brief resurgence of the Cult of the Raven-Lord, an ancient form of black animism that predated the founding of the Order. Having read accounts of its associated practices, Forgoyle began to be convinced of the very real possibility that the rod was a product of a similar kind of necromancy.

And so he was grimly unsurprised when, three-quarters of the way through the book, he came across a symbol that matched the runes engraved upon the rod.

The room seemed to be getting darker. Scowling at the crabbed script on the page before him, Forgoyle adjusted the valve on the lamp so that the flame surged up again in a yellow flare. He propped the book open against a stack of other volumes and leaned forward so that he could read the words more easily:

> Herein ys recorded an accounte of the fashionyng
> of a charme of seekyng, as was discribed before
> thys courte by a practissioner of the sayme. . . .
> Tak ye the blode of that which thou wouldst let
> from straying—cowe or kynde or whatsoever thyng

thou list—and let thys blode be fyltred into a vessall
of thy chosyng, withe al the propre rites and spekyngs
as thy maistre sall teche thee.

And thereaftre sall that thyng no more departe,
but thou mayst knowe by the charme wheresoever
yt sall go. . . .

'' 'As thy maistre sall teche thee. . . .' ''
His face darkening, Forgoyle took his magestone in his
right hand. Oblivious for the moment to the guttering of the
lamp, he took up the rod in his free hand.

It felt slick to the touch. Holding it suspended between his
fingers, Forgoyle felt a prickling sensation through his skin.
Drawing a deep breath in readiness, he closed his eyes,
invoking the power of the Magia to explore the nature of the
artifact he held before him.

Where it had come from . . .

Who had made it . . .

And why . . .

Peripherally, other things in the room yielded savors of
their origins. He knew the oaken desk as a distillation of
acorns and leaf mold, the books as concentrates of wood and
mineral pigments. As he focused his senses in Orison upon
the rod itself, all other impressions were abruptly submerged
in an aura of foulness, like the reek that clings to a picked
bone.

The stone of which the rod was made had been hollowed
out, and the core infused with human blood.

The impact of this discovery was physically sickening.
Steadying himself with an effort, he probed deeper.

And fetched up sharply against solid blankness.

The shock was as great as if he had actually stumbled
blindly into a stone wall. Backing off from it, he paused to
recover his equilibrium before extending himself more carefully.

For all its apparent impenetrability, the barrier was fluid
rather than static, breathing like a living membrane. Slowly
at first, Forgoyle began to assert the force of his will against

it, gradually bringing to bear the concentrated force of the Magia to create a gap where none had existed before.

It was like trying to force a blunt knife through raw, stinking meat. After a shuddering expenditure of effort, he became abruptly aware of a weakening in the noisome barrier before him.

His naked intent honed to a scalpel's edge, he struck out and felt the fabric of the wall give way. The rift opened like a surgeon's incision, and through it he looked out over a sea of visual impressions.

A board painted with the image of a claw-footed beast with a human head.

A darkened room.

A man's heavy face, coarse features frozen in an expression of fascinated awe as its owner gazed raptly at the dagger he held in his hand.

Thin as a reed and rippled like a serpent, the dagger dripped blood at its tip. The man named Haskel Tohr muttered something in a low voice, and the air behind him went dark.

The darkness carried an uncanny suggestion of presence. As Haskel raised the dagger in his grip, a tongue of shadow flowed up his arm, reaching toward the hilt like a second hand. As the black fingers took hold, Haskel's face and form paled like an image in stagnant water and faded into the shadow's hungry embrace.

It was an act of devouring. As Forgoyle looked on aghast, the darkness shot up like a gust of black flame and two molten eye sockets appeared in the massed black of the skull.

Their lashing gaze took in his presence at a glance. The fire in their depths flared out like coals in a forge, and the shadow pounced like a snatching hand.

The force of it sent him hurtling back through the corridors of Power. Shot like a straw through a gale, he spun out of his chair and landed with a crash on the library floor.

The green rod flew out of his hand and skidded away from him. As he made a groping effort to retrieve it, a thin plume of black smoke sprang up hissing from the wand's pointed tip.

Within seconds, the trickle had become a fountain. Gushing in pulsating jets, like blood from a severed artery, the dark rose and spread, blotting out everything it touched.

The air reeked with the stench of old corruption. Choking, Forgoyle raised himself to his knees and made another lunging dive to recover the wand.

It was like seizing the limb of a week-old corpse. It took every shred of willpower he possessed to retain his grip on it against an almost overmastering revulsion. The malevolent air sucked the breath from his chest. His lungs pumping futilely, he clutched his magestone to his heart and poured out the full force of his trained intent in a single-minded effort to drive back the dark.

And destroy its gateway into the waking world. His pulse pounding wildly against his temples, he felt the presence waver and, in that instant, struck back to seal off the gap he himself had created.

From the other side of the gap, his adversary leaped to oppose him. The rod quivered under the strength of two conflicting wills. Then, in a sudden collapse of its physical nature, it exploded.

The backlash slammed Forgoyle back against the bookcase. He gasped aloud and discovered that the air was clean and that he could breathe again. It was the last thing he remembered before he subsided into black unconsciousness.

Forgoyle Finlevyn was late for his appointed rounds at the hospital the following morning.

Surprised, his colleagues went about their own business, expecting at any moment to receive word explaining his absence. None came and as the morning wore on they became increasingly concerned.

Ulbrecht Rathmuir dispatched his own responsibilities as quickly as professional thoroughness would allow. Then he set out at a brisk pace for Forgoyle's house.

He arrived to find the curtains still drawn and the door

locked tight. His anxiety mounting, he beat an insistent tattoo on the door and, when that failed to elicit any immediate response, backed into the garden and flung a handful of pebbles at the nearest upstairs window.

There was a protracted pause. Ulbrecht was seriously considering attempting to pry open one of the downstairs casements when the curtains veiling the upstairs window slid back and a white face appeared behind the glass.

The face was Forgoyle's. Its owner levered open the window and leaned out. "Ulbrecht? What are you doing here?" His speech was slightly slurred.

"Looking for you," said Ulbrecht. Then added sharply, "Are you all right?"

"Yes. Yes, I think so." Forgoyle drew himself up. "Wait a moment. I'll be down to let you in."

It took longer than one might have expected. When the door finally swung inward, Ulbrecht crossed the threshold at a bound. Assessing Forgoyle's appearance at a glance, he declared roundly, "You look terrible!"

"I've been lying upstairs senseless since late last night—I only came to when I heard you knocking at the door." Forgoyle ran a hand across his forehead. "What time is it?"

"Nearly noon. Forgoyle, what's the matter with you?" asked Ulbrecht.

"Nothing that won't pass once I've had something to eat and a breathing space," said Forgoyle. "Come into the kitchen and I'll tell you all about it."

His account of the events of the previous night was brief but alarming. "Of all the foolhardy things to do!" exclaimed Ulbrecht when he had finished. "You, of all people, should have known better than to tamper with an artifact like that. At the very least, you should have reported your findings to An'char before proceeding any further."

"I know," said Forgoyle grimly. "My curiosity got the better of me."

"Judging by the look of you, something else very nearly did, too," said Ulbrecht. "An'char is going to be far from pleased about this."

"I believe I can justify having taken the risk," said Forgoyle.

There was the throb of suppressed excitement in his voice. Ulbrecht elevated an expectant eyebrow. "Why," continued Forgoyle, "would anyone fashion a necromancer's tool for the sole purpose of keeping track of a mere bond-servant?"

"I don't know," said Ulbrecht. "Unless the boy happened to be of some unique significance . . ."

His voice trailed off abruptly.

"I may be wrong, of course," said Forgoyle. "But you must admit, the connection is already there."

He got up from the table. "Come with me. I think it's time young Rhan Hallender was treated to a thorough medical examination."

From Forgoyle's house, they made their way to Margoth's small apartment. But when they got there, they found the place empty.

CHAPTER 33

The Players

On the day before Caradoc Penlluathe was to be executed, the Seneschal of Ambrothen issued an edict proclaiming the occasion as a day of solemn obligation for the city at large.

Mungo Holbeyn, lute-maker, who owned a modest establishment facing out over Manciple Square, was not pleased to learn that he was expected to close up his shop and release his apprentices from their duties in order to witness the morrow's grisly spectacle. Faced with the prospect of losing a day's business, he grumbled his way through the morning, little dreaming that the afternoon's events would contribute significantly to his existing grievances.

Lunch passed uneventfully enough. Returning to his workshop shortly after two o'clock, Mungo retired to the back room of his studio to do some inlay work on his latest creation. He had been at it for less than half an hour when the elder of his two apprentices poked a tousled head around the doorframe and announced his presence with an apologetic cough.

Mungo disliked interruptions. Scowling, he laid aside his tools and demanded to know the reason behind the intrusion. His apprentice, an overgrown adolescent with poor teeth and worse skin, shuffled a pair of enormous feet, and said hesitantly, "Begging your pardon, sir, but would you mind stepping out front for a moment?"

Mungo eyed his apprentice with disfavor. "What for? I didn't hear any customers ringing the bell."

His apprentice hunched rounded shoulders. "It isn't a customer, sir. It's . . . there's a man and a woman outside. They arrived a few minutes ago with a handcart and began setting markers on the cobbles. I tried to get them to go away, but they only laughed at me. I think they intend to stage some kind of performance. . . ."

Mungo came erect with a start. His brows beetling over his nose, he growled, "Indeed. Well, we'll see about that."

He hitched himself off his workbench and marched out to the front of the shop. His other apprentice was standing by the window, pug nose nearly touching the glass. "Master Holbeyn, they're already drawing a crowd," he announced over his shoulder.

Peering, Mungo could see for himself the press of interested spectators gathering practically on his front doorstep. Phrases of indignant protest forming on his tongue, he took three purposeful strides toward the outer door. As he reached for the latch, the sound of music broke out and rose with sweet and rollicking precision above the bustle of movement and curious voices.

It was the music of a lute, crisp and clear, mellow as strong cider. The rich golden tone of the instrument marked it for what it was—the work of a master-craftsman. Transfixed between admiration and envy, Mungo paused for a moment to listen and realized with dawning disquiet that there was something hauntingly familiar in the player's musical style.

He opened the door and stepped out onto the porch. The lutanist had mounted the broad brick wall surrounding the covered well in the middle of the square. From thirty feet away, Mungo caught a fleeting glimpse of a clean-featured profile beneath the drooping brim of a fanciful, parti-colored hat before an outcry of masculine approval and a ripple of applause from the onlookers diverted his attention to the musician's female counterpart.

A lissome and leggy redhead, bodice cut down to reveal a daring expanse of white skin, she was striking enough to rivet the eye. But it was not her looks that compelled the fascination of her audience. As Mungo stared at her, half-scandalized, half-mesmerized, she whirled about in a flurry of patchworked skirts and sent a stream of small, sharp-bladed knives dancing into the air.

Her movements perfectly complemented by the music of her accompanist, she caught them as they descended and sent them aloft again in a series of ever-changing configurations. Spellbound in spite of himself, Mungo remained where he was until she captured the last knife with an elegant twist of the wrist, and the music came to a magical close.

Both performers bowed deeply to the ensuing burst of cheers and hand-clapping. As the lutanist straightened up again Mungo caught his first full view of the other man's face.

His teeth came grindingly together as he recognized his uncle's former journeyman, whom he himself had dismissed. For a moment he remained rooted to the spot, his features congealing into suety immobility. Then, rousing himself, he bounded ponderously to the foot of the steps and set out, like a bullock through daisies, for the makeshift stage.

Shouldering other members of the crowd out of the way, he arrived just as the two performers were exchanging lute and colored balls for an assortment of wooden rings. Bootheels grinding to a halt on the cobblestones, Mungo folded his arms and intoned ominously, "Serdor Sulamith!"

The woman's slender harlequin companion relegated his instrument to the safety of the handcart before turning around. Long-lashed grey eyes lit up in pleased acknowledgment. "Why, hullo, Mungo," said the minstrel cheerfully. "What a nice surprise. You're looking very well. The extra weight suits you—"

"What the devil are you doing here?" growled Mungo. He cast an irate glance at the lute Serdor had just laid aside, and added sharply, "You've got no business playing that thing in a public place."

The minstrel raised pained eyebrows. "Well, you can hardly expect me to make a living playing it in the privacy of my own room. How are you coming on in the trade? Have you made guild-master yet?''

Someone jostled Mungo's elbow from behind and he realized that the audience was pressing forward hoping to hear better. His face went a darker shade of dull crimson. "Don't get clever with me," he snapped. "The day I do become a guild-master, I'll see the likes of guttersnipes like you whipped out of this city at the cart's tail. In the meantime, I'll thank you to pack up your things and move along before I send for the constable."

There was a murmur of protest among the bystanders. "Don't be such a spoilsport, Mungo!" called an anonymous voice from the fringe. "They're not doing any harm."

"Not doing any harm?" Mungo wheeled, his big shoulders thrown back. "I'll have you know they're breaking the law."

"In what way?" demanded another voice in candid skepticism.

"They're performing in public without a writ of authorization from the Musicians' Guild," said Mungo with righteous finality.

This declaration provoked a scattering of derisive catcalls. "How d'you know they haven't got a writ? I didn't hear you ask 'em," said the same voice argumentatively.

Mungo made an explosive noise at the back of his nose. Turning to the minstrel, he sneered, "What about it, Master Malapert? Have you got the proper sanction from the Guild?"

Serdor flipped a wooden ring into the air and caught it behind his back. "No," he said blithely.

He tossed another larger ring to his dazzling companion, who seized it deftly. Leaving Mungo puffed up with undischarged spleen, they stepped aside into the clear area marked off with strings of fluttering rags and took up their places facing each other across ten feet of empty space.

Fingers quicker than the eye, they created a blur of motion between them as the hoops shot accurately from hand to hand. Sending one small ring sailing through a larger one tossed by his partner, the minstrel called over his shoulder,

"All we need now is a dancing bear. Care to join us, Mungo?"

Laughter broke out on all sides. His small eyes ablaze, Mungo clenched a fist and waved it menacingly at the lithe, dancing figure of his tormentor. "Go ahead! Have your fun while you can. Just remember it'll be me who's laughing when the sergeants-at-arms string you up at the pillory and take the lash to your impudent back!"

He turned on his heel and stormed back across the cobbles to the sanctuary of his own shop. Serdor and Margoth completed the juggling routine with a flourish of interchanges that left the spectators gasping. Stooping side by side with Serdor as they collected the coins off the street, Margoth breathed out of the side of her mouth, "Do you think he's angry enough to do as he threatened?"

Serdor's expressive lips tightened a fraction. "Don't worry— Mungo Holbeyn's a man of his word. We should have time for a dance and perhaps another song before they get here. . . ."

His estimate proved accurate enough. Plucking out a fluid coranto, Serdor spotted the flash of metal accoutrements while the five-man patrol was still fifty paces distant. Catching Margoth's eyes as she pirouetted, he gave her a brief nod and gathered up the final measures of the dance into a rippling cadenza.

The hand-clapping and foot-stamping died abruptly away as the liveried guardsmen penetrated the crowd from outside. Serdor waited until they drew even with the front ranks of the audience, then broke the music with a resolving chord that brought Margoth to a standstill.

Trailing Mungo Holbeyn behind him, the sergeant of the patrol came to a halt several feet from the base of the wall on which Serdor was standing. He lifted a helmeted head and raked the minstrel with a disenchanted pair of pale blue eyes. "All right, you can stop right where you are," he said.

Serdor paused in the act of sidling away. "It appears," continued the sergeant sourly, "that you don't have much regard for the statutes of this city."

His grey gaze marginally more ironic than it had been a moment before, Serdor shrugged his shoulders. "On the contrary, sir, I have every respect for laws and statutes—as long as they are justly conceived. In this case, I do not consider it equitable that I should be denied a living for want of a mere scrap of paper."

"Is that so? Well, like it or not," said the sergeant, "that 'mere scrap of paper' happens to represent the civil authority of the Most Worshipful Company of Ambrothen Musicians—to which all reputable members of your profession belong—"

"Reputable? Hah!" This scathing exclamation came not from Serdor, but from his red-haired companion. Her blue eyes flashing, she pointed an uncompromising finger at Mungo. "If the Musicians' Guild were as reputable as it's made out to be, they never would have let *him* in, when everyone knows you could get more music out of an empty barrel than you could out of any instrument *he's* made—"

"Why, you brazen-faced hussy—" Bristling with rage, Mungo lunged forward, only to be hauled back by two of the sergeant's men. Undaunted, the red-haired woman planted her hands on her hips and threw back her head. "Shall I tell you the real reason why he wants us arrested? It's not out of any regard for the law, or the Guild. No, it's because he's jealous—jealous of a *true* craftsman!"

This spirited declaration drew cheers from the spectators. Foaming, Mungo made another struggling attempt to break past the guardsmen. Fingering the bridge of his nose with the air of a man at the end of his patience, the sergeant snapped, "That's enough! Haryld! Loryn! Arrest those two ragamuffins before they provoke a disturbance. And you—Holbart, or whatever your name is: if I hear any more outbursts from you, you'll be sharing their cell tonight up at Ambrothen Keep."

He wheeled about and gestured curtly to his men. Striding forward, they laid hands upon the two street-performers. Serdor yielded up his lute with no visible sign of emotion. He was just submitting to having his hands bound behind his

back when a new voice, shrill with youthful outrage, burst
above the general hubbub of the dispersing crowd.

"Beasts! Cowards! Leave my brother alone, you white-
livered swine!"

His spine breaking out in icicles, Serdor whipped around
as a brown slip of furious movement windmilled into the
midst of the guardsmen and began indiscriminately kicking
shins.

His eyes meeting Margoth's in a stark instant of angry
incredulity, Serdor twisted free of the grip on his bound arms
and made a lunging dive for the boy. A heavy backhanded
cuff intended for Rhan glanced painfully off his shoulder as
he cannoned into his young protégé and forced him back.
Shielding the boy with his own body, he hissed, "You little
duffer, what the *hell* do you think you're doing?"

Rhan's expression was grimly determined. "Trying to get
myself arrested."

"You'll do no such thing," breathed Serdor in a wrathful
undertone. Hands tore at his clothing from behind, but he
managed to shake them off long enough to give the boy
another admonitory shove with his elbow. "Get out of here,
or I swear I'll—"

A booted foot hooked itself between Serdor's ankles and
sent him pitching toward the cobbles. Unable to break his
own fall, he landed bruisingly facedown. He caught a fleeting glimpse of Rhan's white face, transfixed between obsti-
nacy and remorse, before the boy spun around and broke into
a run.

For one blessed instant of relief, Serdor thought his young
associate was going to yield to reason and take flight. Then
Rhan abruptly changed direction, doubling back toward where
Mungo Holbeyn was standing in front of his shop.

Serdor made an abortive attempt to scramble to his feet,
but a large boot planted itself hard between his shoulder blades
and pinned him to the ground. Forty feet away, Rhan skidded
to a halt in front of Mungo. "You bloody coxcomb, this is
all your fault!" he declared, and stooped for a loose
cobblestone.

"Rhan, *no!*" shouted Serdor. An instant later, the front window of Mungo's studio imploded in a scintillating shower of broken glass.

Mungo's howl of dismay clashed with a concerted rush of booted feet toward the site of the disaster. There was a brief, token scuffle. Then Rhan was hustled out of the midst of the destruction he had wrought.

"It seems your brother has more loyalty than sense," said the sergeant to Serdor. To the guardsmen with him, he added, "All right. Bring the brat along. He's done more than enough to earn a night in the Keep prison. . . ."

CHAPTER 34

The Prison

Escorted by the sergeant and his four men-at-arms, the three miscreants arrested in Manciple Square were paraded ignominiously along the city's High Street and through a gap in Fortingal's Dyke, a grass-grown earthwork marking out what had once been the castle's outermost ring of defenses. A cobbled causeway led away from the Dyke, through a furlong of alternating ditches and terraces, up Castle Hill to the west barbican. A chain's length below the fortified gatehouse, they struck a cart-track that branched off to the left, carrying on along the curtain wall to an iron-wrought postern, sheltering at the base of a tall, flanking tower.

There were two guardsmen in the livery of the Du Bors family on duty at the postern gate. After an exchange of passwords, the arresting sergeant and his party were ushered through the port onto a broad half-moon of turf that led to a flight of stone steps.

The steps brought them up to the level of the Keep's intermediary ramparts. Inside, within the compass of the walls, the hill rose steeply toward the flat plate of open ground that capped the bluff overlooking the beach and the harbor. There lay the castle donjon and the cluster of residential buildings that made up the heart of the Keep. Between the donjon and the outer walls were scattered a number of other buildings—the barracks, the armory, and the stables of the castle militia; the headquarters of the city heralds; and the extensive network of cells and corridors that made up the city gaol.

Partially incorporated into the damp lime-rock of the escarpment, the prison occupied more than a single story. Scanning the climbing array of barred window-slits, Rhan shivered slightly, wondering how they were going to locate Margoth's brother among this beehive collection of vaults.

Though that was probably going to prove the least of their worries, once they were inside.

"There are only two ways in—or out—of the prison," Serdor had said. "The first is, of course, by means of the main entrance on the first level. The other is on the upper level: a stairway and passage connecting the prison complex with the Seneschal's Great Hall of Justice. We'll be going in by the one and—if our luck holds—out by the other."

How the minstrel had come to know so much about the interior layout of the prison was something of a mystery, but one or two passing remarks from Margoth had led Rhan to suspect that his friend had acquired his information firsthand during his childhood association with the city's fraternity of thieves. Serdor's studious reticence on the subject had warned Rhan against asking the obvious questions, but he still hoped Margoth might enlighten him further. If they were given the chance.

He cast a strained glance over at Serdor's unyielding profile, and his spirits wavered. The minstrel, it seemed, had not yet forgiven him for his recent breach of orders.

The main door to the prison was reinforced by an iron yett. Once admitted to the gaol precincts, the prisoners were relegated to a small alcove adjoining the guardroom while one of the officers of the watch went off to report their arrival to his superior. Keeping a wary eye on the averted back of the guard who had remained behind, Serdor muttered between his teeth, "Well, Master Hallender, I suppose you think you've been very clever."

His remark lost none of its sarcastic bite for being delivered in an undertone. Bracing himself, Rhan set his jaw. "I did what I had to do."

"Indeed?" Serdor turned to glare at his uninvited accomplice. "Do you, then, take me for a fool?"

Prepared for a wholly different line of attack, Rhan paused and blinked. "N-no."

"Then what else," inquired the minstrel, "made you decide to tamper with an entire set of rather delicate plans that did not include you?"

Rhan wriggled uncomfortably and dropped his eyes. "I've already told you: I want to help. I owe it to you—"

"Disregarding the fact that there's another man's life at stake here. If you're referring again to your 'honor,' " said Serdor, "let me remind you that true 'honor' is largely a matter of humility and obedience—two virtues which you seem conspicuously to be lacking."

It registered as a hit. Drawing himself up, Rhan said in a low, tight voice, "All right. Don't call it honor. Call it duty."

"The obligation to do what you know is right," interposed Margoth's soft voice, "even when it means being punished for it." Her gaze met Serdor's. "I think you already understand the principle."

It had the effect of reducing the minstrel to silence. Encouraged by Serdor's suddenly thoughtful expression, Rhan reached out a tentative hand and touched his friend's worn sleeve. "Please don't be angry," he said, "I *had* to come. I would rather have you send me back to Haskel than leave me behind when you're going into danger."

Serdor was not proof against the appeal in the boy's subdued voice. His expression softened. "Oh, very well, you incorrigible brat," he sighed. "We'll say no more about it. Just promise me one thing."

Rhan gave him a lopsided grin. "What's that?"

"Promise me," said Serdor, "that from here on out, you'll do exactly as you're told—no questions asked."

*   *   *

From the guardroom they were taken to a second detention area, where they were methodically searched. Margoth submitted to handling with a wiggle and a small shriek of protest. Standing a few feet behind her, Rhan caught an infinitesimal glint of metal through her fingers as she momentarily appeared to lose her balance. She clutched the sleeve of the nearest guard and clung there for a moment longer until he had finished with her. When she righted herself again the implement had vanished.

After being searched, they were conducted down one dimly-lit corridor and up another to a wide oaken door surmounted by a metal grid a foot square. As the turnkey jangled through the keys at his belt, there was a sudden crash and an outcry of protesting voices from inside. A woman's painted face appeared at the grid. "For God's sake, sir—those heathens are at it again," she moaned tearfully. "Please take 'em away an' put 'em somewhere else so the rest of us can get some peace!"

There was another crash, and the woman vanished with a shrill squeal. A massive set of fingers took hold of the bars in a grip that rocked the door on its hinges. The guardsman to the right of the turnkey swore. He whipped the cudgel from his belt and dealt the fingers a shrewd crack. There was a bellow of rage from the other side of the door, and the hand was withdrawn.

Trembling slightly in his haste, the turnkey fitted the key to the lock and gave it a sharp turn to the left. With the officer in charge barking orders, the three prisoners in the corridor were seized and stuffed precipitantly through the marginal gap in the doorway.

The door slammed shut behind them. Tumbling head over heels across the floor, Serdor caught a dizzy impression of torchlit walls and other cowering human shapes before landing flat on his face, eight inches away from an enormous pair of sandaled feet.

He raised his head and encountered a fierce pair of hot black eyes. An instant later, a hand like a clutch of tree-roots locked itself into his collar and hauled him unceremoniously to his feet.

It was then that he realized that the big man was not alone.

None of the four were Garillan. All of them, including the towering leader, had the swart, burnished skin and intense aquiline features of the Children of Mohrab, Most Holy Prophet of Pernatha.

Head shaven smooth except for a tightly-twisted topknot of night-black hair, the leader stood a good seven inches taller than the other men with him. A broad gorget of enameled copper plates glimmered against his dark skin, and more copper, in the form of interlacing loops, hung from the lobes of both ears. Gesturing around him, he rumbled belligerently in cracked Garillan, "Here—where?"

Serdor could see that the big man bore a fresh and ugly clout-mark over his left ear. His companions showed similar signs of having been recently involved in a brawl. "Him an' his mates don't seem t' understand they've been had up by the Watch," wailed the woman who had pleaded with the guards at the grating. "Me an' Loysse, we been tryin' to explain it to 'em, but it jest don't get through somehow."

"Ye wouldn't happen to know any of their language, would ye?" inquired her companion, a small man with a broken nose. "They've already smashed up three pallets, a stool, and the only slop basin we had. I hate to think what might go next, if they keep on much longer."

Serdor's knowledge of the Pernathan tongue was limited to what he had been able to glean from a study of the Pernathan manuscripts available in the Hospitallers' library. Faced now with the prospect of having to carry on a spoken conversation on colloquial terms, he experienced a strong qualm of misgiving. "I know a little—not much," he said. "I'll do my best, but don't expect miracles."

He drew a deep breath and switched, haltingly, to Pernathe. "I have some small . . . acquaintance . . . with thy . . . speech. What is it that . . . thee . . . wishes to know?"

The big Pernathan's black eyes lit up in a blaze of joyful

ferocity. He clapped the minstrel hard on both shoulders and burst into a booming torrent of Pernathe.

Highly charged with angry emotion, the words tumbled over each other. Serdor's inexperienced ear failed to catch more than a few fugitive phrases. He was still three sentences behind when his counterpart thundered on through a whole series of invectives, then came to a halt, watching him expectantly.

Serdor felt as if he had been bracing himself against a strong wind. "Well? What's he on about?" demanded the woman anxiously.

"I'm not sure. It went by me too quickly," said Serdor. He pulled a face. "I'll see if I can get him to repeat it."

"No, don't bother," said Rhan. "I can tell you what he said."

Both Margoth and Serdor turned to stare at him in blank astonishment. "His name is Houssein," Rhan continued. "He's the pilot on board the galeass *Yusufa,* which anchored here a week ago. Last night he and his men were gaming in an inn down by the waterfront when they caught sight of someone who had gotten their whole crew into trouble a few months back. When they tried to apprehend him, a fight broke out. The next thing any of them remembers is waking up here."

"And Houssein, of course, wants to know where 'here' is," said Serdor. He sucked in a mouthful of air, feeling a little as if someone had elbowed him in the midriff. "I suppose you'd better tell him."

Rhan's expression was queer, almost frightened. "Yes," he said. "I'll do that."

Coming forward to Serdor's side, he paused a moment, as if to collect himself. Then he embarked on what was obviously a fluent explanation of their present circumstances.

There followed a lengthy exchange of questions and answers. At the end of an explosive disquisition, Rhan nodded and turned back to Serdor. "Houssein says he knows he and his men were wrongfully arrested. He swears he's got to get back to his ship to warn his captain that they may be in for a bad time if they don't act fast." He paused. "What do you think?"

"I think," said Serdor thoughtfully, "that we may have found ourselves some very useful allies. . . ."

Once the Pernathans understood the plan, they accepted it with wolfish enthusiasm. "I'm glad they're on our side," said Serdor with feeling. He turned to Rhan and grinned. "Remind me never to underestimate you again. I had no idea you could speak Pernathe like a native."

"If it comes to that," said Rhan, "neither did I."

Arrested by the harshness of his tone, Serdor stared at him. "I beg your pardon?"

Rhan twisted thin hands together. "I can speak Pernathe; you just heard me do it. But I can't remember where I learned it."

Seeing his friend's bemused expression, he dismissed the question with a vehement shake of his head. "Never mind. It doesn't matter now. We've got far more important things to worry about at the moment."

He sounded very definite. "All right," said Serdor. "I'll take your word for it."

It was quiet now in the passageway outside. The Pernathans were ready, their dark eyes watchful. The minstrel turned to Margoth and raised an eyebrow.

She smiled and held up her hand. A small lockpick glittered between her fingers. Serdor gave her a fleeting grin. "This is where you come into your own," he said.

Going to the door, Margoth first examined the lock, running her fingertips lightly over the metal casing until the impression of the mechanism's internal workings solidified in her mind. With this impression to guide her, she inserted the pick-end into the keyhole, working it delicately into position until she located the gear wheel controlling the lock's spring latch.

Jimmying the wheel with the point of the pick, she coaxed it to the right. A moment later, the tongue-bolt slipped back from the keeper with a well-oiled click.

The sound drew the attention of the man called Loysse. He

sat up with a start and glared at the party clustered around the door. "Here! What're you lot up to?" he demanded.

"We're leaving," said Serdor.

"My God, you're not joking." Loysse goggled at him, then said flatly, "Don't do it. Ye'll not get fifty paces—"

"A rose noble says you're wrong," said Serdor. "Care to join us?"

The remaining inmates of the cell exchanged wary glances. "Not me," said Loysse with a shudder. "I'd rather take the six months they gave me for nickin' a purse than risk a flogging for breakin' gaol."

"Aye, me, too," agreed the woman with the painted face. The others murmured and nodded in support of her.

"Tell ye what," said Loysse. "We'll gi' ye ten minutes' head start before we raise the alarm."

"Generous, but unnecessary," said Serdor. "As far as we're concerned, you can give the guard a shout right now. . . ."

Having completed their circuit of the ground-floor cellblock, Sergeant Regan Ap Ruarch and his two subordinates were about to return to the guardroom in the northwest corner of the building when a series of bangs and an outraged howl from the cell at the opposite end of the corridor made them wheel around in their tracks.

"That'll be those Pernathan bastards the wharf patrol brought in last night," growled Regan. "They've done nothing but cause trouble ever since—"

"But that's one of the other prisoners, sir," protested one of the privates. "I thought I heard something about a knife."

"Did you?" Regan wrested the cudgel from the loop at his belt. "Well, whatever's afoot, we'll soon put a stop to it."

With the sergeant in the lead, they started back down the hall at a trot. Thudding to a halt in front of the cell from which the noise was emanating, Regan struck the grate a ringing blow with his stick. "Here!" he snarled. "What's going on in there?"

An instant later the door burst open.

It slammed him flat to the wall. Struggling out from behind it, he discovered that the corridor was suddenly full of bare-chested Pernathans.

The two privates were already down, thrashing about on the floor under smothering masks of dirty straw. Inflating bruised lungs, Regan tried to croak out a warning shout but had his air supply abruptly cut off by a bronzed pair of throttling hands.

In a moment, it was all over. Leaving Margoth to keep an eye on the far end of the passageway, Serdor knelt down next to the fallen officer. "This one's uniform ought to do," he said to Rhan. "Help me unlace his doublet. . . ."

While the Pernathans despoiled the two unconscious privates of their weapons, he and Rhan stripped the sergeant to the waist. He began to show signs of life before they were quite finished. Holding the man's own dagger to his throat, Serdor said incisively, "Right. Tell me quickly: where are they holding the prisoner Caradoc Penlluathe?"

The sergeant started to sneer, then abruptly changed his mind. Gulping past the point pricking into his windpipe, he rasped, "Cell Nine . . . Level Three."

"Thank you. That will do," said Serdor, and rapped him on the temple with the butt-end of the baton he had appropriated.

They consigned the unconscious guardsmen to the cell they had just vacated, and Margoth relocked the door. Buckling on the sergeant's helmet, Serdor said, "This, I think, is where we part company with our Pernathan friends. Rhan, tell them how to find the way out on this level. The diversions we create between us ought to keep the staff occupied to our mutual advantage. . . ."

CHAPTER 35

The Diversion

The stairway leading up to the second level of the prison was located in the southeast corner of the complex. Caradoc's would-be rescuers arrived to find the stairwell unguarded. "So far, so good," muttered Serdor, scanning the torchlit walls overhead. "Follow close behind me, and watch your feet: there are trip-steps built into most of the stairs in this place."

The topmost step gave way onto a narrow landing, with a solid oaken door set into the wall facing the stairs. Light from a taper set in a sconce to the right of the doorframe showed up a complicated lock-and-latch arrangement in place of a door handle.

"That's funny. This door opens *into* the stairwell," murmured Rhan, peering at the placement of the hinges. "Shouldn't it open the other way?"

"You forget where you are," whispered Serdor. "These doors aren't designed to keep invaders out, they're designed to keep prisoners *in*."

He scowled at the portal. "There used to be a storeroom opposite the stairs on this level. Let's hope nobody's changed the layout."

Motioning his two companions to stand back, he tried the latch. When it shifted loosely in his hand, he touched a

242

warning finger to his lips and pushed the door open a cautious crack.

The sound of voices at once became audible as a soft
semiarticulate buzz on the dim air. Fitting one eye to the gap,
Serdor located a lighted room at the end of the passage that
branched off to the left of the landing.

The door to the room was standing ajar. From his vantage
point, Serdor could make out in silhouette the head and
shoulders of a man sitting with his back to the corridor.
Drawing breath softly, he opened the crack an inch farther
and directed his gaze along the opposite wall until he found
the door he was looking for.

A door that lacked the usual grating and food-slot. A door
marked with the citadel's coat of arms.

He drew back and closed the door to the landing. "Well?"
whispered Margoth.

Serdor leaned over, his lips almost brushing her ear. "Tricky:
there are at least three men—maybe more—quartered in the
guardroom not thirty paces from here. If any one of them
happens to look up at the wrong moment, he'll spot you
cold." He paused, then said, "*Not* the ideal situation. I can
try my hand at this one, if you like."

"It'll be quicker if I do it myself," said Margoth in a
breathless undertone. "Don't worry: I'll manage."

The corridor beyond was only dimly lit. Margoth covered
the distance from one door to the other in two swift steps and
flattened herself to the wall next to the doorframe.

The man sitting by the guardroom door shifted in his chair.
Her heart leaped into her mouth as she waited for him to turn
around. Ten seconds thudded by before she realized he was
still occupied with whatever was going on in the room before
him. Drawing breath shakily, she unbent and gave her attention to the lock on the storeroom door.

A cursory inspection told her it was similar in design to the
one on the cell-door downstairs. That fact alone made her
task that much easier. Smiling grimly to herself, she pin-
pointed the release-mechanism in a matter of heartbeats. She
set her teeth and tripped it.

The click as the spring turned in place seemed to split the air like a thunderclap. Flinching, Margoth shrank against the wall, her nerves jangling like keys on a wire. Seconds passed and nothing happened. She exhaled slowly, steeled herself, and whisked like a moth for the safety of the landing.

Serdor was waiting for her. Slumping gratefully against him, she whispered, "All clear."

He gave her a tight smile. "Well done. Now it's my turn." Looking from her to Rhan, he added, "The pair of you stay here. If something goes wrong—if I'm seen—make for the main entrance. I'll join you if and when I can."

He caught up the torch from beside the door and muffled the flame with a fold of his borrowed cloak. While the embers were still smoldering dully between life and death, he stole a quick glance in the direction of the guardroom and slipped like a cat across the passageway.

The interior of the storeroom smelt of leather, sawdust, and chemicals. And singed wool. He flicked the torch free of his mantle and beat out the sparks with a gauntleted hand. Then, by the light of the brand's reviving flame, he looked around him.

The sputtering glare revealed a mountainous jumble of ropes and cables, crates and barrels, tools and spare pieces of soldiers' equipment. Sniffing, Serdor caught, above the pervading odors of metal polish and neatsfoot oil, the bitter tang of saltpeter.

The six kegs of gunpowder were stacked at the far end of the storeroom under a protective sheet of bunting. Marking their position, Serdor did some further salvage work and came back with an empty powder-flask, a box of nails, and a length of slow match.

Using the point of his dagger to pry the bung from one of the powder kegs, he shook several ounces of corned powder into the flask and added the tacks. He bound the improvised fuse into place with a twist of wire, then retreated to the open space by the threshold.

With one eye on the door, he set the flask down on the floor and picked up a coil of rope. Slinging it over his shoulder, he kindled a straw from the torch and held it to the end of the match. With the sound of its angry spitting loud in his ears, he risked another swift glance outside, then darted back to where his companions were anxiously waiting.

Unraveling the coil of rope, he passed his dagger to Margoth. "Here. Cut me off about ten feet of this," he whispered.

Margoth nodded. While she was sawing at it, he whipped the loose end of the line through the latch-grip on their side of the door and made it fast in a lightning series of knots. "It's an old trick," he murmured over his shoulder to Rhan. "Here's how it works . . ."

The gaoler with the ginger hair was just about to deal his fellow cardplayers a fresh hand when a rattling boom from the opposite end of the adjoining corridor startled him into scattering cards in all directions.

"God's holy fingerbones, what the hell was *that*?" exclaimed the private sitting to his left.

His two fellow guardsmen sent their chairs toppling as they lunged for the door. "Whatever it was, it came from the storeroom," shouted one of them on the way out. "Move your bloody arse, Cedwyn! If something's caught fire in there, there'll be the devil to pay!"

The gaoler at their heels, the three guardsmen pelted down the passageway and hurled themselves at the storeroom door. It yielded without resistance, and they tumbled across the threshold to find the room luridly awash with firelight. "Hey! I could have sworn I locked this!" called the gaoler, following them in.

His companions ignored him. Racing after the thin lines of spreading fire, they danced about in circles, trampling the flames beneath their boots. Cedwyn was grinding out the last spark when he stumbled upon the exploded remains of a powder-flask.

"Here—look at this!" he exclaimed, and as they gathered around him, indicated the telltale powder-burns on the torn casing. "Somebody set that off deliberately!"

The four of them looked at each other. In the same instant, the door banged shut behind them.

Charging, they tried to pull it open. To their highly vocal chagrin, it refused to budge.

Outside in the corridor, Serdor winched the rope's end through the handgrip over the keyhole and braced it while Margoth tied the knots. After she had finished, the minstrel stood back and tested the tension on the line stringing the opposing doors together. "That should hold them," he said. "Let's go."

Rhan was waiting for them at the bend in the passageway. As they joined him, he held up two warning fingers and pointed vehemently in the direction of the adjoining corridor. Nodding, Serdor passed his cudgel to Rhan and shrugged off his cloak.

Holding it up in front of him, he waited until the striding footsteps were practically on top of them, then threw it. The leading guardsman staggered as the muffling folds of material settled over his head. Momentarily blinded, he went down with Serdor on top of him.

His companion leaped back into the shelter of the nearest doorway and ripped his sword from its sheath. Before he could attack, a thrown dagger pinned his cuff to the doorframe.

Swearing, he tried and failed to free himself with a single jerk. The red-haired woman who had thrown the dagger snatched off one of her cork-soled shoes and hurled it at his head. As he threw up his free hand in an instinctive attempt to deflect it, the boy at her side fewtered his cudgel like a jousting spear and rushed him.

The point of it struck the guardsman just below the breast-bone. He grunted and doubled over. The boy sidestepped and brought the cudgel down on the crown of his helmet with a crack. The guardsman's vision splintered and he folded to the floor.

Grappling on the flagstones with his victim, Serdor took a shrewd jab in his left kidney. Wincing, he rammed one forearm under the other man's chin and boxed him sharply under the ear with his free hand. The guardsman bucked

violently and almost threw him off. One knee trapped under
the other man's threshing body, the minstrel gritted through
his teeth, "Somebody, hit him—I can't hold him forever."

Leaving Margoth to recover her dagger and her shoe, Rhan
dispatched their other victim with a well-placed thump. As
Serdor staggered to his feet, he asked, "Now where?"

The minstrel was massaging his back. "Up another flight
of stairs," he said, and stooped to retrieve his cloak. "This is
where we find out if this uniform was worth stealing. . . ."

Insulated from the floor below by thick ceilings and stone
flagging, the officer on duty on the third detention level was
unaware that there was anything amiss until a disturbance
broke out in the hallway down the passage from his office.

Sweeping aside the report he was working on, he clapped
on his sword-belt and strode out to see what the noise was
about. Three of his men were clustered around a fourth at the
head of the stairs. The fourth man was gesticulating wildly,
his voice cracking with excitement. "Don't ask me how
those foreign bastards got loose! We can sort that one out
once they're back under lock and key—"

"What's going on?" demanded the lieutenant.

The man in the sergeant's uniform wheeled and saluted.
"Sir, some prisoners have broken out of one of the cells on
the lower level. They're armed, and they're dangerous. We
could use all the help we can get."

The sergeant's clothes were in a telling state of disarray,
and his helmet had been knocked askew. Catching their
superior's eye, the three privates moved toward the stairs.
Motioning the sergeant to accompany him, the lieutenant
asked sharply, "Where are they now? . . . Level Two? All
right, we'll see if we can pick them up."

He turned on his heel, then paused and looked back.
"While we're at it, you'd better be trying to come up with
some plausible excuses for yourself. You and your men are
going to have some explaining to do."

It was dark at the foot of the stairs. The men in front
checked and looked back for instructions. "Goddammit, some-

body's doused the torches," growled the lieutenant. Glancing
back at the sergeant who was following one step behind him,
he snapped, "Don't just stand there. Go back and fetch a
light."

"Yessir," said the sergeant, and rammed hip and shoulder
sideways into the lieutenant's body.

Caught off guard, the lieutenant lost his footing and slammed
into the man below him. Clutching at each other, they both
overbalanced and shot into space.

They crash-landed two steps down and tobogganed the rest
of the way, sweeping the two other men with them. Fighting
to keep upright, neither of the privates saw the rope stretched
out across the floor at the foot of the stairs until it leaped off
the ground and caught them around the knees. Already hope-
lessly intertangled, the pair went down together with a clatter
like so much scrap metal.

Shadows flitted past them in the dark. By the time the
lieutenant and his men had sorted out their limbs and their
weapons, their assailants were already securing the door at
the top of the stairs.

The lock was a mate to the one on the storeroom door.
Under Margoth's practiced manipulations, it tripped and held.
Shredding the hem of his shirt, Serdor pressed a ball of
threads into her hand. "Stuff this in the keyhole. If they've
got a key with them, it'll keep them from using it."

The cells on the third level were laid out in a rectangle
girdled by corridors. The doors were consecutively numbered. Skating around the southwest corner of the passage,
Rhan gave a suppressed whoop of triumph. "Look! There it
is—Number Nine!"

"I'll stand guard here while you open the door," said
Serdor to Margoth. To Rhan, he said, "You take the far end
of the corridor. You'll be able to see the stair leading up to
the main hall from there. Make for it on my signal. And
don't wait around. Understand?"

Rhan nodded and slipped away. Drawing the sergeant's
rapier, Serdor took up his station, watching the stairs. A
series of bangs and curses told him that the guards had

initiated their assault. He hoped the lock would hold long enough to buy his party the time they needed.

A scuffling sound at the door and a voice calling his name snapped Caradoc out of a black reverie. Casting aside the dark meditations of despair, he rose to his feet, his breath quickening.

The lock on the door rattled, then clicked. Husky with incredulity, Caradoc said, "*Margoth?*"

The cell door flew open. "No, it's the Great Khan of Vladistock," said his sister, and flung her arms around him.

Clinging to her in sheer bewilderment—"What the hell are you doing here?" asked Caradoc.

"Getting you out of trouble," said Margoth. Worming herself free of his embrace, she seized him by the hand and pulled him toward the corridor. "Come on! We haven't got much time!"

Stumbling after her, Caradoc balked at the sight of a guardsman in livery. "Never mind—that's only Serdor," said Margoth. "Here, this way."

Her last words were drowned in a tumultuous crash from the other side of the cellblock. "That was the door! Here they come!" shouted Serdor. "Make for the stairs!"

The minstrel was already in motion. After one quick backward glance to make sure his friends were following, Rhan abandoned his post and sprinted ten feet to the base of a broad flight of steps leading upward. The air was ringing with cries and pounding feet. Overriding a possibly fatal impulse to linger, he raced for the cover of the landing.

He reached it a split second before half a dozen soldiers hammered past in a blur of flashing accoutrements. Aghast, Rhan stared after them, the blood congealing in his veins as he realized that the others in his party had just been cut off.

CHAPTER 36

The Race

Overtaking Margoth and Caradoc, Serdor led the way toward the stairs. They were still two doors away from the bend in the corridor when he heard, above the patter of their own feet, the thunder of heavy boots converging on them from around the corner.

He skidded to a halt before a bristling thicket of drawn swords. "That's far enough," said a cold voice from behind the ranked guardsmen.

The voice was familiar. Stepping back, Serdor scanned the array of stony faces before him, and recognized the lean, lantern-jawed visage of the captain of the guard he had last encountered at the city gates.

Their eyes met, and the other man lifted a pale eyebrow. "Well, well. Master Sulamith, if I remember rightly," said Captain Du Coverlay. "I also seem to recall that *music* was your trade."

The light of the nearest torch struck steel as he drew his sword and stepped forward. His men edged aside to let him pass. Blade-point glinting at eye-level between them—"You appear to have taken up a new career," said the captain. "Let's see how proficient you are at it." Holding his subordinates at bay with a sidewise gesture he added gently, "En garde," and his rapier lashed out. Serdor recoiled, jerking his own blade upright. Metal grated as the two swords met.

"Not a very impressive parry, Master Sulamith," said the captain. "See if you can do better this time—"

His weapon licked out again. A split second too late to deflect it, Serdor took the point of it in a raking line along the crest of his left shoulder.

He caught his breath sharply and staggered back. Spurning the protection offered by Serdor's body, Margoth spat, "You *bastard!*" and let fly with her poniard.

It took the captain between armpit and collarbone, hurling him back among his men. Their ranks broke as his falling form crashed through the armored file. There was a brief paralyzed moment before the captain's men gave a collective roar and surged forward from both sides.

The only refuge offered was a door a few feet to their left. "There! Get back!" panted the minstrel, pointing.

Caradoc swept the torch from the wall overhead and thrust it into the face of his foremost attacker. Kicking the legs out from under a second would-be assailant, he seized his sister by the arm and thrust her toward the door Serdor had indicated.

It was not locked. Tumbling across the threshold, she fetched up hard against a heavy wooden table. "Get ready!" shouted her brother.

Snatching the sword from Serdor's hand, he slashed a whistling arc of fire in the air between themselves and their attackers. Momentarily daunted by the length of his reach, the guardsmen hung back a critical split instant. With no time to spare on courtesy, Caradoc spun his wounded friend unceremoniously through the doorway and dived in after him. Margoth slammed the door shut behind them in the faces of the pursuers.

There was a thick iron bolt on the inside. His shoulder jammed against the door, Caradoc shoved it firmly into place. A tattoo of purposeful fists broke out on the other side.

They were inside what appeared to be a receiving area for stores and provisions. Kneeling on the floor, Serdor drew a hissing breath and swore out loud. Glancing around, Caradoc saw that he was gripping his left shoulder. The cloth under Serdor's clenchéd fingers was crimson.

The door shuddered under a blow from outside, but the bolt held firm. Caradoc left his post and dropped to his haunches beside Serdor.

"Take your hand away," he ordered, and when the minstrel obeyed, widened the tear in Serdor's sleeve, laying bare the wound beneath.

Bleeding freely, the deep gash ran across the minstrel's upper arm and continued along his left shoulder blade. Caradoc ripped a two-inch strip from the hem of his own shirt. Wadding the extra material of the shirt against the wound, he bound it tightly in place, disregarding Serdor's involuntary protests. "That ought to hold the bleeding," he said above the mounting tumult from outside. "Now all we have to do is devise a way to walk through walls."

Margoth paused in the act of dragging the table across the doorway. Panting, she said between breaths, "What . . . about Rhan?"

"I didn't see—or hear—him," said Serdor. "He may have reached the stairs in time."

"Who's Rhan?" demanded Caradoc.

Serdor closed his eyes, his face ashen. "A boy I met on my travels—"

The air in the room shivered with a splintering, staccato crack. The door jumped on its hinges, its timbers fraying under a fresh form of assault. Wincing as stroke followed stroke, Caradoc said, "How astute. Someone's gone and fetched an axe. Worry about your young friend later. We've got more than enough trouble of our own just now."

Serdor picked himself up in a sequence of jerks. "Don't give up yet. What's that over there?"

Following the line of Serdor's pointing finger, Caradoc caught sight of a recess set into the left-hand wall. The recess was backed by a wooden panel three feet long and two feet high. "That looks like it would move," said Caradoc, scowling. "Let's see if it leads anywhere."

The panel opened sideways. Beyond lay a dark opening redolent of cooking-fat and woodsmoke. Turning his head to look up a long dark shaft, Caradoc gave an experimental sniff. "Unless I miss my guess, this connects with the kitchen!"

Serdor flinched at a crash from outside. "That's good enough for me."

"Can you climb a rope with your arm like that?" protested Margoth.

"I won't have to. The delivery platform is here at the bottom. We'll ride up on that," said Serdor. "Get in."

It was direly cramped inside the shaft. "I'll need some help working the ropes," said Caradoc. "Margoth, can you manage it?"

"I can if you give me a few inches more space," said Margoth. "Duck your head, Serdor—oh, God, the outside door's starting to split!"

Whining, the pulleys ground into motion. "This thing was never meant to bear so much weight," grunted Caradoc. "Let's hope it holds out!"

Below them the sound of the shouts and axe-strokes rose clearly through the dead air in the shaft. "Hurry up!" urged Serdor, peering over the edge of the platform. "If they break through before we reach the top, all they've got to do is cut the rope and we're done for."

The platform continued to rise with agonizing slowness. The shaft echoed eerily with their labored breathing. Seconds drained away. Then, squinting upward through the darkness, Caradoc picked out the distorted but definite outline of a second doorway, limned in the light of the room beyond.

Working like troglodytes, they drew even with it a moment later. Caradoc struck the door a blow with his fist, intending to leap out as soon as they stopped moving. To his chagrin, the panel refused to yield.

"Damn! Somebody's snibbed it on the other side," he hissed. "I'll have to see if I can break it."

The platform rocked precariously as he threw his full weight against the door. On the fourth try, it gave way with a splitting bang. He knocked the shards of veneer out of the way, groping for the latch with a long arm. He found it and released the catch.

Margoth was first out of the shaft. "All clear!" she whispered back. Caradoc swung himself headfirst through the opening and somersaulted onto the floor. Pivoting from a crouch, he extended one arm to the minstrel. "Here," he said. "Steady now . . ."

As Serdor rose from his knees, a sudden upsurge in the noise from the room below announced the delayed arrival of the Ambrothen Regulars. He leaped for the open door. In the same instant, the planking beneath his feet shuddered and shot out from under him.

Caradoc heard the crash as the platform rebounded off the wall of the shaft on its way down. Aghast, he lunged forward, half expecting to see nothing but the end of a severed rope.

Instead, he caught sight of the minstrel's head and shoulders eddying in circles two ells below the level of the door. "Hang on!" he called down.

Serdor closed his eyes tightly against the dark, dizzying spin of the rope and the burning strain on his torn shoulder. His back muscles rigid with tension, Caradoc braced himself hard against the sill and caught the hanging cable in both hands.

"Hurry!" pleaded Margoth, wringing her hands.

"I can't," gritted Caradoc. "If I move too sharply, he may fall."

They were within two feet of each other. With an agonizing clarity of vision, Caradoc could see his friend's clenched fingers sliding downward toward the last dwindling foot of the rope's end. His forearms trembled with strain as he took in line hand over hand. His whitened knuckles were within an inch of Serdor's when his grip slipped.

The backlash slammed Serdor's injured shoulder into the wall. He gasped and lost his hold. In the same heartbeat, powerful fingers viced themselves around his right wrist and clung tightly.

His elbow and shoulder straightened with a snap as Caradoc reared back against the force of his plunging weight. For a second or two it seemed as if they would both topple over into the shaft. Hands dug into Caradoc's belt from behind. "Brace yourselves!" panted Margoth, and pulled back.

Together, they achieved counterpoise. Adding the failing strength of his left hand to Caradoc's saving grip, Serdor scrambled for a foothold on the wall of the shaft and succeeded in flinging an elbow over the doorsill. Dropping one hand, Caradoc caught him by the back of his shirt and hoisted. A breath later, they both tumbled sideways to safety.

Margoth stood back as they disentangled themselves. Her eyes were brimming with fright. Serdor gave her a wan grin. " 'At the backe of a goode manne ys to bee founde a bettre womanne. . . .' *Not* my finest moment, but it's over now."

She grinned shakily back at him. "We'd better be going," said Caradoc. "It won't take much imagination to figure out where we've gone—"

He cut himself short. There was a series of squeaks and rattles and a sudden heavy bump against the door in the opposite wall.

A hand tripped the latch from the other side. They made a scrambling lunge for the back of the door and flattened themselves to the wall as it opened.

There was another rattle, and two white-clad figures backed through the doorway, towing behind them a wheeled hand-cart laden with tin plates and mugs. Caradoc waited until they were clear of the door before collaring them from behind.

There was an unnerving thud as their heads came together. Knees nervelessly buckling, the two unconscious cooks sagged toward the floor. "Close the door!" hissed Caradoc, and hooked the handcart out of the way with his foot.

The kitchen beyond, for the moment, was deserted. Serdor turned his attention to their two victims, anonymous in bleached smocks and peaked white caps. Eyeing the taller of the two men critically, the minstrel said to Caradoc, "He's near enough your size," and he twitched the man's cap from his head. "Here: put this on. . . ."

CHAPTER 37

The Lost Sheep

Shortly before sundown, Delsidor Whitfauconer, Lord Warden of East Garillon, accompanied by a dozen armed attendants, rode out through the main gate of Ambrothen Castle, ostensibly to dine at the home of the city's Lord Mayor. That he had a later, far more dangerous appointment to keep elsewhere was a secret he shared with no one, not even the men who were with him.

His wife watched his departure from an upper window of the castle's guesthouse, a luxuriously-appointed annex overlooking a broad sweep of formal garden. Once the gates had closed behind him, she lingered a moment longer, her expression arrested in thought. Then she dismissed her maid and went off to confer with her brother, the Seneschal of Ambrothen.

Fyanor Du Bors had some important covert business of his own to transact that night. He was in the act of drawing on his gloves when his sister was admitted to his presence. Waiting until the servants had gone, Gwynmira spoke, her voice brittle as glass, "I see you still intend to go ahead with this miserable charade. Is there no way I can persuade you to give it up?"

Fyanor's color rose slightly. Twitching the gem-stitched sleeves of his doublet into place, he said acidly, "I would be

257

only too ready to do so, sister dear, if you could present me with a reasonable alternative.''

"It is an outrage that you should allow yourself to be used in this manner,'' said his sister.

Fyanor shrugged. "I fail to see that we have any other choice—unless you would prefer to brave your husband's avenging wrath.''

Gwynmira's chiseled face was hard as ivory. "It might be preferable to enduring this present indignity. I'm not afraid, even if you are, to challenge Delsidor on his own ground.''

"Aren't you? I pay tribute to your nerve, but not to your wit,'' said her brother candidly. "Permit me to point out that bravado is a poor substitute for adequate military support. Until we find ourselves in a position to consolidate our alliances, we would do better to play the game by the brigand's rules, little though we may relish the idea.''

He plucked a dark cloak from the back of the nearest chair ard cast it about his shoulders. Then, seeing his sister's rigid disapproval, quirked an ironic eyebrow. "Contrive to exercise a little patience, my heart. Sooner or later, one or the other of our adversaries is bound to make a mistake, and when that happens, I promise I shall make the most of the opportunity.''

He took his leave of her then, after kissing her hand with punctilious courtesy. Gwynmira did not immediately return to her own quarters. Alone in her brother's study, she took a restless turn about the floor, pausing before a half-length mirror to see the signs of recent tension sharply reflected in her own face.

It was a bitter revelation to discover that she looked fully the thirty-seven years of her age. This situation must not be allowed to continue, she told the image in the mirror. And her mind turned vindictively to the boy none of them had seen in weeks.

She was still standing before the mirror when Commander Ildevek arrived with the news that several prisoners had escaped from the West Tower.

The commander's beetroot complexion betrayed his shocked

incredulity that such a thing could have happened in spite of his careful routines. Gwynmira, however, was in no mood to be sparing. "This is a serious breach of vigilance," she said cuttingly. "Are you prepared to account for it?"

The commander drew himself up stiffly. "The prisoners may have had some outside assistance, milady. All of them are thought to be still at large within the castle grounds." He added, "In the absence of both Lord Fyanor and His Grace the Lord Warden, the authority of command rests with you, milady. I have taken the liberty of mobilizing the garrison. Beyond that, my men and I wait upon your orders."

"Have you doubled the guard on the outer walls? Very well. Then the rest must be divided up into smaller search parties. I understand that many of your own men are on temporary assignment outside the Keep as a result of the recent criminal investigations," said Gwynmira. "Those members of our own retinue who are not presently with my husband will be placed at your disposal until the prisoners are recaptured. . . ."

Lieutenant Cergil Ap Cymric had not been included in the Warden's escort. Less than well-pleased at having been left behind on routine guard duty, he welcomed his new orders when they came.

The fact that the escaped prisoners included none other than Caradoc Penlluathe fired Cergil with a sense of keen and personal commitment. Leaving three privates behind to guard the entrances to the Warden's quarters, he sent the rest of the men under his command to join the patrols along the castle's perimeter. He himself, with his sergeant in attendance, took the more direct route through the castle gardens.

It was by then after nightfall. Pausing in the dark shelter of a trellised arbor, Cergil was about to comment disparagingly on the amount of noise coming from the direction of the West Tower itself when his ears picked up a subtler sound—the rustle of furtive movement in the shadow of an ornamental hedge not far away.

Motioning Sergeant Runlaf to take up a flanking position, Cergil remained where he was, watching and waiting. A moment later a dark shape emerged from beneath the hedge and scuttled across open ground toward a second line of shrubbery. Grinning mirthlessly in the twilight, Cergil slid lightly into action, arms gripped tightly to his sides to muffle any betraying jingle of chain mail.

He was not quite stealthy enough. Warned, the figure abruptly changed direction. Shouting for Runlaf, Cergil abandoned stealth and broke into a run. His quarry, coursing like a hare, gained the shadows and vanished. Coming to a baffled halt under a bay tree, Cergil scanned the moon-silvered tangle of trees, then caught sight of the fugitive again, limned in moonlight against a backdrop of blackberry bushes.

Cergil gathered his muscles and sprang. Thin branches snapped as his weight carried him crashing through the bracken. He caught his victim broadside in a flying tackle, and the two of them went cannoning into the bushes, flailing for balance among thorns sharp as ferrets' teeth.

Cergil's arms closed around a slight, threshing body. His adversary went limp and slithered through his grasp like a wet eel. Cergil dropped with him, trying to pin the other's slender frame to the ground.

He encountered a blow on the point of his chin that brought the water to his eyes, then grunted as a sharp-boned elbow rammed home against his ribs. His armor took the brunt of the second blow, but it was enough to tell him that his frail-seeming opponent was not wholly unskilled in the art of self-defense. Gritting his teeth, Cergil relinquished all delicacy and set about subduing his wildcat counterpart by fair means or foul.

It wasn't easy, despite his superior strength. His adversary fought him with a kind of prodigal desperation that demanded all the energy he had in reserve as they rolled back and forth over a lacerating bed of broken brambles, kicking and clawing like cats in a gutter.

Finally he got a grip on his opponent's jutting collarbone and held on tightly. His victim writhed under the pressure of his fingers, then struck out at him.

He caught the flying fist and twisted it so that arm and shoulder were forced agonizingly out of alignment. His prisoner sobbed once on a ragged note and abruptly stopped struggling as Cergil's controlling hands bore him to the ground.

Cergil pinned his captive's wrists with one hand while he blinked the congealing sweat out of his eyes and tried to recover his temper. The fugitive lay unresisting in his grip, drawing breath in retching, tumultuous gasps.

Listening, Cergil realized, with a tentative pang of concern, that his unknown adversary was exhausted to the point of nausea from his part in the struggle. Investigating by touch, he came to the startling conclusion that his prisoner was only a boy.

He called out to Runlaf, then waited. A moment later a dark lantern uncovered itself beyond a screen of dense bushes and came bobbing toward them like a will-o'-the-wisp.

The boy on the ground shrank away from the groping touch of the light. "Why, he's just a young 'un," exclaimed Runlaf, peering. "Where did he come from, sir?"

"I don't know," said Cergil, "but he's going to tell me double-quick. Aren't you, my lad?"

The buff-blond head remained obstinately averted. Cergil took hold of one shoulder and gave him an admonitory shake. "I asked you a question: how did you get in here?"

Lying prone on the grass, Rhan took a moment to prepare himself for the inevitable. Then he rolled over onto his side and looked his captor squarely in the eye with all the defiance he could muster.

He was dumbfounded when his captor's expression underwent an astonishing transformation. The guardsman blinked once, then drew himself up, his face as white as his shirt. He swallowed, and said on a single, constricted note, *"Evelake . . ."*

The other guardsman made a small movement. "My God! Are you sure, sir?"

Cergil squared his shoulders. His color had not yet returned. "As sure as we're standing here."

His subordinate goggled at him. "How the devil . . . ?"

"I don't know," said Cergil. "And he doesn't seem disposed to tell me."

"What's wrong with him, sir?" asked Runlaf. "If he knows you, he doesn't act like it."

"He doesn't know me, or himself, at the moment," said Cergil grimly. "That renegade mage swore something like this had been done to the boy. He appears to have been telling the truth."

The boy sustained the sergeant's wondering gaze in rebellious silence. "What are we going to do with him, sir?" asked Runlaf.

"Get him inside, for starters," said Cergil. "And then we'd better send for the Lady Gwynmira."

When Gwynmira received word by way of one of her husband's guardsmen that her presence was urgently required back in her own quarters, she was both surprised and displeased. Regarding the young private before her with hard eyes, the Warden's consort said with icy neutrality, "You will be so good, sir, as to explain to me what this is all about."

The private shuffled his feet uncomfortably. "Begging your pardon, milady, but I don't know any more than I've told you. All Lieutenant Cergil said was that he'd made a discovery that called for your immediate attention, and that he hoped you'd understand once you'd seen it for yourself."

The sheer presumption of the request—coming as it did from one of her husband's junior officers—argued that the matter might, after all, be worth looking into. "Very well. I shall come," announced Gwynmira. "But if I find that my time has been wasted, you and your officer will answer for it."

When they approached the guest-wing, her guide made for the side door adjoining the kitchen, where they were met by Sergeant Runlaf. Relinquishing his post to his subordinate, he said, "Thank you for coming, milady," making his obeisance. "If you will please come this way . . ."

He led her upstairs and down half a length of corridor.

Pausing at the door of the morning room, he gave three measured raps on the outside paneling.

The door opened immediately. "Milady!" exclaimed Cergil, and bowed deeply. Stepping aside to allow her room to enter, he added fervently, "Thank God you've come! Perhaps you'll be able to get through to him."

The object of this reference stood bristling against the adjacent wall. "I haven't been able to get so much as a syllable out of him," continued Cergil. "When I offered him water to clean himself up, he threw the basin at me and tried to jump out the window."

Gwynmira stared at the hostile, highly-strung guttersnipe, then drew a short, sharp breath as the realization hit her.

Without taking her eyes off the boy, she said softly, "Where did you find him?"

"Here—in the gardens, milady."

"How . . . how on earth did he get there?"

"I don't know. I don't think he has any idea who he is."

Gwynmira's face was bloodless. "Who else has seen him like this?"

"No one, milady—apart from the sergeant and myself," said Cergil. He paused, then added hesitantly, "Perhaps I've been unnecessarily circumspect, but it seemed to me that it might not be a good idea to publicize the fact before the mages have had a chance to examine him."

"I commend your discretion, lieutenant," said Gwynmira. The taut lines in her neck relaxed. "You are quite right: too many questions too soon could only aggravate his present confusion."

Her gaze returned to her stepson's scratched, defiant face. "Poor boy—we can only guess at the strain of his condition. Until the Grand Master of Ambrothen can be summoned to tend him, all we can do is try to make him comfortable."

She had recovered her air of decision. "None of the servants must see him like this. Keep him in here and let no one enter. I shall order a refection for myself and bring it here. Perhaps some wine would help to relax him. I'll make sure he is provided with the refreshment he so obviously needs, and meanwhile, if you would kindly remain with him in my absence, I would be most grateful.''

She returned a short time later, carrying a laden tray. The boy watched her in stony silence as she set it down on the nearest table. ''You must forgive me if it isn't perfectly served,'' she said with a gentle smile. ''I am not accustomed to such work. The quality of the wine, however, will be above reproach.''

When he still remained stubbornly aloof, she drew up a chair and beckoned to him. ''You are tired, and I can see that you're hungry. Please sit down. What harm could there be in availing yourself of our hospitality?''

When she continued to wait with every appearance of expectation, he gave her a long look. Then he walked stiffly over to the table and took the seat she offered him.

''That's better,'' said Gwynmira approvingly. She poured wine into a goblet and set it before him, then filled two others to the brim. These she presented to Cergil and Runlaf. ''I think perhaps our young friend will feel more at ease if you keep him company. There's plenty of wine. Please don't be shy of sharing it.''

Feeling extremely self-conscious, Cergil lifted the glass to his lips and took a swallow. The sergeant did the same. ''I must leave you now,'' said Gwynmira, her eyes following their movements. ''I have pressing duties waiting for me back at the donjon, and I have been away too long as it is.''

She moved toward the door, then paused, hand on the lintel. ''You need fear no intrusions—I've seen to that. I shall return, myself, as soon as I may. . . .''

CHAPTER 38

The Revelation

Coming away white-lipped from his meeting with the lady. Gwynmira, Commander Ildevek marched off to the West Tower to supervise the proceedings in person. In his absence, his subordinates paired up, according to instructions, and began roving the halls of the main buildings.

They searched the state rooms on the ground floor of the west wing one by one. The two privates assigned to the environs of the state dining hall made a thorough survey of the premises. They were just leaving by the north door when two figures in white came around the bend in the corridor from the direction of the kitchen.

They were carrying between them a canvas sling suspended from their shoulders by wide straps of leather. The sling, covered by a sheet or tarpaulin, was piled with goods. "And just where do you think you're going with that?" demanded the stockier of the two privates.

The two kitcheners stopped dead in their tracks. The shorter of the pair, who happened to be in front, widened grey eyes ingenuously. "Back to the Warden's kitchen, sir."

"Back?" The private glared at him suspiciously.

"Oh, aye: the steward sent us across to collect the supplies he'd requested for the Warden's table," explained the kitchener. His curiosity plainly aroused, he added, "Is anything wrong, sir?"

"There are some escaped prisoners loose somewhere within the castle grounds," said the stockier of the two privates shortly. "We'll escort you back to the annex to make sure you don't run into any trouble on the way."

A long, cloisterlike gallery connected the east wing of the citadel with the annex that had been assigned to the Warden and his staff. Pausing before a pair of oaken doors at the gallery's end, one of the privates had a sudden thought. "Put that sling down for a moment," he said to the taller of the two kitcheners. "I want to see what's in those sacks."

The kitchener looked surprised. "It's only sugar and flour and the like, sir."

"You heard me," snapped the private.

The kitchener blinked. "If you insist, sir."

He traded glances with his companion. Together they lowered their burden to the floor and shrugged themselves free of the harness.

The stocky guardsman hunkered down next to the litter and lifted one corner of the concealing drapery. As he did so a lashing foot hooked him under the chin and sent him flying.

Caught off guard for a fatal split instant, the other private spun around and took a balled fist squarely in the midriff. As he doubled over wheezing, his assailant kneed him under the jaw. He grunted and collapsed in a muted clank of chain mail.

His colleague was lying half-stunned in a heap by the nearest wall. Serdor hit him hard enough to finish the job before rejoining the others. "God, you do favor the near-run thing, don't you?" said Margoth, throwing off the coverlet. She stood up and surveyed the two fallen guardsmen. "We'd better hide the evidence."

After a brief reconnoiter, they dragged the two guardsmen through the double doors into a branching corridor. They deposited their prey in what turned out to be a broom closet. Closing the door, Serdor muttered, "We've got to find a way out. Rhan knew the plan was to cut through the gardens. If he's still free, that's where he'll be waiting."

"And if he's not there?" whispered Caradoc.

"Then I'll have to go looking for him," said Serdor grimly, and abruptly shut his mouth as Margoth's fingers clamped down hard upon his arm.

There were measured footsteps coming toward them along the right-hand branch of the passageway.

There was a stairway behind them. Beating a hasty tiptoe retreat, the fugitives gained the flight above the landing before the other party turned the corner. Crouching on the steps out of sight, Caradoc heard a door open and close, followed by silence. Turning, he was about to signal that the coast was clear when he realized that Serdor and Margoth had disappeared.

Picking himself up, he bounded to the top of the stairs and discovered Serdor and Margoth bending over something that was piled untidily, like so much bunting, against a door twenty feet away.

It was the body of a man in the livery of the Farrowaithe Guard. Caradoc knelt and laid two questing fingers over the artery in the throat. "He's dead!" he murmured.

Margoth's blue eyes widened. "But there's not a mark on him."

"No. Just at a guess," said her brother, "I'd say this man was poisoned."

"That doesn't make any sense," protested Serdor. "Unless someone has taken advantage of all the excitement to settle an old grudge. . . ."

"Serdor?"

The voice, oddly muffled, came from the other side of the door. Serdor snapped upright. "Rhan?" he said on a sharp note of incredulity.

"Yes, it's me! Please—get me out of here!"

The boy's tone was shrill with fearful urgency. "All right, I'm coming," said Serdor.

Margoth fumbled at the dead man's belt. "Here are the keys," she said, pressing them into Serdor's hand. "That's the right one."

Serdor fitted the key to the lock. The mechanism yielded and he flung the door open. "Serdor! Oh, God, I'm glad to see you!'' declared Rhan, and threw himself into the minstrel's quick, hard embrace.

Entering behind Serdor, Margoth saw a pair of booted legs sprawled out on the floor beyond a small cluster of chairs. ''Look!'' she said, and pointed. Ignoring for the moment Serdor's young counterpart, Caradoc strode over to investigate.

Rhan was shivering violently. ''What's wrong?'' demanded Serdor. ''What have they done to you?''

Rhan pulled himself away. ''I'm all right,'' he said shakily. ''But I think he's dying.''

Following the trembling line of his pointing finger, Serdor became aware for the first time of the man lying prone on the carpet. ''Easy now—Caradoc will know what to do for him,'' he said quietly. ''Tell me what happened.''

Rhan covered his face wearily with his hands. ''You were right not to want to bring me,'' he said through his meshed fingers. ''The lieutenant caught me as I was making for the port. He and the sergeant brought me here . . . I—I'm sorry.''

''It doesn't matter,'' said Serdor gently. ''What happened after that?''

Rhan lifted his head. ''There was a lot of talk I didn't understand. Then a woman came to see me. . . .''

He shivered, his face white beneath the bruises. ''I don't know how to explain it, but the moment she entered the room, I felt a terrific wrench inside me—as if I were going to fly into pieces. It hurt so much I thought for a moment I was going to faint, though I don't think any of them noticed—''

He broke off abruptly. Serdor wrapped a steadying arm around Rhan's quaking shoulders. ''Don't worry: strange things often happen to people in times of stress. . . .''

''You don't understand!'' protested Rhan vehemently. ''I *knew* she wanted me dead. That's why I refused the wine when she brought it.''

Serdor stared at him in mute astonishment. ''I refused, but the guards didn't,'' continued Rhan, his words tumbling chokingly over each other. ''Not ten minutes after she'd gone, the poison started to take effect. . . .''

He swallowed hard and drew a deep breath. "Serdor, why should a woman I've never met before want to kill me?"

"I don't know," said Serdor frankly. "Have you any idea who she was?"

"The guardsmen addressed her," said Rhan, "as 'Lady Gwynmira'—"

"Good God!"

The exclamation came from Caradoc. Startled by the tone in his voice, Serdor whipped around to find his friend staring at Rhan in dumbfounded amazement. Gripping the edge of the nearest table as if he felt badly in need of its support, Caradoc said, "That's not the boy who accompanied you in here."

The words carried an odd inflection. "Yes, it is. What the devil's the matter with you?" snapped Serdor.

"Nothing . . ." said Caradoc, and gave himself a shake. He added, "I'll tell you later, once we're well away from here."

For an instant Serdor was tempted to press for an immediate explanation, but a glance at Caradoc's face made him think better of it. "What about him?" asked Rhan, pointing toward the form of his erstwhile captor.

Caradoc had not taken his eyes off the boy's face. "He's still breathing," he said. "But I don't know how much longer he'll be able to hang on without the offices of a mage."

"Can't you do anything?" asked Margoth.

"Not without my magestone," said Caradoc.

"Well, we can't just leave him here," said Serdor. "Anybody got any ideas how to attract some attention without getting ourselves captured in the process?"

Caradoc's gaze swept the room and lighted upon the curtains at the window. A reminiscent gleam came into his eye. "I believe I might have a suggestion," he said. "A trick I learned from an acquaintance of mine. . . ."

It required only minimal preparations. While Serdor and the boy carried the lieutenant to the threshold, Caradoc borrowed helmet, cuirass, and sword from the dead man. Nipping Serdor by the sleeve on the way out, he whispered, "I know now why these guards were poisoned. Your young friend there has some dangerous enemies."

"Rhan?" Serdor looked totally bemused. "But he's only a serving-boy."

"That's his story," said Caradoc. "His real name—though you never would have gotten it from him—is Evelake Whitfauconer. . . ."

As the search for the missing prisoners continued unrewarded, every arms-bearing man in the Keep was eventually drawn into the chase. Called out along with the remaining members of the Warden's retinue, Gudmar and Harlech strapped on broadswords for the sake of appearances and went off, reluctantly, to do what was expected of them.

By then, two cooks belonging to the castle's kitchen staff had been found stripped, bound, and gagged behind a row of flour sacks in the main pantry. This, coupled with the fact that two of Ildevek's men had gone missing, presented the problem in a whole new light. "Ye've got tae give our laddie his due," said Harlech, watching with mordant appreciation as the two hapless turnspits were shepherded away to put on some clothes. "He's learnt a thing or twa since Lauristen."

"Oh, I'll allow Caradoc doesn't want for wit," said Gudmar. "I just hope he survives long enough to cultivate some sense."

With two of their own unaccounted for, Ildevek's men departed to scour the building with fresh fervor. Counting Ambrothen Regulars in double figures, Harlech said with a sniff, "There's that many scarlet cloaks clumbering up and doun the halls, they'll be trippin' over each other's swords before long. How would ye fancy a breath o' fresh air just now?"

They left the citadel by the main entrance. The grounds beyond were flecked with bobbing yellow lights. As Gudmar surveyed the scene from the low terrace fronting the entryway, his eye caught an anomalous sputter of crimson from an upstairs window in the nearest of the citadel's outbuildings: the Warden's annex.

Someone had set a fire in the room adjoining Delsidor's assigned apartment.

Vaulting low bushes like hurdles, Gudmar reached the front door well ahead of Harlech. Shouting to the two soldiers on duty, he charged up the main stairway and followed the trail of escaping smoke around the corner toward the morning room.

Two guardsmen were sprawled out in the hall beyond the morning-room door. The air was pungent with the stink of burning wool. Catching the foremost of his followers by the elbow, Gudmar pointed him toward the room beyond, where the walls were dyed with firelight. "Quick! Douse those curtains!" he ordered. "I'll see what I can do for these men."

One of them, he discovered with a chilling shock, was beyond all mortal aid. The other wasn't much better off. Clattering to a halt behind him, Harlech puffed, "Bloody hell!" and peered over Gudmar's shoulder at the dead man's livid face. "He's a mite young t've died of the apoplexy."

"I'm sure the mages would agree with you," said Gudmar. "There's something very strange going on here."

Rising off his haunches, he stepped over the corpse into the room. The guards had the curtains down and were trampling on the resurgent flames. The carpet by the window, oddly enough, had been soaked through. More striking still was the fact that the table in the center of the room had been furnished for a meal. Scowling, Gudmar stalked over to take a closer look.

The meal, evidently, had been intended for three people. There was one empty wineglass standing by one of the place settings, and another lying on its side among the litter of broken bread and cutlery. The third wineglass was still full to the brim.

His frown deepening, Gudmar picked up the untasted goblet, sniffed it cautiously, and set it down again. Then he reached for the decanter in the center of the table.

There was wine still left in the bottom of it. Holding it up to the light, Gudmar could make out thin flakes of some oily substance clinging like fish scales to its surface.

"If that's claret, it shouldna ha' a skin to it," said Harlech's gravelly voice in his ear.

"No," agreed Gudmar thoughtfully. Glancing over to make sure the guards were still occupied, he passed the flagon to Harlech. "Take care of this for now, will you? We've got to get the lieutenant there to St. Welleran's—and once we've done that, I intend to ask one of the magisters to test out that wine."

An outburst of running footsteps and heavy breathing signaled the arrival of reinforcements. Stepping out to meet them, Gudmar said, "It's all right. We've just about got the fire out," he continued, surveying half a dozen Farrowaithe Guards. "Unfortunately, both your officers were overcome by the smoke before we got here, and the sergeant seems to have succumbed. If you would please report his tragic death to your superiors, my friend and I will see to it that the lieutenant is taken at once to the hospital. . . ."

CHAPTER 39

The Decision

The fugitives left the Warden's annex by one of the windows at the back of the building. They hid in the shrubbery until the fire alarm was sounded, then, leaving the confusion behind them, made for the Falconer's Port.

There were six Regulars on duty at the Port, but the growing noise from the vicinity of the Warden's quarters suggested that something important was afoot. After a brief debate, the party split up and three of them went off to see what all the excitement was about.

The remaining three had just resumed their stations when a shout from off to their left brought them to attention. As one, they abandoned their sentry boxes in time to see one of their colleagues making a mad dash across the open grass in pursuit of a fleeing civilian in a drab-colored cloak.

The foremost sentry, alert to the implications of this, gave a whoop and promptly joined in the chase. His two companions fanned out in opposite directions to cut off the fugitive's line of retreat.

The guardsman caught up with his quarry just under the wall itself, several yards from the Port. The two of them struck the ground in a flying whirlwind of flailing limbs and proceeded to indulge in a fierce bout of fisticuffs.

The first sentry and his more fleet-footed comrade arrived shortly afterward, panting and eager to help. They were very much astonished, a second or two later, when both guardsman and fugitive turned on them and attacked without compunction.

By the time the third sentry got there the two attackers had been joined by two more. Grimly following the dictates of duty, the sentry launched himself into the fray and got his fingers under somebody's throat latchet.

He yanked, and the helmet came off in his hand. Red hair showed like a bonfire in the torchlight from the gate before its owner adroitly tripped him up.

His fall was punctuated by a clip on the head from behind. By the time he was able to get to his feet again, the mysterious intruders were nowhere to be seen.

Calling for lights and assistance, the sentry snatched up a lantern and dashed through the Port. Fifty yards away, the ground fell way steeply into a grass-grown ditch. Beyond the ditch, the slope continued on toward the Dyke, through terrain amply suited to offering cover. Shouting for his auxiliaries to follow, the sentry set off down the slope at a run.

Meanwhile, scuttling like rats along the curtain wall to the right of the Port, four dark figures gained the shadow of one of the watchtowers overlooking the castle-cliffs. Forty feet below them, the tide slapped and gurgled among the inland rocks that fronted the narrow strip of beach.

Serdor was the last to arrive. Catching a glimpse of his face over her shoulder as he stumbled to a halt behind her, Margoth reached forward and caught Caradoc by the sleeve. "You'd better give him a hand, if he'll let you," she whispered.

Cursing himself inwardly for his own negligence, Caradoc fell back a pace. To the minstrel he said, "Your arm—how is it?"

Serdor was obliged to breathe before answering. "I'll be all right once I get my second wind."

From his other side, Rhan's thin whisper piped up in sudden anxiety: "Serdor? . . ."

"Nothing serious," Serdor whispered back reassuringly. Caradoc wondered if the boy heard the fatigue in the minstrel's voice as clearly as he did.

He peered over the cliff's rocky edge. "It's going to be a steep climb . . ."

"Don't worry about me," said the minstrel. "You lead the way."

Overhead, feet pounded along the inner gallery of the tower and rattled en masse to a halt. Voices exchanged a rapid-fire series of questions and answers. There was a disciplined clash of weaponry and the boots hammered into motion again. Edging past Margoth, Caradoc dropped to his hands and knees and eased himself backward through a gap in the supporting rock of the cliffside.

His feet, skidding, found a ledge. Balancing precariously, he squinted down between his legs and marked three more footholds below. Anchoring himself by handgrips, he dropped another six feet and hissed, "Come on!"

Margoth came next, and Rhan after. Serdor brought up the rear. A twenty-foot crab-walk along a tilting slash in the rock brought them to a point where the tide had undermined the foundations of the escarpment. Beyond, the cliff-face divided into two heavy bulwarks that sloped away from each other at acute angles.

Knees tucked under him, spine arching outward, Caradoc wormed his way into the defile, gripping the back-slanting inner face of the cliff with taut fingers. Strain tugged at the small of his back as he shuffled sideways, toes digging into the slanting floor of the hollow. Ten feet farther along, he came to a vertical trough leading down to the beach.

Shifting onto his belly, he let go with his hands and slithered to the bottom in a cascade of small pebbles. Margoth joined him a few seconds later. As he guided her to safe footing, the sound of shouting broke out on the wind.

He looked back sharply and saw pale asters of torchlight blooming along the line of the clifftop in the direction from which they had come. A rattle overhead signaled Rhan's arrival. Plucking the boy bodily off the wall into a black pool of shadow, Caradoc whispered harshly, "Where's Serdor?"

The face of the Warden's son showed a white flash of alarm. "Right behind me—"

In the same instant there was a sudden crackle of loosened rock. Something dark tumbled outward off the cliff-face and landed with a thud among the boulders twenty feet away.

Rhan stifled a cry behind his hands and sprang forward. Catching him by the shoulders, Caradoc forced him back. Giving his sister a fierce warning look, he gritted, "Stay here! I'll go—"

Then he shrank back as the beach beyond came suddenly to life with dancing lights.

Voices filtered down to them out of the general confusion of movement and discussion, and the rocks along the water-line sprang into sudden stark relief as a long tongue of yellow light swept across the sand. "Close your eyes!" hissed Caradoc in Rhan's ear, then ducked low among the weed-encrusted rocks as torchfire flickered past his head.

Shoulder to shoulder, they waited breathlessly for the shout that would mean their discovery. After an eternity of seconds, the lights washed back up the cliff-face and the boots trampled on.

Squirming, Rhan made an effort to break free of Caradoc's restraining grip. "Not yet!" breathed Caradoc. "Hold still and listen!"

For a long moment neither of them moved while the gruff conclave of guardsmen's voices gradually faded away in the distance. Straining his ears in the darkness, Caradoc caught above the soft slap of the incoming tide a small scuffle of movement and an aspirated murmur of pain.

They found the minstrel half-sitting, half-lying in the shelter of a large boulder a few feet from the base of the cliff. "What happened?" demanded Margoth, flinging herself down on her knees beside him.

Serdor shifted his weight and winced. "It was either jump for it, or get caught like a fly on a wall. I decided to jump."

"It looked to me as if you fell," said Caradoc, helping him to his feet. "Are you all right?"

Serdor nodded. "Just a bit shaken up, that's all."

There was a wet patch over his left shoulder blade. "You're bleeding again," said Caradoc.

He scanned the shoreline to the northwest, where the cliffs leveled out. A stretch of beach and a shallow estuary separated them from the watchtower on a neighboring spur of high ground. Its outline looked blurred against the dim sky. "There's a fog coming in. If it gets thick enough soon enough, we just might be able to make it to the cathedral."

"The cathedral!" Serdor's drooping head came up with a jerk. "You can't be serious. You'd be spotted before you got within a stone's throw of the gate. . . ."

"Which is why I intend to go in over the back wall. Listen," said Caradoc. "You need medical attention and I need to talk with Forgoyle. If we hurry, there's every likelihood that he'll still be on the premises. I'll wait for you in the crypt. Once he's had a chance to patch you up, have him come and meet me there."

To discuss how best to safeguard the life of Evelake Whitfauconer. . . .

CHAPTER 40

The Cathedral

The shallow stream known as Drumlyn Burn flowed through the city from the cannon-gate to the beach, where it debouched into Ambrothen Bay a quarter mile north of the castle. Engineers of a century earlier had erected a bridge over the Burn when a road had been built from the castle to Drumlyn Tower, a secondary fortification occupying a neighboring spit of high ground. Beneath the bridge, the water-weeds tugged seaward in the pull of the light current.

The waters of Drumlyn Burn were cold. Squelching along with the stream washing past his thighs, Caradoc kept a watchful eye on the banks ahead of him where the large houses of some of the wealthiest men in Ambrothen showed dim lights above stone retaining walls.

He had parted company with his three companions at the Mercat Street viaduct, two furlongs upstream of Drumlyn Bridge. His own course was taking him another furlong farther inland, to the place where the grounds of St. Welleran's cathedral ran down to the water's edge.

He knew he had reached his goal when a darkening in the mists ahead of him gave way to tree-shapes overhanging the streambed. A muddy scramble up the embankment left him dripping and shivering among the roots of a tall willow. He did his best to wring the worst of the water from his breech-hose, then set out across the tree-grown expanse of the

278

Hospitallers' park toward the wall enclosing St. Welleran's itself.

Built solidly of stone, the wall was eight feet high. Launching himself from the ground in a standing leap, Caradoc got a firm grip on the copestones and chinned himself to the top.

He was overlooking the cathedral orchards. The cathedral itself loomed beyond, its spires rising to obscurity in the thickening mist.

A quick glance confirmed that there was no one around. He let himself down on the inside of the wall with the aid of an espaliered apple tree and made for the pool of shadows flanking the north transept.

Here the walls bowed outward in the ascendant hemisphere of leaded glass that was the Masters' Chapel. The chapel itself was unlighted. Huddled at the base of a soaring lancet of darkness, Caradoc paused to reconnoiter, then moved on.

Leaving the outer wall of the Masters' Chapel behind, he rounded the three-quarter arc of St. Chlara's, the first of three side chapels on the north side of the cathedral nave.

There was a small side door set into the wall between St. Chlara's chapel and St. Birgitta's. Under a carven frieze, the masonry receded to form a porch six feet deep. Lamps burned on either side of the portal. Caradoc drew a deep breath and backed around the base of the wall into the shelter of the overhang.

Shadows leaped up from the floor, whirling skittishly around him like a convocation of goblins. He gingerly tried the latch, breathing a sigh of relief when it shifted in his hand. With a reflexive glance over his shoulder, he slipped inside.

The door opened into the side aisle of the nave, where massive columns of grey stone soared like pillars of cloud toward the ribbed and vaulted roof. Remote at the eastern end of the nave, the high altar shimmered in a candlelit aura of incense and antiquity.

Dwarfed by dimensions of height and darkness, Caradoc made his way forward beneath the piled arches of gallery and clerestory. The tall candles on either end of the altar beckoned to him out of the shadows. He mounted the steps to the chancel and entered the sanctuary through the gate in the altar rail. A curtained alcove behind and to the left of the altar led to the door of the cathedral crypt.

The crypt was, in fact, a vast, sprawling labyrinth of vaults and passageways, some natural, some man-made, underlying the cathedral and its environs. A place of cold shifting airs and muttering darkness, where dead men's bones lay moldering under effigies in granite and marble. A place where a living man could hide among the tombs.

There were three prayer-stations arranged along the south wall of the chancel. Caradoc took a pair of votive tapers from the aumbry above the first lectern he came to. One of them he tucked into his belt. The other he lit at the altar before turning toward the crypt.

He half expected the door to be locked, but it opened quite easily when he tried it. A gust of dank air escaping over the threshold set his candle-flame guttering. Shielding it with his hand, he stepped through the doorway onto a stone landing. Beyond it, flagged steps descended into utter darkness.

He closed the door behind him and came forward to the head of the stairs. The realization that he could not guess the depth of the stairwell was faintly unnerving. Dismissing a sudden reluctance, he took a firmer grip on the taper and started down into the gloom.

The weak flicker of the candle-flame showed up a rough-hewn shaft, pitted at intervals with wrought stones to mark where the bodies of former Hospitallers had been interred in the walls. The air was heavy and chill. By the time he reached the bottommost step, he was shivering with cold.

The stairwell opened into a low, barrel-vaulted chamber lined on either hand with stone sarcophagi. A rounded archway in the wall opposite the stairs gave access to a lightless passageway beyond. The presence of more marking-stones indicated other graves beneath the floor. His footfalls echoing hollowly off bare rock, Caradoc walked the spaces between them to the corridor's mouth.

After twenty feet the tunnel took an acute turn to the left. Stalked by his own following shadow, he crept past the first of many side vaults and turned another corner into another, longer passage. Keeping close to the left-hand wall, he counted his steps. Forty paces farther, he discovered another burial chamber at the junction of a new tunnel.

As he drew even with it he met with a cold draft that blew drearily past him in long hissing sighs. Listening to its eerie soughing, Caradoc felt his flesh creep. The shadows before him seemed haunted with the whispering voices. He had, suddenly, the uncanny feeling that he was not alone.

The sense was so overmastering that he instinctively whipped around to look behind him.

In the same instant, something struck him an explosive blow on the side of the head.

The spires of St. Welleran's cathedral were lost in the incoming fog. Leading the way up a narrow side street away from Drumlyn Burn, Margoth halted at the point where the lane intersected a larger thoroughfare, and looked back toward her two companions. Pointing toward a faded signpost, she called back in a low voice, "Kersey Street—it's not far now."

Serdor nodded and squared his shoulders. His face in the gloom was a pallid blur. Trying to repress his growing concern, Rhan glanced nervously behind him. He wished he shared Margoth's confidence in the mages of Ambrothen.

Kersey Street was virtually deserted. With Margoth still going in front, they hurried along the length of it and turned into the Mercat High Street.

The buildings that lined the High Street looked surreal in the mist, their lights glowing pale and spectral behind distorted, black facades. The few people still abroad were visible only as flitting ghosts, hurrying into doorways and side streets with almost furtive haste. As they approached the broad square fronting the cathedral gates Serdor muttered, "It's unusual for this quarter of town to be so quiet."

Rhan looked ahead to where the buildings parted. It seemed to him suddenly that there was an oppressive quality emanating toward him out of the darkness—a sense of brooding menace, indefinable, but elusively familiar. His feet, unbidden, dragged to a standstill. "Serdor," he whispered, "let's go back."

"Go back?" Serdor stared at the boy in frank astonishment. Then he saw the shadow of fear in Rhan's brown eyes.

It was an expression he had seen before, on the infrequent occasions when Rhan had forced himself to talk about the nightmares that haunted his sleep. "Rhan, what is it?" he asked quietly. "What's the matter?"

Rhan hunched his angular shoulders in painful indecision. "I don't know. It feels as if we're walking into a trap."

Serdor frowned across the spacious courtyard toward the lights from the cathedral gatehouse. "What sort of trap?"

"I—I can't say." Rhan was looking more distraught than ever. "I know it doesn't sound rational, but—"

"Serdor! Serdor, is that you?"

The voice, coming out of the shadows at their backs, made them both start. Ahead of them, Margoth faded swiftly into the gloom between two buildings. Nudging Rhan into the shelter of the nearest doorway, Serdor braced himself upright and turned around. "Who's there?" he demanded.

"Who do you think it is?" snapped Forgoyle Finlevyn, stepping out into plain view. "Is that Rhan with you? Good: I'll want a word with him presently."

He turned his head and called back over his shoulder, "Arn! I've just found our truants."

A second figure appeared around the corner of the closest building and showed a light. Blinking into the glare, Serdor discovered he was feeling suddenly far from well. He said lamely, "Were you looking for us?"

"Only all afternoon," said Caradoc's teacher tartly. "Ulbrecht Rathmuir was with us, too, until he received word by one of his novices that someone up at the castle needed a mage, and went off to answer the summons."

"We decided we might as well come back here as go on wearing out our boot-leather," said Arn. He scowled accusingly at Serdor. "Now suppose you up and tell me where Margoth's got to."

"I'm right here," said a decidedly female voice from the

murk twenty paces away. A figure separated itself from the surrounding darkness. "What's the matter? Didn't you get my message?"

"Yes, I got your message—for all it was worth," snapped Arn. "You and that brother of yours are a precious pair for handing out gibberish as if it were sense. What do you mean you're 'terminating your employment as of tonight'?"

"I should have thought that was plain enough," said Margoth. "Serdor and Rhan and I are leaving Ambrothen."

"Tonight?" Arn was bristling. He glared at Serdor. "If this is any of your doing . . ."

The minstrel was looking paler by the moment.

"Leave Serdor alone! Can't you see he's hurt?" cried Rhan.

Forgoyle's keen gaze narrowed. Taking a closer look at Serdor, he said, "What the devil have you been up to?"

All the angles in the street were looking fuzzy. "I'll be happy to tell you everything," said Serdor indistinctly. "But can't we please do it inside?"

He was weaving where he stood. "Arn—give him a hand. We'll sort this out later," said Forgoyle.

"We certainly will," said Arn. There was a purposeful glint in his eye as he took Serdor firmly by his good arm and steered him away toward St. Welleran's. Margoth fell into step beside them. Forgoyle turned to Rhan.

The boy was watching Serdor with worried eyes. He made no move to follow. "Aren't you coming?" asked Forgoyle.

Rhan swallowed hard. "I—I can't," he said huskily.

The tone in his voice betrayed an irrational depth of reluctance. Calling up his own hidden strength, Forgoyle laid both hands upon the boy's bony shoulders. "There's nothing to be afraid of," he said, projecting reassurance through his hands and his voice. "While you are with me, you are quite safe."

After a moment, the boy's expression lightened, and he breathed a sigh of relief. "Are you feeling better now?" asked Forgoyle.

"Yes. I'm sorry—I don't know what came over me," said Rhan rather self-consciously.

"Never mind—it's probably nothing," said Forgoyle, with a watchful glance at the boy's face. "Let's catch up."

The servitor on duty at the gatehouse took one look at them and waved them inside. The ordinaire at the door of the hospital did the same. Steering Serdor toward the nearest vacant treatment room, Forgoyle said, "Rhan, you look as if you've just spent three days in a dustbin. Tell the ordinaire over there that I said to show you to one of the bathing-rooms."

"Why can't I stay with Serdor?" demanded Rhan.

"Because his wound is deep enough that I'm going to have to call upon the Magia, and your presence might interfere with my concentration," said Forgoyle blandly. "Now do as you're told."

Rhan looked as if he would have liked to protest further, but he obeyed. "What about me?" inquired Margoth softly.

There was an enigmatic glint in Forgoyle's deep eyes. "Arn asked you for an explanation. I don't think it would come amiss for you to give him one."

Margoth gazed back at him. "All right," she said. "He and I can keep each other company until you're finished."

She turned away, and Forgoyle closed the door. Turning to Serdor, he plucked the bloodstained cloak from the minstrel's shoulders and guided him across the room to a waiting cot. "Your shirt will have to come off as well," said Caradoc's teacher crisply. "Who's responsible for the damage?"

Submitting to the magister's assistance, Serdor said, "One of the guards at Ambrothen Keep." He gasped aloud under Forgoyle's hands.

"Ambrothen Keep." Forgoyle's tone was fatalistically calm. "Now what business could possibly have taken you there?"

"We—Margoth, Rhan, and I—were hoping to save Caradoc from the gallows," said Serdor, and grinned through his pain. "You may be interested to learn that we succeeded."

"Oh, my God," said Forgoyle, and cocked an eyebrow. "Are you sure it's wise to confide in me?"

Serdor answered him by quoting canon law. " 'What passes between the healer and his patient must always be considered confidential.' Even if this weren't the case, we need your help.''

"Ah," said Forgoyle noncommittally.

"It's not just Caradoc," said Serdor. "There's something else you ought to know. I only found out myself tonight—"

He hesitated. "This revelation," said Forgoyle thoughtfully. "Does it happen to have anything to do with young Rhan?"

Serdor's grey eyes flew wide. Then he nodded his head in mute acknowledgment.

"So Caradoc has identified him for who he really is: Evelake Whitfauconer," said the magister. He poured a measure of herb-scented liquor into a bowl and passed it to Serdor. "Here. Drink this."

Serdor numbly accepted the cup. "How did you guess?" he asked.

"The rod you gave me turned out to be a necromancer's tool," said Forgoyle. "Once we had established that much, it wasn't difficult to infer the rest. Now, tell me the whole story. . . ."

CHAPTER 41

The Crypt

Unconsciousness was timeless. Caradoc awoke, with difficulty, to the realization that he was cold, and sick, and
acutely in pain.

He was lying facedown on an icy grave-slab in a small
burial chamber. Light entered the room in a pale wedge from
the adjoining cell. Gazing blearily into the light, he attempted
to sit up and discovered that his wrists had been bound
behind his back.

His bonds were torturingly tight, but his feet were still
free. Gritting his teeth, Caradoc shifted onto his side and
worked his legs over the edge of the coffin-lid. In the same
instant, a tall figure stepped soundlessly into the doorway and
stopped, black robes lifting and falling in the unquiet, fune-
real air.

Staring into the opaque black pit of the other man's face,
Caradoc felt his throat close up in a choked instant of premo-
nition. "What a pleasant surprise," said a familiar voice with
hateful cordiality. "I always knew," continued Borthen
Berigeld, "that one day you would come back to us."

The brigand's mocking words triggered a surge of unrea-
soning fear and rage. Bound hands notwithstanding, Caradoc
hurled himself off the slab and lunged at Borthen in a blind,
headlong charge.

A well-timed kick in the knee shattered his stride. Skipping clumsily over his own feet, Caradoc blundered abrasively into the wall and clattered to the stones below.

A large shadow moved above him. Fingers looped themselves into his hair and yanked. Caradoc left the floor, gasping, and came face to face with Muirtagh.

Borthen's leviathan lieutenant bared strong yellow teeth in a tight leer. Then he drove a fist like a mallet under Caradoc's unguarded ribs.

Retching helplessly, Caradoc doubled over. "That will do for now," said Borthen smoothly. Muirtagh growled and stepped back.

Glaring up at the brigand-leader through a red haze of pain and fury, Caradoc croaked, "You bloody bastard! What the hell are you doing here?"

"I was about to ask you the same question," said Borthen thoughtfully.

His gaze caressed the young man on the floor. "Almost, you convince me to believe in Divine Providence. One wonders how the castle guards were so lax as to permit your escape."

Caradoc gave a futile tug at his wrist-bonds. "You could always go and ask them," he said through his teeth.

"I would much rather hear it from you—when the time comes," said Borthen. "At the moment, however, I have an important appointment to keep. Charmed though I am by your discourse, I'm afraid it must be my painful duty to silence your tongue."

The menace was unmistakable. Matching eyes with his enemy, Caradoc felt his seething moil of emotions coalesce suddenly into a cold core of defiance. "What are you threatening me with, Borthen? I'll warn you, I am no helpless boy. While I may not challenge you on equal terms, I was trained as a mage, and I still possess at least the strength of will to resist you."

"Bravely spoken," said Borthen, "but you are more vulnerable than you suppose. You see, I am in possession of your magestone."

Moving unhurriedly, he plucked open a small pouch at his

belt. "Behold the source of your once-vaunted potency," continued Borthen with a chilly smile. He held out his open hand, a smaragdus pendant resting in the cradle of his palm.

At the sight of it, Caradoc's heart gave a sick lurch of yearning. "It was not so very difficult to master the use of it," said Borthen. "Nor, while I wield it, will it prove so very difficult to master you."

He raised his other hand, and the ring on his finger flashed with sullen radiance. Under Caradoc's stricken gaze, the brigand-leader brought the ring and the pendant together in a soul-wrenching conjunction of powers.

Light sprang up between them in a viridescent arc as the two stones kissed and parted. Eyes half-lidded in some remote ecstasy of mastery, Borthen reached out and laid a hand on his victim's forehead.

The shock of contact racked Caradoc's bones in their ligatures. In that instant he felt his tongue cleave to the roof of his mouth.

He fought back, pouring out his will in a desperate bid for autonomy. But the affinities between himself and his magestone were too strong. Even as his intellect cried out in outrage, his subtler faculties consented helplessly to the intrusion of an alien directive.

Writhing, he tried to vent his anguish in a scream. His dry mouth worked, but no sound came out. Choking on his own silence, he realized, with abject fury, that his resistance was crumbling. With capitulation came release—not relief, but a profound sense of violation.

He had no clear idea how long the nausea lasted, but when it finally passed, he became aware of voices in the next room.

Two voices. One of them Borthen's. The other less resonant, less controlled—somehow familiar. Catching the brittle cadence of anger, Caradoc began to take notice.

"I want to see the boy," declared the voice that wasn't Borthen's. "That was part of our agreement."

"Yes." Borthen sounded quite unperturbed. "Your desire to see your nephew's rival reduced to stripes and servitude is only natural. Unfortunately, it has proven quite impractical to have him brought here, without the danger of spoiling the fruits of my labor.''

The second voice swore. "Damn your labor! I took quite a risk coming here tonight. . . ."

"A fact of which I am not unaware," said Borthen smoothly. "The breach of contract is mine. Therefore, I am prepared to offer what I fancy you will consider a very handsome alternative.''

"And what is that?'' sneered the second voice.

"You wanted Evelake Whitfauconer—if not dead, then incapacitated," said Borthen. "I propose to give you his father as a substitute.''

There was a long pause. "Delsidor!'' exclaimed the second voice.

"Why not?'' said Borthen. "Your desire from the outset has been to seize control of the Wardenship through your sister's son. I am merely presenting you with a more direct pathway to power than the one you envisioned.''

"While you continue to hold Evelake as hostage against my good behavior," said the second voice bitterly. There was another seething pause. Then Borthen's visitor said, "And just what inducements are you offering Delsidor to lure him into this trap?''

"A bargain," said Borthen doucely. "Your name in exchange for the person of Caradoc Penlluathe.''

"My name!'' The second voice was spitting with indignation.

"Only a fool would have failed to perceive the political implications associated with Evelake's disappearance—and Delsidor is no fool," said Borthen. "What he doesn't know is that Caradoc Penlluathe is already in my possession. Since I now have what I want, I have no objections to your taking the life of your esteemed brother-in-law. He should be arriving shortly. If the prospect attracts you, I will do what I can to expedite the venture. . . ."

Lying on the floor by the doorway, with Muirtagh in watchful attendance, Caradoc mutely watched Borthen depart with his visitor. But he had already recognized the second man by his voice as Fyanor Du Bors, Seneschal of Ambrothen.

While Forgoyle bathed his wound, Serdor furnished a bald account of their activities. By the time he had finished, Forgoyle's expression was black.

"In view of the danger, Caradoc thought it would be safest to bring the boy here, until his father could be informed of his condition and whereabouts," said Serdor.

"I agree—though I shudder to think what the consequences will be," said Forgoyle grimly. "Where is Caradoc now?"

"If I tell you, will you go to him in secret?" asked Serdor.

"Yes," said Forgoyle. "He's earned the right to my discretion, at least."

"Good," said Serdor. "He's waiting for you in the cathedral crypt."

"We'll go to him as soon as I've finished here," said Forgoyle. "Lie back: I'm going to seal up the gash in your shoulder."

Serdor obeyed, and Caradoc's teacher drew out his magestone. As Forgoyle's Orison encradled him, Serdor felt the healing tingle of the Magia through the magister's long fingers, drawing the throbbing fire out of his injury. By the time Forgoyle had finished, his arm felt as good as new and his strength had returned.

"Now we'd better go see what Caradoc's been doing with himself," said Forgoyle. He reached under the bed and drew out a folded hospital smock, which he handed to Serdor. "Put this on. It'll keep you warm until you have time to get your shirt washed. Soiled or not, you'd better take your cloak as well: it may be chilly underground."

"What about the others?" asked Serdor.

"I'd just as soon leave them out of this for the moment," said Forgoyle. "If only to minimize the risk of our calling attention to ourselves before I've spoken to Caradoc."

Taking a lamp with him, Caradoc's teacher led the way through a side door and along the length of a dim corridor. A second door at the far end of the passageway opened into a small stone antechamber between the hospital and the cathedral's south transept. The portal to the transept was closed. To the right of it, a narrow archway opened black as a wormhole into the thick surrounding masonry.

Feeling a cold draft of air on his right side, Serdor shivered and stole a glance through the opening into the small stone cell beyond. "In the early days, this cubicle was used as a leper's squint," said Forgoyle, shining the light inside. "You can see the sanctuary clearly from here, and sound carries quite readily—"

He broke off short. Shoulders stiffening, he frowned and stepped into the cell. "What is it?" whispered Serdor, moving into the space behind him.

Forgoyle's lined features showed sharply defined in the lamplight. "I'm not sure," said Caradoc's teacher, his eyes roving, disfocused, along the dark stone walls of the leper's squint. "Do you smell anything queer in here?"

Serdor sniffed. "Nothing but damp. Why? What's wrong?"

"I don't know," muttered Forgoyle, his gaze still abstracted. "I thought for an instant I smelled something foul— like carrion . . ."

His voice trailed off. Watching as the magister pivoted slowly in place, Serdor felt a sudden chill creep up the back of his neck. He was about to suggest that they withdraw when his ears caught, sharp as an echo over snow, the distant sound of a door opening and closing, and after that, footfalls.

Both sounds came from the far end of the cathedral nave. Firm and deliberate, the footfalls paced the length of the long aisle, growing louder as they approached the vault before the altar.

Moving closer to Forgoyle, Serdor bent and peered out through the squint, toward the chancel. As he did so, a tall figure stepped into the hemisphere of light pooled before the altar rail, and there remained, outlined in the glow of the altar-candles.

The shadows beyond the reach of the chancel-lights seemed to hold a lurking menace. His muscles involuntarily tightening, Serdor looked around and saw that Forgoyle had set the lamp on the floor. Before he could whisper the question on the tip of his tongue, another voice broke the dark silence from the borders of the sanctuary, chilling the restless air with its perilous mockery.

"Good evening, my most noble lord. Your timing is impeccable. I hope this trysting-place meets with your approval."

The man standing before the altar threw back his head, yielding a strong profile to the light. "Your arrogance is equaled only by your profanity. I suggest we get to the point as swiftly as possible—before I forget my word of honor and summon my men to arrest you."

"There is no need to threaten me: you were not forced to come here tonight," said the first voice coolly. "If you have considered my proposal, give me your verdict. Otherwise, you are welcome to try to take me by force—provided you are prepared to abide the consequences."

"I am not impressed by your pretensions as a sorcerer," said the man by the altar. "Nor by the articles of your suggested bargain. You have offered me the name of Evelake's betrayer in exchange for Caradoc Penlluathe. If you want this young miscreant, he is yours, but I want more than a mere scrap of information in return: I want my son back—alive and well."

It was only then that Forgoyle realized the identities of the men who were speaking. A small involuntary gasp from Serdor told him that the minstrel had reached the same conclusion. In the same heartbeat, Borthen's cold laughter scattered the echoes of the Lord Warden's voice. "You should have acted sooner, my lord—while Caradoc Penlluathe was still a prisoner in your custody."

His voice biting as honed steel, Delsidor Whitfauconer said, "You play a dangerous game."

"But one full of surprises: having contrived to escape from the Keep tonight, my ingenious protégé made his way here—to me," said Borthen. "Would you care to discuss some other arrangement—such as what you would be prepared to offer in exchange for your own life?"

There was a deadly pause. Trading aghast looks with

Forgoyle, Serdor whispered, "Is there another entrance to the crypt?" and when Forgoyle nodded, hissed, "How do I get to it?"

"Through the mortuary—at the far end of the east wing of the hospital. What are you doing?" breathed Forgoyle.

"Borthen can't be two places at once," said Serdor. "Save Evelake's father—if you can. I'm going after Caradoc."

Before Forgoyle could remonstrate, Serdor was gone. Out of the shadows on the edge of the sanctuary, Borthen spoke again to the still figure standing before the sanctuary. "Have you nothing at all to say, my lord? Surely your life must be worth something."

Delsidor drew himself up to his full height. Then, with sudden violence, he threw back his cloak. "More, at any rate, than yours, Borthen Berigeld!" he snarled, and whipped his sword ringing from the sheath at his belt.

His lunge carried him hurtling over the altar rail. As he landed, the air between the floor and the vault exploded into sudden virulent radiance.

The blast swept the housings from the altar. Braving the backlash, Forgoyle threw open the door to the transept and raced for the chancel.

The Warden was lying prone on the stones before the altar. There was a robed figure standing over him, casting its elongated shadow to the far wall. Warned by the sound of footsteps, the figure turned its head as Forgoyle stumbled to a halt at the base of the sanctuary. A serpentined dagger flickered like poison in one gloved hand.

Light from the guttering candlesticks on the floor reflected upward under the cowl of the dark hood. Gazing into the half-revealed face of the man holding the dagger, Forgoyle named him aloud in horrified dismay. "Fyanor Du Bors . . ."

Beyond the altar, a tall shadow moved. "My Lord Seneschal, your moment of triumph is upon you," said Borthen Berigeld. "I give you leave to strike."

His face remote above his bloodless lips, Fyanor knelt and raised the dagger between his two clasped hands, holding it above the Warden's open breast like a high priest at sacrifice.

His forearms tensed to strike. "Stop! I forbid this!" cried Forgoyle in tones of ringing command.

Fyanor froze. "*You* forbid it!" sneered Borthen, stepping into the compass of the light. "Old fool! You forget you have yet to reckon with *me!*"

He raised his hand. A shaft of darkness stabbed downward from the center of his palm. Plunging like a javelin, it struck Forgoyle squarely in the chest and hurled him off his feet.

Pinned helpless to the floor, Forgoyle watched the fabric of his robe shrivel away. When the last threads crumbled, the skin over his breastbone began to burn.

The air stank of corruption. Writhing in his anguish, Forgoyle clawed instinctively at his chest.

Where his fingers passed through the beam, the flesh puffed and whitened like the belly of a corpse. As he stared at his knuckles, the skin began, before his very eyes, to decay. But now his scrabbling fingers touched his magestone . . .

CHAPTER 42

The Crucible

Serdor was still a dozen strides from the entrance to the east wing of the hospital when a blast of something that wasn't wind caught him from behind and hurled him against the left-hand wall. The impact jolted the air from his lungs. As he fought to keep his feet, the shock passed over him like a tidal wave and roared on down the passageway.

There was a series of splintering explosions as the lamps in the main hall went out in spitting fountains of glass. The ensuing darkness crackled with startled shrieks and the raw sounds of mass breakage. Picking himself up with a jerk, Serdor covered his ears and dashed for the doorway.

The flagstones of the main corridor were awash with burning islands of lamp oil. The lurid glare of the flames showed up cots overturned and doors wrenched open. Near at hand, two grey-robed mages were trying to raise a fallen man off the floor, while several others raced toward rooms farther down the hall where the cries of panic were mounting.

The reek of scorched cloth warred with a nauseating stench of putrefaction. Fingers pressed hard against his lips, Serdor sidestepped a smoldering mattress and set off running for the far end of the corridor.

From all sides, the babble of bewildered voices rose in hysterical inquiry. Fighting his way past a fear-stricken stream of hospital inmates making for the outer door, Serdor rounded a corner and skidded to a halt as a short stocky figure stepped out of a side room into his path.

It was Arn. Pitching his voice against the din of confusion, Serdor put his mouth to the innkeeper's ear and shouted, "Rhan and Margoth—where are they?"

Arn jerked a thumb over his shoulder. "In there—I was just going for help."

Serdor darted through the doorway he had indicated. Rhan was lying in a tumbled heap on the floor. A few feet away from him, Margoth was just dragging herself to her knees.

Her face was empty of color. Racing to her side, Serdor knelt and gathered her into his arms. "Margoth, what happened?"

She shook her head dazedly. "I—I'm not sure. I didn't see anything, but Rhan suddenly cried out and collapsed. When I bent down to touch him, something hit me—a jolt of some kind. I felt as though I were bursting into flames. . . ."

She shuddered and broke off. Beyond her, Rhan stirred and moaned. Like Margoth, he was deathly pale, but he seemed to be breathing normally enough. "What the devil's going on?" demanded Arn from the doorway.

"There isn't time!" barked Serdor. "Get them out of here, will you, and whatever you do, *stay with them!* I'll meet you in the park by the Burn. . . ."

Leaving Arn to help Margoth to her feet, Serdor rescued a candle from a fallen candlestick and shot out into the hall again.

The door to the hospital mortuary was swinging crookedly by one hinge. Pausing outside to light his taper at one of the fire-pools, Serdor stepped across the threshold.

A cold rush of stinking air called his attention to an open trapdoor in the far corner. The opening gave access to a dark flight of stairs. Gripping his light tightly, Serdor started down.

The air grew more turbulent as he descended. As his foot left the bottommost step, an icy gust struck at him out of the labyrinth, and his candle flickered out.

The breath sawing backward through his teeth, he flattened

himself to the stair-rail. A heartbeat later, he discovered that he could still see.

An eerie phosphorescence was clinging to the walls, filming the masonry with dim light. Grave markers stood out in sickly relief against the shadowy stones behind. Catching a hint of movement in the ghost-glimmer of the tombs, Serdor felt the sharp prickle of cold sweat between his shoulder blades. Gulping air, he stood away from the steps and made for the archway to the adjoining chamber.

It yielded to two diverging passageways. Serdor paused at the intersection and moistened his dry lips. In the full knowledge that he was taking a dangerous chance, he called, "Caradoc! Caradoc, where are you?"

Lying bound hand and foot on the floor among whispering drafts of icy air, Caradoc started out of a half swoon, thinking he had heard the sound of his own name.

Despite sickness and exhaustion, his heart leaped within him. Serdor! he thought with blind certainty. He's down here looking for me!

Struggling into a sitting position, he propped one numbed shoulder against the wall, his mind reaching out to his friend in desperate, yearning appeal. Here—I'm *here!* he thought. But though he strained to catch the minstrel's voice again, he heard nothing but the sibilant hiss of air snaking over stone.

His newfound hope guttered toward extinction. I must only have imagined it, he told himself dully and laid his aching head against the frame of the door.

Consciousness lapsed. As he drifted back into half-fainting sleep, a series of sharp impressions forced their way through the cloud of ugly dreams . . .

Light feet pattering hesitantly along stone corridors. . . .

An eager profile turning this way and that. . . .

"Caradoc!"

This time, the sound was unmistakable. Nerves leaping to life, Caradoc wrenched himself upright. This way! he urged, straining without voice to communicate his need. This way!

The anguish of uncertainty stung him into action. Dropping onto his belly, he wormed his way across the threshold into the next room, and came to a halt at a thick pair of booted legs.

He had forgotten Muirtagh.

A kick in the side slammed him helplessly against the wainscot. Borthen's massive lieutenant paused long enough to give him an unpleasantly knowing grin before sauntering over to the door in the opposite wall.

Muirtagh was armed with a knotted quarterstaff the thickness of his own wrists. Balancing it purposefully between his huge hands, he took up station to the left of the architrave, his colorless eyes watchful and intent.

"Caradoc!" Carrying clearly through the neighboring vaults, the minstrel's voice was ragged with anxiety. His heart thudding against his bruised ribs, Caradoc writhed in a torment of frustration. I've got to warn him off, he thought wildly.

His lips framed the minstrel's name, but his attempt to shout died stillborn. Lungs pumping, he tried again, to no avail.

His throat was burning under the tension between his own will and Borthen's deadly constraint. Quaking with effort, he made another desperate attempt to throw off the shackles of obedience, and again knew the agony of defeat.

"Caradoc?"

Drenched in his own ice-cold sweat, he became aware, suddenly, of Borthen's inimical presence. Air and darkness swirled before his eyes—pillars soaring toward impossible heights above a desecrated altar. Screaming defiance in the depths of his own mind, he rent the vision asunder, squandering his remaining strength in a blistering moment of rejection. The images flared into nothingness, and he knew that he was free.

A spare figure stepped from the passage into the shadow of the doorway. *"Serdor, look out!"* screamed Caradoc.

Warned, the minstrel hurled himself sideways as the blow intended for his head struck chips off the doorframe. He came up crouching, dagger in hand. "Get out of here, you fool! He'll kill you!" shouted Caradoc. But Muirtagh had already stepped between the minstrel and the door.

Taking a fresh grip on his weapon, he began to advance. The staff sliced the air in a murderous arc. Dodging under it, Serdor made a valiant passing swipe with his knife-hand.

The point scored a thin line of blood on the brigand's sleeve. Snarling, Muirtagh leaped forward, whipping the staff between his hands like a thresher's flail.

There was nowhere to run to. His eyes never leaving the deadly flick of the quarterstaff, Serdor retreated until his back met the wall. Grinning down at him, Muirtagh paused, feinted, and lashed out, not for the head, but for the legs.

The blow caught Serdor between the hip and knee. He cried out and staggered, his face wrenched with pain. His leer broadening, Muirtagh stood back. Watching in sick helplessness, Caradoc realized that the big man was only playing with his prey.

Winded and half-crippled, Serdor sagged against the wall. The stone seemed to be trembling under him. Knowing himself beaten, he took it for a sign of his own weakness. Then it came to him that there was more to it than that.

Before he could think it through, the ground underfoot gave a deep, subterranean rumble. As it rippled upward, the walls around them began to shake.

Serdor looked up into a sifting rain of loosened mortar. There was a grating sound of granite on granite as the building-stones began to separate.

The trembling increased until the chamber was visibly rocking. There was an ear-splitting roar and a crack appeared along the floor, racing for Muirtagh's splayed feet.

Small eyes ablaze with sudden panic, Borthen's lieutenant dashed Serdor to the ground with a sweeping backhand blow and lumbered for the door.

He vanished to the right. A moment later, there was a rending crash and the dim air fountained backward in a bellying implosion of loose earth. "The ceiling's beginning to cave in! Cut me loose—we've got to get out of here!" panted Caradoc.

Dragging himself half-stunned to his knees, Serdor crawled to Caradoc's side and hacked at the ropes that bound him.

Behind them, the inner tomb was filling up with collapsing rock.

The last strands parted with a snap and Caradoc made a floundering effort to stand up. "I can't walk—my circulation's gone!" he gasped. "You'd better leave me—"

"Not on your bloody life!" rasped Serdor. "Here—give me your arm."

Working their hobbling way along the wall under the stinging bombardment of crumbling masonry, they gained the passageway beyond mere seconds before the roof crashed down in a broken slab. The tunnel to the right was already buried. "We'll have to make for the cathedral exit," wheezed Caradoc, "if the way is still open. . . ."

Helping each other along, they stumbled down passages half-clogged with broken stones and shattered graves. Light glimmered spectrally among the upturned sarcophagi. "What is that? Where's it coming from?" gasped Serdor.

"Don't ask—just keep going," muttered Caradoc.

The stairway to the chancel was cracked and twisted, but still passable. "This is it," breathed Serdor. "Up we go."

Behind them, the greenish glow from the tombs was growing stronger. They were nearly at the summit of the stair when the door to the cathedral apse erupted off its hinges and rocketed down the steps on a shrieking gale of black wind.

Serdor and Caradoc threw themselves flat as it splintered off the wall above their heads. Pouring through the opening, the maelstrom ripped the gravestones from their settings and sent them booming ruinously down the shaft as it tore into the heart of the crypt below.

A sickly light trickled like ichor out of the cavities left behind. Wrenching his horrified gaze away from the pools that were forming on the steps, Caradoc caught Serdor by the arm and jerked him to his feet. "Come on!" he choked. "Don't let any of that touch you!"

The shadows around the doorway lashed at them like vipers. Clattering across the landing, they burst through the opening into the sanctuary, and there came to a shuddering halt.

Before the altar a dark figure knelt as if in prayer over the still form of Evelake's father. At the sound of their entry, the figure turned its head, and Serdor recognized the face of the Seneschal of Ambrothen.

Fyanor's gloved hands were locked around the hilt of a long dagger. The blade itself was buried to the handguard in the Lord Warden's chest. Beyond the sanctuary, light glinted dimly off helmets and hauberks: Delsidor's bodyguards had not survived their lord.

Moving like an automaton, the seneschal released his grip and stood up.

"You may go now. Your work is done," said a cold voice from the shadows of the apse.

Stricken, Caradoc wheeled in the direction of the voice. "The price of folly—you should have warned your associates not to meddle with me," said Borthen Berigeld, stepping out of the darkness. "Your teacher was fool enough to think he could hinder me—and there he lies."

He gestured toward the outer edge of the chancel, and Caradoc glimpsed for the first time the torn grey figure lying motionless at the altar rail. His blood turned to ice. "Forgoyle?" he whispered. Then rounded on Borthen, his voice quivering with grief and loathing. *"What have you done to him?"*

"Allow me to demonstrate," said Borthen, "on the person of your young friend."

Before Caradoc could move or cry out, Borthen raised his arms and flung them wide, fingers spread like striking talons. Twin bolts of darkness leaped together from his hands.

Knocking Serdor out of the way, Caradoc lunged for the floor and screamed as the edge of the bolt raked his back. Dragging the minstrel with him, he rolled under the altar rail and tumbled to the foot of the steps.

Serdor landed limp and did not move again. His shoulders scored as if with acid, Caradoc struggled to his knees and turned at bay. Advancing to the edge of the sanctuary, Borthen said, "I have been gentle with you long enough." His arms mantled like great dark wings.

Gazing into his enemy's implacable eyes, Caradoc steeled himself for the agony of dissolution. Darkness clove the air in a murderous downstroke. In the same instant, light blazed athwart its path in a dazzling countershaft. There was a deafening crackle as force met force, and the shadow burst into splinters. "You crow too soon," said Forgoyle Finlevyn. "This battle isn't over yet."

His face and body were ravaged as with leprosy, but his haggard eyes were unwavering and his magestone burned like an oriflamme between his hands. As Borthen, snarling, turned on him, he opened his fingers and light billowed forth in a glistering wave.

Igneous as molten glass, it swept Borthen into a blinding embrace. The brigand-leader writhed like a moth in a holocaust, his body straining toward extremity. Then, mastering himself, he brought his hands together, and out of his palms sprang a spinning black wind.

Shrilling like a whirlwind, it smashed against the wall of dancing radiance, ripping into it like claws. Sparks flew from the rents in spattering waves until the air was clogged with warring motes of light and dark. Buffeted blind, Caradoc cried out and buried his face in his hands. Above the shrieking cyclone of conflict, a voice howled in a sudden anguish of capitulation, and abruptly, all was still.

An insistent hand pulling at his arm roused Caradoc from his frozen immobility. Moving stiffly, he lifted his head and found himself gazing up into Serdor's bruised face.

Cold, sea-smelling air filled the ruined vault through the shattered remains of stained glass windows. His throat too tight for speech, Caradoc mouthed one fearful question. "Borthen?"

"He's gone—I don't know where," said Serdor. He swallowed hard and added unsteadily, "Forgoyle . . . Caradoc, Forgoyle's dead." He turned away and bowed his head.

Caradoc drew two sharp breaths, then closed his eyes, feeling the molten surge of tears against his lids. It was a long moment before he mastered himself enough to move.

Leaving Serdor where he was, he rose to his feet and crossed the floor to where his teacher's body lay.

Forgoyle was lying on his back, holding at his torn breast a handful of silver-green dust—all that was left of his magestone. Apart from the marks of malice, there was no sign of strain or torment left in his face. Kneeling, Caradoc took one quiet hand in his own, his throat constricted with grief. "Thank you," he whispered through the ache in his chest. "It was bravely done . . . almost a perfect victory—"

His voice broke then, and he covered his eyes. He heard distantly, as over some remote gulf of time and space, the clash of weaponry and the hoarse calling of voices, but it seemed less real to him than the memory of the man who had taught him so much.

Serdor touched his shoulder. "There are soldiers coming," said the minstrel. "We've lingered long enough."

When Caradoc did not respond, Serdor plucked him by the sleeve. "Caradoc, please—for Margoth's sake, and for Evelake's: we're all the protection they have left, and they *need* us!"

A heartbeat later Caradoc nodded and drew himself up. Releasing Forgoyle's hand, he laid it gently to rest on the stones. "You've shown me the way," he told his teacher in silence. "From this moment, like you, I will fight to the death, if I must. And so, goodbye. . . ."

And after looking for the last time upon the face of the man he had loved as a father, he turned away and followed Serdor out of the sanctuary.

EPILOGUE

The fog rolled turgidly along the waters of Drumlyn Burn. Crouching in the damp grass in the shelter of a thick brake of small trees, Margoth hunched a borrowed blanket more closely around her shoulders and leaned closer to Rhan.

Rhan was anxiously watching the dueling interplay of lantern-beams beyond the wall that divided the park from the cathedral grounds. "How are you feeling?" whispered Margoth.

They could hear the confused clash of voices from the direction of the cathedral. Without turning his head, Rhan said, "I'm all right." He fidgeted where he sat. "Where *is* Serdor?" he muttered between set teeth. "Maybe I ought to go back to look for him—"

"Oh, no you don't," said Arn Aldarshot. "You're going to sit right there and wait, like you were told to do."

"But he and Caradoc might be in trouble—"

"If they are, there's precious little *you* could do about it," said Arn. "Give 'em another ten minutes. If they haven't turned up by then, I'll go take a look around—"

A twig snapped in the undergrowth. The three people in hiding caught their breath and drew instinctively closer together. Another twig snapped and someone swore in an aspirated undertone. Her ears pricking up, Margoth exclaimed

304

in a whisper, "That was Caradoc!" She rose to her knees and spoke his name aloud. "Caradoc!"

There was a stir in the bushes and two heads appeared momentarily silhouetted against the patchy backdrop of firelight. "Margoth?" breathed a tentative voice that she recognized as Serdor's.

Her heart felt as if it might break with relief. "Down here!" she hissed, then broke from cover to meet them.

Serdor was in the lead. Fervently returning his embrace, Margoth murmured, "Thank God you're both safe!" Then she caught sight of her brother's stricken face. "What's happened?" she asked sharply.

Caradoc's mouth twisted. He turned his head without speaking. Thin fingers gentle against her cheek, Serdor said, "There was a fight. Forgoyle was killed in the struggle."

Her heart lurched against her chest. "Forgoyle? Dead?" she faltered, and looked to Caradoc for further enlightenment.

Again, her brother's face told her nothing but the depth of his own shock and grief. "It's not safe to linger here," said Serdor. "Suffice it to say for the moment that we're only alive because of him. We'd better go while we still can and save the story for safer surroundings."

Striking out upstream, they made for the water gate that ran under the walls to the west of the city. It was silent at the guardposts along the ramparts. "The news must not have reached this far yet," muttered Serdor, and ploughed out, shivering, for the deeper water as it flowed under the teeth of an iron portcullis in midstream.

Dripping and shuddering, they made their way to the north bank and climbed out onto dry ground. "We left packs with food and spare clothes at the old brickyard," said Serdor to Arn and Caradoc. Then softly, "My God, it seems like years ago." There was a silence. Then he moved and they followed him.

Located a quarter of a mile outside the city walls, the abandoned brickyard had been one of Serdor's childhood refuges. Picking their way now among the dilapidated huddle of half-fallen buildings, they arrived at last at the brick-kiln.

Three packs were lying just inside the doorway. Dragging them out, Serdor began handing out dry blankets. While he was helping Rhan and Margoth redistribute the loads, Caradoc took Arn aside.

He told their story in short, stark phrases. When he had finished, Arn gave him a sober look. "Your friends have done you proud, lad. I suppose now you're bound away."

Caradoc nodded. "Tonight."

"It won't be an easy journey," said Arn. He glanced over at Rhan. "Why not leave the boy behind with me? I'll see to it that he stays out of trouble."

"That's not possible," said Caradoc flatly. "He's as deeply caught up in what happened tonight as I am. And perhaps in even greater danger."

Arn's black eyes narrowed uneasily. "You might explain that."

"It's safer for you—believe me—if I don't," said Caradoc. He clasped Arn's shoulder. "Will you do something for me?"

"All you need do is ask," said Arn. "What is it?"

"I want you to carry a message for me," said Caradoc, "to a man called Gudmar Ap Gorvald."

"Gudmar Ap Gorvald." Arn rolled the name around on his tongue. "What's his direction?"

"I don't know. But he shouldn't be hard to find," said Caradoc. "He's a friend of the Lord Warden. A big man with a golden beard—you'll know him by that when you see him."

"I'll manage," said Arn. "What's the message?"

"Just this," said Caradoc. "Tell him from me, 'Your friend's son is alive, but in peril. If you want to see him safe, meet us at Holmnesse.' "

Arn repeated it. "Is that all?"

"That's all," said Caradoc. "He'll find a way to do the rest."

The others were lashing up their bundles. "All set," Serdor called over. "We'd better be on our way."

Caradoc held out his hand, and Arn took it. "I don't know

when—or if—we'll meet again. But thank you for your friendship. For the rest, we can only hope.'' He released Arn's hand and abruptly turned away. Joining the others, he shouldered his pack and set out in the lead for the broken gate.

Watching as the four dark figures faded away into the fog, Arn Aldarshot said softly, "Goodbye . . . and God speed you. . . .''

interzone

SCIENCE FICTION AND FANTASY

Quarterly   £1.95

- *Interzone* is the only British magazine specializing in SF and new fantastic writing. We have published:

BRIAN ALDISS	GARRY KILWORTH
J.G. BALLARD	DAVID LANGFORD
BARRINGTON BAYLEY	MICHAEL MOORCOCK
GREGORY BENFORD	RACHEL POLLACK
MICHAEL BISHOP	KEITH ROBERTS
RAMSEY CAMPBELL	GEOFF RYMAN
ANGELA CARTER	JOSEPHINE SAXTON
RICHARD COWPER	JOHN SHIRLEY
JOHN CROWLEY	JOHN SLADEK
PHILIP K. DICK	BRIAN STABLEFORD
THOMAS M. DISCH	BRUCE STERLING
MARY GENTLE	IAN WATSON
WILLIAM GIBSON	CHERRY WILDER
M. JOHN HARRISON	GENE WOLFE

- *Interzone* has also published many excellent new writers; graphics by **JIM BURNS, ROGER DEAN, IAN MILLER** and others; book reviews, news, etc.

- *Interzone* is available from specialist SF shops, or by subscription. For four issues, send £7.50 (outside UK, £8.50) to : **124 Osborne Road, Brighton BN1 6LU, UK.** Single copies: £1.95 inc p&p.

- American subscribers may send $13 ($16 if you want delivery by air mail) to our British address, above. All cheques should be made payable to *Interzone*.

- "No other magazine in Britain is publishing science fiction at all, let alone fiction of this quality." *Times Literary Supplement*

— —

To: **interzone** 124 Osborne Road, Brighton, BN1 6LU, UK.

Please send me four issues of *Interzone,* beginning with the current issue. I enclose a cheque/p.o. for £7.50 (outside UK, £8.50; US subscribers, $13 or $16 air), made payable to *Interzone*.

Name _____

Address _____

_____